Iris M. Ford

ALSO BY JAMES PONTI

The Framed! series

Framed!

Vanished!

Trapped!

The City Spies series

City Spies

Golden Gate

Forbidden City

DEAD CITY SAGA

Dead City
Blue Moon
Dark Days

JAMES PONTI

ALADDIN

NEW YORK LONDON TORONTO SYDNEY NEW DELHI

This book is a work of fiction. Any references to historical events,
real people, or real places are used fictitiously. Other names, characters, places,
and events are products of the author's imagination, and any resemblance to
actual events or places or persons, living or dead, is entirely coincidental.

ALADDIN
An imprint of Simon & Schuster Children's Publishing Division
1230 Avenue of the Americas, New York, New York 10020
This Aladdin paperback edition June 2021
Dead City copyright © 2012 by James Ponti
Blue Moon copyright © 2013 by James Ponti
Dark Days copyright © 2015 by James Ponti
Cover illustrations copyright © 2012, 2021 by Nigel Quarless
All rights reserved, including the right of reproduction in whole or in part in any form.
ALADDIN and related logo are registered trademarks of Simon & Schuster, Inc.
For information about special discounts for bulk purchases, please contact
Simon & Schuster Special Sales at 1-866-506-1949 or business@simonandschuster.com.
The Simon & Schuster Speakers Bureau can bring authors to your live event. For more
information or to book an event contact the Simon & Schuster Speakers Bureau at
1-866-248-3049 or visit our website at www.simonspeakers.com.
Cover designed by Tiara Iandiorio
Interior designed by Lisa Vega
The text of this book was set in Adobe Garamond Pro.
Manufactured in the United States of America 0521 OFF
2 4 6 8 10 9 7 5 3 1
Library of Congress Control Number 2021934868
ISBN 978-1-6659-0245-8 (pbk)
ISBN 978-1-4424-4128-6 (*Dead City* ebook)
ISBN 978-1-4424-4133-0 (*Blue Moon* ebook)
ISBN 978-1-4814-3638-0 (*Dark Days* ebook)
These titles were previously published individually.

CONTENTS

Dead City   1

Blue Moon   285

Dark Days   619

DEAD CITY

For Denise:
Wife, muse, and all-around cool chick

Acknowledgments

Only one name goes on the title page, but so many people go into bringing a book to life. I am beyond grateful for the entire Aladdin team, who did everything from undangling my modifiers to designing the look of the book. Triple thanks to my guardian angels, Fiona Simpson and Bethany Buck. If I had an Omega Team of my own, you'd be the first two I'd pick.

I leaned heavily on a small circle of dedicated readers who offered encouragement and suggestions along the way. This was especially true of Kim, Kim, Wyatt, and Adam. I'm leaving off your last names because I don't want any other writers to steal you. And I leaned even more heavily on my amazing literary agent, Rosemary Stimola. In addition to being accomplished in three separate careers, you're quite the amateur psychologist, strategic planner, and friend.

And finally, while all of the undead characters in this book are fictional, there were many sleep-deprived nights when I began to exhibit the traits of the worst Level 3 zombies. I cannot say enough about my wife and kids for putting up with it all. You amaze me every day.

You're Probably Wondering Why There's a Dead Body in the Bathroom...

I hate zombies.

I know that sounds prejudiced. I'm sure some zombies are really nice to kittens and love their parents. But it's been my experience that most are not the kind of people you want sending you friend requests.

Consider my current situation. Instead of eating pizza with my teammates as they celebrate my surprise victory at the St. Andrew's Prep fencing tournament, I'm trapped in a locker-room toilet stall.

With a dead body.

It's not exactly the Saturday I had planned. I wasn't

even supposed to compete in the tournament. Since most of the girls on the team are juniors and seniors and I'm in seventh grade, I was just going to be an alternate. But Hannah Gilbert didn't show up, and I filled in for her at the last moment. Five matches later my teammates were jumping up and down and pouring Gatorade on my head.

And that was the first problem.

I may not be the girliest girl, but I didn't really want to ride the subway with sticky orange hair. So I decided to clean up while everyone else headed down to the pizzeria to get a table and order a couple of large pies.

I had just finished my shower when I heard zombie noises coming my way. (I know, they hate to be called the z-word, but I hate being attacked in the bathroom, so I guess we're even.)

At first I thought it was one of my teammates playing a joke on me. But when I saw the reflection of the walking dead guy in the mirror, I realized it was Life playing a joke on me. I mean, is it too much to ask for just a couple hours of normal?

To make matters worse, this zombie and I had something of a history. During an earlier encounter, I sort of chopped off his left hand. I won't go into the details, but trust me when I say it was a "have to" situation. Anyway, now he was looking to settle a grudge, and all my gear was in a bag on the other side of the locker room. Too bad, because moments like these were the reason I took up fencing in the first place.

He looked at me with his cold dead eyes and waved his stump in my face to remind me why he was in such a bad mood. All I had to protect myself with was the towel I was wearing and my flat iron. Since I was not about to let Mr. Evil Dead see me naked, I went with the flat iron.

My first move was to slash him across the face, which was a total waste of time. Yes, it burned a lot of flesh. But since zombies feel no pain, it didn't slow him down one bit. Plus, no way was I ever going to let that flat iron touch my hair again, so I was down thirty bucks and I still had a zombie problem.

Next, he slammed me against the wall. That hurt unbelievably bad and turned my shoulder purple. (A color I like in clothes, but not so much when it comes to skin tone.) On the bright side, when I got back up I was in the perfect position for a *ballestra*, my favorite fencing move. It combines a jump forward with a lunge, and it worked like a charm.

The flat iron punctured his rib cage and went deep into his chest. It got stuck when I tried to yank it out, so I just started flicking it open and shut inside his body. This distracted him long enough for me to grab him at the base of the skull and slam his head into the marble countertop.

I don't know how much tuition runs at St. Andrew's, but their bathrooms have some high-quality marble. He went from undead to just plain dead on the spot.

All told, it took about forty seconds. But that's the problem with killing zombies. It's like when my dad and I make spaghetti sauce together. The hard part's not so much the doing as it is the cleanup afterward.

If this had been a public-school locker room, there would have been some gray jumbo-sized garbage cans nearby, and I probably could've taken care of cleanup by myself. But apparently the girls of St. Andrew's don't throw anything away, because all they had was a tiny wastebasket and some recycling bins. There were bins for paper, plastic, and glass, but none for rotting corpses. Go figure.

That meant I had to drag the body into a stall, text my friends for help, and call my coach with an excuse about how I had to go straight home. Now I'm stuck here sitting on a toilet, my hair's a total mess, and after two bottles of hand sanitizer, I still feel like I've got dead guy all over me. And don't even get me started about how hungry I am!

If you had told me any of this a few months ago, I

would have said you needed to visit the school nurse. That's because before I was Molly Bigelow, superhero zombie terminator, I was just an invisible girl in the back of the classroom who you'd probably never notice.

I'm sure none of this makes any sense. I mean, it's still hard for me to understand, and I'm the one who just did it. So while I wait for help to arrive, I'll try to explain. I understand if you don't believe it, but trust me when I say that every word is true.

It all started more than a hundred years ago, when an explosion killed thirteen men digging one of New York's first subway tunnels. But my part didn't begin until one day last summer, when I was hanging out at the morgue. . . .

Ω

That Weird Bigelow Girl

It was the last Friday of summer vacation, and I was running late. I'd made it halfway out the front door when I heard my dad call out from the kitchen.

"Molly, you forgot something."

"I took the trash out last night," I answered.

"Not the trash."

I started to run through a quick mental list of my chores. "I've got my lunch right here," I said, holding up my brown bag.

"Not your lunch."

I rolled my eyes and walked back to the kitchen doorway to look at him. He'd worked the late shift and was still wearing his navy blue paramedic's uniform as he hunched over a bowl of cereal.

"You want to give me a hint?"

He smiled that goofy dad smile and raised his cheek up to be kissed.

"Seriously?"

"What?" he answered. "You're worried someone might see you in our apartment? Worried that it could ruin your reputation?"

"It's not that. It's just that I'm not a little kid," I explained. "I don't need a kiss every time I go outside."

"Notice the cheek," he said, tapping it for emphasis. "I get the kiss, not you."

It was pointless to argue, so I walked over and gave him a peck on the cheek. As I did, he turned his head and gave me one too.

"Gotcha," he said with a movie villain's laugh. "By the way, last night I used those same lips to give mouth-to-mouth resuscitation to this really old woman. She was scary looking and had bad breath. She even had a little mustache thing going on." He added a couple of hacking coughs. "I hope I didn't catch something."

"You see what I mean?" I said with exasperation. "Nothing in my life can be normal."

"Normal?" He laughed. "Aren't you the girl on her way to hang out . . . at the morgue?"

I tried to give him my scrunched-up angry face, but I couldn't help laughing. He kind of had a point, so I rewarded him with an unsolicited good-bye hug.

He smiled. "Was that so hard?"

"Can I go now?"

"You can go. Say hi to Dr. H for me."

"I will," I answered as I hurried out the door and down the hall.

I do realize that it's not normal for a girl my age to hang out at the morgue. (Okay, I realize that it's not normal for a girl of *any* age to hang out at the morgue.) But I guess the first thing you should know about me is that I'm not exactly a cookie-cutter kind of girl. Even if I wanted to be, I think my mother had other plans.

When I begged her to put me in ballet class, she somehow convinced me that Jeet Kune Do was a better fit. So after school on Tuesdays and Thursdays, when the rest of the girls were learning *pirouettes* and *grand jetés*, I was down the hall mastering the martial art of the intercepting fist.

And when I wanted to join the Brownies, she signed me up for the New York City Audubon Society's Junior Birder program instead. As a result, I don't know a thing about cookies or camping but can identify sixty-eight different varieties of birds known to inhabit the five boroughs.

She even led me to the morgue.

My mom was a forensic pathologist for the New York City Office of Chief Medical Examiner. When the police needed help figuring out precisely how somebody died, they called her. She was really good at her job. The best. Sometimes she was even on TV or in the newspaper when she had to testify at a murder trial.

I know it sounds gory and gross, but she loved it. She liked to say that "even after someone dies, they still have a story to tell."

One Friday when I was seven years old, my grandma was supposed to watch me. At the last minute she couldn't make it, and Mom had no choice but to take me to work with her.

I can still remember how terrified I was as we rode the subway into the city. I'd always pictured her office looking like something out of a horror movie, with dead bodies scattered all over the place. But it wasn't like that at all. It turned out to be the most amazing science lab I could have ever imagined. I liked everything about it, except for the dead bodies. But they were mostly kept out of the way.

Going to the morgue became our thing to do. During the summers I went to work with her every Friday. She was careful not to let me see anything too gross, because she didn't want to give me nightmares. But she taught me all kinds of experiments and showed me how to use the cool equipment. Eventually, I even got less and less freaked out by the dead people.

"Death is part of the natural order of life," she would explain. "You shouldn't be scared of it. You should be respectful of it."

A couple of years later, when they diagnosed her cancer and she started going to chemotherapy, she used the morgue to help prepare me, in case she died. She explained that while the human body was amazing, it had limitations. She wanted me to know that when her body gave out, her spirit and soul would still live on in me and my sister.

Mom died two summers ago. It was a Sunday morning, and I remember every single thing about that day. I remember the smell of the pretzels for sale outside the hospital and the mechanical sounds of the monitors in her room. I remember that everything about her looked pale and weak and unrecognizable—except her eyes.

My mom had mismatched eyes. It's called "hetero-chromia," and I have it too. My left eye is blue and my right is green, just like hers. She said it was our special genetic bond.

That day, I looked deep into her eyes. Everything else was failing, but they still looked as sharp and bright as ever.

"Even after someone dies . . . ," she whispered.

"They still have a story to tell," I finished.

She smiled and then added, "That's right, and my story is going to be told by you."

I was amazed by how many people came to her funeral. The policemen who worked with her on cases and the paramedics and firemen from my dad's station house were all there wearing their dress uniforms. They looked so big and strong. And every one of them cried.

Everyone cried that day . . . but me.

The following Friday, I rode the subway into the city and went to her office like I always had. I don't really know what I was thinking or expecting. It was just a habit. But nobody said anything about it or asked me why I was there. They just acted like I belonged.

That day I hung out with Dr. Hidalgo, my mom's best friend. I've been going back and hanging out in his office on summer Fridays ever since. And because this was the last Friday of summer vacation, I didn't want to be late.

"Waiiiit!" I yelled as I raced down the hall.

I sprinted the last few strides and managed to jam my hand inside the elevator just as the door was closing. When it sprang back open to reveal who was riding it, I wished that I had just slowed down and waited for the next one.

There was Mrs. Papadakis, whose two favorite hobbies are gossiping and tanning. Judging by her bathing suit, which was inappropriate by at least thirty years and sixty pounds, she was on her way to the courtyard to do both with a group of old ladies I call the Leather Bags. You always have to be careful about what you say or do around her, because anything slightly embarrassing is bound to be the talk of the building by the end of the day.

Next to her were Dena and Dana Salinger, twin sisters from down the hall who like to do everything together—especially torment me. One time they pinned me in the elevator and forced me to ride all the way to the fifteenth floor. They pushed me out into the hallway, even though they knew I was terrified of heights and never went above the third floor.

Today they wore leopard-print bikini tops and matching short shorts and were headed to Astoria Park, a huge public pool just down the street from our apartment building.

But the person I dreaded most was the girl with the Salingers. The one who was giving me the stink eye.

It was my sister, Beth.

Normally, Beth and I have an "ignorance is bliss" policy when we cross paths away from home. She ignores me and I'm blissful about it. It's not that we don't love each other. It's just I'm in middle school, and she's in high school. I'm brainy and nerdy, and she's cool and popular. But as I stepped into the elevator, I was pretty sure she was going to say something.

"What do you think you're doing with that jacket?" she demanded.

Did I forget to mention that while everyone else looked like they stepped out of the swimsuit edition of *Queens Apartment Living*, I was wearing jeans, a long-sleeved T-shirt, and, most important to Beth, carrying a bright pink ski parka.

"You know," she continued, "the jacket that belongs in *my* closet."

Bank vaults had nothing on my sister when it came to protecting her clothes. That's the reason I was running late. I'd waited inside the apartment for nearly forty minutes after she'd left, just to avoid the possibility of bumping into her. Now I was stuck with her on the world's slowest elevator. Apparently, it had taken the Salingers longer than usual to spray on their fake tans.

"It's Friday," I explained. "You know how cold it gets in the morgue."

"The morgue?" Mrs. Papadakis screeched, her Queens accent exaggerating the word. "Did somebody die?"

"No," I answered sheepishly.

"Then why are you going to the morgue?"

I didn't know what to say, so I just told the truth. "I like to hang out there."

Beth cringed. It was bad enough that her little sister was "that weird Bigelow girl from the third floor." She didn't need everyone to know how weird I really was.

"You hang out at a morgue?" Dana said.

"Your sister is a *total* freak, Beth," Dena added.

Beth shot them a look that seemed almost protective of me. But then she gave me one that was even angrier. "What's wrong with *your* jacket?"

"I got cadaver juice on it last week," I said as though that was a normal conversation topic. "I've washed it seven times, but it still stinks."

Mrs. Papadakis almost threw up at the mention of "cadaver juice."

"So your brilliant idea was to get some on mine?"

"No. I won't. I promise. Dr. H isn't even doing an autopsy today. I called and checked."

"It doesn't matter what Dr. H is or isn't doing," she said, "because you are going upstairs and putting it back in my closet where you found it."

"If I don't have a jacket, it'll be too cold in the morgue," I pleaded.

She gave me that "condescending older sister" look. "Then I guess you won't go."

I thought about it for a moment before I flashed my "evil little sister" smirk and then said, "Okay. I guess I won't. Maybe I'll go swimming at Astoria Park instead. I can work on my butterfly stroke. It's kind of awkward, and I splash a lot, but who cares if people stare. Besides, I can always ask for help. You know, from the boys you'll be flirting with. Then the four of us girls can hang out."

Both Salingers shot Beth a look, and I knew I had won.

"Fine," Beth said curtly. "You can borrow it. But if you get so much as a drop of water on it, you're buying me a new one."

"Deal," I said as we stepped into the lobby.

I only made it a few steps before Mrs. Papadakis decided she just had to butt in. She put a caring hand on my shoulder, like we had some sort of close relationship . . . which we don't.

"Darling, it is not appropriate for a girl your age to visit the morgue. I know your mother—"

The mention of my mother was as far as she got.

Beth literally stepped between us and said, "Mrs. Papadakis, my mother thought you were a joke. I'm sure she wouldn't want either one of us to take advice from you. So save yourself the trouble."

Mrs. Papadakis's eyes opened wide. "Well, aren't you so very rude?"

"Really?" Beth said, not backing down. "Because I thought it wasn't nearly as rude as a woman your age trying to bully my little sister into feeling bad about herself."

Did I forget to mention that despite our many differences, my sister totally rocks?

Popsicles and Vanilla

Mornin', Molly," the security guard said as I entered the lobby of the morgue. Jamaican Bob was tall and thin and wore his dreadlocks pulled back in a ponytail. "You know, it's a good thing you got here when you did," he continued. "The building's going to be jam-packed today."

"Why is that?" I asked as I emptied my pockets into a plastic tray and walked through the metal detector.

"Haven't you heard about the morgue?" he said with a booming laugh. "Everybody's *dying* to get in."

Bob always told the corniest jokes, but I had to laugh because he got such a kick out of them.

"Have a good day," I said as I took my backpack from the X-ray machine.

"I will," he answered with a big smile. "As long as I stay up here and away from that freezer of yours."

Like a lot of the people in the building, Bob was freaked out by the freezer, which is what we called the body storage area, located three floors underground.

I guess it takes a while to get used to the idea of being surrounded by dead bodies.

Even when you do get used to it, there are two things you need to bring with you whenever you work in the morgue. The first is a jacket, because the bodies are refrigerated well below freezing. (If yours is not available, you can always steal your sister's.)

The second is vanilla extract to fight the smell. My mom taught me this trick the first time I went to work with her. Now I always bring a bottle with me when I come to the morgue. I swipe a finger of it under my nose every hour or so. (Unfortunate side effect: Vanilla milk shakes now make me think of dead people.)

"Somebody got a new jacket," Natalie said when I entered the lab.

"That's because somebody spilled cadaver juice on my other one," I reminded her.

"Oh yeah," she answered with a sheepish grin. "Sorry about that."

"I had to steal this one from my sister's closet," I explained. "If anything gets on it, I'm going to end up with the Popsicles." (That's what we call the dead bodies.)

Natalie is Dr. Hidalgo's intern. Like me, she's a student at MIST—the Metropolitan Institute of Science and Technology, a science magnet school that draws kids from all over New York City.

MIST is made up of two separate schools. The Lower School is for sixth, seventh, and eighth grades, while the Upper School is for ninth through twelfth. I'm in the Lower School and Natalie's in the Upper. Normally, high schoolers don't mingle with Lowbies, but since Nat and I were often the only living people in the room, we had gotten to know each other pretty well during the summer.

Natalie talks like a total science geek but looks like she belongs on the cover of a fashion magazine. Not only does she discuss everything from DNA sequencing to nanotechnology, but she does it with perfect hair, flawless skin, and the cutest clothes you ever saw.

Our backgrounds are different in nearly every way. Natalie lives on the Upper West Side. She never flaunts it, but you can tell her family has serious money, with doormen in the lobby and park views from the terrace. Her parents are both surgeons, and everything about their life has a feeling of fabulous about it. She even owns a horse named Copernicus that she rides some weekends.

Despite our differences, we'd become real friends over the summer. Or at least I hoped we had. I've never been great at judging social situations. I wondered if the friendship would continue back at school or if it was just convenient since we're both at the morgue.

"What's on the schedule for our last day?" I asked.

"A surprise," answered a voice from behind me.

I turned to see Dr. Hidalgo entering the room.

"We're going on a field trip," he continued, heading to his desk and grabbing his medical bag.

Natalie and I gave each other a "did he just say what I think he said" look. We never left the lab. *Never.* A field trip could mean only one thing.

"To a crime scene?" she asked, trying to mask her obvious excitement. "We're going to a crime scene?"

"Yes." He took a camera from a shelf and then slipped it into his bag. "We are going to a crime scene."

"And you're cool with us being there?" I asked. "Nightmare-wise?"

"I give you my no-nightmares guarantee," he assured

us as he held three fingers in the air like a Boy Scout taking an oath.

A few things you should know about Dr. H. First of all, he's awesome. He's been like family my whole life. Second, he has obsessive-compulsive disorder and is the neatest, most organized person I have ever met. He has wire-rimmed glasses and always wears a bow tie that matches his socks. He keeps his nails perfectly manicured and gets the same haircut from the same barber every other Thursday.

He has a way to do things, and that's the way he always does them. My mom once told me that's why he's such a brilliant medical examiner. He's so obsessive that he notices when any detail is out of place.

One example of his OCD is that whenever he leaves for a crime scene, he follows the exact same routine. First, he pulls a new legal pad from the supply cabinet and writes the case number, time, and location across the top three lines.

Next, he calls the staff secretary and gives her the same information, so that she can open an official file. Finally, he grabs his doctor's bag and the keys to Coroner's Van #3 and drives to the crime scene. He says he likes #3 because it has the best radio.

This time, however, he didn't do any of those things. He just rushed out the door.

"It will be quicker if we walk," he explained as we scrambled to stay with him in the maze of hallways that snake through the basement. "I know a shortcut."

I thought I knew my way around the morgue pretty well, but I was ready to start leaving bread crumbs so we could find our way back, when he suddenly popped open a door and we stepped out onto First Avenue. I had no idea how we got there, but I couldn't help noticing that his shortcut let us leave the building without anyone else knowing.

Dr. H didn't say anything about where we were going or what type of crime scene to expect. He just did his speed-walking thing while we tried to keep up. He spent most of the walk on the phone, arranging for someone to meet us. "This is it," he announced as he came to a stop in front of an alley on Second Avenue.

If this was a crime scene, I was underwhelmed. There were no detectives looking for clues. There was no mob of people trying to figure out what had happened. There wasn't even any of that yellow police tape. There was only a tall iron gate blocking off the alley.

"Someone should be here any minute to let us in," he continued.

The sign at the top of the gate read NEW YORK MARBLE CEMETERY. INCORPORATED 1831.

Just then, Natalie noticed something stuck between the edge of the sign and the top of the gate. "What's that?" she asked, pointing at it.

The sun was directly above us, so when we looked up, it was impossible to see clearly.

"Let's find out," Dr. H replied.

He grabbed a silver pointer from his bag, extending it until it was long enough to reach the sign. Then he put his arm through the bars and tapped at the object from behind so that it fell on our side of the gate.

"Got it," I said as I went to catch it.

"You might not want—" was all he got out before it was too late.

I caught it, and when I looked down, I realized it was a severed human finger. So much for the no-nightmares guarantee.

". . . to touch that," he said, completing his sentence.

I tried not to gag as I hot-potatoed it over to him.

"Impressive catch, though," he added. "Especially with the sun in your eyes."

Without missing a beat, Natalie grabbed a bottle of hand sanitizer from her backpack and gave it to me.

"Thanks."

"Left hand, ring finger," Dr. Hidalgo concluded instantly.

I was impressed. "You can tell that without the other fingers to go by?"

He held it up for us to see. "The wedding ring kind of helps."

Sure enough, there was a gold band around the base of the finger. I stared at the finger for a moment. Something about it seemed wrong. Then I realized what it was. There was no blood.

Dr. Hidalgo slipped the ring off the finger and checked the inside for an inscription. "*Amor Fidelis*, Cornelius," he read aloud. "Faithful love . . . Cornelius. Not a name you hear every day."

Once again, Dr. Hidalgo broke standard procedure. Rather than putting the finger into an official evidence bag and then labeling it, he slipped it and the ring into a plain plastic baggie and then dropped it into his doctor's bag.

A few minutes later, the caretaker of the cemetery arrived to unlock the gate for us. He told us he had to rush back to the office and asked Dr. Hidalgo if he could lock up when we left.

That meant we were all alone.

The cemetery looked like a small park. A tall stone wall wrapped around the edge. The only way in or out was through the gated alley.

"Look for anything out of the ordinary," Dr. H said as we began to spread out and scour the grounds.

"How's this for out of the ordinary?" I offered. "This cemetery doesn't seem to have any tombstones or graves."

"That's because a law was passed in the early 1800s that banned earthen graves in Manhattan," he explained. "The fear was that yellow fever would pass from the dead bodies into the soil and make its way back among the living."

"Then where are the bodies?" Natalie asked.

"They're in underground death chambers," he said.

"Death what?" I asked as I stopped in my tracks and processed yet another image for my sleepless nights.

"Marble rooms where they could place the corpses underground without having to worry about their decay contaminating the soil. Think of them as studio apartments for the afterlife. There's another cemetery just like it around the corner."

"And how is this a crime scene?" Natalie asked.

"Last night the police received a dozen phone calls complaining about loud noises coming from here."

"The crime is *loud noises*?" I asked.

"You saw how hard it was to get in." He motioned back to the alley. "Those gates are unlocked only one Sunday a month. Don't you wonder what was causing all the commotion?"

"Not particularly," I answered, getting a little spooked. Severed fingers, death chambers, and scary noises. As far as field trips went, this rated well below the Museum of Natural History. (But it was still better than our class visit to the wastewater treatment plant.)

"This is where the death house was," said Dr. H, coming to a stop. "A shed where the bodies were stored until they were buried. Kind of like the nineteenth-century version of our freezer at work."

"And you know all of this because . . . ?" I asked.

"Are you kidding?" he replied. "I'm a New York City medical examiner. I learn this stuff for fun."

Natalie and I both laughed, which made Dr. H laugh too. Then he noticed something.

"Check this out," he said, kneeling down.

A large square of grass looked like it had been pulled up and laid back down. It didn't stand out from a distance, but up close it was impossible to miss.

Dr. Hidalgo snapped a picture. Then he peeled back the corner of the grass to reveal a large stone slab. "It's a fieldstone cap," he said as he took another photograph. "Someone must have gone down into this entry shaft to reach one of the vaults."

I began to get a sinking feeling that he was expecting us to do the same.

"Look at this," he said with a smile. "They were in a hurry and didn't put the cap all the way back. We can slide it open."

"Lucky us," I said, trying to force a laugh.

Dr. H sat down, ignoring the threat of grass stains on his perfectly pressed pants, wedged himself into the ground, and started pushing the slab with his feet. It was a strain, but after a minute or so, he managed to move it far enough to reveal a dark shaft in the ground.

"You're not going down there, are you?" I asked.

"No," he said, to my momentary relief. "I'm much too big to fit in there. It's going to have to be one of you two."

"Seriously?" I said. "What about your no-nightmares guarantee?"

"I'll go, Dr. H," Natalie volunteered. "Molly's too scared to do something like that."

Instead of feeling relieved, I felt challenged. "I didn't say anything about being scared," I corrected. "Just let me think about it for a second."

I sat on the edge of the shaft and dangled my legs through the opening. "Okay, now I've thought about it. I'm in."

Dr. H and Natalie shared a smile.

"I'm very proud of you," he said as he handed me a small flashlight.

Natalie reached into her backpack again and pulled out the hand sanitizer. "I'm ready the moment you get back."

I gave her my sister's jacket. "Protect this with your life. If I take it down there, I might as well just stay in the vault."

A small ladder was built into the wall. I slowly climbed down into the shaft. Actually, I tried to do it slowly, but I lost my grip and fell into the darkness. I landed on my butt, and when I looked back up at them, the sunlight around their heads looked like halos.

"Are you okay?" Dr. H asked.

"I found the floor," I answered.

"There should be a door to the vault just to your left," Dr. H told me.

"I really can't believe I'm doing this," I said as I stood up and brushed the dirt off my hands. I pushed on the door and was surprised by how easily it swung open. The sunlight didn't quite reach here, so the vault was just empty darkness. It had a disgusting smell that made me wish I'd brought along my vanilla extract.

"What do you see?" Dr. Hidalgo asked.

"Nothing yet," I answered as I turned on the flashlight.

The shaft of light cut through the darkness. I knew that if I could do this, I could overcome almost any fear. I stepped all the way into the vault and looked around.

Thirty seconds later I stepped back out into the shaft and looked up at their still-haloed faces.

"Well?" Natalie asked nervously. "What did you see?"

"It's what I didn't see that's interesting," I replied. "Shouldn't there be dead people in there?"

The Reason I Hate Swans

After taking a deep breath and realizing that despite my worst fears, I was not going to uncover a pile of maggot-riddled corpses, I took Dr. Hidalgo's camera and went back into the burial vault for a second, slightly longer, look around. I counted enough slabs to hold ten bodies; each one was empty. Still, the vault rated pretty high on the creep-o-meter, so I took a few quick pictures and then climbed back up to the surface.

While the doctor scribbled some notes and I put the hand sanitizer to good use, Natalie went over to the wall where there are plaques that correspond with each of the vaults.

"According to this, there should be eight people buried in there," she said, reading from one. "All from the Blackwell family."

Dr. H nodded and wrote this down on his pad. "The Blackwells were an important family in the early history of New York," he said. "In fact, Blackwell's Island was the original name of Roosevelt Island."

Natalie and I shared a smile at the mention of Roosevelt Island. It's a thin strip of land in the East River that runs alongside midtown Manhattan. Hardly anyone lives on it and nothing much happens there, so most people never give it a thought. Natalie and I smiled because Roosevelt Island is a big part of our everyday lives. It's where our school is located.

"By the way," Dr. H asked Natalie, "are any of the Blackwells that are supposed to be in the vault named Cornelius?"

Natalie laughed, but she stopped cold when she looked at the plaque. "Yes!"

"Interesting," he replied as he made a note.

Natalie and I were stunned.

"How can that be?" I asked.

Dr. H looked up from his pad and answered, "My

guess is grave robbery, but that's something for the police to figure out."

We looked around the cemetery for a little while longer, but found nothing else that seemed out of the ordinary. Since it was our last Friday of the summer, Dr. Hidalgo treated us to lunch at Carmine's, where we shared big bowls of pasta and laughed at the retelling of my descent into the Blackwell crypt.

Despite Dr. H's promises, I did have a couple of bad dreams. But over the next few days the worries that kept me up at night went from severed fingers and robbing graves to fitting in and making friends. The first day of school was looming, and even in a student body filled with science geeks, I wasn't particularly skilled at social situations.

Every year more than a thousand students from across New York's five boroughs apply to MIST.

Only seventy get in.

Applying never would have occurred to me if not for the fact that my mother was a MIST grad. She'd always talked about me maybe going there, and just filling out the application made me feel closer to her. Even though I'm a good student, I was totally shocked when I was accepted. So now, in addition to our mismatched eyes, MIST is something special that the two of us share. Sometimes during lunch I like to sneak into the library to look for pictures of her in old yearbooks.

The student body isn't the only thing that makes MIST unusual. The campus looks like something out of a horror movie. The school is made up of four buildings that originally housed a mental hospital in the late 1880s. (That little tidbit is left off the brochure.)

In other ways, though, MIST is just like every other school—filled with cliques and rivalries, which is why I had an uneasy feeling as I got ready that morning. I even ignored all scientific reasoning and brought along a good-luck charm: a necklace with a little horseshoe on it that I had found in my mom's old jewelry box.

The first few classes went fine, but the moment I'd been dreading was lunch. That's where my solo status was at its most glaring. Unlike most middle school girls, who traveled in packs and coordinated their lives and wardrobes with their BFFs, I tended to do things by myself. This hadn't always been the case. For one three-and-a-half week period, I was part of a group.

I'm embarrassed to admit how much I liked it.

It started last year, right around Thanksgiving. Every day at lunch I sat at a table with the same six girls. We were all new to the school and were pretty intimidated, so we found our strength in numbers.

One day one of the girls, Jessica, said that our group should have a name. I wasn't sure if she was joking or not, but some of the others agreed with her, and suddenly finding a name became a big deal. Everyone tried to come up with one that would fit us.

Surprisingly, *I* was the one who did. It was the holiday season, and I had Christmas carols in my head. I blurted out, "Seven swans a-swimming."

"I love it," Jessica announced. "We're the *Swans*."

Pretty soon the bell rang, and I didn't think any more about it. But the next day when we sat down, Jessica had a surprise for us. She opened her lunch box and pulled out seven silver swan charms. She gave us each one and told us we should keep them in our backpacks. They would mark our secret sisterhood.

For reasons that I still cannot fully understand, I thought this was the coolest thing ever. Suddenly I was part of something special. Something secret. Sometimes I'd walk into a classroom and see that another one of the girls had drawn a little swan in the corner of the chalkboard, and I'd smile. It was our code.

Everything was great until Olivia came along. She

wanted to join the group, which seemed easy enough. We all liked her and, after all, there were eight seats at each cafeteria table. No one would even have to move.

But that's not how Jessica saw it.

"It doesn't make sense," she said. "She'd make eight, and there are only seven swans. Eight would make us maids a-milking, and I am not a maid."

Seriously, that's what she said.

I told her that the song didn't really matter. I reminded her that *I* had been the one to make up the name in the first place. But her mind was set. Seven swans, not one more or one less.

My mistake was thinking that all swans were created equal. I didn't realize that some were more equal than others and that Jessica had become our leader. In a show of protest I reached into my backpack, pulled out my swan, and slapped it on the table. I thought five other girls would join me in pointing out how ridiculous this was and do the same.

No one did.

They just sat there and stared at me like I was the world's biggest traitor. Before I knew it, Olivia had my swan charm and was sitting at the table with the other girls while I was all alone in a corner of the cafeteria. I was living a reverse fairy tale. I'd gone from swan to ugly duckling.

At Christmas, Jessica even gave me a nickname. She started calling me Partridge. "Because in 'The Twelve Days of Christmas,' the partridge is the one that's all alone."

Nine months later, I still felt anxious as I walked past their table to my corner spot.

When I sat down, I noticed Jessica giving me her usual superior look. But then a funny thing happened. Her smirk became a look of surprise with maybe even a hint of jealousy mixed in. I turned to see what had caused this and was amazed to find Natalie and two of her friends standing by my table, holding their lunches.

"Mind if we join you?" she said.

Lunch is one of the rare times when Upper School and Lower School students are together in one place. Even so, they hardly ever mingle. A Lowbie sitting at a lunch table with high schoolers is practically unheard of.

"Not at all," I said with a smile as I looked back at Jessica.

Natalie sat down and did some quick introductions.

"Molly, meet Alex and Grayson. Guys, this is Molly Bigelow."

"Nice to meet you," Grayson said.

"We heard you like to hang out at the morgue," Alex added with a smile. I wasn't sure if he was teasing me, but at the moment, just knowing that it was killing Jessica was all that mattered. Suddenly, I thought of Jamaican Bob, the security guard with the bad jokes.

"Well, you know what they say about the morgue," I said as coolly as I could. "Everybody's dying to get in."

It took a moment, but they all actually laughed. Although I had never met Alex or Grayson, I knew both of them by reputation. Alex was a boy version of Natalie. He had supergeek brains in a quarterback's body, and I wondered if they might be boyfriend and girlfriend. Grayson, on the other hand, looked more like you'd expect a science geek to look. A ninth grader, he was known as the school's resident computer genius, which is saying something at a place like MIST.

When he sat down, the first thing he did was look at me and say, "You're heterochromatic."

"What?" I asked.

"Heterochromatic," he repeated. "It means your eyes are different colors."

"I know what it means," I said. "It's just kind of an odd way to start a conversation."

"Grayson doesn't have much of a social filter," Natalie warned. "You get used to it."

Alex, meanwhile, was busy pulling out an amazing array of food from what had to be the world's largest lunch box. He had two ham-and-turkey sandwiches, a bag of chips, string cheese, two bananas, a box of crackers, raisins, and a can of soda.

I don't know if I actually said "wow" out loud, but I certainly thought it.

"Oh yeah," Natalie added. "And Alex eats more than any three people you've ever met. Try not to stare, he's very sensitive about it."

"I am not," said Alex as he chewed off the end of the string cheese.

"You should be," Grayson interjected.

"Is that so?" Alex said with a laugh. "You think *my* eating habits are embarrassing. You won't eat any food that's white. As if color affected the taste."

Grayson slumped. "We just met her."

Alex ignored him and turned to me. "I'm not joking. He won't eat mayonnaise, milk, eggs, vanilla ice cream, sour cream . . . anything white."

"I eat bread," Grayson offered.

"Only if it's toasted."

Grayson laughed and then added, "It tastes better toasted."

"So, now you know a little something about us," Alex said. "Let's find out about you."

"I eat almost anything," I said. "Except I don't like pickles or peaches."

"Because they both start with the letter *p*?" Grayson asked hopefully.

"No," I answered. "Because I don't like how they taste."

"How very reasonable," Alex said.

The joking and friendly teasing continued throughout lunch. I have to say that this group was a lot more fun than the Swans. I couldn't quite figure out how the three of them became friends, but I could tell they really were.

I also couldn't help but feel a little self-conscious. Throughout lunch, they kept asking me questions like they were interviewing me for the school paper.

They asked me about my friends (what friends?) and my taste in music (anything with a girl who plays guitar). They even wanted to know about the Junior Birder program. Part of me liked the attention but another part was exhausted by how relentless it all was.

"What do you want to be when you grow up?" Grayson asked.

"A doctor."

"Why?" asked Alex.

"That's kind of personal, don't you think?"

"I don't know," he said. "Is it?"

"It is to me," I explained. "A few years ago my mother died from cancer. During those last six months, I spent a lot of time in hospital rooms watching doctors work."

"And now you want to be like them?" Grayson asked.

I looked him in the eye and shook my head. "Didn't you hear me? I said she died. I'm going to be *better* than them."

And with that both Grayson and Alex smiled, and the questions stopped.

Natalie gave them a look and said, "Didn't I tell you?"

They both nodded.

"Tell them what?" I asked.

"Just that you were cool and that we should get to know you," Alex said.

Okay, no one ever called me cool before.

"We're really glad to have met you," Grayson said.

"Definitely," added Alex. "We've got to go help set up for the assembly, but we'll see you around. I promise."

They got up and left me alone with Natalie.

Once they were gone, I asked, "You want to explain what that was all about?"

"They're just a couple of friends of mine," she said. "I'd been talking about getting to know you over the summer, and they wanted to meet you. Don't worry. They're good guys."

Then something caught her eye. She leaned over and looked at my necklace. "Where'd you get that?"

"I found it in my mom's old jewelry box," I said. "Why?"

She looked a little concerned and then seemed to force a smile. "No reason. I just didn't remember your wearing it this summer."

"Yeah," I replied. "I thought a horseshoe might bring me some luck."

She nodded. "Let's hope so."

After lunch everybody went to the auditorium for the start-of-the-school-year assembly. As always, it began with an inspirational speech from our principal, Dr. Gootman.

"Immortality," he intoned as he gripped the podium. "The pursuit of science is the quest to render obsolete the boundaries of our mortal beings. It is the search for immortality." (No one talks like this, right? But Dr. Gootman really pulls it off.)

"Although scientific advancements have dramatically increased our lifespan, death is still inevitable. You cannot live forever." He took a long dramatic pause before adding, "Or can you?"

He held up a test tube so that it shimmered in the light. "This vial contains a strain of the bacterium *Saccharomyces cerevisiae*."

A girl sitting next to me gulped like it was some deadly form of anthrax.

"It's more commonly known as yeast," he continued, much to the girl's relief. "And as long as yeast is fed a steady diet of flour and water, it will live forever.

"This particular strain was created here at MIST as part of a chemistry experiment . . . in 1904."

He let the words sink in.

"Today we will do what has been done on the first day of each fall semester since then. We will eat bread made from this yeast. In doing so we will continue a meal that has included every student and teacher in this school's history."

He stopped and looked at the test tube for a moment. There was a touch of emotion in his voice as he continued. "The students from that chemistry class died long ago. But more than a century later, their experiment still thrives. Immortality.

"At most schools the mascot is some sort of cartoon animal—a ram or a bear on a football helmet. Welcome to the only school whose mascot is a single-celled bacterium. Welcome to MIST."

Ω 4

Why I Floss on a Daily Basis

Before I go any further, I should probably explain my intense fear of heights. It started with the scariest moment in my life. One evening when I was five years old, my mom and I had just left a movie theater and were walking down the street when a lunatic charged up to us and grabbed her purse. They had a quick tug-of-war, and when the purse strap broke, he fell to the ground. In a flash, my mom swooped me up into her arms and started running. Even though he had the purse, he still chased after us.

I was crying my eyes out, but Mom stayed cool and calm. She was concerned, but she was in control. First she ran into a building that was brightly lit. When he continued toward the building, she started to run up the stairs. I can still remember the sound of his shoes echoing in the stairwell as he ran up after us. Because I was facing back over her shoulder, I got a good look at his face.

I will never forget that face.

When we got to the top of the stairs, we burst through a door and onto the roof. My mom was still cool and calm. She set me down and picked up a brick. At first I thought she was going to use it to hit him when he came through the door. Instead, she used it to smash the door handle, breaking it so it wouldn't work.

Seconds later we could hear him pounding on the other side of the door. Her trick worked, and he couldn't get it to open. Eventually, he went away.

We were no longer in danger from the lunatic, but we had another problem. My mom had done such a good job of breaking the door, *we* couldn't open it either. And since her phone was in the purse that was stolen, we couldn't call anyone for help. We wound up stuck on the roof for the entire night. It was cold and rainy, and I was terrified. I was scared that if I fell asleep, I would somehow fall off the top of the building. Ever since, I've tried to avoid anything higher than our third-floor apartment.

This is why I've spent my entire life in New York without ever stepping foot in the Empire State Building or the Statue of Liberty. And it's why, when the assembly ended and school let out, I wasn't one of the kids headed for the Roosevelt Island tram.

The tram is the most popular way for people to get on and off the island. Up to a hundred and twenty-five people at a time get into the tram car (I like to call it the death cage) and take the four-minute ride over the East River. My problem is that along the way, the tram dangles from a cable about two hundred and fifty feet in the air.

I get ticked when people say I have a phobia. Phobias are based on irrational fears. My fear is rooted in a true scientific understanding of gravity. That's a big tram and that's a big drop.

Luckily, Roosevelt Island also has a subway station. It's not very busy, but the F train runs through it on the way to Queens, so it works perfectly for me. Well, it would be perfect if it weren't for the escalators.

Roosevelt Island Station is the second deepest in the entire subway system. It's like an upside-down ten-story building, and you have to ride a trio of unbelievably steep escalators to get down there. It's not the ideal thing for someone terrified of heights, but still *way* better than the tram.

That day, like most others, my solution for dealing with the escalator was to grab the handrail as tightly as I could and close my eyes until I reached the bottom.

If my eyes had been open, I might have seen the creepy guy a little bit sooner. Instead, I didn't notice him until after I had just missed the train and plopped down onto a bench to wait for the next one.

Or, put another way, I didn't realize he was there until I was completely alone and unprotected in a subway station one hundred feet below ground.

Once the rush of the departing train died down, the station fell virtually silent. The only noises were the buzzing of the lights hanging from the ceiling and the occasional crackle of electricity along the train's third rail.

Looking around, I noticed this guy sitting on another bench, staring right at me.

He was tall like a basketball player, and superthin. His hair had been dyed shoe-polish black, and he had dark circles under his eyes. He wore mismatched earrings and, judging by the splotches along his jawline, he also wore makeup. Very bad makeup. Even by New York subway standards he was weird.

Then he smiled and got even weirder. His teeth were an unforgettable blend of orange and yellow. Not one of them was straight. I suddenly realized I had seen them earlier that morning. He'd been standing on the platform and smiled at me when I got off the subway on my way to school.

Now it seemed like he had been waiting all day for me to come back. I know that sounds paranoid, but that's what it felt like.

I smiled politely as I stood up and headed for the escalator. I wasn't moving particularly fast because I didn't want to alert him and also because my backpack was loaded down with all the new textbooks that had been handed out on the first day of school.

Even though I was going away from him, I could hear his boots thud as he walked across the floor behind me. He was moving faster than I was, and the sound was getting closer.

I needed to slow him down, so I decided to use all those textbooks to my advantage. Just as I heard him about to reach me, I swung around with my backpack at the end of my outstretched arm to build as much force as possible. I was going to slam it right into the side of his head.

He didn't even flinch. He just reached out and stopped my bag with an open hand. For a skin-and-bones–looking guy, he was unbelievably strong. He ripped the backpack out of my hand and flung it across the floor.

Cool and calm, I told myself.

He made a move for me, and out of nowhere I flashed back to my Jeet Kune Do classes. I turned my body to the side, and when his fist went past me, I punched him right in the ribs. It must have been pretty hard because I actually heard ribs break.

I smiled because I knew this would knock him to the ground and let me run for help. Unfortunately, he didn't seem to know this. The broken ribs didn't bother him at all. He just stood there and flashed that crazy Crayola smile of his.

Cool and calm was no longer an option. It was time to be *freaked and frightened*!

He grabbed me by the shoulders and slammed me against the wall. I screamed for help, which got no response from him or anyone else. And just when I thought he couldn't be any creepier, he started to sniff the air around my face like he was some sort of wild animal.

"What do you want from me?" I wailed.

He tried to talk, but it was a struggle for him to form a word. Finally, he gurgled something that sounded like "Omaha." Then he yanked off my mom's necklace. The chain cut into the flesh along the back of my neck.

He started to say something else when a voice called out.

"Dude, you'll want to give that back. It's a family heirloom."

Creepy Joe and I both turned to see my rescuer. It was Natalie. Oddly enough, he seemed to recognize her. Because the second he saw her, he let go of me, smiled, and started sizing her up.

"I can tell by your genius expression that you know what I am," Natalie barked. I had no idea where this tough-girl attitude was coming from, but I was happy to see it on my side.

"What do you have to say for yourself?" she taunted. "Come on! Use your words!"

This frustrated him. He kept trying to say something, but the struggle was too hard. After a few tries, he gave up and just charged at her. He was fast. Right when he was about to slam into her, she twisted to the side and used his momentum to slam him into the tile wall.

"I'll call the police!" I yelled.

"Don't," Natalie said, looking right at me. "I've got this."

She turned back to face Creepy Joe, who was picking himself up off the ground. There was now a huge cut across his forehead. But for some reason there was no blood. He also had three fingers completely dislocated and pointing in different directions. This didn't seem to bother him either, as he calmly snapped each one back into place. When he was done he smiled again.

Natalie was completely unfazed.

"If you think you're some sort of tough guy Level 2 who can make his reputation by taking me out, you are sadly misinformed," she said. "You're an L3, and that's all you'll ever be. I don't know what you've heard, but there's no climbing back up the evolutionary ladder."

I had absolutely no idea what she was talking about. But he seemed to. And the taunting made him even angrier.

He ran straight at her again. This time she leveled him with an elbow across the face that sent him sprawling on the floor.

When she saw her sleeve, she was not happy.

"Look what your cheapo makeup did to my favorite shirt," she said as she pointed at a smear by her elbow. "I love this shirt. It's my first-day-of-school shirt. And that will not come out."

This time he was too woozy to get up. The blow to the head had really shaken him, and Natalie took advantage of this. She stepped over him and kneeled down so that her knees pinned his shoulders to the ground.

He snarled and spat and tried to break loose, but it was useless.

"Did he sniff you?" she asked.

At first the question didn't register.

"Did he sniff you?" she demanded more emphatically.

"Yeah," I said, creeped out by the memory. "Like a dog."

She looked down at him and shook her head.

"Get the vanilla," she told me, pointing at her bag on the floor. "It's in the front pocket."

"The vanilla extract from the morgue?" I asked, confused, as I dug around for it.

"It's more useful than you might imagine."

I found the bottle and then handed it to her. She jammed it up each of his nostrils and squirted until he sneezed and gagged.

"That should take care of that," she said. Next, she pulled one of his earrings tight, so that it stretched out his lobe. "Now, do I have your attention?"

He nodded.

"The way you roughed up my friend over there was not cool. I want to give you a little reminder so you don't make the same mistake again."

Without warning she yanked on the earring and in the process ripped off most of his ear. That's not an exaggeration. More than half his ear was now dangling from the earring in her hand.

"I want you to go back to where you belong and spread the word among all your little troll buddies that if any of you mess with me or my friends, some very bad things will happen. Very bad! Do you understand?"

He nodded slowly.

"Go ahead," she said. "Use your words."

He took a deep breath and, with a voice straight out of another world, slowly answered, "Un-der-stand."

"Good," she said as though everything was bright and cheery. "I'm glad we had this chance to talk. Now give me back her necklace."

She jerked the necklace from his hand and got off him. He scampered to his feet and ran away. In the final element of freaky, he didn't head for the exit. Instead, he ran into the subway tunnel toward Manhattan.

"Don't forget your ear," she called out to him. If he heard her, he was not coming back. Natalie tossed the ear into the darkness of the tunnel. Then she turned to me, and I did the only thing that seemed appropriate: I started to throw up onto the subway tracks.

"Go right ahead," she said. "It's really a lot to take in all at once. I threw up my first time too. Did he say anything to you?"

"Omaha," I said between retches.

61

She shook her head. "Not Omaha," she replied. "Omega."

"Why Omega?"

"It's actually a longer story than we have time for at the moment. But I promise I'll tell you everything. For right now, though, we need to get you aboveground quickly."

"Where are we going?" I asked.

"The tram."

"No way," I declared. "I am not riding in the dangling death cage."

"What?" she said with a smirk. "Are you really willing to take a chance that the next thing out of that tunnel is the F train, and not the creeper with a dozen of his friends? Because frankly, I don't think we're ready for that yet."

I looked into the darkness of the subway tunnel, and was terrified.

"Okay," I said softly. "Maybe the tram's not as bad as I think."

5

I'd Better Get Used to Creepy Guys Who Want to Kill Me

It turns out I was wrong about the Roosevelt Island tram. Riding it was *far more terrifying* than I had ever imagined. The floor rumbled, the cables creaked, and the entire car swayed from side to side in the wind. And just in case I forgot that I was dangling two hundred and fifty feet in the air, there were giant windows conveniently located on each side of the car to remind me. Luckily, I still had the subway attack fresh in my mind to keep me distracted.

"Just relax," Natalie whispered. "It's going to be all right." She was standing right next to me, trying to act normal while still being reassuring.

Whenever I went to ask her a question, she just waved me off. "We'll talk about it all when we get there."

"Can I at least ask where we're going?"

"Grayson's."

"Grayson from lunch?" I didn't quite see how a computer geek scared of white food was going to be of much help against an underground killing machine. "Why?"

"First of all, don't be like everybody else and underestimate him," she said. "Grayson is awesome. He's smart, funny, and talented. And he's off-the-charts loyal. Plus, he lives in Brooklyn, and we have got to get you out of Manhattan."

The next thirty minutes were a blur. I can only remember bits and pieces. I do know that somehow I survived the tram ride only to be told that we next had to take the subway to Brooklyn.

"We're going back underground? I thought you said that was bad."

"It will be safe," Natalie assured me. "Even if the creeper guessed we were coming here and ran full speed, it would take him at least another twenty minutes to reach this station. The tunnels don't intersect anywhere near here."

I guess it should have struck me as odd that Natalie knew so much about the layout of New York's subway tunnels. But I was too busy clinging to the "it will be safe" portion of her statement to notice.

Safe or not, she insisted we sit in the very front of the first car. And she turned so that she was in front of me and could see if anyone was coming toward us.

I was still in a fog when we made it to Grayson's. He lives in a brownstone in the Fort Greene section of Brooklyn.

"Come on in," he said when he opened the door. Then he shot Natalie a look. "You're only *three* days early."

"Sorry about that, but we kind of had to speed things up," Natalie said as we entered. "Are we alone?"

"Yes, but I don't know for how long," he answered, obviously frustrated. "I had arranged for everyone to be gone on Friday—"

She cut him off. "I know. This was supposed to happen in three days. Deal with it."

"How am I supposed to do that?" he asked, exasperated, nodding toward me. "I'm not ready for her to be here."

"You know, I'm in the room and can hear you," I reminded him.

"As I told you at lunch," Natalie said, "Grayson's a little lacking in the social skills."

"Oh, right, and you're so good. How about the social

skills in this text you sent?" He picked up his phone and read it aloud. "'Molly's orientation. Thirty minutes. Grayson's.' No explanation. No 'please.' No verbs."

"Listen, she was attacked in the subway station," Natalie said, cutting to the point. "He was a bad guy, and I don't think it's wise to leave her out there without some support and information. Besides, I kind of outrank you, so get over it."

"Attacked?"

"By a Level 3."

"You might have mentioned that in the text," he said, suddenly concerned. He turned to me with caring eyes that were surprisingly reassuring. "Are you okay?"

"I'm not sure," I answered honestly. "I don't really understand what's going on."

He gave me a quick look over, checking for any bumps or bruises. "What happened to your neck?" he asked.

I had forgotten about that. I reached up and ran my finger along the cut. The sting had dulled but still hurt. "He yanked off my necklace."

"We'd better clean it," he said. "Come on."

He led me into the kitchen. I leaned over the sink and held up the back of my hair while he ran some cool water over the wound.

"How do you know he's a Level 3?" he asked Natalie. "The teeth?"

"They were some kind of special," she said. "Quite the ad for daily flossing."

I stood up from the sink, and he handed me a paper towel. "Pat this gently along the wound. Don't rub, just pat."

"I know," I said with a smile. "My dad's a paramedic. He's kind of obsessive when it comes to first-aid training."

Grayson smiled. "First-aid training. That will come in handy."

Natalie nodded.

"Hey, I know what would come in handy," I said.

"What?"

"If you guys would stop talking about this like any of it makes sense and explain it to me instead."

"I'm sorry," Grayson said with a sigh. "It's just all so complicated. I don't know where to begin. That's why I've been working on my presentation for the last few weeks. So that we could explain all this in a way that would make sense to you."

"How can you have been working on it for weeks?" I asked. "We just met today."

He smiled and shared a look with Natalie. "Actually, we've been checking you out for nearly a year."

"Checking me out for what?" I asked.

"Why don't you just do the presentation," Natalie said, prodding.

"It's not—"

"I know," she said. "It's not perfect. But you're Grayson the Great. I'm sure it's still amazing. Way better than I could do with months to prepare."

"Okay," he said with a bashful smile, the flattery working like a charm. "But we'll have to watch in my room. It's still loaded on Zeus."

"Zeus?" I said.

"His computer. He named it." Then she whispered conspiratorially, "He acts like it's a person."

"I do not," he said as we walked down the hall toward his room.

"You gave it a birthday party," she said.

Grayson stopped walking for a moment. "Annual hard-drive maintenance and software upgrades do not count as a birthday party."

"No," she said. "But singing 'Happy Birthday' to it does."

He took a deep breath. They'd obviously been through this before. "You know I was testing the new voice-recognition software."

Natalie looked at me. "Birthday party."

I laughed for the first time since the attack.

"Pardon my messy room," Grayson said as he opened the door.

"Yeah, I know," I answered. "You weren't expecting me for three more days. I'm fine with a little mess."

Okay, "little mess" turned out to be something of an understatement. The room was a maze of books, maps, and electronics.

One wall was covered with a giant subway map. It wasn't like the color-coded ones on the walls in each station that show you which train to take. It was technical, with elevations and measurements. It also had stations marked that I didn't recognize. They were ones that had been closed down long ago.

The star of the room, though, was definitely Zeus, which took up an entire third of the floor space. It was an odd mix of high-tech and homemade. Different computers and custom parts had all been connected into one giant supercomputer, with three large high-def monitors.

"Tell him hello," Grayson whispered to me.

"Tell who?"

"Zeus."

"You want me to talk to your computer? Seriously?"

Natalie nodded for me to do it. So, even though I felt ridiculous, I went with it.

"Hello, Zeus."

"Hello, Molly," it answered in a human-sounding voice. "Welcome to Omega."

Again with the Omega, but more than a little cool that Zeus recognized my voice. My yearbook picture even popped up on-screen. Grayson was grinning proudly.

"How'd you pull that off?" Natalie asked.

"I recorded her voice today at lunch," he answered.

"Will somebody tell me what Omega is?" I demanded, trying to get them to focus on what was going on.

"That's what I'm about to explain," Grayson said. He pulled out a chair from his desk and offered it to me. He signaled Natalie to sit on the corner of his unmade bed.

Grayson picked up some index cards and stood by the computer like he was about to give a speech. Just before he started talking, he turned to check his appearance in a mirror on his dresser and fixed his hair with a comb he pulled from his back pocket.

"Good evening," he said, reading from the first card. (Apparently, Friday's session was scheduled for evening.) "For your safety and ours, what we're about to tell you must stay private. You can't tell anybody. First of all, no one would believe you. Second, it would put them in danger as well. Do you understand?"

I didn't, but I nodded anyway. "I think so."

Just then the door to the room flew open. I let out a frightened yelp that startled Grayson and sent his index cards flying.

"Did I miss it?"

I turned to see Alex. He was breathing heavily and had obviously been running.

"No," Natalie told him, "we're just getting started."

"I thought this was supposed to be on Friday," he said as he caught his breath.

"*Deal with it*, people," Natalie replied, her temper rising. "She got attacked by a Level 3."

Alex nodded and looked at me. "You okay?"

"I think so," I answered.

"Can we get on with this?" Grayson asked as he picked up his index cards. "My parents could come home at any minute with Wyatt and Van."

Natalie turned to me and shuddered as she said, "His brothers . . . pure evil."

"Sorry," Alex said. "I'll just clear off a spot over here."

He pushed an armful of junk off the edge of the bed

and sent it clattering across the hardwood floor. He took a seat and motioned for Grayson to resume.

"Where was I?" Grayson said as he tried to put the cards back in order. He checked his reflection in the mirror again and ran the comb back through his hair. Then he looked back at me.

"After much consideration, Natalie, Alex, and I would like to extend a formal invitation for you to join our Omega Team. The team's name comes from the final letter in the Greek alphabet because it's our responsibility to be the final word."

"The final word on what?" I asked.

Grayson shot a look at the other two and then back to me. "The final word on the undead."

I don't know how long I sat there with the big doofus expression on my face, but I'm sure it was for a while. Finally, I was able to ask, "You mean, like, zombies?"

"Actually, they hate being called that," he said. "But yes, that's what I mean."

I turned to Natalie and Alex. They both nodded. My first thought was that this was all a big practical joke. I didn't know why they would go to so much trouble to embarrass me, but that was the only thing that made sense.

"Since its founding," Grayson continued, "MIST has

been training select students to police and protect the undead citizens of New York City."

I'd had enough.

"Very funny," I said, with a combination of hurt and anger. "I get that I'm weird and people like to tease me. And maybe I was too eager to have new friends to notice that you were making fun of me. But you really shouldn't have gone to the trouble."

I started to get up, but Alex put a hand on my shoulder to stop me. "This isn't a joke," he said. "We know how hard this is to believe. Each one of us has been where you are right now. And each one of us had the same reaction. But trust us when we say it's true."

"That there are zombies living all over New York?"

"Not all over," Grayson said. "Only in Manhattan. And mostly underground or in the bottom floors of buildings. But that's getting a little ahead of ourselves."

"And just how many of these zombies are there?" I asked mockingly.

"One thousand one hundred and thirty-two," he answered. "According to the last census. But I think there are a lot more than that."

"The census?"

"Not the government one," Grayson said. "The 'Census

of the Undead' is taken by the Omegas every five years. It's one of our responsibilities. The problem is that most of them don't want to be counted."

"You guys really expect me to believe all this? You must think I'm the dumbest Lowbie of them all."

"Actually," Alex said, "we think you may be the smartest. That's why we want you on our team."

"Think about the guy in the subway today," Natalie said. "Nothing made him bleed. Nothing hurt him. Not even broken ribs or fingers twisted in every direction. It's because he isn't really alive. He's a zombie."

"If you join our team," Alex said, "we'll train you and teach you. The four of us will work together."

"To police and protect the undead?"

"That's right," Grayson answered. "There are three levels among the undead. Level 1s look and act just like us. For the most part, they want to live normal lives. That's where the *protect* comes in. We make sure they're able to do that."

"Level 2s look and act like us too," Alex said. "But they have no soul, which means they have no sense of right and wrong. That's where the *policing* comes in. Sometimes they can get out of hand and need to be stopped."

"And the Level 3s?" I asked. "Is that what you called the one who attacked me?"

"They're degraded 1s and 2s barely clinging to whatever bit of life they have," said Natalie. "They're more like the zombies you see in movies. A lot of them don't even realize they're undead. They can't pass for human too well, so they stay mostly underground and avoid coming out in the light of day."

"The presentation I have will take you through the whole history and explain what we know about them," Grayson said. "But we can only show it to you if you take a leap of faith. If you decide to join us."

"If you decide against it, we understand," Natalie said. "You can go back to your regular life, and we'll act like none of this ever happened."

I thought about this for a minute or so without saying a word. They stayed silent too and just sat there and watched me think it over.

"If this is true," I said, "which I don't believe, I don't really have a choice, anyway. I was already attacked for being an Omega even though I'm not one."

"It was a mistake," Natalie said. "Level 3s aren't too smart, and since I covered your scent with the vanilla, it won't happen again."

"Why would he even think I was one in the first place?" I asked.

Natalie held up my necklace. "Because you wore this."

"My mother's horseshoe necklace?" I asked, unable to make a connection.

"It's not a horseshoe," she said. She turned it upside down and I recognized the symbol instantly.

"It's an omega!" I said, realizing.

Natalie nodded.

"But why would my mom have . . ."

That was the exact moment when I started to believe.

"She was one, wasn't she? My mom was an Omega!"

"I can't tell you that," Natalie answered.

"Because you don't know? Or because you won't tell me?"

Natalie shook her head. "Because the identity of any Omega past or present cannot be revealed to anyone outside the group. That's for everybody's safety."

"Then you can tell me," I answered instantly. "And, Grayson, you can start your presentation. I'm in!"

6

Things You Should Never Touch in a Subway Tunnel and Other Lessons

When I told them I wanted to join, they exchanged happy looks and smiled. But before anyone could respond, we heard Grayson's parents come in the front door.

And they weren't alone.

To say that Grayson's little brothers are loud is like saying jet engines are kind of noisy. They sounded like a troop of howler monkeys as they raced down the hallway toward his room. Natalie told Alex to block the door to let me have a chance to reconsider.

"Are you sure?" she asked as the brothers started

slamming their bodies against the door to force their way in. "It's a big decision."

There wasn't much time to think about it. But I didn't really need any. I had never been more certain of anything in my life.

"Positive!"

Just then Alex lost the battle, the door flew open, and the brothers tumbled into the room. They were much smaller than their volume and strength had suggested. Both had big curly hair, thick glasses, and matching elementary school uniforms. They were arguing about whether or not dinosaurs were warm- or cold-blooded and wanted their big brother to settle the dispute.

"Stop!" Grayson quieted the pair as he pointed an angry finger at them. "How many times do I have to tell you about this?"

It was the same angry tone my sister uses whenever I interrupt her and her friends. Except, Grayson being Grayson, the interruption wasn't the part that he was angry about.

"Cold-blooded and warm-blooded are inaccurate terms," he continued. "It's 'endothermic' and 'ectothermic.' Got it? You're not in second grade anymore." (Okay, this was so unlike any argument I had ever had with Beth.)

The scolding quieted them for a few seconds until they

started another argument about who was to blame for using the wrong terms.

Eventually they left the room long enough for me to see Grayson's presentation. Even in its incomplete state, it was as impressive as Natalie had promised.

It was a full multimedia production, complete with pictures, graphics, and video. Some of it even had music and fancy editing. It explained the three levels of zombies and the history of the Omegas.

It was almost done when Grayson's brothers came back to argue about something else, and we decided to move out onto the stoop for some privacy.

I sat down on the top step and asked the one thing I was dying to know. "So tell me, was my mom an Omega?"

Natalie shook her head. "No, she was not *an* Omega." Then she flashed a huge grin. "She was *the* Omega."

"Seriously?"

"Absolutely," Grayson said. "She's a total legend."

"Depending on whether you were one of the living or one of the undead, she was either the most revered or most feared Omega ever," Alex added.

"Feared?" I could hardly believe it. "We're talking about my mom, right? The woman who made snickerdoodles for my birthday?"

"I haven't heard anything about her baking skills," Natalie answered, "but I have heard that she was the ultimate Zeke."

"Zeke?"

"It's from 'ZK,'" Alex explained. "Abbreviation for 'zombie killer.'"

I let this sink in for a moment and couldn't resist smiling. My mom was quite the mix: room mother, soccer coach, medical examiner, zombie killer. No wonder I turned out the way I did.

And now I was following in her footsteps.

Over the next six weeks, Omega training dominated my world. And while my complete lack of a social life left me with plenty of free time, training ate up enough of it that it affected my studies. This led to an oh-so-fun lecture from my dad about my midterm grades.

I blamed it on watching too much television and promised to fix them before my next report card. I don't normally lie to my dad, but I couldn't possibly tell him the truth. It's not like MIST wasn't already superdifficult. It turns out it's even harder when you have to squeeze all of your homework and studying in between training sessions with names like "Seven Ways to Kill a Zombie," "How to Remove Dead Flesh from Open Wounds," and my all-time fave: "Things You Should Never Touch in a Subway Tunnel." (Spoiler alert: "Pretty much everything.")

My new teammates took turns, so I worked with each one on different days.

Mondays and Fridays, I learned history and procedures from Grayson. To avoid interruptions from his brothers, we usually took long walks around Brooklyn while we talked. He explained that the Omegas were more like spies than police and that there was an unknown number of other teams. The only person who knew all the identities was the Prime Omega. The identity of the Prime Omega was top secret, and we had to communicate with him through special encryption software on Grayson's computer.

One Friday, Grayson told me the story of how the zombies originated. We were walking through the Prospect Park Zoo and had just stopped in front of the sea lions.

"It all began in 1896," he started to explain. "A group of miners was digging one of New York's first subway tunnels when an explosion killed all thirteen men in the crew."

He stopped midstory when a family came up and stood next to us at the railing.

"Let Daddy take your picture in front of the seals," said the father.

Grayson turned to him, and, knowing what I knew

about his lack of social grace, I fully expected him to correct the father by pointing out that they were, in fact, sea lions and not seals. I was pleasantly surprised when instead he offered to take their picture so that the whole family could be in it.

"Everyone smile," he said, before adding, "including you *sea lions*." (All right, so he couldn't totally resist. After all, this is Grayson we're talking about.)

He took the picture and handed the camera back to the father. A few moments later, they were walking toward the next exhibit, and I said to Grayson, "I knew you were going to correct him."

Grayson just smiled and resumed the story of the subway miners. "Anyway, the explosion that killed them also blasted open a deep pocket of Manhattan schist."

"What's Manhattan schist?" I asked.

"It's an extremely dense and strong type of bedrock," he answered. "The only place on earth it's found is underneath Manhattan. Without it, New York couldn't have all of its skyscrapers. It's what makes the city possible. And it's also what makes the undead possible."

"What do you mean?"

"Some energy force from the minerals in that bedrock brought the miners back to life," he explained. "But they weren't really alive. They were *undead*."

"And Manhattan schist is still what keeps them from dying?" I asked.

He nodded. "That's why the undead can't leave. And why they stay mostly at ground level or below. That rock is like their oxygen. The farther away from it they are, the weaker they get."

We looked out at the sea lions for a minute, and I pointed out something that I had observed.

"You never call them zombies, do you?"

He shook his head and smiled, maybe a little pleased I had noticed. "No, I don't."

"Why not?"

"Because they don't like it," he said simply. "At least the ones I've talked to. When you hear the word 'zombie,' you think of bad horror movies and flesh-eating monsters. That's just not accurate. I figure if they don't like it, the least I can do is respect that."

"Just like sea lions don't like to be called seals," I pointed out.

"That's exactly right." He turned to a sea lion and called down to it, "You hate that, don't you?"

The sea lion barked back, almost as if he was answering, and we both laughed.

Unlike Grayson, Alex had no problem using the

z-word. That was pretty obvious when I showed up for my first lesson: "Seven Ways to Kill a Zombie."

Don't get me wrong. Alex is a total sweetheart and an incredibly nice person. I just think four years of hand-to-hand combat with the undead have made him not too worried about hurting their feelings.

Alex was in charge of my physical training. We did martial arts together on Tuesdays, and for Thursdays he convinced me to join the school's fencing team. He said it would be good to get weapons practice. I thought I'd hate it, but it's awesome.

"Zombies feel no pain, and most of their organs are no longer functioning," he told me that first day. "So most traditional methods of fighting are useless. When it comes to killing zombies, it's all about going for the head."

We were lined up on the mat in traditional combat positions.

"I'm going to come at you like a zombie," he said. "I want you to show me what you can do."

I looked up at him. Very up. He was at least six inches taller and a hundred pounds heavier.

"It's not exactly a fair fight," I offered.

"It never is," he answered with a confident smile. Of

course he was confident; he didn't know that I had been a star pupil in my Jeet Kune Do class.

The last thing he said as he moved toward me was "Remember to go for the head."

The philosophy of Jeet Kune Do revolves around fluid motion. You are taught to imagine yourself to be like water, which is exactly what I did as he approached me. I dipped down low, spun to the left, and popped up right next to him. This caught him completely off guard. Before he could react, I landed two punches on his jaw and sent him sprawling across the mat.

"You mean like that?" I said, more than a little pleased with myself.

It took him a moment to answer, but when he did he was smiling. He was rubbing the side of his face, but he was smiling.

"Yeah," he said. "Like that."

Wednesdays and Saturdays I did field practice with Natalie. She was great. She taught me how to identify the undead, how to follow someone without being seen, and how to find "indicators." Indicators are beyond cool and are what you use to find former Omegas.

Once you're an Omega, you're one for life. The saying is "Omega today, Omega forever." When you graduate from MIST, you become what's known as a "sleeper." Sleepers are available to help current Omegas. But since everyone's identity must be kept secret, you have to use a code to find the sleepers. The key element of that code is an indicator.

I saw my first indicator one Saturday morning when Natalie pointed out a small red Omega symbol that had been spray painted on the sidewalk.

"Here's one," she said.

"That's an indicator?" I asked. If you didn't know what you were looking for, you'd think it was just a stray mark left over by a work crew.

"No, that's called a 'standpoint,'" she said. "But if you stand on that spot, you should be able to see the indicator."

"Isn't that kind of dangerous?" I asked. "The symbol being so public?"

"The key to indicators is that they're hidden in plain sight. If they weren't, we wouldn't be able to find them. Besides, I think you'll see that it's not as easy as it sounds."

We'll call that an understatement.

I stood on the symbol for about five minutes, look-ing in every direction, searching for anything that might be an indicator, but nothing looked like a code or a clue to me.

"Okay," I finally admitted. "I give up."

Natalie smiled. "What about that shop right over there?" she asked as she pointed at a plant and flower store called Home Gardens.

"What about it?"

"Take the last three letters of 'home' and the first two of 'gardens' and what do you get?"

"O-m-e-g-a. Oh my God, it spells 'Omega'!" I couldn't believe it. Suddenly it seemed so incredibly obvious, like when you find out how a magic trick is done and can't believe that it fooled you.

"You got it," she said. "The woman who runs the shop was an Omega about ten years ago. She comes into the school sometimes to lecture to the botany class."

"Do we go inside and introduce ourselves?" I asked.

"No! The rule is that you only make contact with a sleeper if there is an imminent need," Natalie explained. "That's crucial. We have to protect our identities and theirs. For now, you just lock it away in your memory until you need it someday."

The concept of hidden in plain sight is important. In fact, the key to virtually every Omega code hangs right out in the open in most of the classrooms at MIST. It's the periodic table of elements.

"You're going to have to learn the periodic table," Grayson told me one day. His parents and brothers were at soccer practice, so we were kicking back and drinking cream sodas in his kitchen.

I cracked a smile. "That's easy. I already know the periodic table. It has one hundred eighteen different elements, and each one of those has an atomic number, symbol, and weight."

"I know you know what it is," he answered. "But I mean you're *really* going to have to know it. Memorize it inside and out."

"That's easy," I said with a laugh as I repeated myself. "I already know the periodic table. If you want to test me, feel free."

He gave me a skeptical look. "Okay. I'm going to list off a series of atomic numbers. I want you to tell me which elements they represent."

It was obvious he thought I couldn't do it, so I just played along and said, "I'll try my best."

Without taking a breath he rattled off, "Four, seventy-four, eighteen, seventy-five."

Just as quickly I answered, "Beryllium, tungsten, argon, and rhenium."

His jaw fell open a bit. He was impressed, but he wasn't

going to quit so easily. "That's good . . . but can you write out their symbols?"

I picked up a pencil and quickly wrote the symbols: "Be" for beryllium, "W" for tungsten, "Ar" for argon, and "Re" for rhenium. When I looked down, I was surprised to see that except for one extra *R*, they spelled out a word: BeWArRe. "Beware!" I said, a bit louder than I had intended.

"Very nice," he said. "To the Omegas the numbers four, seventy-four, eighteen, seventy-five are code for 'Beware.'"

I thought it was a pretty cool little code.

"Can you do it in reverse?" he asked. "What code would you use to say 'Help'?"

"I'd go helium, lithium, and phosphorus. That's two, three, fifteen."

He shook his head. "How did you know that so quickly?" he asked. "You haven't taken chemistry yet."

"My mom," I answered. "She made me memorize the periodic table the summer she was in the hospital. She drilled me on it over and over again. I had to know all the parts, but I got fifty cents for every one I got right. The periodic table earned me fifty-nine dollars."

Grayson thought about this for a moment and smiled. "That explains it."

"What explains what?" I asked.

"Your mom," he answered. "She was training you."

"What do you mean?"

"For this," he said as if it couldn't be more obvious. "She was giving you a head start on your Omega training."

I wondered if that could possibly be true. Did my mother suspect I would end up here? If she did, some of her decisions suddenly made more sense. The Jeet Kune Do classes came in handy when Alex and I were training.

And when we were in the field, Natalie said I had to know my way around every inch of Manhattan. I had to know which subways ran to which stations and where all the little parks were located, because they were favorite meeting spots of the undead.

Brownies and Girl Scouts may not know the parks, but Junior Birders do. My time with the Audubon Society had taken me to every little park and green space on the island.

I realized that Grayson was right. My mother had been preparing me for this my whole life. Maybe, just maybe, I could go from geek to Zeke.

The last day of my training was a Saturday. Natalie and I were walking in midtown, not far from the morgue, when I found a standpoint on the sidewalk. Someone had used a stick to draw an Omega symbol into the sidewalk when the cement was still wet.

"Standpoint," I said.

Natalie looked down and smiled. "I've never seen this one before."

After a second, we both said it at the same time: "Race you!"

We stood on the standpoint and scanned the neighborhood for the indicator. It only took about forty-five seconds until I said, "Got it."

I gave Natalie a couple of minutes, but she couldn't find it.

"I don't see it," she said, her pride a little wounded.

"That's because you didn't spend five years in Catholic school," I explained.

I pointed out a bakery across the street. In the corner of the window was an old New York license plate.

"Kind of a strange place for a license plate," I said.

"I guess," she replied. "Maybe it was from their first delivery truck."

"R-E-V-2-2-1-3," I said, reading the plate aloud.

"What about it?"

"It's a verse from the Bible. 'REV' is the book of Revelation, then chapter twenty-two, verse thirteen. 'I am the Alpha and the Omega.' Check out the name of the bakery."

Natalie looked at the sign above the door. "Alpha Bakery. Very nice."

"Thank you," I said, trying to convey modesty but failing miserably.

"Do you know what that means?" she asked.

"That my teacher has done a great job showing me how to spot an indicator?"

"Well, yes. But it also means something much more important."

I looked at her expectantly. "What?"

"It means you're ready for your final exam."

Ω 7

Killing Time

I don't mean to brag, but as far as training goes, I pretty much killed it. Grayson told me it normally takes six to eight weeks to finish, and I was done in four. Of course, most Omega trainees haven't been secretly prepared for it by their zombie-hunter mothers, so I tried not to let it go to my head. Still, it was kind of cool. And if you haven't noticed, "cool" and "my life" aren't very well acquainted.

The biggest advantage to finishing early was that the team wasn't ready for my final exam. That meant, with the exception of Thursday's fencing practice, I had a week completely free to catch up on schoolwork. And, yes, I do realize being excited about having time to catch up on schoolwork might explain why "cool" and "my life" are such strangers.

Of course, having time to catch up and actually taking advantage of it are two totally different things. It seemed that no matter how hard I tried to focus, I could not stop thinking about my mom, the Omegas, and what my life as a zombie killer might be like. Then, after fencing practice, I did something really stupid.

I went back to the Alpha Bakery.

I know that Natalie told me there should be no contact unless there was an *imminent need*, but I *needed* to do something Omega based or I thought I would burst. Besides, I wasn't actually planning on making contact. I had an excuse. It was my father's birthday, and although there are about a hundred bakeries closer to our apartment, I needed a cake.

Before I went in, I stopped at the standpoint to make sure I hadn't misread the clue. I hadn't. The only thing that could possibly refer to Omega was the license plate with the coded Bible verse. My plan was to go into the bakery, get a cake, and get out. Since the baker would never know I was an Omega, there would be no hint I had broken any rules and I would still have the thrill of making a secret connection.

I walked in, and a bell over the door announced my arrival. The smell was delicious. A man looked up from a sheet of fresh-baked cookies.

"Can I help you?" he asked.

I was determined to play it cool. "I'm looking for a birthday cake . . . for my pops." (Apparently, something in my head suggested "pops" would sound cool. It didn't.)

"We have a book over here with different cakes you can order," he said. "How soon is his birthday?"

"Today," I said sheepishly.

"All right," he offered with a smile. "Let's skip the book and see what we've already got made."

There was a display case with about eight cakes in different sizes. They all looked amazing, and I started to worry about the price. Then he gave me something much bigger to worry about.

"So, you go to MIST."

I panicked. My *brilliant* plan relied on him not knowing I was an Omega. But somehow he had spotted me. Then I realized my mistake. He must have seen me go to the standpoint and make the ID. When I came in, he thought it was a signal that I was in trouble.

"I'm sorry," I stammered. "I don't really need . . . I mean, I do need a cake, but there aren't any . . . you know . . . zombies.

I mean, *undead*. It's just, I figured out the code about Revelation, and, you know Natalie, my trainer, missed it, and I'm waiting for my test and I thought . . ."

This was when I noticed the look of absolute confusion on the man's face. Something was terribly wrong. So I just stopped talking, as if I had reached the end of a sentence or had at least completed a coherent thought.

He waited for a moment before asking, "What are you talking about?"

I very cleverly responded with, "What are *you* talking about?"

"I thought we were talking about a birthday cake."

I put my hands on my hips. "Then what made you ask if I went to MIST?"

He gave me a "duh" look and pointed at my shirt. That would be the shirt that read MIST FENCING. (The shirt is actually kind of cute. On the back it says, FENCERS ARE SHARP, but that's really not important to this part of the story.)

"Oh," I responded as I quickly tried to think of a way out of the situation. We've already established that thinking fast on my feet isn't exactly a strength. Luckily, a rescuer came from the back room.

"Tommy," he said, putting a hand on the shoulder of

the guy with the perplexed look still on his face, "can you help unload the boxes from the delivery truck? I'll take care of this customer."

He turned to me and continued his save. "You're looking for a birthday cake, right? With a zombie theme?"

"Right," I answered, relieved. "My pops is really into zombies." (Again with the "pops." Argghhh.)

"Sure thing," Tommy said as he disappeared into the back, no doubt thrilled to be away from the psycho.

Once he was gone, the man behind the counter looked down at me and actually glowered.

"You're only supposed to make contact when you have an imminent need," he reminded me. "Do you have one?"

"I really do need a birthday cake," I said before adding, "imminently."

He leaned forward with an even angrier look. "Let me rephrase that: Do you have a need worth the risk of possibly exposing the identities of two Omegas?"

I shook my head. Then I began to worry that this might lead to actual trouble. During one of his procedures lessons, Grayson described a whole suspension process with review boards. I wasn't even a full member yet, and I might have already blown my chance.

"Please don't tell anyone. I promise I won't do it again."

I gave him my best pleading eyes, which seemed to do the trick. There was something in the way he looked at me. A recognition.

He stared for a moment, lost in a thought as a smile slowly grew across his face. Then he put a name to that memory: "Rosemary Collins."

Now it was my turn to smile.

"My mother," I said, confirming what he already knew. "We have the same mismatched eyes."

"No," he replied, shaking his head. "You have the same everything. It's like I'm back in the eighth grade."

I knew I had my mother's eyes, but to hear that we shared other features was nice. Also nice was the fact that it seemed to have changed his mood for the better.

"You knew my mom in eighth grade?"

"That's when she asked me to be on her Omega Team," he answered, a large part of his attention still pleasantly reliving the memory.

"Did you think it was a practical joke when she asked?" I wondered. "I did when they asked me."

"Absolutely," he said with a booming laugh. Then he stopped and looked more serious. "But it isn't a joke. It's important. And so is following the procedures and protocols."

"I know," I answered. "I really am sorry. Please don't tell."

"You should know better," he replied, although less harshly than before. "How long have you been an Omega?"

"I just finished my training," I answered. And then, realizing I might not be able to brag about it to anybody else, I added, "It took me four weeks."

He did a double take, and smiled. "You completed all of your training in four weeks? You've got more in common with your mom than your looks."

This actually made me blush.

"Now, is it really your dad's birthday?" he asked.

I nodded. "Yes, sir."

"Let's get him a cake."

We picked out a red velvet cake with cream cheese frosting—Dad's favorite. The baker gave me a huge discount and reminded me I should not come back unless the situation truly demanded it.

As I headed out the door, I turned back and asked him a question. "Out of curiosity, what made you become a baker?"

He smiled. "What do you think?"

"Does it have something to do with the lecture on the first day of school? When everybody eats the bread?"

He nodded. "It has everything to do with it." Then he winked at me, and I hurried home.

Beth was not pleased that I was forty minutes late, but her mood brightened considerably when she saw the killer cake.

She was hard at work at the stove and waved a wooden spoon toward a cutting board on the counter. "Start chopping mushrooms."

We were making beef Stroganoff, which is kind of an inside joke in our family. My mom had many talents, but cooking was not one of them. Baking she could do, but actual meals, not so much. Dad has always run the kitchen, which is great because part of his job as a paramedic is taking turns cooking for the other guys in the station house. He's an awesome cook.

One year he even won a contest for the entire New York City Fire Department and was asked to do a cooking demonstration on a local morning TV show. Beth and I got to skip school and go to the studio. It was a big thrill. As he was cooking, the host of the show asked him if there was anything he couldn't make, and Dad joked that he knew how to make everything but beef Stroganoff.

Mom latched on to this in the way that only she could. She decided that she would master beef Stroganoff and make it her one specialty. She researched online, consulted friends, and even took a class at a cooking school, just to learn that one recipe so she could surprise my dad on his birthday. Of course, it never occurred to her that the reason Dad didn't make beef Stroganoff was because he didn't like it. And, of course, it never occurred to Dad to tell Mom. So every year, on his birthday, she pretended to be a gourmet chef and he pretended to like beef Stroganoff.

We've offered to make him something he actually likes, but he insists, so that's what we make.

He also insists that for his birthday, there are no friends or relatives, no Internet or phone calls—just the three of us and the Stroganoff.

The deluxe cake, though, was a welcome addition. Before he blew out the candles, he closed his eyes to make a wish. Then he turned to the living room to see if it had come true.

"Drat," he said. (Only Dad still uses a term like "drat.")

"What did you wish for?" I asked.

"Mrs. Papadakis and the Leather Bags . . . in their bathing suits."

Even my sister laughed at that one.

We had a great evening, talking, laughing, and just being goofy. And because of his no-phones-or-Internet rule, I didn't get the message from Natalie until the next morning.

In typical Natalie fashion, the message wasn't chatty. There was just an address, a time, and two words in all capital letters: FINAL EXAM.

Ω8

If You've Ever Wanted to Know a Good Place to Meet Zombies...

Just as I'd suspected, Natalie's building had a doorman. His maroon jacket and cap had gold braid that matched the stripe down each side of his pants. His name tag said "Hector" and his smile said that he had no idea he was giving me such bad news.

"What was that?" I asked with a gulp, hoping that I'd misheard him.

"They're waiting for you in apartment 12-B," he repeated. "You can take the elevator to your left." Unfortunately, that's exactly what I'd heard the first time too.

"Thanks," I mumbled as I began my walk of doom toward the elevator.

I hadn't even thought to ask Natalie what floor she lived on. The message had her address and said to be there Saturday at four o'clock. I'd assumed we were going to meet in the lobby and go somewhere for my final exam. Now Hector was telling me the meeting was a full nine floors above my normal limit.

My knees got weak just thinking about it.

Confession time: While I wasn't lying when I said I'd killed it during training, I may have glossed over the fact that my fear of heights had been a major problem. That's because sometimes the only way to escape the undead is to go up into buildings high enough that the Manhattan schist no longer gives them power. That usually means about ten to fifteen floors. My instinct to do everything but go up was something I'd have to conquer. I knew this.

I just didn't know I'd have to conquer it so soon.

But I realized that as much as I dreaded it, there was no way I could possibly pass my final exam without actually going to Natalie's apartment to take it. So I got on the elevator, pressed the button for twelve, and held my breath.

I eventually made it to 12-B. Alex opened the door,

greeting me with a big smile. "Come on in," he said. Then he called out to an unseen room, "She passed the first part!"

"What was the first part?" I asked.

"We weren't sure you'd make it up this high."

"I'm still not sure," I answered, only half joking. "Either you're wearing makeup or it's actually affecting my vision."

"No, your vision's fine," he said with a laugh. "I *am* wearing makeup. It's part of the test," he added cryptically.

Before I could begin to figure out what that meant, he led me through an apartment that was so amazing, I almost forgot my fears. There was a music room with a grand piano and cello, and a library with overstuffed chairs and floor-to-ceiling bookcases. The living room even had a wall of windows with a balcony that overlooked Central Park.

"Crazy, isn't it?" he said, shaking his head and pointing at the balcony. "It's like something out of a movie."

"Yeah," I answered as I stepped back to avoid the dizzying view. "A *horror* movie."

We reached a large bathroom with side-by-side sinks. Natalie was leaning over one to check the mirror as she carefully applied eye shadow. Grayson was at the other, rinsing his mouth with some orange liquid. The fact that all four of us fit comfortably in the bathroom is a pretty good sign it was nothing like our place in Queens.

"Look who made it," Alex announced as we walked in.

"I told you," Grayson half spoke and half gargled.

"Perfect timing," Natalie said as she turned to us. "How does my makeup look? Be honest."

I hoped this wasn't part of the test, because she looked terrible. My experience with makeup was absolutely zero, but even I could tell this was bad. Luckily, Alex answered first.

"Awful," he said. "You look like a corpse."

I expected Natalie to slug him, but instead she smiled and asked, "You're not just saying that, are you?"

Grayson spit the mouthwash into the sink and then patted a washcloth across his lips. "Nope. You look totally dead."

"But still cute," she added.

"Oh yeah," Alex answered, rolling his eyes. "Dead . . . but cute."

"What about me?" Grayson flashed a big smile, revealing that the liquid had turned his teeth the same blend of yellow and orange as the teeth of the zombie who had attacked me in the subway station. "Do I look cute too?"

"No. You look hideous."

"Nice," he replied. "Hideous is exactly what I was going for."

I couldn't have been more confused. "Let me get this straight," I said, trying to hide my nervousness by sounding carefree and humorous. "For my final exam we're doing really bad makeovers?"

Natalie gave me a finger wag. "You wish it were that easy. No, for your final exam, we're going to a party. The makeovers are so we can get in."

"What kind of party needs bad makeovers?"

"A *flatline* party," Alex said.

"I'm guessing that's not some kind of Sweet Sixteen."

"Flatline parties are for the undead," Grayson explained. "Their name comes from the flat line that appears on a heart monitor when a patient dies. These parties are their only opportunity to come together in a group and just be themselves."

"They like to say that the only thing with a beat is the music," Alex added. "Strictly zombies. No breathers allowed." ("Breather" is undead slang for the living.)

"Which is why we need to look dead," I answered, finally getting it. "So we can crash the party."

"Exactly," Natalie replied. "As part of your final exam, you have to pass yourself off as undead for thirty minutes."

"Great," I said halfheartedly. "Acting and makeup. My two favorite things."

Suddenly, I was worried. I'd thought my test was going to be about finding standpoints and breaking codes. Things I knew I could ace. I had absolutely no confidence I could convince a group of zombies that I was one of them. What if I failed? I wondered if any retakes were allowed.

The three of them took turns helping me with my makeup. They used foundation, powder, and eye shadow to give my face a hollow, bloodless appearance, and then rubbed some gel in my hair to make it look dried out and frizzy.

When they finished, they scanned me over to make sure they hadn't missed anything.

"How do I look?" I asked.

Grayson smiled and then answered, "To *die* for."

The others groaned as they turned to him.

"You've been waiting all day to use that joke, haven't you?" Natalie asked.

"It's funny," he said. "Why should it matter when I thought of it?"

"Because it matters," Alex said.

While they continued to give him a hard time, I stood

up and looked at myself in the mirror. Surprisingly, I did look kind of dead. Maybe I could pull this off after all. "So, where is this party?"

"Good question," Alex answered. "As part of the whole no-breathers policy, they keep that information pretty secret."

"But we can find out," Grayson added. "That is, *if* you know how to get to J. Hood Wright Park."

He said it like a challenge, and I couldn't help but laugh. Alex and Grayson had been trying to stump me ever since Natalie bragged that I knew the city parks better than they did.

"Is this part of the test?"

"Why?" asked Alex. "Don't you know the answer?"

"Yeah," Grayson said eagerly. "Don't you?"

I paused for a second to get their hopes up and then said, "Actually, it depends on whether you want to enter by the rec center on Fort Washington Avenue or near the overlook on Haven Avenue," dashing their hopes. "Personally, I'd recommend the rec center. To get there we can get on the C train at 72nd Street. Switch over to the A at 168th. Continue north toward Washington Heights and get off at 175th."

Natalie cackled. "You only make yourself look silly

when you try to stump her," she said as she gave me a fist bump. "I told you she was a natural."

A natural, I thought. My confidence was growing.

We got to the park at that time of day when the city is its most beautiful. It was just before sunset and the sky had an orange glow that made the George Washington Bridge look like a painting at the Met. I was able to admire it for all of about thirteen seconds before Natalie took charge.

"The test starts now," she said. "Find the zombies."

A lump formed in the back of my throat. This was really happening.

I tried to come up with a strategy. The park stretches for three blocks on each side. Because a cluster of buildings in the middle blocks your view, you can see only about a third of it at a time. I decided to start in one corner and walk toward the center.

"Don't make it obvious that you're looking," Alex said. "Act natural."

Yeah, I thought. *Nothing's more natural than hunting zombies in a park full of children.*

On the playground, kids were chasing one another back and forth across a mini-size version of the George Washington Bridge. Their laughter filled the air, and I felt the urge to protect those children. I scanned the parents watching them play, but didn't see anyone who looked out of the ordinary.

We walked through an archway to the other side of the buildings and came to a table where three white-haired men were playing an intense game of dominoes. One was singing along with a Spanish song that played on the radio. They may have been old, but they were very much among the living.

Trying to act "natural," I pretended to watch the domino game. Meanwhile, I was able to scan another third of the park. A group of kids was playing baseball, a family was cleaning up after a birthday party, and a couple was pushing a stroller along the walkway. Once again, all were living.

I was stumped.

I turned to the others, who were also pretending to watch the domino game.

"Are you certain?" I asked them quietly.

Natalie nodded.

Then I remembered something.

"Schist," I said.

All three of them smiled.

In the corner of J. Hood Wright Park is a large outcropping of Manhattan schist. In fact, it's one of the largest aboveground formations anywhere. I looked toward the rocks and then toward Natalie. She nodded again.

The domino game ended, and I gave a little polite applause for the winner. Then I started to walk to the southwest corner of the park.

The rocks were the color of pencil lead, and had been smoothed by centuries of wind and rain. Two little kids were climbing on one corner of them, and on the opposite side were two couples.

At first glance you wouldn't think there was anything unusual about the couples, but I remembered my field training with Natalie. The first thing I noticed was that despite warm weather, all of them were wearing long sleeves. The undead often do this to protect their skin. Then I saw that one of the guys was wearing makeup and had done a bad job blending it in along the neckline. Finally, when one of the girls laughed, I saw that her teeth looked just like Grayson's.

I sat down on a bench across from them, and the others joined me. We acted normal, like a group of friends having a relaxing Saturday.

"Nice work," Grayson whispered.

"Are they going to have the party here?" I asked.

Alex shook his head. "No. This is just where they meet

before they go. We're going to have to follow them to the party."

And just when I thought the test couldn't get harder, he added, "We'll have to go down into Dead City."

The City That Really Never Sleeps

We're going into Dead City?" I asked nervously. "Really?"

Alex gave me an encouraging pat on the back. "Don't worry. It's not as bad as it sounds."

"Good," I replied. "Because it sounds creepy, gross, and disgusting."

"Oh," Natalie chimed in, "then it *is* as bad as it sounds."

"Yeah," added Grayson. "Creepy, gross, and disgusting pretty much nails it."

The three of them laughed.

"I'm glad my final exam amuses you all," I said as I joined them and laughed too.

Dead City, or DC, is what the Omegas call the maze of abandoned tunnels, sewers, aqueducts, and catacombs that wind their way underneath Manhattan. It's where zombies are free to move around without attracting attention from the living and where the bedrock walls of schist to recharge their bodies.

Dead City is also incredibly dangerous.

Omegas are allowed to go there only in groups of three or more. Natalie, Grayson, and Alex talked about it during training, but this was going to be my first actual visit. And if I'm totally honest, I'll admit that as creepy, gross, and disgusting as Dead City sounded, part of me was excited to see what it was like.

First, though, we had to keep an eye on the four zombies in the park. They were our key to finding the flatline party. For a group of undead, they were a pretty lively bunch. They were joking and laughing about something when a man approached them. He talked to them for a moment before he continued walking toward the middle of the park. The four of them, however, headed in the opposite direction, toward the street.

"Here's the next part of your test," Alex said. "He just told them where the party is. What do we do?"

The three of them looked at me.

"Follow," I said.

"Him or them?"

I hesitated for a second, worried that it might be a trick question. "Them."

"Okay," Alex said. "Show us what you've got."

I looked at Natalie, and she gave me a confident nod. I knew I had to take charge and show them the surveillance skills she had taught me.

"A-B shadow technique," I said, using the terminology from training. "Grayson and me in the first group, Natalie and Alex in the second."

From her smile I could tell that I was off to a good start.

Grayson and I waited on the bench for about thirty seconds before we began to follow the four zombies to the street. Thirty seconds after that, Natalie and Alex started following us. That's the key to A-B shadow technique. Because they were following us, Alex and Natalie were too far back to be seen by the people we were following. Every two blocks our two groups swapped places, making it less likely for them to notice any of us.

"You're doing great," Grayson said as we walked away from the park down Haven Avenue. "Really great."

"Thanks." I figured Grayson might offer moral support. That was partly why I picked him to be in my group.

We followed for about six blocks until the four of them turned down an alley. I kept an eye on what they were doing while Grayson bent over to tie his shoelace. This was the signal for Alex and Natalie to catch up to us.

One of the zombies lifted a grate from the ground, and the four of them quickly climbed down through the opening. The last one pulled the grate back over his head as he disappeared underneath. By the time Natalie and Alex reached us, the zombies were gone.

"Right over there," I told them. "All four went down through a grate in that alley."

"What do we do now?" Natalie asked.

"We've got to hurry up and go down there so we can follow them underground," I said.

"How do we do that and keep them from seeing us?" asked Alex.

This one stumped me for a moment before I figured it out. "It won't matter if they see us down there, because they'll assume we're undead, just like they are."

"Good answer," Alex said. "You're thinking like an Omega."

So far the test was going well, but I knew it was about to get a whole lot tougher once we got underground.

Alex pulled up the grate, which turned out to be much heavier than it looked. It opened up on a narrow shaft that went deep enough into the ground that I couldn't see the bottom. Iron rungs had been built into the side of the shaft and formed a ladder.

"I'll go first," Grayson offered.

"No," I said. "It's my test. I'm going first."

Alex pointed his flashlight down, but even with the light, I still couldn't tell how deep it was.

"Piece of cake," I said confidently, trying to convince myself as much as them.

I took a deep breath and started climbing down. One by one the others followed, with Alex going last. He was just pulling the grate back on at the top when I reached the bottom.

It took a minute or so for my eyes to adjust. Even when they did, everything was still mostly darkness and shadows. A few hundred yards away I could see a faint light bobbing up and down. It was a flashlight being carried by one of the zombies we had followed.

"This way," I said, pointing down the tunnel.

I started to walk, and my first step was right into a pool of water. Luckily, Natalie managed to grab my arm and kept me from falling in. As it was, my jeans were soaking wet all the way up above my left knee.

"Please tell me this isn't sewage," I said.

Alex laughed. "Believe me, you'd know if it was." He shined his flashlight across the ceiling. We were in a rounded tunnel about eight feet high in the middle. It must have been old, because instead of concrete it was made out of bricks. "It's just rainwater. I think we're in the Old Croton Aqueduct."

His light illuminated a narrow walkway on one edge of the tunnel. On the positive side, it was above the waterline, so it was mostly dry. On the negative, the curve of the wall made you walk with a severe tilt to the left. Within a few minutes my neck was starting to hurt.

As we walked, I tried to keep a mental map of where we were, but without buildings and streets to go by, it was impossible. Even though one of the world's busiest cities was only thirty feet above our heads, it felt like we were all alone on some alien planet.

Eventually the aqueduct met up with an abandoned subway tunnel, and we were finally able to stand up straight and stretch out. I rubbed my throbbing neck as I tried to figure out which way to go.

"Remember not to rub your neck at the party," said Grayson. "Zombies feel no pain, which means their muscles don't ache."

I would have completely forgotten that. Still, since it was just the four of us now, I kept massaging it. There was some lighting in this tunnel, which made it easier to see where we were going. Unfortunately, it also made it impossible to see the zombies' flashlight.

We were on our own. I wasn't sure about the grading scale for the exam, but I was pretty certain it'd be an F if I got everybody lost in Dead City.

"What next?" Alex said.

"First of all," I snapped, angrier than I intended, "I need you to be quiet and still."

Alex smiled, not at all offended by my attitude. He was happy that I was taking charge.

We all stopped moving and talking, and Dead City became even eerier. I closed my eyes, and one by one I tried to identify and eliminate the sounds I heard.

First was the steady flow of water along the aqueduct. If you forgot where you were, it sounded just like a waterfall up in the mountains. Next I could hear the faint echo of a subway train rushing along a distant tunnel. One by one I went through the sounds until I heard the one I was searching for.

"Got it," I said.

The others hadn't picked up on it yet. "Got what?" asked Natalie.

"The only thing with a beat." I pointed down the abandoned subway tunnel toward the faint thumping. "Music."

They listened for a moment and then smiled when they heard it too. We followed the sound, which gradually got louder as we got closer. Along the way, we met up with more zombies coming from different directions toward the party. I got nervous but tried to hide it. I also kept telling myself the same thing over and over.

Do not rub your neck!

When we finally reached the party, I was speechless. I'm not sure what I was expecting to find, but I know it was nothing like what we actually came across.

First of all, it was beautiful.

The party was being held in an abandoned subway station unlike any I had ever seen. The walls and archways were covered with gorgeous tiled mosaics, while the ceiling had brass chandeliers and stained-glass skylights.

"What is this place?" I asked, staring up at the dazzling ceiling.

"Subway stations used to be a lot fancier," Grayson said. "They closed this one back in the 1940s when the trains went from five to ten cars long. Ten-car trains are too long to fit in the curve."

"So they just left it empty?"

"It's called a ghost station," Natalie said. "There are ten in New York. This one's my favorite."

The flatline party took full advantage of the location. On one side of the tracks, zombies of all ages were socializing. There were some Level 3s hanging out on the fringes of the group, but most everyone looked like normal, everyday people. They certainly didn't look dangerous.

On the other side of the tracks was a long row of tables where merchants had set up shop. Strands of white lights hung from archway to archway, giving the whole station the look of an outdoor street festival or farmers' market.

"You're going to have to make it for thirty minutes on your own," Alex said.

Suddenly, I was overcome with panic. "You're not going to leave me here, are you?"

"Of course not," Natalie reassured me. "We'll stay close by and keep an eye on you."

"And if anything goes wrong, we'll step in," Grayson

added. "But the whole point is for you to pass yourself off as undead without any help."

"Remember the no-breathers policy?" Alex asked.

"How could I forget?"

He looked me in the eye. "They take that seriously. So be careful."

I nodded.

Just like that, they disappeared into the crowd and I was all alone. And here's the hard part. Even if everyone at this party was alive and it was being held in the courtyard of my apartment building, I'd still have trouble fitting in. Social situations baffle me. I never know what to say or do.

I figured I'd have a better shot dealing with the merchants, so I made my way to their side of the tracks. Most of them were selling items to solve problems specific to the undead.

I watched a man demonstrate a tiny but high-powered flashlight. He pointed it down the subway tunnel, and it illuminated much farther than I would have thought possible.

I couldn't help thinking that a light like that would have come in handy in the aqueduct. I was admiring it when a pair of hands suddenly grabbed my shoulders from behind. I tried to pull away, but the grip was too tight.

Then this unseen person leaned up and whispered into my ear, "Makeup like that won't get you too far."

I couldn't believe it. I hadn't even lasted fifteen minutes. I was trying to figure out an escape plan when she whispered something else.

"Come to my booth, and I'll show you how to pass for the living."

I looked over my shoulder and saw the smiling face of a woman who wore way too much makeup. She hadn't blown my cover at all. She was just trying to make a sale.

She led me to a table filled with homemade beauty supplies and tried to convince me that I just "had to have" some of her special lotions and creams. She called them Betty's Beauty Balms.

"Look at your hands," she said with mock terror. "There's no way you could pass those off as live human flesh. No offense."

"None taken," I replied, trying not to laugh.

"They're too pale," she explained. "But try a dab of this, and you'll see a miracle."

She scooped out a glob of coffee-colored cream and smeared it all over the back of my hand. Making it the same color as the Salinger sisters after one of their spray-on tanning sessions.

"See what I mean?" she said. "Now you almost look human."

"Almost," I said, still trying not to laugh. "Like you promised, it's a miracle."

"Great, so how many jars do you want to buy?" she asked hopefully. "Just ten dollars each."

"I'll have to think about it," I answered, trying to be polite. "Let me get back to you."

She went to show me something else, but I just turned away. I walked along the row of booths and stopped at a table where a man was selling something I thought should be in high demand in Dead City: toothpaste.

At least that's what I thought it was until he held up a tube and asked, "Hungry?"

I was confused until he squeezed a dollop of brown paste onto a plastic spoon and I realized that it was food. Or at least the undead version of food.

Alex and Natalie had both warned me about this. Unless they were trying to pass themselves off in front of the living, the undead didn't eat normal food. Instead, they usually ate a paste enriched with key vitamins and nutrients. They told me it wasn't harmful to the living, but since the undead had heightened senses of taste and smell, what was pleasing to them was not to us.

"Lots of calcium and vitamin D for your bones," he said, offering it to me. It was so unappetizing, it made cafeteria food look tasty. But I was worried that rejecting it might give me away.

I thought about the no-breathers policy and forced a smile. "Thanks. I'd love to try some."

My plan was to take it all in one big bite. I tried to suck it down quick enough to keep from actually tasting it, but that didn't work.

It tasted kind of like a big glob of wasabi I once ate by accident at a Japanese restaurant. As I forced myself to swallow it, I felt a burning sensation in my mouth and tears welling up in my eyes.

"Delicious, isn't it?" he asked.

I couldn't speak, so I just nodded and went, "Mmmm."

Fearful of what might have been waiting next, I bypassed all the other tables until I reached the end of the row. There, I came upon a guy who looked like he might be in college, giving a speech to anyone who would listen. He was bald and had a long scar that ran along his cheek and up to the top of his scalp. I wondered if it was the result of whatever had killed him. He passionately argued for the undead to stand up for their rights.

"Why should we hide underground like frightened

moles?" he demanded. "We did not choose to be this way. We did not ask to lose the sweet taste of fresh air and the warm comfort of sunlight against our skin. We have as much claim to this city as the living. We need to come together and march forward as a group with one voice, to confront those who scare us so."

"You'll certainly scare them back with that scar of yours," someone heckled him.

It didn't seem to bother him that no one was agreeing with him. Some of the people laughed, and a couple tried to goad him into an argument, but he just kept making his points. That's when I realized something.

He was absolutely right.

I thought back to the day the others had asked me to become an Omega. They said it was our responsibility to police *and* protect the undead. Training had focused a great deal on the policing part, but this trip to the flatline party and this speech had reminded me about the need to protect as well.

Most of the people at this party weren't dangerous to anyone. They just wanted to live in peace. Even if their version of living was different from what we're used to, it seemed like a fair request.

As others continued to give him a hard time, he looked

into the crowd for a friendly face, and he settled on mine.

"What about you? Do you think the living know more than we do?"

I thought about it for a second. "No," I answered honestly. "I think they know less than we do."

He cocked his head to the side, surprised by what I had said. "What do you mean?"

"They only know what it's like to be alive," I replied. "We know that too. But they have no idea what it's like not to be alive. That's something they'll never understand."

He smiled and nodded. "Absolutely. This one speaks the truth."

I was pleased . . . and a little freaked out. Not only was I able to pass myself off as undead (pleased), I was beginning to think that I might fit in better among them than among the living (freaked out).

Just then another hand grabbed my shoulder from behind. This time it wasn't a vendor. It was Alex.

"We told you to blend in," he said with a laugh. "Not stand out."

Natalie and Grayson walked up from the other side.

"You made it to thirty minutes," she said, pleased. "Let's get out of here before you wind up running for zombie council."

She laughed, and I could tell by their expressions that they were happy with how I had done.

"How do we get out?" I asked. "The same tunnel we used to get here?"

"Nah," Alex said. "We should go straight to the surface. I know a shortcut."

As we followed Alex, Grayson leaned toward me and whispered, "I liked what you said about the living and the undead. You're absolutely right."

Alex led us to one of the subway station's old stairwells. It was blocked off by a metal gate, which he managed to pry open a little.

"This should take us up to the street," he said.

We had to squeeze through the opening one at a time. I was the last one in our group, and there was a zombie right behind me using the same exit.

I smiled at him, but he didn't respond. If I had to guess, I would have said he was a Level 3, but I wasn't sure.

When it was my turn to squeeze past the gate, one of the metal links scratched a cut all along my forearm. It burned with pain, but I remembered not to cry out or make any pained expressions.

After all, only breathers feel pain.

What I wasn't able to control, unfortunately, was the

trickle of blood that started to run from my elbow to my wrist.

I looked back and saw the zombie staring first at the blood and then at me. Even in the darkness, there was no mistaking the orange-and-yellow glow of his teeth as he smiled and prepared to attack.

It's Time to Get My Zeke On

Guys, we've got a problem." I tried to sound calm, but the squeal of my voice was a dead giveaway that I was anything but.

Natalie was right in front of me. When she turned, she could see the blood on my arm and the look on the zombie's face. She yanked me through the gate and tried to slam it shut on the Level 3 killing machine before he could come after me.

"Get out! Get out!" she barked.

Natalie did her best to hold the gate closed while the rest of us started to run up the stairwell. The last thing we needed was a fight with a zombie at a flatline party. Considering we were outnumbered about four hundred to four, there was no way that could turn out well.

It's amazing how fast and strong you are when you're properly motivated. I was able to clear three steps at a time as we raced up the stairs to the next level. Unfortunately, when we got there, we ran into a dead end.

"I thought you said this was a shortcut," I wailed.

"You know, I may have been thinking about the ghost station over on Worth," Alex offered sheepishly. "I get them confused."

Seconds later, Natalie was barreling toward us.

"He's coming and he's unhappy!" she exclaimed. "We have got to move!"

She bolted out onto the mezzanine, and we were right behind her. I could hear the party going on below; luckily, they couldn't see us from where they were. We ran full speed toward an exit that led to the street.

The zombie, however, was amazingly fast. He caught up to us halfway across the mezzanine and managed to kick my ankle in midstride. Both of us crashed and skidded across the floor.

He was a little slower getting up, though, which gave the four of us enough time to surround him. He sat there for a moment, looking from person to person, trying to figure out what to do.

"Make sure no one followed us," Alex told Grayson.

"Got it," Grayson replied as he hurried over to the stairwell.

At this point I expected Alex to show off his skills and wipe the floor with this guy. Instead, he walked over to Natalie and then whispered to her. The zombie, meanwhile, slowly stood, and with everyone else suddenly busy, he began to size me up.

"Hey, guys," I said, trying to redirect their attention back to the situation. "You want to check this out?"

Grayson came back from the stairwell. "We're clear. It's just us."

The zombie was now striking a combat pose. He looked just like Alex did when we practiced martial arts at the YMCA. Only he had terrifying teeth and very angry eyes.

"Seriously, guys," I pleaded. "How about a little help here?"

Alex looked at me and smiled. "Nope."

I've got to say, that's not what I expected to hear.

"What do you mean, 'nope'?"

"You're on your own," he answered. "This will be the final portion of your exam."

I turned back toward the Level 3. He was full of hate, and he was about to attack.

"C'mon, guys," I begged. "Enough with the joking."

"We're not joking," Natalie said. "You can do this."

"Use what we've taught you," Grayson added. He made a clapping motion with his hands to remind me of CLAP. CLAP is the memory tool Omegas are taught for the proper procedure when confronting the undead. At a moment like this, it seemed a little . . . *inadequate*.

"CLAP?" I said, disbelieving. "Seriously?"

"It works," Grayson promised. "Go through the steps."

I scanned their faces, desperate to see a smile or a laugh, but when I saw their serious expressions, I realized I was going to have to fight this guy.

I turned back to the Level 3 and flashed a phony smile as I ran through CLAP in my head. *C is for "calm,"* I thought. The first thing an Omega is supposed to do is calm the situation.

"Hey," I said all friendly-like. "Let's start over. First of all, I want to apologize for my behavior. I should not have come to your flatline party. That's my bad. Totally on me. But now I've left the party, right? So the problem's solved. And I promise I won't come back."

He snorted and started to move toward me. I kept my distance by matching every step of his with a step backward.

"Besides, did you hear me in there? I gave a pretty strong argument *in favor* of the rights of the undead. I'm on your side. I want to be a friend."

I offered my hand in friendship. He moved toward it, but instead of shaking, he slapped me across the palm. It stung and instantly started to throb.

So much for *C*. It was time to move on to *L. L is for "listen."* An Omega is supposed to listen and try to understand what's causing the zombie's anger.

"Maybe 'friend' is too strong a word," I continued. "But I can see that you're upset. Why don't you tell me why, so we can work out a solution and settle this peacefully?"

He yelled something impossible to decipher as he charged me again. This time he was swinging wildly, and one swing slammed against my head and shoulder, knocking me to the floor.

"Level 3s aren't big talkers," Natalie advised from the sidelines. "Especially when it comes to their feelings. You might want to skip to the next step."

"Thanks so much," I said sarcastically as I stood up

and brushed the dust off my hands and legs. "Seriously."

"Glad to be of help," she shot back with equal sass.

A is for "avoidance." An Omega should do everything possible to avoid a physical confrontation.

"I can tell we're not going to be able to work this out," I said to the zombie. "So I'm going to leave."

I moved toward the exit, but he grabbed me from behind and slammed me against the wall. Pain shot through my body. I was hot and sweaty and not in the mood to take this anymore.

"Can I go to the last step now?" I asked as clearly as I could with my face pressed up against the tiled mosaic.

"Yes," Alex said. "Start with the first thing I taught you."

I pushed back from the wall and shoved the zombie away to create a little space between us. "Bad news, buddy," I said with as much attitude as I could muster. *"P is for 'punish.'"*

Alex's first lesson was simple: *Go for the head.*

The zombie came at me, and I delivered a punch right into his face. It caught him completely off guard and knocked him to the ground.

I should have finished him off then, but I didn't. The problem was that despite all my training, I had never been in a fight. I was used to pads and sportsmanship. This was all-out war, and I was being too polite.

Alex, Grayson, and Natalie continued to watch from the sidelines, offering nothing more than moral support as the zombie and I traded blows. I was using a combination of Jeet Kune Do, fencing, and everything that Alex had taught me.

The zombie was wild and undisciplined, which made it hard to fight him. He didn't land too many punches, but I couldn't predict how he was going to fight.

At one point he threw a punch at me. I was able to move out of the way and grab his arm. I held on to it tight and tried to do a judo throw. When I did, his arm literally came out of its socket and off his body.

As if it wasn't gross enough to have an actual severed arm in my hand, my teammates now found humor in the situation.

"I'd give you a hand," Grayson offered, "but it looks like you already have too many."

"Now *that* was funny," Natalie said with a laugh as she gave him a high five.

"Thanks," he said.

I tossed the arm at them, and they had to jump out of the way to keep from getting hit. I turned and then charged right at the zombie and threw a punch that broke through his rib cage and inside his chest.

When I pulled out my fist, it was dripping with purple-and-red goop that almost made me throw up. It was like the worst biology lab ever.

This, of course, brought only more laughter from my so-called teammates.

"Are you guys just going to sit there and laugh all night?" I snapped, a little peeved.

"That depends," Alex shot back. "Are you just going to keep goofing off? Or are you going to use what we've taught you?"

He was right. This zombie was a bad guy, and I was going way too easy on him.

"Seriously, how hard can it be to go for the head?" Natalie pointed out. "He's only got one arm."

The zombie moved toward me again, slime coming out of his chest and his arm socket. I thought back to my first class with Alex and the Jeet Kune Do move I had done to him.

I tried to move as fluidly as possible as I dipped down low, spun around, and popped up right next to him. He didn't have a chance. I delivered three quick punches to the head, and the zombie dropped like a rock.

I was stunned, unsure of what had just happened. But he wasn't moving. He was dead. My first instinct was to feel bad. I think Grayson was the one who realized this.

"Don't," he said to me. "Don't feel guilty for one second. He was bad. He was looking to hurt you, us, anyone who looked at him the wrong way."

"Yes, but . . ." I motioned toward the party as I tried to put my feelings into words. "I was just arguing for zombie rights."

"His existence and his behavior put all those good people in danger," continued Grayson. "You helped them today."

"He's right," Alex said. "That's what we have to do when they become dangerous."

I was too stunned to think through it all, but I knew they were right. He was bad and had to be stopped.

"We'd better go," Natalie said.

"What about cleanup?" I asked.

Grayson shook his head. "We don't clean up in Dead City. Down here the undead take care of their own."

"Yeah," Alex said, moving toward the exit. "Let's get out of here . . . Zeke."

At first I didn't catch it. Then I realized what he had called me.

I was no longer a trainee. I was a full-fledged Omega. And just like my mother before me, I had become a "zombie killer."

I was a Zeke!

Ω 11

I Get Called to the Principal's Office ... and It's a Good Thing

Learning about the Omegas, going through weeks of intensive training, and traveling underground to defeat a Level 3 zombie in hand-to-hand mortal combat was pretty life-changing stuff. So it shouldn't have been a surprise when I went back to school the following Monday, everything was totally . . . the same.

It turns out the one drawback of having a supercool secret identity is that you have to keep it a secret. Becoming a Zeke can't make you popular if none of your classmates even know what a Zeke is.

But I didn't mind the lack of popularity so much. After

all these years, I was kind of used to it. Even the fact that nobody knew I'd been to Dead City and fought a zombie didn't bother me. The thing that was driving me crazy was the fact that *I* knew I had been to Dead City and fought a zombie and couldn't seem to get back there again.

Once the initial shock had worn off, I was ready for more. Except Omegas can't just go looking for trouble. Until we receive word there's a problem that needs to be solved, all we can do is wait.

Every morning before school I met up with Natalie, Alex, and Grayson to find out if we had an assignment. And every morning for the next few days the answer was no.

It was beyond frustrating.

Then one day I was in the middle of an English class discussion about *The Outsiders* (a great book once you get over the characters having names like Pony Boy and Soda Pop) when I got called down to the principal's office.

Dr. Gootman's office is . . . different. It's a converted cottage on the edge of campus. A hundred years ago, when this was all a hospital, the cottage was where the chief doctor lived. Today it still feels like a home, only now one that belongs to a mad scientist.

It's surrounded by gardens where he grows bizarre-looking flowers and vegetables as part of his crossbreeding experiments. Inside, the kitchen has been converted into a chemistry lab, and what once was the living room now holds his desk and a conference table.

"Ah, the fair Miss Bigelow," he said with a smile as I came through the door. "Until this morning, I wasn't aware you were part of this study group."

I had no idea what he was talking about until I saw Natalie, Alex, and Grayson seated at the table. Apparently, our Omega Team was calling itself a "study group."

"I just joined," I told him, unsure what, if anything, he might know about what we really were.

"An excellent choice," he said to Natalie as he motioned for me to sit with the others. "Natalie tells me that you are working on an experiment as part of a research project," he continued.

"That's right," said Natalie. "And while we would normally never ask to leave the campus during school hours, it's very time sensitive. There's been a change in the weather, and I'm afraid if we wait until later to collect the data, the experiment will be compromised."

He mulled this over for a moment. "Well, we can't have that, can we?" he said. "Are you certain it has to be now?"

Natalie didn't blink. "Yes, sir."

That was all the certainty he needed. "Then I'll inform

the dean and your teachers that you'll be back by fifth period."

"Yes," she said. "We should be able to do that."

"It wasn't a question," he corrected.

"Yes, sir," she said. "We'll be back by fifth period."

He handed Natalie four passes and gave us all a final stern look before heading out the door. "Makeup work will be done immediately."

We all agreed.

He kept up the tough guy act, but when he turned away from us, I could see his reflection in the mirror, and he had a sly smile. He'd said what he needed to say, but he also had our backs.

The final thing he said as he walked out the door was "Be careful."

I waited for the door to close before I turned to Natalie and queried, "Study group?"

"What was I supposed to call it?" she asked. "Zombie-hunting team?"

I laughed. "Does he know about the Omegas?"

"We've often wondered," Natalie said.

"He's been principal at MIST for as long as anyone can remember," Grayson added. "I think he must know something. But he doesn't ask."

144

"Yeah," Alex added with a laugh. "He didn't even make Nat describe her experiment."

"What would you have said?" Grayson asked.

"Something about weather and soil samples," she said with a flip of her hand.

Alex shook his head. "That would have been convincing."

"So, what's the real reason?" I asked. "Why are we leaving campus during school hours?"

All eyes turned to Natalie.

"It's our first assignment as a team," she said.

The Prime-O—or Prime Omega—is the only person who knows the identities of all active Omega Teams. He's the one who gives us our assignments.

"A hunt job?" Alex asked, referring to an assignment in which we'd track a zombie who was causing problems.

"Nope," she said. "Strictly research at this point. Three dead bodies were discovered in a park right here on Roosevelt Island."

Grayson had a confused look. "Aren't dead bodies more of a police thing than an us thing?"

"These bodies aren't your normal variety," she said cryptically. "According to the coroner on the scene, they had no blood and appear to have been dead for quite some time . . . like, years."

"Okay, that is a little weird," Alex said. "But it still doesn't sound like our line of work."

"Maybe you should look at the picture the Prime-O sent," Natalie added as she handed her phone to Alex. "The bodies were arranged in a very particular fashion."

Alex was surprised by what he saw. "Is that what I think it is?" he asked.

She nodded. "Yes."

Grayson looked at the picture and also nodded. "I guess it is an us thing."

Finally, the phone got to me. When I saw the picture, I couldn't believe my eyes.

The three bodies were arranged in the shape of a giant omega.

Ω 12

How to Set a Trap

T ry to relax," Alex said as we followed the brick pathway that wraps around Roosevelt Island.

I was just about to lie and tell him I *was* relaxed
when I realized he wasn't talking to me. I was so caught
up in my excitement, I hadn't noticed that Natalie's hands
were clenched into nervous fists or that she was taking
long, fast strides like an Olympic speed walker.

"I am relaxed," she snapped in a voice so tense that
Grayson actually laughed.

That's when it dawned on me that in addition to this
being my first assignment as an Omega, it was also Natalie's

first one as a team leader. Even though Alex is older, both he and Grayson had insisted that she take the position when the team's previous leader graduated last year.

"I'm serious," Alex said as he put a friendly hand on her shoulder. "We picked you for a reason. You're going to do great, but you need to relax."

She started to disagree again but caught herself and took a deep breath instead. She stayed quiet for a moment before she managed to smile and say, "Thanks."

I had never seen Natalie flustered before. You could tell her mind was racing in a million different directions.

"We're just supposed to do research at the crime scene, right?" Grayson said. "That should be easy enough."

"It should be," she said, thinking something over. "But I'm worried it might be a trap."

Both boys stopped for a moment to consider this.

"What makes you think that?" I asked.

"Whoever positioned those bodies into a giant Omega knows we have to come check it out," she explained. "Maybe the whole point is just to get us out there so that they can see who we are and figure out our identities."

"So while we think we're spying on them . . ." Alex started.

"They're actually spying on us," finished Natalie.

"Hadn't thought of that," Grayson said, impressed.

Alex smiled at her. "See what I mean? That's why we picked you. You're brilliant."

We stopped talking for a moment as we walked past a couple of old men who were casting their fishing lines into the East River. Then we rounded the corner, and the crime scene came into view.

We were right on the edge of a park that overlooked the water. On the other side of the park was an old wooden farmhouse that was now some sort of history museum. (I'd walked past it a million times and never paid any attention.) In the grass right in front of the house's porch, yellow police tape marked the area where the bodies had been found.

Needless to say, the discovery of three dead bodies in a public park had attracted a crowd. In addition to the police, there was a television news crew and some pockets of people who'd been passing by and stopped to find out what was going on.

"The crowd's good," Natalie said. "It should help us blend in."

"But what if it *is* a trap?" asked Grayson. "What should we do about that?"

Natalie thought for a moment, and then something

caught her attention: the fishermen. She looked at them and nodded.

"We set a trap of our own right back at them," she answered, getting some of the swagger back in her voice. "Molly and I will approach the scene and find out as much as we can. Maybe we'll even get lucky and there will be someone we know from the morgue. If there are any zombies in the crowd, they'll know we're there."

"Sounds like exactly what they want," Alex said. "What will Grayson and I be doing?"

"You'll be circling the crowd, looking for whoever's watching Molls and me. They'll see us, but they won't see you. You'll be able to see where they go."

I looked over at the fishermen and realized what had inspired her. "So we're bait?"

Natalie smiled. "Yeah."

"I like it."

"Sounds good," Alex said. "I'll start left, Grayson, you go right."

Alex and Grayson began circling the park and checking out the different groups of people. Natalie and I waited a moment, and then we walked right toward the middle of it all.

"Trap or not, someone is sending us a message," she

said. "Look for any clues that might tell us what it is."

I nodded.

We eavesdropped on the TV reporter as he broadcast, but didn't learn anything except how to be overly dramatic. "Action News reporter Brock Hampton reporting from Roosevelt Island, where three men met an unlucky fate . . ." (Personally, I thought "unlucky" was a bit of an understatement.) We also heard two detectives talking about shoe print evidence they had found.

"It doesn't make any sense," one of them said. "There were three sets of shoe prints, and each one matches a pair of shoes on one of the dead bodies."

"What's wrong with that?" asked the other.

"What about the guy who arranged the bodies?" the first one asked. "Where are his shoe prints?"

Natalie and I shared a look when we heard that. We both shook our heads as we tried to figure it out. He had a point.

There was no one left from the coroner's office. Apparently, they had already loaded up the bodies and were taking them back to the freezer at the morgue.

We were standing off to the side talking when Natalie got a text from Alex. She handed her phone to me so that I could read it too. It said YANKEES CAP. YELLOW JACKET. SOUTHSIDE COFFEE SHOP.

Our trap had worked. Alex discovered someone watching us.

"Be cool," Natalie whispered as we both casually looked toward the south side of the park. There we saw a woman in a baseball cap and yellow jacket standing by a coffee shop. The colors made her look a little like a bumblebee. Like many of the other lookers-on, she was taking a picture with her phone. But unlike the others, she wasn't taking a picture of the crime scene.

She was taking a picture of us.

She noticed us looking right at her and got spooked. She slipped the phone back into her jacket pocket and quickly began to walk away.

"Do we follow her?" I asked urgently.

"No," Natalie said. "That might be part of the trap. She spotted us but not Alex. He'll tail her and see where she goes."

Even though Natalie had predicted it, I was a little spooked by the fact that someone had been watching us. Suddenly, I felt paranoid about all the people gathered around the park and wondered if any others were spying on us. I turned to scan the people's faces, and that's when an idea hit me.

"What if it's a standpoint?" I asked.

"What?" answered Natalie.

"When we want to find a past Omega, we have to find a standpoint and look for an indicator," I said.

"Yeah," she said drily. "I'm pretty sure I'm the one who taught you that."

"A standpoint is an Omega symbol," I continued. "Maybe that's what the bodies were supposed to be. A standpoint we were certain to find."

Her eyes opened wide as she considered this. "That's . . . interesting," she said, warming to the idea. "The problem is, there's no way you're going to be able to actually stand on the point with all those policemen around. See how close you can get and start looking."

"Me?"

"Remember the bakery?" she said with a laugh. "You're better at it than any of us."

I smiled at the compliment.

Over the next ten minutes, I positioned myself in a couple of spots as close as I could get to where the bodies had been found, and looked for any sort of coded message or indicator.

"Any luck?" Natalie asked when we regrouped.

"No," I answered, discouraged. "Sorry."

"Don't be. It was a good idea. It still is. Maybe after all of this clears up, we can come back and look again."

Grayson and Alex were headed our way, and we walked over to meet them.

"Did you follow her?" Natalie asked.

"Did I follow her?" Alex replied, a little offended. "Of course I did. She was definitely undead. She was also pretty clever . . . and paranoid. I don't think she knew I was there, but she still used hard-core evasive techniques. She went down into Dead City by way of that old pumping station near the ruins."

"Well done," Natalie said. "We'll have to go back and check that out."

"I wasn't nearly as successful," Grayson said, shaking his head. "I didn't find any undead and I didn't learn any-thing when I poked around the Blackwell House."

It took a moment for the name to register.

"What's the Blackwell House?" I asked.

He gave me an "are you kidding me?" look.

"Haven't you ever noticed the two-story wooden farm-house before?" he said, pointing at it. "You walk by it every day on the way to school."

"I've noticed it," I said. "But I didn't know what it was called."

Of course, Grayson being Grayson, he not only knew what it was called, but also its entire history. "It's one of the oldest houses in New York. The Blackwells built it right after the Revolutionary War, when this island was their farmland."

Natalie and I shared a look. Grayson had no idea that he'd discovered the key bit of evidence.

"What?" asked Alex.

"Yeah," added Grayson. "Why does the name of the farmhouse matter?"

We both said it at the same time: "Cornelius Blackwell!"

"Who's Cornelius Blackwell?" Grayson asked.

"A body that's missing from the Old Marble Cemetery," I said.

"And now three bodies turn up at the Blackwell House," Natalie continued. "That can't be a coincidence."

"Technically, it can," Alex said. "And even if it's not, how could you ever know for sure that Cornelius Blackwell is one of the bodies?"

"All we have to do is find out if any of them is missing his left ring finger," Natalie offered.

"Cool," I said, realizing she was right. I even gave her a fist bump. "We can pay a visit to the freezer and count some fingers."

"Absolutely," she answered.

We were happy, but the guys were completely confused. As we headed back to school, Natalie began to fill them in on what had happened when we went to the Old Marble Cemetery with Dr. Hidalgo. If the finger we'd found at the cemetery was from one of the bodies found here, we'd know for sure.

But then something caught my eye and stopped me in my tracks.

I held my hand up for Natalie to stop talking and asked, "How many numbers do they draw for the lottery?"

"Oh, don't ever play the lottery," Grayson said, shaking his head. "The odds of winning are less than the odds of—"

"I know that," I said, cutting him off. "I don't want to play it. I just want to know how many numbers they draw."

"Six," he answered.

"And how high do they go?"

"Sixty," Alex said.

"That's what I thought," I replied.

"Then what's the problem?" asked Alex.

"That."

I pointed to the window of the coffee shop. Earlier, when I'd been looking for an indicator, I couldn't see it because a tree was blocking my view. Now it was clear as day. And it was perfectly in line with where the bodies had been arranged.

It was a sign with the winning lottery numbers written on it. Only they couldn't have been the actual numbers because there were only four of them, and two of those were higher than sixty.

They were 4, 74, 18, 75.

It was the first Omega code I had learned in training.

"BEWARE!"

13

I Meet the One and Only
Cornelius Blackwell

As we walked back to school, we tried to figure out the meaning of the "beware" message. I suggested the most obvious explanation.

"Someone's trying to warn us about something."

"Maybe," Alex said with a shrug. "But what? If they want to warn us, why be so mysterious? Why make us waste time trying to figure it out?"

Grayson considered this for a moment. "Maybe they want us to waste time," he reasoned. "Maybe they're not warning us at all. They're just trying to distract us from solving the real mystery—the one about the three bodies."

"Kind of like an *appel*," I said.

Grayson raised an eyebrow. "What's an *appel*?"

It wasn't very often that I knew something Grayson didn't, so I savored the moment.

"It's a fencing maneuver," I explained as I acted it out. "A fake out. You start to make a lunge, but instead of going through with it, you just stomp your lead foot. The motion and noise distract your opponent and create an opening so you can go in for the kill."

"That sounds ominous," Alex said.

"Worse than that," offered Natalie. "Because if it is some sort of fake out, it means one of the bad guys knows our code."

This troubling possibility quieted us as we thought about what might happen if a zombie could read our code.

Finally, Grayson broke the silence when we reached the campus. "Well, there is one thing we know for sure."

"What's that?"

He looked us each in the eye before answering, "That we need to be careful."

Natalie nodded. "You've got that right. Which is why I'm putting us on the buddy system. Until we know more, we go to and from school in pairs."

We all moaned.

The moans had nothing to do with not wanting to be together. The problem was that according to proper procedure, we would now have to meet up in alternate locations each morning. In my case, this meant I'd have to wake up about forty-five minutes earlier than usual.

"I don't want to hear it," Natalie said. "It's a safety issue."

"You're right," Alex agreed. "After school I'll go with Grayson and help write up our report for the Prime-O." All our messages to the Prime Omega had to be sent through Grayson's computer.

"Meanwhile," Natalie replied, "Molly and I will head over to the morgue to see if any of those bodies is missing a finger."

"Actually," I said sheepishly, "I have to go to fencing practice first."

Natalie gave me a "seriously?" look and the others laughed like they were in on a joke that I didn't know.

"I thought fencing was on Thursdays," she protested.

"We've got some tournaments coming up," I explained. "Coach Wilkes doubled our practice schedule."

Natalie took an exaggerated breath. "I guess that means I'll go watch Molly dance around with her little sword," she said as she did a goofy fencing impression. "And then we'll go to the morgue."

"It's not dancing," I declared defensively. "It's combat."

"Combat?" she said, having fun with it. "And what type of combat training are you doing today?"

I waited a moment before answering meekly, "We're practicing our footwork."

Everyone laughed, including me.

"Sounds like dancing to me," she called out as we split up and headed toward our fifth-period classes.

Despite the teasing, I knew they thought it was good for me to be on the fencing team. Not only was I learning how to use a sword, but more important, I was learning battle strategies.

For example, our footwork lesson that day centered on the *in quartata*. It's an evasive maneuver that requires you to step back and turn out of the way while simultaneously moving under your opponent's blade and into position to make a counterattack. The footwork is really tricky, and I was still running through it in my head after practice as Natalie and I rode the subway to the morgue.

"As I said," she joked, "it looks like dancing."

I looked down and realized that I wasn't just doing it in my head. I was actually going through the steps in the aisle of the subway car. "It's a cool move," I offered in my defense. "That is, it *would be* a cool move if I could figure out the footwork."

She pointed at my back leg. "You need to step back farther with your left foot, so that you can maintain better balance and counterthrust."

I couldn't believe my ears. I stopped and pointed an accusing finger. "You were on the fencing team?"

She laughed. "You obviously don't know my father. I couldn't *just* be on the fencing team. I had to have private lessons . . . a personal trainer . . . three weeks in Colorado Springs with the Olympic developmental team."

"Wow," I said, blown away. "How good are you?"

"*Were*, past tense," she answered. "I was good enough to get to the point that I hated every second of it. It finally got to be too much, and I burned out. I quit cold turkey last December. A little Christmas disappointment present for my dad."

"How'd he handle it?" I asked.

"The same way he always handles it when I let him down," she said with a combination of anger and embarrassment. "He refused to talk about it and ignored me just a little bit more than usual."

I had never heard her talk this way.

"My dad just says 'Don't get your eye poked out.'"

She smiled and looked almost envious. For the first time since I'd met her, it occurred to me that the fabulous life might not always be as fabulous as it looks. I dropped the subject, and we made small talk until we got to the morgue.

Considering it was after hours, we weren't sure how we were going to get downstairs and into the freezer to check out the dead bodies. I knew luck was on our side when I saw my favorite security guard working the main desk.

"I got this," I whispered to Natalie as we walked toward him.

"Good golly, Miss Molly," Jamaican Bob greeted me. *"Wagwan?"*

It had taken me most of one summer to figure out that *"Wagwan?"* is Jamaican slang for "What's going on?"

"Not much," I said, happy to see him. "What's going on with you?"

"Same old," he said.

"You remember Natalie, don't you?"

He gave me a wounded look. "As if I could forget her. How are you, Natalie?"

"I have too much homework, but other than that I'm doing great," she said with an easy smile.

So far, so good. But normally, this was when Bob would

tell one of his famously bad jokes. This time, though, there was no joke. There was just a question.

"What are you two doing here this time of day?"

It was more curious than suspicious, but I knew we had to be careful.

"We came by to see Dr. Hidalgo," I said, knowing full well that one of Dr. H's obsessive-compulsive habits was that he always left at precisely 5:45. "Is he still around?"

"He left about an hour ago," Bob said, giving me a skeptical look, as though he thought I should know the answer. "Same time as always."

"That's what I figured," I said, trying to cover. "We're supposed to pick up something for school, but fencing practice ran long."

"Fencing?" he said with a laugh. "You're taking fencing."

"Yeah," I said, happy that this had distracted him. "I'm on the school team and everything."

Now came the tricky part. I had to act like nothing was up, but still get us downstairs by ourselves.

"Since Dr. H isn't here, can you escort us to pick it up?" This drew a desperate look from Natalie, but I knew what I was doing. "It's down in the freezer."

That's why I knew I had him. No way would Bob go

near the freezer. Sure enough, he shook his head at the mere suggestion.

"Why don't you two just go by yourselves," he said as he waved us in. "The only way they're getting me in that room is when they wheel me in."

We put our book bags on the X-ray machine and walked through the metal detector. Just when I thought we were clear, he reached over and grabbed me by the wrist.

My heart jumped, but I tried to stay cool.

"One thing you should know," he said.

"What's that?" I asked with a gulp.

"Without you hanging around, it's been really *dead* around here." He let out a booming laugh, and I knew we were golden. Natalie and I both laughed with him as we grabbed our bags and disappeared down the hall.

"Nice work," Natalie said as we headed toward the stairs.

We went down three floors and made it to the door that led to the lab and freezer. I pulled the bottle of vanilla extract out of my backpack and swiped a finger of it under my nose. Natalie did the same.

"As if this place wasn't spooky enough during regular business hours," I said as we entered the lab.

A row of security lights flickering on the far wall gave the room an eerie green glow. I reached for the main switch, but Natalie stopped me.

"We don't want to advertise what we're doing," Natalie warned.

"Good point." Even in partial darkness, I knew every inch of the lab, inside and out. I went straight to the autopsy room and flicked on a small desk lamp while Natalie headed for the refrigerator.

"Here's the guest book," I said, picking up a ledger that listed the arrival and departure of every corpse that came through the office. I flipped it open to the page with the most recent entries.

"'Three John Does found on Roosevelt Island,'" I read aloud from the book. "They're in freezer drawers seven, eight, and nine."

"And look what I got from the fridge," Natalie said, holding up a little plastic bag and shaking it.

"I'm guessing it's a finger," I said with a smile.

"Don't forget the wedding ring," she added as we entered the freezer. We walked over to a wall of drawers. They're numbered from top to bottom, and the three we wanted to check were one on top of the other.

Natalie grabbed the handle to drawer number seven

and turned to me. "I'd like to introduce you to Mr. Cornelius Blackwell."

She pulled it open with great dramatic flair. But the moment was ruined when the drawer turned out to be empty. Natalie gave me an "okay, that's a little strange" expression. She tried the introduction again with drawer number eight.

"I'd like to introduce you to Mr. Cornelius Blackwell."

Drawer number eight was also empty.

So was nine. It was the Old Marble Cemetery all over again. You expect dead bodies, and then there aren't any.

"Are you sure you got those numbers right?" she asked me with an arched eyebrow.

"I'm positive," I said. "Check the cards."

Next to the handle of each drawer was a card with basic info about that particular body. Sure enough, all three drawers had cards that read "John Doe. Roosevelt Island."

Dr. Hidalgo pays close attention to every detail of his morgue. There's no way three bodies were not where they were supposed to be in the freezer.

"It just doesn't make any sense," Natalie said.

And it didn't make any sense . . . until we heard the loud crash coming from the next room.

Ω 14

Careful What You Wish For

The crash sounded like a bookcase tumbling over and spilling everything from its shelves. Our first reflex was to freeze, not because we were scared, but because we were the only ones on that floor and we worried that we had somehow caused it to happen. Then we heard another crash, followed by shattering glass, and realized that we weren't alone after all.

"Who is that?" I asked, in that way you whisper something you really want to scream.

Natalie considered it for a second before a look of realization came over her. She motioned to the empty drawers in front of us. "They're not dead. . . ." She pointed toward the noise and finished her thought. "They're undead."

Suddenly, it seemed so obvious.

"I think you're about to put your combat training to use," she continued.

The first thing that came to mind was how frustrated I had been that morning because we hadn't had any zombie action. I guess you should be careful what you wish for.

We each took a deep breath and nodded that we were ready. We moved silently from the freezer into the lab. The flickering security lights cast our shadows at odd angles across the examination tables.

The noise was coming from a small library, where Dr. H kept his medical books and journals. I remembered that the bookcases had locks on them, and it sounded as though someone without a key had decided to unlock them by smashing them to bits.

"There could be as many as three of them in there," Natalie reminded me. "They've got us outnumbered, but we've got surprise on our side."

"Surprise . . . and training," I said, trying to ease the tension and to reassure myself at the same time.

"And training," she agreed with a nod.

"Do we go in?" I asked, motioning toward the library door.

"No." She pointed to where she wanted me to stand, a spot about five feet from the door. "We let the fight come to us. We're going to wait for the door to open and then try to take control of the situation before they even know what hit them."

"Got it."

"You're ready for this, I know it," she reassured me. "But don't be afraid to ask for help if you need it."

"I won't," I promised.

From the sound of things, all the bookcases had now been pulled over, and someone (or up to three different someones) was digging through the rubble. After about thirty seconds the digging stopped, and we heard an inhuman laugh that sent chills down my spine.

"Brace yourself," Natalie whispered. "Here it comes."

My heart was racing so fast, I had to force myself to take short steady breaths to calm my nerves. A metallic taste filled my mouth as adrenaline rushed through my body.

The door flew open to reveal a giant man wearing one of the hospital gowns we drape over dead bodies while they await autopsy. The room was too dark to get a good look at him, but his eyes burned orange like coals in a fire, and he didn't seem the least bit bothered by the large chunks of glass sticking out of his cheek and forearm.

The light in the library allowed me a full view of the destruction behind him. More important, I could see that no one else was in there. As he stepped through the doorway, he held a book above his head triumphantly and started to call out with some sort of guttural wail.

I thought back to the *appel* maneuver from fencing and decided to try a modified version.

"He's alone!" I called out to Natalie as I jumped toward him and stomped my foot as loudly as I could.

He turned to look at me, and was too distracted to see her coming. Natalie ran right at him and delivered three rapid-fire kicks right into the side of his knee, crumpling him to the ground.

He bellowed and started yelling some sort of zombie gibberish. I didn't understand it, but I could tell he wasn't yelling at us.

He was calling for help.

His extreme height advantage was gone for as long as he writhed on the floor. It was the perfect chance for Natalie to finish him off with a solid kick to the face. But as she went to do it, she caught a glimmer of the green security light reflecting off the shards of glass in his cheek.

She stopped herself midkick in order to keep from cutting up her leg and foot.

This hesitation bought him enough time to get his bearings and stand up straight. Or at least as straight as you can stand with one of your legs bent at a forty-five-degree angle to the side.

He swung a fist and with it an armful of broken glass; Natalie easily ducked it. She countered with a flurry of punches to his stomach that sent him staggering back toward the library.

Watching her, I was mesmerized. She was amazingly tough and brave. I wondered if her "disappointed" father had any idea of what she was truly capable of.

I snapped out of it when I heard a crash behind us. I spun around to see another zombie in a hospital gown coming our way. Apparently, this group of undead was all from the *supersize* side of the menu, because he too was massive. Adding to his intimidating effect was the fact that one half of his head had wild red hair that tentacled in every direction while the other half had been completely shaved in preparation for his autopsy.

"I'll take care of this one," I called out to Natalie.

"Just remember there's another one around here somewhere," she said. "Quick kills are vital."

Easier said than done.

I could hear Natalie and Glass Face fighting behind me as I approached Big Red. I remembered the way Natalie had taunted the Level 3 in the subway station and how much it had frustrated him. I thought I'd give it a try.

"What's up with your haircut?" I asked, trying to sound cool and tough like the stars in those action movies my dad watches. "Did the barber have a half-off sale?"

Okay, so the joke didn't really work, but in my defense, it was my first day as an action hero. Being able to deliver cool lines in tense situations takes practice. Besides, I didn't really need to do anything to get him worked up. Turns out he was more than mad enough just at my being there.

He charged right at me, and I probably should have been more scared than I was. But while he had the size, I had the home-court advantage. This was *my* lab, and I knew everything in it!

I calmly grabbed the corner of a gurney, popped the wheel brake with my foot, and spun it around so that it was in front of me like a shopping cart.

I rammed it right at him as he charged at me, and we collided like two trains coming at each other on the same track. The force of it knocked me back onto my butt and cut him off at the waist so hard, he slammed face-first into the gurney.

I jumped up and then grabbed a large metal bowl Dr. H uses to hold human organs when he weighs them (I know, gross, but you get used to it), and I slammed it into the clean-shaven side of Big Red's head. I was hoping this would finish him off.

It didn't.

Instead, he stood up and swiped at the gurney with the back of his hand, sending it skittering off to the side. I could hear his neck bones crack into place as he cocked his head, side to side. Then he looked at me and my bowl and laughed.

(Okay, if you're ever looking for a scary Halloween costume, it turns out "giant laughing zombie with a half-shaved head in a hospital gown" is both inexpensive and effective.)

I held up my bowl like a weapon and refused to back down. As silly as it sounds, I thought if I could get another whack at his head with it, I might at least be able to daze him.

He charged at me again, and I instantly thought about fencing practice and the *in quartata* maneuver I had learned that day. This was the perfect situation: I'd turn out of his way, avoid him, and go from defense to offense with a lightning-quick blow to the back of his head.

At least, that's how I imagined it.

Unfortunately, I still couldn't get the footwork right, and I tripped over myself. Instead of the bowl against the back of his head, the only slamming was my nose and face against the concrete floor.

Big Red flipped me over, grabbed me by the shoulders, and picked me up like a doll. He lifted me all the way up, so that my eyes were even with his. Then he grossed me out by doing that thing where he sniffed me like a dog.

I cannot stress enough how much I hate that.

I squirmed and struggled but could not break loose. I had no idea what to do. Then I heard Natalie call out.

"What did I tell you about asking for help?" she said, frustrated.

"I know, but you looked kind of busy," I said, short of breath and struggling. "And I wanted to prove to you that I could take care of things myself."

"How's that working out?"

I squirmed some more, but still had no luck getting free. "Not so good."

"You might want to try a head butt," she suggested.

It wasn't exactly Jeet Kune Do, but it sounded like a

plan. I smiled and snapped my head forward, right into his face. Upside: It worked and he let go. Downside: It really hurt.

I slammed against the floor (again), and this time I didn't even bother getting up. I just used my small size to an advantage and started to scramble under the tables to get away from Big Red.

From my vantage point I could see Natalie was still going at it with Glass Face. His right leg was now barely attached below the knee, and it flopped around as he moved. Despite this, she hadn't been able to finish him. The broken glass was working like a booby trap in his face. As to fighting, he seemed more concerned with protecting the book than hurting her.

Suddenly all the lights came on, and I looked over at the door where Zombie Number Three had just flipped the switch. He was not quite as big as the others but was still plenty horrifying. He had changed from his hospital gown into street clothes and was carrying clothes for them as well. If I had to put my money on it, I'd say he was the brains of the operation.

He barked something at them, obviously upset they were wasting time fighting a couple of girls. Then he saw the book and smiled. He went straight for it.

Everything was different with the lights on. Especially because now the zombies could see all the equipment. The needles, scalpels, and blades that were normally just the tools of a medical examiner suddenly looked more like weapons. Big Red flashed a hideous orange-yellow smile as he grabbed two large blades from a table.

Zombie Number Three didn't care about us. He was only interested in the book. He snatched it from Glass Face and smiled broadly as he looked at the cover to see that they had the right one. As he held it, I got a good look at his hand and noticed something interesting.

He was missing his left ring finger.

I'd like to introduce you to Mr. Cornelius Blackwell.

He snapped at them again, and they turned their attention away from us and started to leave.

"The book," I pleaded with Natalie. "I don't know what it is. But we can't let them take it."

"You know some way to get them back?" she asked as she tried to catch her breath.

I looked down at the table and saw the answer in a little plastic bag.

"Hey, Corrrrneeeeliusss," I sang out. "Did you happen to lose a finger? And a wedding ring?"

He stopped and turned around. He looked right at me,

and I dangled the bag in the air. I even gave it an extra shake.

"We found this at the cemetery where you left it," I said. "I hope that wedding ring doesn't have any sentimental value for you. Especially with that sweet inscription from your wife and all. I can't decide if I want to melt it down, give it away, or just throw it in the river."

He was furious, which is exactly what I was hoping for.

"Or did you want it back?"

He started coming right at me, and when he got close, I tossed the bag onto the far side of the table I was next to. When he reached for it with his right hand, I grabbed a metal handsaw that Dr. H uses for (actually, you don't want to know what he uses it for, just know that he uses it) and with the best saber technique I knew, I chopped off his left hand at the wrist.

The hand, and more important, the book, fell to the floor. I grabbed them both (the hand was still kind of clutching the book) and raced toward the rear exit, snatching my backpack on the way.

As I ran, I pried the dead fingers off the book, which I then shoved into my bag. Natalie caught up with me at the door and we ran down the hallway. We made it around the corner and almost all the way to the stairs before we had to stop.

Big Red and Glass Face had beaten us there and were blocking our escape.

A few seconds later Cornelius Blackwell came out of the lab. He had the bag and the severed hand. And, understandably, he was in a pretty bad mood.

I turned to Natalie and finally took her advice.

"Help."

15

Big Zombies, Little Women

We were trapped. Glass Face and Big Red blocked the stairs and elevator while Cornelius Blackwell stood between us and the lab. To say that they were angry would be an understatement. I'd bashed in the side of Big Red's head, and thanks to Natalie, the lower half of Glass Face's left leg was now barely attached at the knee.

But the angriest was Blackwell.

Not only had I chopped off his hand, but I had also stolen the one thing he'd come to get. He approached us slowly, careful not to make any sudden movements. And while it was a struggle for him to form the word, I knew exactly what he was trying to say.

"Boooookkk."

"What book?" I answered, trying to play dumb. "I don't have any book."

He snarled and motioned to the others to start closing in. As they did, Natalie turned so that we were back-to-back, our shoulder blades pressed against each other, ready to fight in any direction. We'd almost run out of time when she cocked her head to the side and whispered the one word capable of bringing a smile to my face.

"Shortcut."

I knew exactly what she meant. The day he'd taken us to the Old Marble Cemetery, Dr. H had led us out of the morgue through a series of basement hallways. He'd called it his shortcut. Now it was our escape route.

First, though, we needed to distract the undead.

"Wait, wait," I said, holding up my hands for them to stop. "I have the book, and I'll give it to you. Just let me get it out."

They held their ground as I slipped the backpack off my shoulder and then unzipped it. I reached in and grabbed the biggest textbook I could find (*Advanced Biology*, hardcover edition), careful to make sure they couldn't see it. Then I looked right into the cold dead eyes of Cornelius Blackwell.

"Is this the one you mean?"

In one fluid motion I pulled out the book and swung it as hard as I could. I caught him squarely under the chin with an uppercut. He staggered backward, and that was all the opening we needed. We turned down the hall and started to sprint at full speed.

"Tell me you remember the way," I pleaded breathlessly.

"Just follow me," Natalie answered as she took the lead, a wild smile on her face.

Not once did I look back to see how close they were. All I did was run. We raced along the narrow hallways, through an old lab that reeked of formaldehyde, and up three mini-stairwells, fighting through the cobwebs, twisting and turning until we reached a door that opened onto First Avenue.

My immediate reaction was to suck in a lungful of fresh air and let out a sigh of relief.

"We're not safe yet," Natalie reminded me. "As soon as they get out of those hospital gowns and into street clothes, they'll be able to follow us anywhere in Manhattan. They have your scent.

"We need to get off the island," she continued. "Now!"

I looked for a cab but didn't see one. It defies all logic, but whenever you actually *need* a cab, they're nowhere to be found. If we didn't need one, they'd be everywhere.

Then I heard the sound of the zombies coming up from the basement, and my heart went into turbo drive.

"I know where we can go!" I blurted excitedly. "Alpha Bakery."

The bakery was only two blocks away. I knew that if we could make it there, we'd get help.

MIST doesn't have a track team, but if it did, Natalie and I would have qualified based solely on our sprint down First Ave. I don't think I've ever run that fast in my life.

When we finally burst into the bakery, we actually knocked the bell from above the doorway and sent it clanging across the floor. Luckily, there were no customers in the store. Only the baker, who was not particularly happy to see me so soon after his warning.

"What did I tell you about coming here without an *imminent need*?" he demanded, his big puffy cheeks red with frustration. But then he saw the panicked expressions on our faces and knew this was not another unnecessary visit.

This was real.

"This *is* an imminent need!" I declared. "We're being

chased by three massive zombies and need to get off the island right away."

Talk about sentences you never imagined yourself saying.

"Quick!" he replied urgently as he lifted a panel in the counter. "Hide in the pantry." We rushed through the opening and into the back of the store.

"Go in there and lock the door," he said, motioning to a small storage room. "Do not unlock it for *anyone* but me."

"How will we know it's you?" I asked as I tried to catch my breath.

"There's a monitor in there for the security cameras," he explained. "You'll be able to see everything in the bakery. Remember, no one but me."

"Got it!" we said in unison.

We rushed in and closed the door behind us. Natalie bolted the lock and then took a deep breath. She relaxed for a second (but only one) before she turned to me and angrily asked, "How come he recognized you? How come he'd talked to you before?"

I didn't have it in me to make up some elaborate excuse or explanation, so I went with the truth. "I broke the rules and came by the bakery. It was stupid, and I know that.

But can you get mad at me after this is over and we know we're still alive?"

There would be explaining to do later; for now she let it go and turned her attention to the monitor.

"Here they come," she said, pointing at the screen, which had images from four different cameras. On one we were able to see the zombies walking up the sidewalk, and on another we saw them as they entered the bakery. They tried to act normal, which was a bit ridiculous considering their appearance. They were colorful . . . even on a black-and-white screen.

Big Red had combed his hair across the bald half of his scalp. Or at least, he'd tried to. It kept flipping back over, so that now it looked like a giant *C* on the top of his head. Glass Face, meanwhile, had taken all the glass shards out of his cheek, so now he would be more accurately called Open Wound Face. He also tried not to limp too noticeably, but the lower part of his left leg kept dragging behind him at odd angles. Finally, Cornelius Blackwell did his best to mask his missing left hand by sticking his arm deep into his jacket pocket. It would have been funny if it weren't for the fact that they were trying to kill us.

And as if their bizarre appearance wasn't already

enough to attract attention, Big Red was sniffing the air like some sort of undead bloodhound hot on my scent. Despite all this, the baker acted like it was just a normal day and they were regular customers.

"Welcome!" he greeted them warmly. He winked at Big Red and offered, "I bet that's the vanilla you smell. Wonderful, isn't it? There's nothing more powerful to the nose than the smell of vanilla. *Nothing in the world*."

Natalie nodded, smiling. "Brilliant!"

"What's brilliant?" I asked.

"He's talking to *us*," she said as she started to search the shelves of the pantry. "He wants us to find vanilla. There's got to be some in here."

The pantry was filled with giant-sized containers of baking ingredients. Twenty-pound bags of sugar and flour were stacked up along one wall while shelves filled with cans of cinnamon, bags of chocolate chips, and boxes of sprinkles lined the others.

"Check it out," Natalie said as she crouched low. She'd found a row with gallon jugs of vanilla. "Triple-strength Madagascar pure vanilla concentrate." She looked up at me with a grin. "This should hide your scent perfectly."

"Great idea," I said with a shrug. "But how do you suppose we'll squirt it up his nose?"

She started to laugh. "That's not what I meant. Close your eyes tight, this could burn."

It still took a moment for me to realize that her plan was to cover my scent by covering *me* . . . with the vanilla.

"No way!" I objected. "You cannot be serious."

"Yes way! And I am."

"But I'll smell for days!"

"You don't have much of a choice," she said as she started to unscrew the cap. "Unless you'd rather smell like Dead City?"

"Well, if you're going to put it that way . . ."

If you've never worked in a bakery before, let me tell you that triple-strength Madagascar pure vanilla concentrate is as much syrup as it is liquid. It made a gurgling noise as Natalie poured it on top of my head. It slowly oozed through my hair, down my face, and, well, you get the picture.

It was pointless to fight, so I did my best to speed up the process by rubbing it in. My one lucky break was that I was still in the gym shorts and T-shirt I'd worn to fencing, so I wasn't ruining any clothes I cared about.

Natalie tried not to smile too much, but she failed miserably. I couldn't really blame her. When I saw my reflection in the stainless-steel door of the pantry, it took everything I had to keep from busting out.

"This is ridiculous," I whispered, trying not to crack up and make any noise that might attract attention.

Ridiculous . . . but also effective.

It wasn't long before the look on Big Red's face became even more confused than usual. He had clearly lost my scent. A minute later he motioned to the others, and the three of them left the bakery.

On the security monitor we saw them linger on the sidewalk, trying to catch a whiff of me. Once they were gone, the baker snuck us out in the back of his delivery truck. He drove to Queens, dropping us off right in front of my apartment building.

Face-to-face on the sidewalk, no longer in danger, the three of us looked at one another and smiled.

"It's been a while since I've done anything like this," he said, pleased to have a little taste of zombie action again. "I didn't realize how much I missed it. So tell me, did you two inflict all that damage? The broken leg? The missing hand?"

Natalie and I looked at each other and then at him. In unison we said, "Yeah."

"I love it," he said with a hearty laugh.

"Thanks for all the help," Natalie said.

"Omega today, Omega forever," he replied. "Anything else you need?"

"You got any tips on how to get rid of the smell of triple-strength Madagascar pure vanilla concentrate?" I asked hopefully.

"Showers, plural," he answered. "Lots and lots of showers."

He started toward his truck but stopped and turned back to us. He thought for a moment, trying to pick out the right words for what he wanted to say. "Molly . . . your mom . . . she was the best."

"Yeah," I said with a nod. "They say she was quite the Zeke."

"Yes, but that's not what I meant," he said, shaking his head. "She wasn't just the best zombie killer. She was the best . . . everything. The best *person* I ever knew. She'd be really proud of you."

A warm feeling came over me (although that could have been the vanilla settling into my pores) as I thought about her. Then I looked up at him. "Thanks."

Natalie and I hurried upstairs. My dad was hard at work in the kitchen. Luckily, the powerful aroma of his spaghetti sauce let me slip by unnoticed. Natalie hung out in my room while I took a quick shower.

Okay, maybe "quick" is not the right word. Despite scrubbing so hard that my skin turned bright pink and washing my hair three times, I still smelled like an ice cream factory. But at least all the sticky goop was off me.

When I walked into my room, I found Natalie sitting on the floor with the contents of my backpack spread out around her. She had a worried look on her face.

"Something wrong?" I asked.

"What happened to the book?" she replied, looking up at me.

"What do you mean? It was in my bag."

"No, it wasn't." She motioned to the piles around her. "They're all either textbooks or from the school library."

"That doesn't make any sense," I said, thoroughly confused. "I know I put it there, and they never got near my backpack. Besides, I don't have any library books. My card was revoked until next semester due to excessive overdue fines."

"Seriously?" she said, shooting me an incredulous look. "How hard is it to remember to return a book?"

"Apparently, harder than it sounds," I responded. "Now, do you mind not passing judgment? Just know that I don't have any library books."

"Well, then, what's this?"

She held up a medium-sized green book and turned it

so that I could read the stamp along the side: "Property of MIST Library."

"Well, I don't know why it was at the morgue," I said, "but that's the book they had. I never saw it before that scary zombie dude burst through the door and held it up in the air."

Natalie cracked a crooked smile as she shook her head. "Then something's really wrong here," she said. "Because it does not make sense that three zombies would climb out of their graves, stage an elaborate death scene, tear up the morgue, and fight to the death to get a copy of this."

She turned the book so that I could see the cover. And when I saw what it was, I had to agree that it didn't make any sense.

The book was *Little Women* by Louisa May Alcott.

16

Geek Mythology

As Natalie stood there holding the book, I tried to think of any reason why three zombies would be so desperate to get a copy of *Little Women*.

"Ever read it?" she asked me.

"Of course," I answered. "Haven't you?"

She shook her head. "Never interested me."

"Really? Not even in fifth grade?"

She laughed. "In fifth grade my favorite book was *Emerging Principles of Nanotechnology*." (Sometimes Natalie almost makes me feel normal by comparison.)

"Well, then, you've really missed out, because the

book is *sooooo* good. It's set in New England during the Civil War and is about four sisters who try to keep up their spirits despite hard times. They take care of their neighbors, go to parties, and put on plays for their friends and family."

"In other words," she answered, "it's the exact opposite of twenty-first-century killer zombies who live beneath Manhattan."

"Pretty much," I said. "So you've got to wonder why they'd go through so much trouble to get a copy of a book they could pick up at any bookstore."

"Well, it's not actually *Little Women*," Natalie said as she opened it to the title page. "That's just what it says on the cover. The full title is *Louisa May Alcott's Little Women, the Theatricals of Jo, Meg, Amy, and Beth March*, by Margaret Key."

She handed me the book, and I flipped through it. Sure enough, a writer named Margaret Key had written entire scripts based on the plays put on by the sisters in the novel.

"Okay, so what, then?" I asked, half joking and half trying to figure it out. "The three of them want to start performing girl plays for their friends down in Dead City?"

Just the thought of them dressing up as the sisters made me laugh out loud.

"Not exactly Shakespeare in the Park," she replied.

"I can tell you, though, who would have loved this book," I added as a happy memory danced through my head. "My mother was obsessed with *Little Women*. It was her all-time favorite novel. She even named my sister Beth after one of the sisters in the book."

I handed it back to Natalie, and she flipped through it some more.

"I get that your mom would have liked it," Natalie replied, "but not why Cornelius Blackwell was so desperate to get his hand on it." She gave me a little wink and a smirk. "Notice I said *hand*—as in only one?"

"I *had* to chop it off," I said defensively. "It was the only way to get the book."

"And you're sure this is the book you pried from the fingers of that severed hand?" she asked, holding it up by the corner as if it suddenly had cooties.

"Positive," I said, replaying the gory scene in my head. "And I specifically remember that he checked the cover to make sure he had the right book. This is what they were after."

She thought about it for a second. "Now that you say that, I remember him checking it too."

We sat there dumbfounded, trying to think of any reasonable explanation and coming up with exactly zero.

"Okay, let's forget for a minute why they wanted it," I suggested, "and try to figure out what a book from the MIST school library was doing in the New York City morgue."

"Change of perspective. Good idea."

We mulled this over for a minute, and then Natalie made that "eureka" face she gets when she comes up with a brilliant idea.

She flipped to the back of the book and carefully slid the library return receipt from the pocket inside the cover. It was brittle and faded, but when she held it up to the light, she could still make out the faint writing. She read it and then laughed. "I know one thing the morgue and MIST have in common."

"What?" I asked eagerly.

"Apparently, you're not the only one in the family who's lousy at returning library books."

Now I realized what MIST had in common with the morgue. "You can't be serious."

"Oh, yeah," she said as she handed the slip to me.

I checked the slip and could not believe my eyes. The book was last checked out nearly thirty years earlier by a

MIST student named Rosemary Collins. My mother.

"You were right when you said your mom would have loved this book. She loved it so much, she checked it out and never returned it."

That's when the doorbell rang.

"I bet that's the boys," Natalie said. "I texted them from the delivery truck and a couple more times when you were in the shower. You were in there for a while."

Sure enough, Alex and Grayson were at the door, relieved to see us healthy and whole. Before we could fill them in on our adventure, my dad popped out from the kitchen.

"Hey, Molly, want to introduce me to your friends?"

"Sure thing, Dad. This is Natalie, Alex, and Grayson. We're working together on a research project for school."

"Nice to meet you all," he said. "I'm making baked rigatoni for dinner, if any of you would like to join us."

Alex, ever the food monster, smiled gleefully. "Is it true that you were selected the best cook in the entire New York City Fire Department?"

Dad, almost embarrassed, nodded. "I don't know how tough the competition was, but yes."

"Then I, for one, would very much like to have baked rigatoni."

"Me too," added Grayson.

All eyes turned to Natalie.

"Do you have enough for three extra people?" she asked sheepishly.

"More than enough," he answered with a smile. "I'll call you when it's ready."

I could tell Dad was thrilled at the prospect of other kids visiting. I think I've made it pretty clear that I'm not exactly a social butterfly (let's be honest, I'm not even a social caterpillar), and whatever friends Beth has, she tends to meet up with them away from home.

Dad went back into the kitchen while we headed to my room. Natalie and I filled the guys in on what happened at the morgue, our escape by way of the bakery, and our utter confusion about the book. That's when Alex caught us all by surprise by announcing, "*Little Women* rocks!"

"Are you serious?" Grayson asked incredulously. "You've actually read it?"

"Multiple times," Alex answered, without a hint of sarcasm or shame. "I have three younger sisters, and I read it to each one when they were little. I even did different voices for the characters. My Jo . . . off the charts."

"If you know it so well, maybe you can figure out why they wanted it," Natalie suggested as she tossed the book to him. "'Cause we sure can't."

Alex opened the book to the table of contents and then flashed a smile that up until that point I had seen him use only while looking at food.

"What a great idea," he said as he read through the play titles. "There's *The Witch's Curse*, that's the one where they perform on Christmas at the start of the book, *The Captive of Castile*, *The Greek Slave* . . ."

His voice trailed off as he continued down the list.

"What's wrong?" Natalie asked.

"Well . . . some of these aren't from the book at all."

"Really?" I asked.

"Like this one," he said. "*Atlas and Prometheus*."

"Now *that* sounds good," Grayson said, suddenly interested in the conversation.

"What do you mean?" asked Natalie.

"I may not know anything about *Little Women*," he answered, "but I know almost everything about Greek mythology."

"You sure you don't mean geek mythology?" Alex asked with a laugh.

"Call it what you want. I used to read myths to my little brothers at bedtime. I even did voices. My Hephaestus would put your Jo to shame."

We all laughed at that.

"Why would there be a play about Atlas and Prometheus in this book," Natalie wondered, "if it's not in the original?"

"Maybe there's something in the myth," I suggested. "What's it about?"

"Atlas and Prometheus were Titans, and they were brothers," Grayson replied. "But when the Titans went to war with the Olympians, Prometheus went against his own kind."

"All right," Natalie said, nodding. "Do you think that might have something to do with three Level 3 goons?"

Grayson shook his head. "Nothing I can think of."

As we looked further into the book, we discovered that most of the plays were not, in fact, from *Little Women*. Despite this, Margaret Key had written them as though they were. Each one featured the four sisters and was written in Louisa May Alcott's style.

We were stumped, staring off into space and trying to figure it out, when my father entered.

"Dinner's almost ready—" he said, before stopping himself and laughing at the perplexed looks on our faces. "Homework's that hard, huh?"

"Yeah," I answered.

"I don't suppose you know anything special about Atlas and Prometheus," joked Alex.

"Just the obvious," my dad said with a shrug, as if we all should know what he meant.

"What's 'the obvious'?" I asked.

"You really don't know?"

"No."

"What kind of New Yorkers are you?" he asked. "Atlas and Prometheus are the two giant statues at Rockefeller Center. Atlas is across the street from St. Patrick's."

"And Prometheus is right in front of the ice-skating rink," Grayson finished. "How did I miss that?"

"Yeah, how'd you miss that?" Alex asked, with a friendly toss of a pillow.

"There's a big statue out in the harbor, too," Dad joked. "Tall lady with a crown and a torch. I think her name may be Something Liberty."

"Very funny, Dad."

"Anyway," he said, with a clap of his hands, "dinner's in about half an hour."

He walked back toward the kitchen, and we turned to one another, our minds digesting this new information.

"Do you think it's a coincidence?" Natalie asked. "Or do you think the play actually has something to do with Rockefeller Center?"

"Let me see the book again." Alex picked it up and turned to the first scene of the play. He stared at it as if something might jump off the page and catch his attention. It took a moment, but something did, and a smile slowly began to form. "That's interesting."

"What?"

"Come here and look at the heading on the script," he said. He motioned to all of us, so we crowded next to him and scrunched together. "Read the top three lines."

PERFORMERS: JO, MEG, AMY, BETH

LOCALES: ZEUS'S HIDDEN APPLE ORCHARD,

TARTARUS, THE CHAMBER OF IAPEDUS

"So?" Natalie asked. "Is something wrong?"

"Not that I can see," added Grayson. "The locations are all from the classic myth."

Alex smiled. "Watch what happens when I cover the edges."

He pressed his hands down flat on the page so that they covered the edges.

"Now read it."

Suddenly a new phrase was visible in the middle.

OMEGA'S HIDDEN CHAMBER

"Omega's hidden chamber?" I said, stunned.

Alex nodded. "I don't think this is a play. I think it's a code."

Book of Secrets

We scoured the book, looking for any possible connections to New York, zombies, or the Omegas and discovered something interesting in a Christmas play called *A Present from St. Nicholas*. In the story, Santa Claus brings a toy to a lonely prince named Belvedere. At first glance, it couldn't have less to do with the undead.

But hidden in the script, we found clues about St. Nicholas Heights, which is where City College is located, and Belvedere Castle, a European castle in the story, but also the name of a building in Central Park.

Still, other than the fact that they are both in New York, we couldn't come up with a connection between the college and the castle until Grayson found it online.

"Here's one thing they have in common," he announced while looking at a website about historic landmarks in the city. "They were both built from the same material."

"Gee, let me guess," I joked. "Bricks?"

"No," he answered, shaking his head. "They're both made entirely from Manhattan schist."

Alex gave him a look. "Seriously?"

Natalie was reading over Grayson's shoulder and noticed something else. "Here's another building made from Manhattan schist," she said. "The Sea and Land Church, down on the Lower East Side."

"And . . . ?" asked Alex, unsure of where this was leading.

"Listen to this." She picked up the book and read one of Belvedere's lines from the script. "'Oh, Saint Nicholas, I have searched my kingdom for this toy all along the *East Side*, across *Sea and Land*.'"

It began to make sense why the undead were so interested in the book.

"What *is* all this?" Natalie said, flipping through the pages.

Grayson took it from her and held it. "To maintain

secrecy, virtually everything we know about the Omegas and the undead has been passed down orally," he offered. "In fact, the only written records we know about are the *Book of the Dead*, which contains all the census information we collect, and the *Book of Secrets*."

"You guys told me about the *Book of the Dead* during training," I said. "But nobody said a thing about the *Book of Secrets*."

"That's because none of us really knows anything about it," Alex explained. "We don't even know for sure it exists. It may just be a rumor passed down from generation to generation."

"Supposedly," Natalie continued, "it contains codes and clues that lead you to a place where you can find the names of all Omegas, past and present, locations of hidden records and information, and even a doomsday plan to eliminate the entire undead population in case of an emergency."

I looked at Grayson. "And now you think *The Theatricals of Jo, Meg, Amy, and Beth March* is a third book that nobody knew about?"

"No," he answered as he held it up. "I think *it* is the *Book of Secrets*. It would be a classic Omega trick to hide it in plain sight right there in the MIST library."

We were all quiet for a moment as we considered the seriousness of what he was saying.

"I think so too," Natalie agreed. "And for some reason, your mother thought it needed to be moved out of the library, so she took it and eventually hid it in the morgue for safekeeping."

We all turned to Alex, who had taken the book from Grayson and was looking at its spine.

"What do you think?" Grayson asked him.

"I think the answer is right here in the Dewey decimal number from the library," he said. He turned it so we all could read the spine.

812.31

KEY

If you look in your local library, you'll see that 812.31 is right in the heart of the drama section. But if you look at the periodic table, you'll also see that it's a coded message: 8 stands for oxygen (O), 12 is magnesium (MG), and 31 is gallium (GA). All strung together it reads:

OMGGA

KEY

"Omega key," Alex said. "The key to all the Omega codes and secrets. I think we've only scratched the surface of what's inside here."

"Then we need to stop looking right now," Natalie said, taking charge again. "Whatever this is, we're not supposed to know about it. Grayson, when you get home tonight, send an emergency message to the Prime Omega. The Prime-O will tell us what to do."

Before she could say anything else, Dad called, "Dinner!" Further planning would have to wait.

Dinner was great. As expected, Dad's rigatoni was a huge hit. Less expected, Beth was actually nice to all my friends. Of course, that may have been because she thought Alex was cute. Then, about halfway through the meal, there was a knock on the door.

"Another guest?" Dad laughed as he got up to answer it. "Suddenly, we have the most popular apartment in the building."

"Word must have gotten out about your rigatoni," Alex mumbled, his mouth full of pasta.

At first I was surprised to see Dr. Hidalgo, but then it kind of made sense. I'd begun to suspect that in addition to being friends and coworkers, Dr. H and my mother had been Omegas together when they were at MIST. This kind of confirmed it. He may have given my dad some excuse about being in the neighborhood and wanting to say hello, but I knew he was there to make sure Natalie and I were all right.

"Alex, Grayson," I said, handling the introductions, "this is Dr. Hidalgo. Natalie and I interned for him down at the morgue. Well, technically, Natalie interned and I was just hanging around . . . you know . . . because I'm weird."

Everyone laughed.

"Nice to meet you both," he said, shaking their hands. Then he turned to me and Nat. "And very nice to see you two looking so well."

He closed his eyes for a second and let out a sigh of relief now that he'd found us safe and sound.

At my dad's insistence, he sat down and joined us for the rest of the meal. It reminded me of the lunch at Carmine's that Dr. H, Natalie, and I had after my adventure into the Blackwell crypt at the cemetery.

"By the way," he said, turning to me. "I was having trouble finding one of my books down at the morgue and wondered if it might have ended up with you by some chance."

I shot a quick look at the others. "I think I know the book you mean," I answered. "It's in my room."

He let out another sigh of relief, and it occurred to me that Dr. H might not be just any Omega. Maybe he was the Prime Omega, which would explain why he had the *Book of Secrets*.

After dinner I gave Dr. Hidalgo the copy of *Little Women*, and he clutched it tightly.

"Natalie and you really saved the day," he said with a mix of pride and appreciation. "You can't imagine how bad it would have been if they'd gotten this. But there's something more that I need from all four of you."

"Anything," I answered.

"Whatever you know, or think you know, or imagine you know about this book," he said, holding it up, "you need to forget. Completely."

I nodded. "Yes, sir."

"You can't just say it," he responded with total seriousness. "You have to mean it. This is for everyone's safety, especially yours. You have to promise me."

"I promise."

And when I said it, I really did mean it. But when I went back to my room, I found something that I could *not* forget.

Earlier, when I'd been in the shower and Natalie was looking for the book, she had dumped everything out of my backpack. Once dinner was over and everyone had gone home, I started sorting through the papers and putting them back where they belonged.

That's when I found the envelope.

My guess is that it must have fallen out of the *Book of Secrets* somewhere between the morgue and our apartment. I instantly recognized my mother's handwriting on the front, where she'd written: 92, 7, 71, 6, 19, 39 Al.

Using the periodic table code it spelled out "Unlucky 13." I know a lot of people think thirteen is an unlucky number. My mother wasn't one of them.

I could feel photographs inside the envelope. Since I couldn't be a hundred percent sure that the pictures were related to the *Book of Secrets*, I wouldn't technically be breaking my promise to Dr. H if I looked.

There were eight pictures in all. Each one had a number and a date written on the back. According to the dates, they had been taken over a period of nearly twenty years.

I didn't recognize anyone until photo number four. It was none other than Cornelius Blackwell, fat and happy, with his fingers and hand still attached. Two pictures later I came across Big Red. But the real surprise was the last picture.

It was a photograph of a man getting into a cab. And

even though it was taken from across the street and he was looking to the side, I recognized him instantly.

It was the man who had stolen my mom's purse and chased us up to the top of that building where we got locked on the roof for the night.

I had always assumed he was just some crazy person and it was a random robbery. Now I wasn't so sure. Why did my mother have a picture of him? And why would she keep it in the *Book of Secrets*? What if he was like Cornelius and Big Red? What if he was a zombie too?

That would explain why she tried to escape him by running up toward the roof. And if he was a zombie, maybe it wasn't random. Maybe he was targeting her.

He certainly didn't look crazy in this picture. He wore a suit and carried a briefcase.

Despite my promise to Dr. H, there would be no way for me to forget this. More important, there would be no way for me not to search for the answers to my questions.

And since I couldn't ask my mom or the other Omegas, there was only one way.

I would have to go back to Dead City.

Alone.

Party Crasher

Over the next few days, I debated whether or not I could really go through with my plan. The idea was to go down into Dead City, crash a flatline party, and show the picture around to see if anyone recognized the creepy guy who had tormented my mother and me.

It sounded simple enough, but it had some major design flaws.

First of all, I wasn't just breaking one of the rules. I was breaking the biggest rule of all. Omegas are only allowed to go into Dead City in groups of three or more. There are no exceptions. But I couldn't ask the others to come with me. We had specifically been instructed to ignore everything about the *Book of Secrets*. Asking them would mean putting them in the unfair position of having to choose between helping me and following the rules.

And since I couldn't ask anyone, I couldn't tell anyone either. When an Omega Team goes underground, they're supposed to notify the Prime-O. Not quite sure how I could have worded that one.

Dear Prime-O,
I'm doing something I'm not allowed to do and investigating something I'm not supposed to know about. Just thought you should know.
Love,
Molly

Needless to say, I didn't send a note. This meant that if something happened to me while I was down there, no one would know where to look. I wouldn't even be able to call or text for help because there's no cell service that far underground.

I was an army of one.

That Saturday afternoon my dad was working and my

sister was off doing whatever it is that popular kids do on weekends. This gave me the perfect opportunity to go into her room and raid her makeup drawer.

I didn't have three people to help me look like a walking corpse as I did at my first flatline party. So I started digging around and experimenting with Beth's extensive cosmetics collection all on my own.

Let's just say there was a learning curve.

I put on some powder that I thought would make me look pale, but mostly it just made me look like a pancake. And then, when I tried to use a mascara brush, I almost poked my eye out . . . twice.

Finally, as if things weren't going badly enough, I was staring at a tube of something called stick foundation, trying to figure out what the heck it was, when the door opened behind me.

"What do you think you're doing?"

I looked up at the mirror and saw the reflection of my sister looming in the doorway. She had the same expression she uses when she catches me trying to borrow her clothes.

"I'm putting on makeup," I offered lamely as I turned to face her.

I was ready for her to explode at me for being in her room and touching her stuff. But that's not what happened. Instead, she just kind of smiled and said, "Well, you're doing it . . . wrong. Very, very wrong."

She disappeared into the hallway, and I stood there frozen, unsure what I should do. I wondered if maybe she was looking for a camera so she could document the evidence of my invasion to show our father later. Instead, I heard her turn on a faucet for a moment.

When she came back into the room, she was carrying a damp washcloth.

"You going to hit me with that?" I asked, both confused and a little worried.

"Yes, because I'm that big a monster," she said, shaking her head. "Just clean off your face so we can start over."

She handed me the washcloth, and I began wiping off all the powder and mascara.

"You should have asked me," she said, motioning to her makeup drawer.

"I know," I answered. "I shouldn't have gone into your room without your permission."

"Well, that too," she said. "But I mean you should have asked me to help you with the makeup. I may be useless when it comes to molecular biology homework, but makeup is kind of in my wheelhouse."

It finally dawned on me that she really wasn't mad.

"You mean you'll show me how to do it?"

"Just like Mom showed me."

Over the next thirty minutes, Beth tutored me in the fine art of makeup for beginners. Granted, these were not the kind of lessons you need when you're trying to look like a corpse, but I didn't care. She had never talked to me this way, and it felt great.

"First of all," she told me, "you don't want to use too much. You're too young and pretty for that. Just a little accent here and there."

I turned and looked at her, totally dumbfounded. "You think I'm pretty?"

"It doesn't change the fact that you're a total freak who steals my clothes," she said. "But yes. And when you fully grow into your looks . . . watch out."

I was stunned.

She took out the stick foundation and drew a little line on each of my cheeks. "Rub this in until it's all smooth and the color blends. It will give your skin a slight glow and will hold the rest of the makeup in place."

"Foundation," I said, finally getting it. "Like how the foundation of a building holds its superstructure in place."

"Yeah," she said with a tilt of her head. "But let's not turn this into an engineering discussion."

"Got it."

I rubbed it in, and she watched closely to make sure I was doing it right.

"That's good," she said, nodding. "Now for a little eye shadow."

She flipped open a tray that looked like a watercolor kit and then dabbed a brush into a light brown shade. "Now close one eye and gently brush this on the lid."

"Like this?" I asked as I tried it.

"Gentle. You don't want to rub it in," she instructed. "Now try the other eye."

She watched me for a moment and then totally caught me off guard when she said, "I used to be so jealous of those eyes."

"Really? Why?"

"Are you kidding? Look at them." She pointed to my reflection in the mirror. "Not only do they look amazing, but they were just one more thing you had in common with Mom. One more thing that made you Mini-Mom. It wasn't enough you were a little brainiac like her. You had to have her eyes, too."

I was quiet for a moment. "Sorry."

"Don't be. I got over it a long time ago. Now I like them. I see them, and they remind me of her."

She handed me another brush.

"Put that in the outer corner of each eye,"

I started applying it on my left eye.

"Now you're getting it," she said as she nodded. "That's real good."

"I know a secret about you," I said cryptically as I began applying shadow to the other eye.

"Because you've been digging around in my room?"

"No," I answered. "Because I know what I know."

She looked at me, waiting to hear what it was. I made her sweat it out.

"Okay, so what's the secret?" she asked.

I stopped again and looked at her. "You're a brainiac too."

She almost looked like she was going to smile, but she swallowed it. I went back to brushing on the eye shadow.

"You try to hide it from everybody, especially the Salinger sisters, but I know what kind of grades you make. And I've read some of your English papers. They're amazing. You are such a good writer."

I put down the brush to signal that I was done.

"So *I'm* smart and *you're* pretty," she said as she checked to see how it looked.

I cracked a sly smile. "I won't tell if you don't."

"Deal," she said with a laugh. "By the way, it looks good."

I don't know if it was the makeup or just the confidence boost from what she said, but I liked the way I looked too. Unfortunately, I was supposed to look like a corpse. Still, it was a nice feeling.

I left the house and headed straight for J. Hood Wright Park. Like the last time, I was looking for some zombies who I could follow to a flatline party. This time the zombies found me first.

They were three girls in their early twenties, and with the exception of a few clues—such as the color of their teeth and the fact that two of them were wearing gloves to hide their skin—they looked totally normal. I wasn't even sure they were undead until one of them spoke up.

"I remember you," she said.

I was worried, but she was smiling, so I just went with the flow. "You do?"

"From the party about a month ago," she said. "You were the only one who agreed with Liberty."

I had no idea what she was talking about.

"Who's Liberty?"

"The crazy bald guy with the big scar," she said. "He goes to every flatline party and argues for equal rights for the undead. He was desperate, and you helped him out."

She laughed, and I wasn't sure how to react. Was she teasing me? Maybe she thought I was crazy too.

"It was cool," she added.

"Really?"

"Yeah," she said with a nod. "You want to go down with us?"

"Sure. That would be great."

I walked over and joined them. One of the other girls looked at me and smiled.

"Your makeup looks great," she said. "I'd never guess you were undead."

"I could never do it alone," I answered honestly. "My sister helped. She's amazing."

The third girl chimed in. "Well, maybe you can get her to help me, because my skin's beginning to look like those old paintings in museums."

"Haven't you tried Betty's Beauty Balms?" I joked, referring to the lame zombie makeup at the last party. They all laughed, and just like that, I was accepted—more than I ever had been by the girls in school.

I was tempted to flash the picture right there. If one of them recognized him, I wouldn't even have to go into Dead City. But I was worried that it might seem suspicious and give me away. So I just did my best to keep up with the conversation. About ten minutes later, a man came up to us and told us the location of the party.

"Abandoned steam tunnel underneath City College," he said. "Do you know it?"

The other girls nodded, so I did too.

My first thought was that City College was mentioned in the *Book of Secrets*. The main buildings were built entirely out of Manhattan schist. I wondered if that had something to do with why the party was there.

This party was much easier to get to than the last one. There were no long tunnels to tromp through and no water to fall into. We stayed aboveground until we reached the campus, where we went into an old maintenance building.

The girl who had recognized me led the way as we snuck into the building and went down into the lowest basement. It was so damp, my hair began to frizz the second we walked in. We bent down and practically crawled under a series of pipes. I was careful not to touch them because I could tell they were hot, and I didn't want to yelp and give myself away.

When we stood up again, we were in an abandoned tunnel underneath the college. It was filled with pipes that no longer carried steam. We followed them for about a block until we reached the party.

It was smaller than the last one but had the same feel. There were vendors lined up against the wall and people socializing wherever they could find space. I stayed with the three girls for a while, and then I went out into the crowd.

I showed the picture to three different people, telling them I was looking for an old friend of my mother's and wondering if they recognized him.

There is a secretive nature to the undead. Even the girls I walked with to the party never offered their names or asked for mine. And it was clear none of these people liked being asked to identify the picture. Each said they didn't know him and instantly moved on.

I was just about to approach a cluster of four women when a man came up behind me.

"You need to stop," he said.

I turned around and recognized him in an instant. It was the man they called Liberty—the one who believed in undead rights.

I smiled when I saw him.

"Hi," I said, with genuine friendliness.

He didn't return the sentiment.

"Did you mean what you said?" he asked me.

"What are you talking about?"

"When you said that the undead deserved rights? Did you mean that?"

"Of course," I answered. "If we don't get our right—"

He cut me off.

"I'm going to ask you again, *breather*," he said, using undead slang for the living. "Did you mean it?"

I was busted. I decided my best strategy was to be completely honest.

"I meant every word."

He looked deep in my eyes, trying to see if I was telling the truth.

"Then you'd better follow me," he said. "Because you're in real danger."

The Wildest Ride in Manhattan

I stood there staring at him, trying to process what he'd just said. I may have blinked, but if so, that was the only movement I was capable of. Beyond that, I was frozen with fear.

"I'm sorry. Could you repeat that?"

"I said you'd better follow me, because you're in real danger."

"And by real danger, you mean . . ."

"The kind that gives Dead City its name," he replied, sending a chill up my spine. "So hurry up, before I change my mind about helping you."

He quickly moved toward a darkened stairwell that led deeper underground.

"No," I implored him. "We need to go up, not down."

"Considering you've already alerted a least a dozen people that you are, in fact, not undead, the first place they'll look is up. Down is our best shot."

He took to the stairs, and after a brief hesitation I followed him.

"*How* did I alert them that I'm not undead?" I wanted to know as I tried to keep up with him.

"You asked them to identify a picture of a man who everyone in Dead City already knows. The fact that you don't was kind of a big hint."

I was in too much of a panic to wonder why every zombie would know the creep who'd chased my mom and me. "If they knew, why didn't they just attack me there?"

We reached the bottom of the stairs, and he stopped for a moment. He looked at me and shook his head, frustrated by my lack of understanding.

"They're not Level 3s back there," he reminded me. "And 1s and 2s don't *just attack*. They discuss and they coordinate."

"And then?"

"And then . . . if you're lucky, the Level 1s win the

argument and you make it back to the surface with only minor damage. But the 2s . . . they hate to lose."

As I was mulling over this little tidbit, I could hear the roar of water rushing nearby.

"Where are we going?"

"The aqueduct," he informed me as he headed in the next direction. "It's the quickest way out. We can ride the current down to Morningside Park and then go up to the surface there."

"Ride the current?" I asked with disbelief. "You have a boat?"

"No," he laughed. Then he stopped for a moment and looked back at me. "You can swim, can't you?"

That's when I realized that we were going *into* the water.

"Yeah, but laps at the Astoria Park pool are one thing. A raging current in a dark underground tunnel sounds a little dangerous."

"Oh, it's not *a little* dangerous," he said. "It's a lot dangerous. But nothing compared to what happens when an undead mob turns on a breather at a flatline party."

Just the thought of that made me shudder. Then we heard some people following us down the stairs.

"Speaking of which," he said, nodding at the noise. He

pointed toward the darkness. "The aqueduct's this way."

We hurried to a narrow crawl space. He squeezed in and I followed. I was smaller than him, so it was easier for me, but I still began to feel a little claustrophobic.

The sound of the water got louder and louder, until we reached the end of the passageway. Once we came out on the other side we had enough room to stand up, but that was about all. We were on a small ledge directly above the water.

The roar echoed through the tight quarters of the tunnel, and he had to speak up as he gave me instructions. "After you dive in and come back to the surface, try to float on your back, feet first, and keep to the middle. You want to stay as close as possible to the air pocket."

Dive. Surface. Air pocket. Argghhh.

It was all too much. But before I had a chance to think it over, he jumped in and started going down the tunnel. Then I heard voices on the other side of the crawl space getting closer, and I decided I had no choice.

I closed my eyes and then stepped off the ledge.

The water was way colder than I expected, and the pace of the current was really strong. I tried to follow his instructions and float on my back, but I kept slamming into the bricks that formed the ceiling of the aqueduct.

I felt like I was riding one of the slides at the water park we went to last summer at the Jersey shore. Only that was fun and exciting, and there were lifeguards everywhere.

This, on the other hand, was dark and terrifying. And the closest thing I had to a lifeguard was an undead crackpot who was already mad at me for crashing his flatline party.

Before I knew it, I'd lost all track of time and direction. There was a long stretch where the air pocket was only a couple of inches high, making me gag water whenever I tried to breathe.

Then the pace picked up, and I really started zipping along until I shot out of the tube and plunged ten feet through the air before splashing into an underground reservoir. When I bobbed up to the surface, I could hear him calling to me.

"Over here!" he yelled out. "Swim hard!"

It was dark, but I was still able to make him out. He was above the waterline, sitting on some rocks, waving for me to come to him. My instinct was to rest for a moment, but that's when I felt the current trying to pull me down into the reservoir.

"Don't let it pull you under!" he warned. "Just swim to me."

I swam with all the strength I could muster, and finally broke through the current and struggled to the side.

He reached down to help me up, but I was so frantic that I almost ripped his arm out of its socket. (A real possibility with the undead.) Finally, I made it up next to him, collapsing on a rock.

"Are you okay?" he asked me.

I hacked some water and tried to catch my breath. I was finally able to sit up partway by resting back on my elbows. "You know how sometimes you're scared of something, but then you do it and it's so exciting that you end up enjoying it?"

"Yeah," he said, smiling.

I shook my head. "This was nothing like that." I hacked a few more coughs. "That was the single worst experience of my life."

Then I looked at him.

"Thank you."

"You're welcome."

That's when I noticed his left hand. His fingers were broken and bent in different directions, and his wrist had been snapped back at an impossible angle.

"Ooooh. Did I do that when you were helping me out?"

"No," he said with a shrug. "I caught it against the wall right before the plunge."

"Oh yeah . . . *the plunge*!" I shook my head. "There's *no* warning for that one."

He laughed. I just sat there and tried to pull myself together. For about a minute or so we were silent, except for the sound of my heavy breathing and the cracking noise his fingers and wrist made as he snapped them back into place.

Finally I asked, "Where are we?"

"Morningside Park," he answered. "You know it?"

I nodded. "Best place in the city to see great blue herons, red-winged blackbirds, and rock doves," I answered, recalling my days with the Junior Birders. "Especially in the pond by the waterfall."

Morningside Park has an actual waterfall. It's not some phony man-made fountain, but a natural fall that drops about twenty feet into a big pond. It's hard to believe it's in the middle of the city.

"I'll give you this," he said, laughing. "You're not like any breather I've ever met."

"And you're not like any . . . *undead person*"—I caught myself before using the z-word—"I've ever met."

He looked at me for a moment before asking, "What do you want with Marek?"

"Is that his name? The man in the picture?"

He nodded.

"When I was a little girl, he tried to hurt my mother and me," I answered. "I want to know why."

"With Marek, there doesn't have to be a reason *why*. The only thing you need to know about him is that he's a bad guy and someone you want to avoid."

"Let me guess," I joked, in the way you joke about something that terrifies you. "He's one of those Level 2s who hates to lose."

He shook his head and with all seriousness answered, "No, he's the Level 2 who never loses."

"How come?"

"First of all," he said, "he's one of the Unlucky 13."

It was the same thing my mother had written on the envelope with the pictures. "Who are the Unlucky 13?" I asked.

"The very first undead," he replied. "They were miners who were killed in the explosion in 1896 that opened the seam of Manhattan schist."

"Those guys are still around?" I said in disbelief.

He nodded. "And you can build a lot of power in more than a hundred and thirty years of living. They're treated like gods down here. Each one is in charge of a different part of the underground."

"And what's Marek in charge of?" I asked.

He smiled. "He's in charge of the other twelve. He was the foreman on the mining crew, and he's still the boss. They call him the mayor of Dead City."

"I imagine he wouldn't be happy if he found out you helped me."

Liberty shook his head. "No, he would not."

"Then why did you do it?"

He thought about this for a moment before answering. "Omega today. Omega forever."

I couldn't believe it. "You're an Omega?"

He nodded. "And Marek is the one who did this to me," he said as he pointed to the scar that ran along his scalp. "He's determined to get rid of all the Omegas, past and present."

"I don't know how I can thank you," I said.

"First of all, you can get out of here in case any of the others followed us." He pointed toward a walkway. "That takes you right out behind the waterfall."

I stood up and started toward the walkway. Then I stopped and turned back to him. "I know you go by Liberty, but can I ask your real name?"

"Liberty is my real name," he said. "My parents were both American history teachers. What about you?"

"I'm Molly."

"Nice to meet you, Molly," he said, smiling. "Now do me a favor. Stay safe and stay away from Marek . . . no matter what."

I thanked him again and then followed the path until it came out by the waterfall. The passageway was wet, and water poured all over me, but I was too soaked to care.

By the time I made it home, I'd decided to give up my search. Part of this was because Liberty had done such a good job convincing me that it was too dangerous, and part was due to the fact that I had run out of ways to look. Even I wasn't stupid enough to go back into Dead City by myself, and you can't exactly look up "Marek" under "zombies" in the phone book.

But a couple of days later, I was over at Grayson's house using his computer to research a biology paper. Zeus really is an amazing computer. It has access to every database you can imagine, and I like the way it recognizes my voice and calls me by name.

As usual Grayson's brothers, Wyatt and Van, stumbled into the room, arguing about something. I think it had to do with whether or not Pluto should still be considered a planet. He moved the debate out into the family room, and in the process left me alone.

That's when it dawned on me that while I couldn't look up Marek in the phone book, I *could* check for him in the *Book of the Dead*.

Unlike the *Book of Secrets*, Omegas did have limited access to the *Book of the Dead* because we're responsible for taking the census every five years. In fact, the five years were almost up, and Grayson had been working on a new program for the next one.

His theory was that the census usually misses a large portion of the zombie population, and he was trying to come up with a better way of counting them. To test the program, he'd been running data from all the past censuses through Zeus.

I accessed the program and then ran a search for the name Marek. Zeus instantly spit out four different entries. Each was from a different year and each Marek had a different last name. The most recent was Marek Fulton in 1975. It seemed like a dead end, but then something about the last names caught my attention. They were Bedford, Linden, Nostrand, and Fulton.

They sounded familiar and I realized why. Each one was also the name of a major road in Brooklyn. They had to be fake surnames used by one person named Marek, trying to hide his identity.

I could hear Grayson and his brothers still arguing and figured I had a few minutes. I ran a search for all the names of streets in Brooklyn, and then cross-referenced them with the name Marek.

I've got to say, Zeus is some kind of powerful, because in about ten seconds a single name was flashing on the screen:

MAREK DRIGGS, CONSULTANT,

NYC SANDHOGS LOCAL 147

There was also a phone number listed.

Normally, I would never have thought of calling because of caller ID. But I had Zeus at my fingertips, and Grayson had set him up with a program that blocked it.

I knew Grayson was going to be back any second, so it was now or never.

I had Zeus dial the number.

Just when I was about to hang up, I heard a click on the other end, then a man's voice.

"Hello?"

20

I Create a Fake Identity

Until now, he had simply been an anonymous face in a recurring nightmare. The face of the man who had chased my mother and me. The man who had terrified me and created my paralyzing fear of heights. But now that face had a name . . . and a voice.

"Hello?" he repeated.

The voice wasn't ominous like I'd expected, but was actually kind of friendly instead. Still, I gulped before answering.

"Is this Marek Driggs? With the Sandhogs?"

"Yes, it is. Can I help you?"

I may not always be a quick thinker, but I was sitting in front of a computer that more than made up for it. After just a few mouse clicks, Zeus was spitting out page after page of information about Marek Driggs and the Sand- hogs Local 147. As the pages filled the trio of monitors in front of me, I came up with a plan.

"I'm working on a project for school," I said, trying not to stammer. "About the Sandhogs."

The Sandhogs are the urban miners who dig the tunnels beneath Manhattan, and Local 147 is the labor union that represents them. The pictures scrolling across Zeus's monitors told their amazing story. At any given moment hundreds of workers are operating giant earth- moving equipment and tunneling machinery underneath one of the busiest cities in the world. And hardly anybody even knows they exist.

"That's fantastic," he said, sounding like he truly meant it. "It's about time the local schools paid some attention to the Sandhogs. You know, without them this city wouldn't be possible."

"They're the men who make New York work," I said, reading their slogan from the website in front of me.

"That's exactly right!"

"That's what I want to write about," I told him, gaining

confidence. "And for the assignment we're supposed to do an interview."

"Well, I'm not with the press office," he replied. "But I don't know anybody who understands the underground quite like I do."

"Well, then," I said, "maybe I could interview you."

And that's how I ended up making an appointment to interview Marek Driggs in his office.

I knew this went against everything Dr. H and Liberty had told me. But for reasons I didn't fully understand, I *needed* to see him face-to-face. Both for me and for my mom. And unlike the flatline party, where I was ill prepared and made stupid mistakes, this time I had a good idea of what I was doing and who I was up against. I was going to be careful and smart.

I spent the next few days learning everything I could about the Sandhogs. The more I read, the more I was amazed by what they do. The Sandhogs are constantly at work underneath the city. And their history made them the perfect hiding place for the undead. The original zombies and some of the earliest Sandhogs both came from the crew of miners who dug the city's first subway tunnel. And what better place is there for a zombie to work than deep beneath the city, surrounded by Manhattan schist?

I wasn't planning to confront Marek. I just wanted to study him and figure out why he and my mother were enemies.

I had one big advantage. He still looked like he did when I first saw him, but I had aged and looked nothing like my five-year-old self.

That Thursday I was totally confident when I left school and went to the union headquarters. It's located in Washington Heights, in the shadow of the George Washington Bridge. Before I went in, I put my Omega training to good use. I walked around the building looking for possible escape routes, just in case something did go wrong. And in my head I ran through my phony identity one more time to make sure I had it down. Unlike with Liberty, I was not about to give this guy my real name.

By the time I walked up to the receptionist, I was completely prepared.

"Hello. My name is Jennifer Steinbach, and I'm a student at Bronx Science," I told her, using the name and school of the girl who'd beaten me at last year's regional science fair. "I'm supposed to interview Mr. Driggs for a research paper I'm writing."

So far, so good.

"Yes," she said with a smile. "You're a few minutes

early. So why don't you sit down with the others?"

It took a moment for what she said to register. "Others?"

She motioned to a nearby waiting area, where I saw the very unhappy trio of Natalie, Alex, and Grayson. I didn't want to let the receptionist see my surprise, so I gave them a smile and a little wave.

"Hey, guys."

Not one of them smiled back. They just glowered as I walked over to join them.

"What are you doing here?" I asked under my breath as I sat next to Natalie.

"Well, considering you couldn't come up with anything better than Jennifer Steinbach and a research paper," she answered, "I'd say we're saving you."

"How'd you even know I was going to be here?"

She nodded toward Grayson. "He told us."

I looked at Grayson. "Who told you?"

He couldn't help but smirk ever so slightly. "Zeus."

I couldn't believe it.

"A computer . . . *tattled* on me?"

"No, but it did generate a report on your unexpected search into the *Book of the Dead*. And the voice recognition software recorded your phone call because it detected a high level of distress in your speech patterns."

"You shouldn't be here," I whispered to them. "This has nothing to do with you. Besides, I can handle it by myself."

"If that's what you think," Alex said, looking right into my eyes, "then you haven't listened to a thing we've tried to teach you. *Omega today, Omega forever.* You can't turn it off and on. We're a team. And by the way, you can't handle it by yourself."

Before I could respond, a well-dressed man in a suit came out to greet us. He had a boyish face with rosy cheeks, and was definitely not Marek Driggs.

"Are you the students for the interview?" he asked with a friendly smile, no hint of New York in his accent.

I stood up to greet him. "Yes, but I thought we were meeting with Mr. Driggs."

"You are," he answered. "I'm his assistant, Michael. I'm just here to take you to his office."

At first I thought it was kind of strange because the headquarters weren't particularly big. It didn't seem like we'd need a guide. But then Michael opened a cabinet and started pulling out red hard hats with the Sandhogs logo on the side.

"What are those for?" Alex asked.

"Didn't you know?" Michael responded. "Mr. Driggs

keeps his office underground, close to the construction site. He always wants to be near the workers, so that he can best address their needs and concerns."

The four of us shared a desperate look, and I was ready to call off the whole thing when Natalie stepped to the front.

"Sounds cool," she said, totally selling it. "How do we get underground?"

Without realizing it, I had put my friends into the impossible situation I most wanted to avoid. In order to help me, they were going to have to break rules they did not want to break. They were about to head into Dead City, and there was no way to alert the Prime-O.

Michael led us out of the building and down the street for a couple of blocks until we reached a construction site. He went to talk to a security guard, which left us alone for a moment.

"I am so sorry," I told them. "I didn't want to drag you into this."

"Well, we're dragged," Natalie said. "So we might as well do this right." She paused for a moment. "We'll deal with how angry we are later."

"What can you tell us about Driggs?" Alex asked.

"He's very secretive and very bad," I told them. "He's

one of the original thirteen zombies dating back to the subway explosion in 1896. And he's the guy who chased my mom and me when I was a kid. The time when we got stuck out on the roof."

"Really?" Grayson was concerned. He knew how much that moment haunted me. "You're certain it's him?"

I nodded.

"Well, that explains why you went crazy," Alex said with a laugh that actually made me feel better. "But I'll tell you, there's one thing I'll never be able to forgive you for."

"What's that?"

"Making us from Bronx Science. They're our biggest rivals. You know how much I hate those guys."

He smiled and winked, and I realized how lucky I was to have the three of them as friends.

Michael came back from the guard shack. "We're all set," he said. "Just make sure you keep on your hard hats the entire time."

He led us to a large freight elevator. Instead of a door, it had a gate that Michael had to pull down until it snapped closed. As the elevator descended, we could look through the links of the gate and see the different layers of rock as we passed them.

"We're going down about thirty floors," Michael said,

his voice rising so he could be heard over the elevator's motor. "But there's only one stop, so it doesn't take long."

When the elevator reached the bottom, we stepped out into a world unlike anything I'd ever seen. We were in a massive cavern at least a hundred feet high. I couldn't even see the ceiling because all the dust from the digging formed a haze above our heads. We practically had to yell to be heard over the rock pulverizers.

"It looks like something out of a science-fiction movie," Grayson said.

I nodded. "Exactly what I was thinking."

"Let's hope it's not one of the science-fiction movies where the aliens eat the arriving astronauts," Alex joked, leaning in.

I looked up and saw a line of giant dump trucks belching exhaust as they climbed through tunnels that spider-webbed in every direction. For the life of me I couldn't figure out how they got all the equipment down here. Michael must have read my mind because he explained it to us.

"A lot of the time, they have to take the equipment apart on the surface, send it down in the elevator in pieces, and rebuild it here. It's amazing, isn't it?"

"Yes, it is," Natalie said, truly impressed.

"Marek's office is right over here," he said as he led us to a trailer on the edge of the construction site.

Seeing a photo of Marek Driggs was one thing. I didn't realize how hard it would be to see him face-to-face. I almost screamed when he met us at the door.

When we locked eyes, I had no doubt he was the man who had chased my mother and me. But I couldn't believe how much he had cleaned himself up. Even down here in an underground construction trailer, he was dressed in a suit like a Wall Street lawyer.

It didn't help that he was incredibly charming and friendly. He greeted each one of us with a big smile and a hearty handshake. He even offered us sodas from his mini-fridge.

"How was the ride down?" he asked us. "Something, isn't it?"

"Yes, sir," Natalie said, taking charge when it was apparent I was too tongue-tied.

"Well, I can't tell you how pleased I am that you all have shown an interest in what we do down here." He turned to his assistant. "Michael, give us thirty minutes. Then they'll need an escort back."

I was frightened simply seeing him, but the really terrifying thing was how nice he was. If I didn't know what

I knew, I would have been totally fooled. He told us about the history of the Sandhogs and some of the important projects they had completed. He pulled out diagrams and blueprints and explained how the tunneling worked and what they did with all the rock they dug out.

He gave us everything we'd need to write a thorough term paper and absolutely nothing that helped me understand why he tormented my mother or why Liberty said he was so dangerous.

I hated to say it, but he seemed awesome.

Then, when there were about five minutes left, he looked right at me.

"You know," he said, "even in the bad light we have down here, you have absolutely beautiful eyes."

It was awkward, and I didn't know how to respond.

"Thank you."

Then he dropped the bomb.

"You look so much like your mother."

21

The Mayor of Dead City

All the color drained from my face.

Marek laughed and flashed a wicked smile before saying, "Well, now who looks like a zombie?"

I couldn't believe he had recognized me. I couldn't believe I had put myself and my friends into this much danger. We were three hundred feet deep in Dead City, alone with the most evil Level 2 zombie of all.

And nobody knew we were here.

"You know, you really do look like your mother," he continued. "And I'll tell you, she would have been proud of you for figuring out who I was and finding me so quickly. The apple doesn't fall far.

"But she would have been disappointed in this: you coming here so unprepared, putting your friends and yourself in danger. She would have been very disappointed."

I started to tremble as I thought about the words that Liberty had used: *"He's determined to get rid of all the Omegas, past and present."*

"Don't listen to him, Molly," Alex said, jumping in. "He's not going to do anything to any of us."

Marek turned to him. "Is that so? What makes you think that?"

"Too many people know we're down here," he said, bluffing. "Our teacher, the Prime-O, the receptionist, your assistant. Besides, we had an appointment. It's marked in your official calendar. Even if you tried to erase it, a computer tech from the police department would find it in less than two minutes. You can't risk those types of loose ends."

Marek nodded, savoring the moment. "First of all, there's no way you told your teacher or the Prime-O; they wouldn't have let you come. As to the receptionist and the assistant, they're both undead, so I'm pretty sure my secrets are safe with them. You are right about the appointment. That would be a problem, except that the appointment was for Jennifer Steinbach of Bronx Science. Lovely girl and *very* much alive. In fact, we had her over earlier today, so the Sandhogs could present her with a plaque in honor of her win at last year's science fair. I even posed for a picture with her, you know, to tie up any loose ends."

Alex slumped. His bluff had been called.

"As far as the rest of the world is concerned, you four might as well be on Mars," Marek said as he turned to me. "You know, it's funny—if only you'd been honest when you made the appointment. You would have saved everyone."

What happened next was unexpected. Grayson stood up and looked at Marek defiantly. "And if you had been honest, it might have saved you."

"What are you talking about?" he asked.

"Just some other loose ends that you've overlooked."

"Really?" Marek said. "We're going to go through this with each one of you? Okay, I'll play along. How many loose ends did I forget this time?"

"One thousand seven hundred and eighteen."

Marek laughed. "That's a specific number. Tell me, what is it?"

"It's the number of Sandhogs Local 147 members who

249

will get e-mails from me tonight if I don't cancel the send command by seven o'clock."

For the first time since we'd arrived, Marek was momentarily speechless as he tried to read Grayson, to see whether he was bluffing too.

"And what do these *alleged* e-mails say?"

"They detail the tens of thousands of dollars you have stolen from the hardworking members of this union over the years. Money that you've deposited into private accounts to spend on whatever it is that freak-show zombies like you do for fun."

It was the first time I'd ever heard Grayson use the z-word. And I have to say it was well-timed, because Marek froze in his tracks.

"What can I say?" Grayson added, with total badass confidence. "I was bored this weekend, and I have a *really* good computer."

Natalie jumped into the fun. "After they arrest you, what do you think the odds are that they'll send you to a prison constructed out of Manhattan schist?" She made a choking sound, imitating what Marek's final breaths would be like.

He considered this for a moment, looked at Grayson, and cocked his head. "Perhaps I underestimated you," he said. "Although I suppose I wouldn't be the first to do that."

"And you won't be the last," Grayson responded, not backing down one bit. "Because my friends and I are going to walk out of here completely unharmed."

Marek nodded and actually looked impressed by what Grayson had done. "That leaves us at something of an impasse. Maybe we should try that memory device you Omegas use in these confrontations? What is it called, CLAP?"

He knew a lot more about the Omegas than I would have liked.

"*C* is for 'calm,' right?"

No one responded.

"I'll take your silence as a yes. Well, we're being calm, so that's a good start. *L* is for 'listen.' So listen to this: Even if you did send those e-mails, I can disappear underground for longer than you can imagine. It may delay my plans a little, but I will come back and I will win. So all you've done is buy yourself time. Don't push your luck.

"As to *A* and 'avoidance,' trust me when I say you want to avoid me from now on. We've had our fun, but it's over and I've got work to do. Which leaves us with *P*, the reason you want to avoid me. Because if you don't, I will punish you in far worse ways than any you've thought of. I won't just hurt you. I will take from you the things you hold dear. Just as they were taken from me."

He leaned close to Alex and whispered in his ear.

"For example, those little sisters you love so much. It would be awful if something happened to them."

Alex shoved him and looked ready to fight on the spot. But Natalie put a calming hand on his shoulder, and he managed to control himself.

"I'm not saying that I'm going to hurt them," Marek continued. "I just want you to understand that the best thing about being a Level 2 is the fact that having no soul means having no conscience. I can do something you find completely reprehensible and not lose a second of sleep over it."

He turned to me and gave me his most evil look yet. "You know, I slept like a baby the night I killed your mother."

I went to instant boil, which is exactly what he wanted. "Don't even try that with me," I snapped. "You had nothing to do with her death. My mother died of cancer."

Marek nodded. "Yes, she did. She died of a very specific type of cancer that occurs when dead human tissue penetrates an open wound and passes along its own sickness and disease to the living. Most people, like your father, think that happened by accident while she was performing an autopsy. But would you like to know where the flesh really came from?"

He slipped off his jacket and unbuttoned his shirt cuff at his left wrist. He slowly rolled up his sleeve to reveal that his arm was covered with hideous scars and gashes. Chunks of rotted flesh clung to exposed bone.

I almost threw up looking at it.

"This is why you came here, isn't it, Molly?" he asked, holding the arm up for me to see. "You wanted to find out something about me. Well, you've succeeded. I am a grotesque monster."

He rolled the sleeve back down and then buttoned it just as his assistant returned to escort us back.

"Perfect timing, Michael," Marek said happily. "We just finished. I think we've all learned some valuable lessons. Don't you?"

None of us felt the need to continue the charade by answering.

"I'll take your silence as a yes," he said, undeterred. "Good luck on your term paper. You should have a lot to write about."

The five of us remained quiet during the entire elevator ride to the surface. I was in a daze, wondering if it was at all possible that Marek had actually caused my mother's death. Even more important, I was worried I had endangered my friends and their families.

Natalie was to my right. She put a comforting arm across my shoulder and gave it a reassuring squeeze.

"It's going to be okay," she whispered. "He was just trying to scare us."

"It worked."

I looked over at Michael and realized that the rosy complexion I had noticed on his cheeks was, in fact, makeup. Marek had told the truth about him. He was undead.

Once we turned in our hard hats and left the work site, Natalie moved to the curb and signaled for a cab.

"Let's give it up for Grayson," Alex said, offering him a high five. "Hero of the day."

"Absolutely," I added with a grin. "I can't believe you were able to break into his banking records."

"About that . . . ," Grayson said. I noticed his hand was trembling.

"What's the matter?" I asked.

"That was all a bluff," he said with a gulp.

"No way," Alex said, even more impressed. "You *are* the man."

"How did you know he'd stolen money from the Sand-hogs?" I asked.

Grayson was still a little shaken. "He's a bad guy with no conscience. I figured he had to have stolen something. Money seemed like the most logical guess."

I shook my head in disbelief. "You guys are something else."

A cab pulled over and we all got in. It was a minivan. Alex and Grayson took the rear seat while Natalie and I got in the middle row.

"Where to?" the driver asked.

"To 520 First Avenue," Natalie said. "The Office of Chief Medical Examiner."

"We're going to the morgue?" I asked.

Natalie shook her head. "No. We're going to see the Prime-O."

Consequences

Like me, Natalie was convinced that, in addition to being New York's best medical examiner, Dr. H was also the Prime Omega. And after what we'd just been through, she knew we needed to go straight to the top. She called him from the cab and said we were coming in.

The final proof he was who we suspected: He didn't try to stop us.

We walked into the building, and if ever I could have used one of Jamaican Bob's corny jokes to break the tension, this was the time. But he must have sensed something serious was going on. Instead of a joke, all we got was a faint smile as he told us, "Dr. Hidalgo is expecting you."

The closest I got to a laugh was right before we walked into the lab. Natalie and I each swiped some vanilla under our noses and offered it to the boys. They looked at us like we were aliens.

"I think we'll be fine," Alex assured us.

"Yeah," Grayson added smugly. "It's not the first time we've ever been in a lab."

It was, however, the first time they'd ever been in the morgue. Within thirty seconds, they were begging for some extract. Natalie and I shared a smile.

It was the last time she smiled at me for quite a while.

More than anywhere else, the key moments of my life occurred within the walls of the lab at the New York City morgue. This is where my mother and I created a bond that made the rest of my family call me Mini-Mom. And when her death turned my world upside down, this was where I started to rebuild my soul. More recently, it was where Natalie and I formed the first true friendship of my life. And even more recently than that, it was where I came into my own as an Omega in a battle with three killer zombies.

Amazingly, in a room everyone else associates with death, my memories of the morgue were everything but. They were all vibrant and very much alive.

Until now.

That's because "dead" is the only word to describe the expression on Dr. Hidalgo's face as Natalie detailed what had happened between us and Marek Driggs. She recounted the entire chain of events, and the revelation about my mother's death and the threats he made against us and our families.

When she was done, I told him the story of my solo visit to Dead City. About how I crashed the flatline party and escaped with Liberty in the aqueduct. I even admitted that I had visited the Alpha Bakery without any imminent need.

I didn't want any more secrets. By the time I was done, I couldn't look any of them in the eye.

"Well," Dr. H said, digesting the weight of what we'd just shared. "I am so relieved you all are safe. And I appreciate the honesty in what you've told me."

He hesitated for a moment.

"You have told me *everything*, haven't you?"

All eyes turned to me.

"Yes, sir," I said, barely able to get it out.

As the Prime-O, Dr. H held all the power. He didn't need to confer or consult with anyone. He didn't even need time to mull it over. He was judge and jury, and wasted no time before giving us his verdict.

"First, for the three of you," he said to the others. "You broke one of our most important rules by going into Dead City without notifying me. The primary purpose of this rule is to keep you from winding up in a dangerous situation exactly like the one you found yourselves in. You should all know better. You did it to protect your teammate in very unusual circumstances, and while that counts for something, there must be consequences."

Alex flinched.

"This team will be inactive until further notice, while we determine the extent of your exposure and danger," Dr. H continued. "I hope you will use this time to consider the seriousness of what you've done. You are not to engage in *any* activities as an Omega Team . . . with one exception."

The "exception" caught Natalie by surprise. "What's that?" she asked.

Dr. Hidalgo took a quick breath, looked at me, and then back at her. "You can get together at the school or at Grayson's house in Brooklyn to discuss candidates to replace Molly."

The word hit me in the gut worse than any punch from a zombie ever could.

"Replace?" I asked weakly.

Dr. H turned to me, and I saw a tear running down his cheek. The only other time I had seen him cry was at my mother's funeral. I knew this was killing him.

"Molly, you're family to me," he said, shaking his head. "But you've shown such bad judgment. You've risked your life and the lives of your teammates. You simply cannot be an Omega. At least, not now. Maybe next year or the year after that. If I think you're ready, I'll let the teams looking for new members know. But until then, you're out."

I was devastated. But I knew he was right. I had to take responsibility for what I'd done.

"Do you understand the consequences of your actions?"

I tried to speak, but all I could do was nod.

Much to my surprise, another voice spoke out for me.

"I'm sorry, but I find that unacceptable."

It was Natalie.

My surprise was nothing compared to Dr. Hidalgo's. He was downright angry.

"I beg your pardon?"

"With all due respect, I find your decision unacceptable." Her voice was cracking a little, but she didn't back down. "I know you have been very close to Molly and her family for a long time. I think the emotions of that connection might be affecting your decision."

Dr. H gritted his teeth and tried to maintain his composure.

"I assure you that they are not," he said.

"Even so, as the captain of this team, I believe I have the right to appeal any ruling to a review board of past Omegas. And that is what I would like to do."

I actually remembered this from one of my training sessions with Grayson. But he had made it sound like it was a technicality, not something that ever happened.

"Do you dispute any of what you and Molly have told me here?" Dr. Hidalgo asked her.

"No," she said.

"Then what do you plan on telling the review board that you think will make a difference?"

I can guarantee you that no friend in my entire life will ever stand up for me as much as Natalie did at this very moment.

"First of all," she began, "I will tell them that Molly is the sole reason why the *Book of Secrets* is not in the hands of the undead. That if it were not for her quick thinking and fast action, the lives of *every* Omega, past and present, would be in danger."

I looked over to her, but she avoided eye contact with me. She kept a laser focus on Dr. H.

"I will tell them that the reason she was able to do this is because she is the most naturally gifted Omega that any of the three of us has ever seen. And that because of this natural ability, she completed her training in record time. I should have realized this speed cut into important lessons that would have better prepared her judgment and adherence to the rules. I didn't realize that she wasn't ready, and as her leader, I should have."

I watched Dr. Hidalgo as his face turned from angry to something else harder to define. He wasn't agreeing with her, but he was listening.

"Most important, I will tell them that up until now, this Omega Team has had an impeccable record and a one-hundred-percent success rate. I feel confident in saying that by any standard, this team is elite. And we have absolutely no interest in finding a replacement. Molly's our fourth. There's no one else we'd want."

"Don't you think you should talk to your other teammates before you make such a claim?" he asked her.

Natalie didn't even glance at Alex or Grayson. "I don't need to. I know what they'd say."

Even if she wasn't going to, Dr. Hidalgo looked to the two of them. They nodded their agreement without hesitation. All three were putting their reputations behind me. I didn't deserve it, but I was beyond grateful.

The room fell silent in the way that only the morgue can be as Dr. Hidalgo thought about this. Once he'd considered it, he looked at her.

"Okay," he said, nodding. "You're correct. You do have the right to appeal my decision to the review board. I will tell you that no panel has *ever* overridden the ruling of the Prime-O. And I see no reason why they'd do it this time. But you obviously feel passionate about this, and I respect that."

I smiled and turned to Natalie, but she still wouldn't make eye contact with me. She was mad, and she had every right to be.

"I will pass along your request," he said, "once my successor has been chosen."

"Your successor?" Natalie asked.

"The identity of the Prime-O must be a secret," he explained. "That is no longer the case. My last order will be to put eyes on you and your families. And more important, I will put them on Marek."

"That's going to be hard," I said. "I don't think he comes up to the surface much."

He flashed a tight-lipped smile. "Molly, you're not the only Omega with natural gifts."

"I'm sorry, Dr. H. I didn't mean anything—"

He silenced me with an upturned hand. Then he addressed us all.

"Until further notice, this Omega Team is dissolved."

23

You're Probably (Still) Wondering Why There's a Dead Body in the Bathroom

Despite their strong support in front of Dr. H, the others didn't exactly welcome me with open arms once we'd left the morgue. I couldn't blame them for being mad. I'd done a lot of things wrong. But the worst may well have been that I did them by myself. I forgot that no matter what, I was part of a team.

For the next few days, I gave them plenty of space at school. I avoided the cafeteria and ate my lunch out on the patio overlooking the river.

They came around. Slowly.

Grayson was the first. By Thursday, he had migrated out to the patio too. He wasn't very chatty, but we sat together and watched the boats traveling along the river. Sometimes he'd forget he was mad at me and would make a joke or tell me some odd piece of trivia.

Alex came next. I was sitting in the library one day when he sat down across the table from me.

"Just tell me one thing," he demanded, a stern look on his face.

I braced for the worst and asked, "What?"

"What's it like to ride in the aqueduct?" He flashed a smile. "I've always wanted to do that."

"It's terrifying," I said with a relieved laugh. "Absolutely terrifying."

"But still fun, right?"

"No! It's not fun at all."

"Really? 'Cause it seems like it would be."

A few days later, I was leaving campus after school and I saw that Natalie was right in front of me. I realized that I was going to have to take the first step toward making things better, so I caught up with her.

"I know I said I was sorry," I started, not waiting for any sort of acknowledgment. "But I also should have said thank you."

"Why?" she asked, still not looking at me. "For challenging Dr. H and forcing a review board? For getting my team dissolved?"

"No," I answered. "For being my friend."

She turned her head ever so slightly, the closest I'd come to any sort of opening.

"I've never had a friend before," I continued, "at least not one that I'd count. And as much as I love being an Omega, and I really love it, it's nothing compared to how much it means to be your friend."

"You've got a funny way of showing it." Her tone was short, but I detected the faintest hint of kindness in her expression. An ever so slight thaw.

"I know. I'm terrible at it. Like I said, this is all new to me. You gave me Omega training, but you should have given me *friend* training. I could have used lessons like: 'Five Ways to Show a Friend You Care' or 'Things You're Not Supposed to Do in a Friendship.'"

"I'll tell you the first one," she answered. "You're not supposed to lie. Ever. And you're not supposed to go behind your friend's back."

She was being honest. But she was also beginning to warm up a bit.

"What about endangering your friends' lives?"

"No," she said, laughing. "You definitely should not endanger your friends' lives."

"You see, now I'm getting it. This is exactly the type of training I needed."

We kept talking until we reached the tram. She swiped her transit card and walked through the turnstile. I was just about to do the same when she turned back to me.

"What are you doing?"

"Swiping my card."

"For the tram?" she said, in total disbelief. "You're terrified of the tram."

"Completely."

Finally, she looked me in the eye and smiled.

"You would ride this tram? The tram that dangles more than two hundred and fifty feet in the air?" she asked, taunting. "Just to show me how much you want to be my friend?"

"I might scream and pass out along the way, but yes, I would."

She reached out to stop me from swiping my card.

"You don't have to," she answered, to my great relief. "I'll see you tomorrow."

That was earlier this week, which brings me to the St. Andrew's Prep fencing tournament where this story began.

If you remember (and I tend to ramble, so I know it's hard to keep up), when I started to tell you about all of this, I was sitting in a bathroom stall with a dead body. That's where I still am. Trapped and waiting for help to arrive.

It is definitely not the way I expected this Saturday to unfold. As an alternate, my job was supposed to be keeping score for my coach. I was also hoping to get a feel for the strategies used by some of the girls from different schools, because I really want to get good at this.

I didn't find out I was going to compete until a few minutes before the first bout. (In fencing, the individual matches are called "bouts.") Coach Wilkes had to turn in our official lineup, and Hannah Gilbert still hadn't shown up. When he couldn't reach her on her cell, he gave me her spot on the team.

The fact that I hadn't had any time to worry about competing in an actual tournament was probably a good thing. There were no expectations and no pressure. Any points I could earn for my team were a bonus.

In my first bout, I fell behind quickly, only to suddenly go on a roll. In an odd way, all the anger, rage, and frustration I had from recent events found their way into my fencing. I didn't give up a single point in the next two bouts, and before I knew it, I was in the finals.

I was up against Saige Simpson, the top-ranked girl fencer in metropolitan New York. She had already accepted a scholarship to fence at Notre Dame and hadn't lost a single bout all season. Everyone assumed she was going to kill me. But I knew better. I looked at her and came to an instant conclusion.

She didn't have a chance.

That's because the way she wins is through intimidation. Every other girl in the city was scared to face her, and that gave her an unbelievable advantage. But I wasn't scared. I'd faced Level 3 killers, survived a twenty-block ride in an underground river, ripped an undead man's arm out of its socket. I mean, the list goes on and on. To me, Saige Simpson is just another girl.

When I won, I don't know who was more surprised—Saige or my coach. Both had tears in their eyes. My team loved it, and pretty soon they were all pouring bottles of Gatorade on my head, which is why I had to take a shower.

I had just finished showering when the zombie arrived. It was Cornelius Blackwell, still mad about me chopping off his hand. I know I wasn't supposed to participate in Omega activities, but I didn't really have a choice. I had to get rid of him. When I was done, I dragged him into the toilet stall and then texted Natalie, Alex, and Grayson for help.

So now you're caught up. When we started I warned you that you wouldn't believe it, but it's all true.

Also true, I wish I had my vanilla because Cornelius's rapidly decomposing corpse really stinks. I don't know how long I've been here, but I'm going stir crazy.

Finally, I hear someone come into the locker room.

"Molly," a voice calls out in a whisper. "Are you here?"

"Back here," I reply. "The handicapped stall at the end."

I get up, slide the latch, and begin opening the door.

"Are you alone?" the voice continues.

I go to answer as I step out into the bathroom. But then I see him and my heart begins to race. I don't know how it's happened, but I am looking right into the cold dead eyes of Marek Driggs.

I try to move my lips but nothing comes out.

"I'll take your silence as a yes."

Reckoning

I stand there, staring at Marek and desperately trying to devise a plan.

"Am I too late for the tournament?" he asks. "I read about it on your team's website and so wanted to watch you compete. Even though you were only an alternate, I had a *feeling* you'd get a chance."

Suddenly it dawns on me that he may have had something to do with Hannah Gilbert not showing up. He reads the panic in my eyes.

"Don't worry," he assures me. "An unfortunate accident, but the fracture was clean, and she should heal nicely."

Marek Driggs is pure evil.

"What did *she* ever do to you?"

"Ab-so-lute-ly noth-ing," he says, drawing out each syllable. "But don't you remember the part about my not having a soul? I needed to get you into the tournament so that you'd be nice and tired by the time we had this little chat. Still, I had no idea you would win. You are a girl of many talents. Hopefully, *reasoning* is one of them."

"We're not in Dead City," I remind him. "There are laws up here on the surface. Trust me when I say you do not want to be caught in a girls' locker room. All I need to do is scream."

"True," he replies, with a thoughtful nod of his head. "But I don't think you want to be caught with a dead body." He motions to Cornelius Blackwell's corpse in the toilet stall. "So let's just keep this between you and me."

It occurs to me that Cornelius was also part of the plan. "Did you send him to tire me out too?"

Marek nods. "Guilty. And I even knew you'd kill him. Truly a terrible thing to do to your own brother. If I had a . . . you know . . . I'd feel awful about it."

I glance at the floor and see my fencing gear. I realize that if I can stall him just a little as I move toward it, I might be able to grab a weapon.

"Cornelius was your brother?" I ask, buying myself time.

"Yes. In fact, there were five Blackwell brothers in that subway explosion. Five among the Unlucky 13 banished to spend eternity half alive and half dead on this wretched island. And I'll let you in on a little secret."

He leans forward and whispers, "One of my brothers . . . is someone you know. Betcha can't guess who."

Marek flashes a wicked grin, and for the first time, I can see that his back teeth have a little orange and yellow to them.

"I seriously doubt that," I say as I take another tiny side step. "I don't really hang out with *your* kind."

He mulls that over for a second.

"I'll make a deal with you. I'll tell you who my brother is. And then I'll spread the word among . . . *my* kind . . . that you are not to be touched. Believe me, if that's what I say, no one will so much as lay a finger on you. Ever."

"And what do you want from me in return?"

"The *Book of Secrets*," he says, his eyes burning orange with sudden rage. "Cornelius said you took it from him, and I want it back."

I shift my weight, as though I'm considering this, and use that movement to cover another mini-step toward the gear. I'm almost close enough.

"Why do you want it?"

"Why do I want a book that will lead me to the identity of every Omega past and present?" he asks sarcastically. "Let's just say I'm planning on throwing a party, and I want to make sure everybody's invited."

"I've got bad news," I tell him. "I don't have it anymore."

"Pity." The smile disappears from his face. "I guess that means I have no use for you."

It's now or never.

I make my move toward the bag. But it's not a real move. It's an *appel*—the fake out I learned in fencing. Rather than reach for the bag, I move in that direction and stomp my foot.

Marek, who has had his eye on the bag the whole time, jumps to cut me off, and in the process winds up completely out of position.

I use one of my favorite Jeet Kune Do moves to introduce my foot to the back of his skull. Before he knows what's hit him, I follow with two quick punches, all the while reminding myself what Alex taught me that first day: *Go for the head. Go for the head.*

He grabs a weapon from my bag and then flails wildly at me. I dodge the blade and grab one of my own.

Real sword fights aren't like you imagine them. And they certainly aren't like you see in the movies. They're quick and messy and confusing. There's no time to think or plan and certainly no time for clever lines.

And while training had made me a better sword fighter than him, he has an advantage that I cannot overcome. I discover it as I make a great move to run my sword right into his gut, only to have the blade make a clanking sound and bend back at me.

I stare at it in confusion as he laughs.

"Oops," he says with delight. "Is this against the rules?"

He raps his chest and there's a loud *thwack*. Then he undoes a button to reveal a layer of body armor.

"It's the kind of thing that . . . how did your friend put it? Oh yeah . . . that freak-show zombies like me buy with our money."

I decide my best strategy is to stop fighting and to escape. Long rows of lockers fill the room, and I duck behind one to try to play hide-and-seek with Marek.

I think back to how Liberty rescued me at the flatline party. He took me deeper when everyone thought I'd go straight for the surface. I use the same logic on Marek. Rather than head for the door, where he expects, I go for the window.

By the time he figures out what's happened, I've already

climbed down to the sidewalk and have a block-and-a-half head start.

As much as I hate heights, I look desperately for a skyscraper to get away from him. But there aren't any in this part of town. It turns out skyscrapers are just like cabs. There's never one around when you need it.

My only hope is to get off the island. That's when I see my salvation: Looming high above me, just a few blocks away, is the George Washington Bridge.

If you've never seen it, the GWB is amazing. It's a suspension bridge that crosses the Hudson River into New Jersey. It's held up by two massive towers made entirely of exposed steel beams.

Not until I am running along the walkway, however, do I realize how impressive it is. The bridge is nearly a *mile* long, and a full day of fencing and zombie fighting is beginning to catch up with me.

As I reach the first tower, I look over my shoulder and see Marek gaining on me. I don't know where the magic line is that he cannot cross without losing the power from the Manhattan schist, but he's still picking up speed and I'm slowing down big-time.

That's when I make a drastic decision.

At the base of the tower I see a maintenance elevator.

Actually, calling it an elevator is a stretch. Technically, it's a cage with a motor and a gear that climbs up a row of teeth leading all the way to the top. I climb in, slam the cage shut, and press the button for up. The motor whines to life, and the gear slowly begins to turn.

Just as the cage starts to climb, Marek grabs on to the bottom. The engine squeals and strains and then begins to pull him up into the air. I stomp on his fingers as they reach through the links and hear a couple of them snap. Finally, he lets go and I start my climb to the top of the tower.

As I go higher and higher, I try my best not to hyperventilate. We studied the GWB in a class about how suspension bridges work, and I learned the towers are sixty-five stories high . . . a fact I now wish I had forgotten.

When I finally reach the top, I step out into a room where all the suspension cables rest. The science geek in me is amazed by these mammoth steel ropes and the fact that they are able to hold so much. The rest of me is just terrified.

The only thing motivating me is that I am certain Marek won't risk coming this high. I'm more than six hundred and fifty feet away from the nearest Manhattan schist. I can wait here until I'm rescued by workers or find a way to call for help.

Just as I start to catch my breath, I hear the engine of the elevator come back to life.

I don't know how, but Marek is coming.

I figure it will take the elevator five minutes to go all the way down and back up again. That gives me five minutes to figure out a plan.

I step out from the room and onto the top of the tower and cannot believe my eyes. There's no railing or protection of any kind. Just a knee-high edge and a sixty-five-story drop in every direction.

I am frozen with fear.

A strong wind howls around me, and I worry it will knock me over. I gasp and fall to my hands and knees, trying to catch my breath. Even if I wasn't scared of heights, this would be terrifying. As it is, it might be more than I can handle.

I hear the elevator returning, and the only plan I can come up with is to wait by the door and hit Marek with everything I've got the second he steps through it. If I can knock him down and get back to the elevator first, I can escape.

Instead of walking, I crawl into position so that I don't have to look over the edge.

When he steps through the doorway, I summon every

ounce of strength I have left and slam him in the chest with my fist.

I'm so nervous and focused that I have completely forgotten about the body armor.

The sickening sound of my bones breaking is quickly followed by my scream. I try to club him with my other fist, but the pain is already radiating through my left arm and spreading. My last effort is a kick into the side of his knee, but the attempt is feeble, and I stumble back and fall on my butt.

Marek smiles but does not deliver one of his usual wisecracks. I realize why when he starts to walk. Being this high has weakened him considerably. He looks to be at about half his normal strength.

I devise a new strategy. I crawl over to where a giant rope is lying and wind my leg and arm through it. If I hold on with everything I have, I don't think he'll be strong enough to lift me.

Maybe I can wait until all his energy is gone.

He spits and snarls as he moves toward me, much more like a Level 3 than a cold-blooded killer. He looms over me, looking down at my swelling hand, and smiles.

Then he lifts his foot and stomps, grinding his heel into the back of my hand as I wail in agony.

Just as he's about to do it again, we both hear the elevator come to life.

I can tell by his expression that he has no idea who is coming. Neither do I.

I run through the possible scenarios. In my wildest dreams, it will be Natalie, Alex, or Grayson to rescue me once again. But there's no way they could know where I am. Then I remember Dr. H had said he was going to have past Omegas looking out for us and keeping an eye on Marek. Maybe, just maybe, it's one of them. But more than likely, it's one of Marek's many followers.

"One of us is about to be very happy," he says in a halting whisper, unsure of what to expect. Then he grins and grinds his heel into my hand one more time as I writhe in pain.

The elevator reaches the top, and we hear the cage door opening. When the figure reaches the doorway, my heart sinks. She's wearing the same yellow jacket and Yankees cap she had on the first time I saw her. It's the zombie who was watching us on our very first assignment.

Marek turns to me and grins. It's frightening because now virtually all his teeth have turned bright yellow and orange.

"Sorry," he says with a hoarse cackle. "One of mine."

He walks toward her as I try to devise a plan to fight the two of them. I'm drawing a blank. And then I hear it.

A scream.

It's Marek. He screams again as he backs away from her. She wastes no time and hits him with a flurry of kicks and punches. If she is weakened by the height, she doesn't show it.

Marek tries one last charge, but she levels him with a fully extended kick, right to the center of the chest. She powers into his body armor and pushes him backward.

Marek stumbles, and my final images of him are of his arms pinwheeling as he falls over the ledge and disappears, plunging toward the Hudson River sixty-five stories below.

Now the woman turns to me. I have no idea why she killed Marek—anyone that powerful has to have enemies—but I still assume I am next. I am too much of a loose end.

As she walks toward me, she staggers and I realize that she is weakening.

I have a chance.

I wrap my arm and leg around the rope as tightly as I can. I look up to see her looming above me. She is just a silhouette, but I can tell that she's studying me. The only sound is her shallow breathing as she tries to keep her strength.

She looks at my swollen hand, and I'm ready for her to crush it like Marek did. She doesn't. Instead, she kneels next to me and lifts it gently before placing it on my chest.

Then she looks at me, and the sunlight catches her face. Her cheeks are hollow and her skin is wrinkled and brown. Nothing about her looks human.

Except her eyes.

They still look the way they do in my memories. The way mine look when I check in the mirror.

One green, one blue.

Both very much alive.

She brushes the hair out of my face and looks down at me. Then she gently presses her lips against my forehead and holds them there for a few seconds.

My mind is racing. My life plays back in my head, and I question everything as I try to make sense of it all.

She doesn't talk. She just stands up and staggers to the elevator.

Finally, I'm able to gather the strength to speak. But as I do, the wind howls over me and I cannot be sure if she hears the single word I call out to her.

"Mom!"

BLUE
MOON

For Alex and Grayson,
who, in addition to being my sons,
are also my heroes

Acknowledgments

Although this is a work of fiction, it was only made possible by some very real people, many of whom, like the characters in this book, live and work in New York City, but none of whom are actually undead. At least as far as I know.

Despite their aversion to excessive adjective usage, the Omega team at Aladdin is amazing, brilliant, talented, kind, thoughtful, encouraging, and fun. It is led by Fiona Simpson and Bethany Buck, and includes Annie Berger, Craig Adams, Jessica Handelman, and Nigel Quarless.

Speaking of adjectives, only superlatives apply to my agent/friend/confidante Rosemary Stimola, who somehow manages to keep her eye on the smallest detail without losing sight of the big picture, and has done more for lowercase letters than anyone since e.e. cummings.

Suzanne Collins is a remarkable writer, but she's an even better person. I treasure her advice, her generosity, and, most of all, her friendship. I count myself lucky that we are the only two who truly understand and appreciate the Egg Mystery.

Most of all, I want to thank my wife and children, who turn the solitary process of writing into something that is truly a family affair. They inspire, solve, challenge, reassure, and proofread. But most important, they fill my heart every day.

Countdown

I've never had much luck when it comes to New Year's resolutions. Last year I only lasted three days before realizing I couldn't survive in a world without junk food. And the year before that, when my sister and I promised not to argue anymore, we didn't even make it to the end of my dad's New Year's Eve party. I'll spare you the gory details, but fruit punch and guacamole were involved. So was dry cleaning.

Here's hoping this year will be more successful. I've skipped the "live healthier" and "live happier" type of resolutions and have settled instead on the just plain "live."

"This year I, Molly Bigelow, resolve to stay alive."

That's it.

I know that sounds fake, like "I won't eat liver" or "I won't get abducted by aliens," but I'm totally serious. In the last five months I've been in eleven different life-or-death situations. Or is it twelve? You'd think I'd know the exact number, right? But it's hard to keep track of them all when you're an Omega.

The Omegas are a secret society responsible for protecting New York City from the undead. It turns out there are zombies all over Manhattan. And while a lot of them hide out underground in abandoned sewers and subway tunnels, even more have lives that seem like yours and mine. (You know, except for the part about breathing.) That's what makes my job so hard. Finding them can be difficult. Despite what you may have seen in horror movies, most zombies look normal.

The two I'm following right now could pass for a hipster couple hanging out in a coffee shop. The girl's wearing skinny jeans and a vintage jacket, and the guy has on a furry hat with earflaps that should be dorky but actually looks kind of cool. There's nothing at all suspicious about them . . . unless you know what to look for.

For example, her jacket is way too light considering it's

already in the low forties and about to get much colder. The undead aren't warm-blooded. They're no-blooded, so temperature doesn't affect them. And he goes out of his way to make sure he never shows his teeth, even when he smiles. A big giveaway for many zombies, because their teeth can turn orange and yellow.

Still, I wouldn't tag them as undead just because of a jacket and a non-smile. After all, she might put fashion before comfort, and he could just be shy. The giveaway was when I spotted them sneaking into the Rockefeller Center subway station from a darkened tunnel that leads to abandoned tracks. You know, as opposed to getting off an actual subway like most people.

I've been tailing them for about five blocks now, and from all appearances they're both Level 2s, which means that in addition to being undead, they have no souls or consciences. This makes them extremely dangerous.

Normally, I try to stay at least a half block away when I'm following someone, but tonight I'm doing my best to keep within fifteen feet because the streets are total chaos. Nearly a million people are trying to cram into Times Square to celebrate New Year's Eve, and if I lose sight of them here I'll never find them again.

Every once in a while, one of the two checks to make

sure they're not being followed and I do my best to blend into the crowd. With all of the people around it's not likely they'd notice me, but I'm still careful not to look right at them. Omega training taught me that it's hard to remember a face if you've never made eye contact.

At Forty-Fifth Street we reach a security checkpoint where the police start herding us like farm animals into barricaded chutes. I almost wind up in the wrong one, but I fight my way against the flow of people and wedge in behind the two suspects.

Eventually, we dead-end into a pen, and once it's full, a policeman puts up another barricade behind us and closes us in. There's no getting in or out for food or bathroom breaks. This is where we're staying for the next four and a half hours until a giant crystal ball drops down a flagpole and signals the start of the New Year. It's a classic New York tradition that dates back to the early 1900s, and the undead have been a part of it since the beginning.

The fact that they've been coming all these years where anyone could see them, yet no one ever has, shows how clever the undead really are. (Another thing the horror movies tend to miss.)

This year, however, it seems as though they may be coming out of hiding and stepping into the spotlight. We know the undead are planning something big for tonight, but we haven't been able to figure out exactly what it is.

That's what has us worried.

All we know for certain is that there are a million people who have nothing to protect themselves with except for noisemakers and paper hats.

And us.

Omegas old and new are scattered throughout Times Square. In fact, there are more Omegas here tonight than have ever been together before. That's because we're determined to make sure everyone else gets a chance to make their resolutions come true too.

I take my spot right behind the couple and wait. They're not going anywhere and neither am I. I have four and a half hours to figure out what their plan is and come up with a way to stop it. That gives me enough time to think back to when this started and try to notice any clues I might have missed along the way.

It all began with the most indestructible zombie ever imagined and a bowlful of British candy bars. . . .

1

Trick or Treat

I mean seriously.

So far this zombie had survived a lead pipe to the head, the total dislocation of his right arm, and a puncture in his stomach that now oozed yellow slime. Yet somehow none of it had slowed him down. He just kept coming right at me doing the wail and flail, which is what we call it when a zombie makes those creepy moaning noises and walks all stiff-legged and jerky. I kept my cool when he flashed the death stare with his milky white eyes. But when he reached out and I saw the chunks of dead flesh dangling from finger bones right in front of my face, I couldn't help myself.

I flinched.

And how did my friends react? How do you think they reacted? They laughed hysterically.

"What?" I asked defensively as I took off my 3-D glasses and realized that I might have done more than flinch.

The zombie was still there, frozen in midsnarl on the giant television screen. Alex, who had just pressed the pause button on the remote, shook his head in total disbelief. "I'm sorry, but aren't you the girl who just defeated Marek Blackwell in an epic battle at the top of the George Washington Bridge?" He pointed at the neon purple cast on my left arm. "Isn't that how you broke your hand?"

"Your point?"

"My point is that you've faced an actual Level 2 zombie," he said. "How can you be frightened by this ridiculous movie?"

"I'm n-not . . . frightened," I said with a stammer even though I was hoping to sound confident. "Why would you even say that?"

"Oh, I don't know," answered Grayson. "Maybe because you went like this." He held his hands in front of his face and cowered as he let out a shriek so ridiculous, I couldn't help but laugh too.

"I guess scary movies scare me," I conceded. "But I didn't squeal. I just *flinched*."

"Keep telling yourself that," Grayson replied.

The truth is I normally avoid scary movies no matter what. It's like a rule for me. But this was no normal situation. Officially our team was dissolved, but we'd managed to petition for a hearing to review the case. For now we were suspended until our fate could be decided. It had been a couple of weeks, and our Omega team was so desperate for any sort of undead action, we were spending Halloween watching a zombie movie marathon in Natalie's apartment. Mostly, we made fun of how fake and unbelievable the movies were. But Natalie's family has a deluxe home theater that's tricked out with a giant 3-D television and surround-sound speakers that make even the cheesiest horror movies seem realistic.

"If you'd like, we can watch some cartoons instead," Alex joked. "Or does it scare you too much when the Road Runner gets the anvil to fall on the Coyote?"

"You are sooooo funny," I replied, mustering all the sarcasm I could manage as I whacked him on the back of the head with a pillow.

That's when Natalie came into the room with a massive bowl of candy. Like they did with everything else, her parents had gone overboard with the Halloween treats.

"Unless there are a couple of hundred kids in the building I don't know about, there's no way we're going to give all of this out tonight," she said as she set it on the table in front of us. "So help yourself to as much as you'd like."

Alex gave the bowl the same look a lion gives a herd of zebras before he quickly began devouring his prey. Grayson, however, picked up a piece and examined its shiny orange wrapper before asking, "What kind of candy is this? I've never even seen it before."

"Well, we just can't have normal candy, can we?" Natalie replied with a phony British accent. "Mum and Dad had to special-order chocolate from England. You know, to impress the neighbors who, by the way, don't have kids and won't ever see it. It's ridiculous."

"It's not ridiculous," Alex mumbled as he tried to talk and chew at the same time. "It's delicious!" He swallowed a bite and announced, "Best. Chocolate. Ever."

"Glad you like it," Natalie said as she settled into the cushy chair next to mine. "So what was that scream I heard when I was in the other room?"

"Grayson trying to be funny," I answered. "And failing epically."

"Not that scream," she corrected. "The one before that."

I slumped.

"*That* was Molly," Grayson said. "Flinching . . . epically."

"She was terrified of him," Alex explained, pointing toward the zombie on the television.

Natalie rolled her eyes. "You can't be serious."

"It's a scary movie!" I reminded them. "You're supposed to get scared watching scary movies. It's considered normal behavior."

"Well, you've only got one more week to be normal," she reminded me. "So get it out of your system."

She didn't need to say anything more than that. I knew exactly what she meant. Our review hearing was set for the following week, and when we presented our case to the panel of past Omegas, we'd have to be much better than normal. We were asking them to lift our suspension, and to do that, we'd need to convince them that we were essential in the fight against the undead. If they ruled against us, our team would most likely be disbanded.

"Is that why you didn't wear a costume?" Grayson asked me. "Because costumes scare you too?"

My lack of a costume had been a running joke all night long. When I arrived at the apartment, I was more than a little surprised to find the others had all dressed for the occasion. Grayson was decked out as a superhero; Alex wore a vampire's cape and plastic fangs; and Natalie went full Bride of Frankenstein, with pancake makeup, a huge wig, and a tattered wedding dress. Meanwhile, I'd come dressed as ... . me.

"Nobody told me we were supposed to wear costumes," I protested.

"It's Halloween," Grayson said. "We kind of figured it was obvious."

(Dear World, when it comes to social situations, what's obvious to you is totally not obvious to me.)

The funny thing is that I was going to wear a costume but decided it would be a big mistake. Since they're all older than me, I assumed they'd outgrown Halloween costumes and that wearing one would make me look too young. I didn't want to be the only one dressed up. So, instead, it turned out that I was the only one not dressed up. Arrgh.

It also didn't help that unlike every previous October of my life, I wasn't really in a Halloween mood. Normally, I spent weeks trying to figure out the perfect costume; but this year it just didn't seem like the thing to do. I'd been in a funk ever since my battle with Marek atop the bridge. This had less to do with the fight and more to do with the fact that I'd been rescued by my mother. That would be the same mother whose funeral I'd attended two and a half years earlier. Once you've discovered that your mom is an actual zombie, dressing up like one doesn't seem like fun.

I haven't told anyone about my mother. I mean, really, what can I say? ("Hey, you know those zombies we're always fighting? Turns out one's my mom!") It's even worse at home. I feel so guilty when I'm around my father and sister, but there's no way to tell them Mom's a resident of Dead City when they have no idea what Dead City is. I'm pretty sure they would call a psychiatrist right around the part where I say, "You see, there are thousands of zombies living underneath New York City. . . ." So I had this huge dilemma, and there was no one I could talk to about it. The only person who could possibly understand would have been . . . my mom. After all, she had been an Omega when she was in school (a legendary one, in fact), and she would be able to help me figure this all out. But she disappeared within moments of saving my life.

I desperately wanted to go down into Dead City to look for her, but I couldn't do that to my friends. *I* was the reason that our team had been suspended, and the three of them had staked their reputations to defend me. If I went underground without permission, it would ruin everything and our suspension would become permanent. So I just had to act like it never happened.

"I'll look for a less scary movie," Alex joked as he started to click through the channels. "Maybe one with rainbows and puppies."

I was about to make a smart-alecky comment when something on the screen caught my eye.

"Wait a second," I said. "Go back."

"Back to the zombie movie?" he asked hopefully.

"No," I replied. "Back to the news."

He flipped back a couple of channels to a local newscast. A reporter with slicked-back hair, professor glasses, and way too much spray tan was sitting at a desk. Behind him was the picture of a man and the headline SUBWAY DEATH.

"I think I know that guy," I said, pointing at the screen. "But I can't remember where I've seen him."

Natalie laughed.

"That's Action News reporter Brock Hampton," she said, doing her best overly dramatic news reporter impression. "Remember? We eavesdropped on his newscast when we went to the crime scene on Roosevelt Island."

I looked at the reporter for a moment and realized she was right. "Hey, that *is* him," I said. "But that's not who I was talking about. I was talking about the dead guy. I've seen *him* somewhere before too."

According to the report, early that morning a man named

Jacob Ellis had been found dead on a subway in Brooklyn, and the police were still trying to determine what had happened. There were two unusual details that made the story newsworthy. One was that his right arm was completely missing. The other was that he was handcuffed to his seat.

"Despite the handcuffs, the police say that Ellis was not an escaped prisoner and, in fact, had never been in trouble with the law," Brock Hampton intoned. "Perhaps it was a Halloween prank gone wrong, or maybe just a case of someone being extremely . . . unlucky."

"Unlucky?" Grayson asked. "I think if you're dead and someone steals your arm, you've gone way beyond being *unlucky*."

"That's it," I said as I grabbed the remote from Alex and froze the image on the screen. I studied the face for a moment. "Jacob Ellis was one of the Unlucky 13."

"The unlucky what?" asked Alex.

"You remember the pictures I found in the *Book of Secrets*?" I asked.

"You mean the ones you weren't supposed to look at or do anything about, but you did anyway, and it led to all of us getting suspended?" asked Natalie. "You mean those pictures?" (She was joking, but there was no denying that she was right.)

"Okay, stupid question," I said. "But those pictures were of the men who were killed in the subway tunnel explosion back in 1896. In Dead City they're known as the Unlucky 13. That guy was one of them. He was one of the very first zombies."

Suddenly, Alex was interested. "Are you sure?"

I looked right into the dead man's eyes on the TV screen. "Positive."

"He's been alive for over a hundred and ten years and he just dies on the subway and gets his arm stolen," Grayson said. "There's got to be a story behind that."

Unlike the movie monsters we'd been watching all night, we'd finally caught a glimpse of a real zombie story. Suspended or not, we began to look at the situation like an Omega team.

"Do you think it's like when the three guys pretended to be dead on Roosevelt Island?" Alex asked. "Do you think maybe he's just faking being dead to get back into the morgue?"

"I would," said Grayson. "But his body was discovered in Brooklyn. He's dead dead."

That's the part that didn't make any sense to me. There's no way the undead can survive off Manhattan and away from the Manhattan schist, so why was he in Brooklyn? That's when it hit me. "Maybe that's what killed him."

"Yeah," Alex said, putting it together with me. "Maybe he was on the subway and couldn't get off before it left Manhattan."

Alex, Grayson, and I all said it at the same time: "Because somebody handcuffed him to his seat."

After a few weeks on the sidelines, we'd possibly made a major Dead City discovery. Needless to say, we were a little excited. There may have been high fives and fist bumps.

"That's really something," Alex said as he opened another piece of candy and popped it in his mouth.

Grayson nodded and asked, "But why would someone steal his arm?"

"Stop it," Natalie said, interrupting. "I've seen you guys like this. You've got undead on the brain and you want to figure out what really happened."

"Of course we do," Grayson said.

"When you think about it," added Alex, "it's the perfect way to kill a zombie."

"No, when you think about it, it's the perfect way to ruin our review hearing," she countered. "We have been told to avoid any and all Omega activity, and that's exactly what we're going to do."

"What about Molly? She killed Marek Blackwell on the bridge. And she killed his brother Cornelius in the locker room after her fencing tournament," protested Alex. "That's all Omega activity."

"No," Natalie corrected. "She defended herself and saved her life. It was an extraordinary circumstance."

"Don't you think this is one too?" Grayson asked. "One of the original zombies getting murdered on a subway train sounds pretty extraordinary."

Natalie was having trouble controlling her frustration, so I came to her rescue. "She's right," I said, interrupting. "I'm just as curious as you guys, but we can't jeopardize our hearing."

"But . . . ," Alex said, starting to argue. Both he and Grayson wanted to disagree with us, but in their hearts they knew we were right.

"What about next week?" Grayson asked. "After the review hearing?"

Natalie smiled. "If we get reinstated, we're all over it. But until then, we've got to act like we've never even heard the word 'undead.' We have to prove that we can follow orders."

We slumped back into our seats and tried to get our minds off the situation. We flipped channels for a while and even went back to watching the zombie marathon. But after a glimpse of an actual undead story, a phony one only seemed that much less realistic. This time it didn't even make me flinch. Finally, Natalie had a suggestion.

"Why don't we go watch the Procession of the Ghouls?"

"Really?" Grayson said, a trace of excitement in his voice. "I thought you had to stay here to give out candy."

"We haven't had any trick-or-treaters for a while, so I think we're done for the night," answered Natalie.

"The Procession of the Ghouls would be fun," Alex said in his best Dracula voice. "But all the costumes might scare Molly." He added a silly vampire laugh.

"I think I can handle it," I assured them. "Let's go."

The Procession of the Ghouls is an annual tradition on the Upper West Side, not far from Natalie's apartment building. It features some of the most elaborate costumes you've ever seen and takes place in the Cathedral Church of St. John the Divine, where the huge pipe organ plays scary music.

As we walked down Amsterdam Avenue toward the cathedral, I couldn't help but think that on Halloween, at least, New York looked like an aboveground version of Dead City. There were scary-looking characters everywhere. Add to this the light mist in the air and the occasional howl of the wind rushing between the buildings, and it began to feel a little eerie. Still, after the flinching incident, there was no way I was going to let on that any of this spooked me.

Luckily, Grayson and Alex got too distracted to pay

much attention to me. They were in the middle of a debate about a science-fiction costume that Grayson said was inaccurate.

"The vest is from the original movie," he pointed out. "But the helmet is from the sequel. Wearing them both at the same time doesn't make any sense. It's like a caveman wearing a business suit."

"Now, that would be funny," Natalie said, egging them on.

"What movie the vest is from isn't important; it's obviously still the same character," Alex said. "Why do you have to be such a snob?"

"I'm not a snob," Grayson responded. "I'm just a costume . . . connoisseur."

"Okay." Alex laughed. "The fact that you call yourself a 'costume connoisseur' proves that you're a snob."

As they continued to bicker back and forth, they missed the moment when I really did flinch. Unlike during the movie, which was just a shocked reaction, this one took my breath away. I kept noticing someone in the corner of my eye and began to worry that we were being followed. Then I saw her reflection in a store window and realized that, mixed in with all of the ghosts and goblins, there was an actual zombie about thirty feet behind us.

It was my mother.

2

The Big Bang

My name is Milton Blackwell, and I am 137 years old. During the Civil War, my father fought in the Battle of Gettysburg, and when I was a young boy, I attended the dedication of the Statue of Liberty. I have witnessed New York City's rise from cobblestone streets to concrete canyons. I was here the day that Wall Street crashed in 1929 and the day Times Square flooded with people celebrating the end of World War II. I've seen parades honoring Charles Lindbergh when he flew across the Atlantic and the Apollo astronauts after they returned from the moon. I've been an observer to so much living history, yet always *that—an observer. That's because I'm not truly alive.*

I'm undead. And I'm not alone.

I'm making this video so a record exists that explains how it came to be that Manhattan has both a living and an undead population. But, before I do that, let me state without hesitation that I alone am to blame for everything that went wrong.

Like the universe, it all began with a big bang. On this date, October 31, 1896, I was one of thirteen members of a crew trying to dig New York's first subway tunnel. The crew was composed entirely of my brothers and cousins. We all worked for Blackwell & Sons, a construction company owned by our grandfather. Our foreman was my eldest brother Marek.

If it is possible to both idolize and be terrified of the same person, then that is how I felt about Marek. He was brilliant and brave but also capable of sudden violence and rage.

I learned this when I was nine years old.

At the time, New York was still a city of dirt roads and horse-drawn carriages. One day, a neighborhood boy playing a prank accidentally spooked a horse, causing it to run wild. I had just started crossing the street and could not get out of its way. I was trampled by the horse and dragged by the overturned carriage.

I was unconscious and barely breathing, my bent limbs lying in every direction in the muddy street. Anyone should have assumed that I had no chance to survive. But Marek was not just anyone. And, luckily, he was the first to reach me.

He scooped up my broken body into his arms and ran for over a mile until we reached a house that also served as a small hospital. He chose it not because of its location—others were closer—but because of its history. The infirmary, as it was known, specialized in caring for women and children. More important, it had been founded by the first female doctor in American history.

Her name was Elizabeth Blackwell.

She ran the infirmary with her sister Emily, and, while our relation to them was distant at best, Marek trusted that, unlike other doctors who might see mine as a hopeless cause, family bonds, no matter how slight, would compel them to fight for my survival. To Marek, nothing was stronger than family, and he counted on them feeling the same way.

"He's a Blackwell," I heard him say as I drifted in and out of consciousness. "And he needs you."

Due to my head injuries and the side effects of nineteenth-century medication, I only have a few brief memories from the two and a half months I spent at the infirmary. I can remember waking up on several occasions with Marek at my bedside, squeezing my hand and repeating the mantra, "Blackwells are strong. Blackwells survive." I also remember overhearing one

313

of the doctors tell my parents that Marek's actions had saved my life. But my most vivid memory from the hospital is of the apology I received from the boy who had accidentally riled the horse.

Like me, he had come to the infirmary as a patient. His arm and leg were badly broken, and his left eye was swollen shut. He limped into my room using a small wooden crutch and took a seat next to my bed.

"I am so sorry, Milton," he said earnestly. "I want to make sure you know that it was an accident."

"Of course it was," I answered. "I don't blame you at all."

"Really?" he said as he let out a sigh of relief. "How are you feeling?"

"I'm doing better," I replied. "How about you?"

"I'm also doing better."

We sat there for a moment, and all the while, a question nagged at me. Something just didn't make sense. Finally, I asked him, "How did you get hurt?"

"The same way you did," he replied with a weak smile. "I was trampled by the horse."

Even though my mind was in a fog, this didn't seem possible. My memory of everything up until the moment of the accident was clear, and I was certain that the horse had run away from him and toward me. I tried to figure out how the horse might have doubled back after I was unconscious, but then I realized what had actually happened.

"Marek?" I whispered, sad that I would even think such a thing about my own brother. "Marek did this to you, didn't he?"

The boy's one good eye opened wide with fear, and I knew that I was right. My brother had appointed himself judge and jury and punished him for what happened to me.

"No," he said with a shaky voice that only convinced me that much more that I was right. "It was the horse." Rather than continue our conversation, he scrambled back onto his crutch and hobbled out the door as he said, "I'll let you rest for now and come back some other time."

He never came back, and I rarely saw him around the neighborhood afterward. He faded from memory until years later when we were trying to dig that first subway tunnel. That's when I saw the same fear in the eyes of my brothers and cousins on the crew. All of them were afraid of being the one who might upset or disappoint Marek.

And all of them were counting on me to make sure that didn't happen.

I wasn't supposed to be part of the crew. Many of the injuries I received in the accident were permanent, and I simply wasn't strong enough for such backbreaking work.

315

Rather than muscle, my value to the family business was to be brainpower. In 1896, when the others started working on the tunnel, I began my third year as a chemistry student at Columbia University.

I wasn't brought on to the project until late September, when the digging had come to a standstill. They had reached an incredibly dense rock formation that geologists called Manhattan schist. To the crew, however, the dark bedrock was better known as black devil.

After failing to break through it with traditional tools and equipment, Marek approached me with an idea. He knew that I'd studied the chemistry of explosives and wondered if I could make one strong enough to "bring the devil to his knees."

It was my proudest moment.

I was the baby of the family, always the youngest and the weakest. And now, in their greatest moment of need, my brothers and cousins had turned to me. This filled me with confidence like I had never known. Confidence that blinded me to some dangers.

I'll never forget my sense of triumph as I walked into the tunnel for the first time. There was little trace of the limp that had dogged me since my accident. I kept the serious face of a scholar as I inspected the rock formation and made detailed notes and schematics. I was determined to be impressive.

"Can you do it?" asked Marek as I reviewed my notes.

"I think so," I told him.

He stared deep into my eyes. "Think is not enough, brother. Can you do it?"

For the first time in my life, I did not back down from him. "I'm certain of it."

It was a turning point in our relationship. Although Marek was still the foreman, in many ways I took charge of the project. I was testing different combinations of black powders and South American nitrates, and he simply could not tell me how to do something he knew nothing about.

At first, I was very cautious. I experimented with small controlled blasts and then slowly added to their strength. I was happy with the results, but I was not moving fast enough for Marek. He was under great pressure from our grandfather. If our tunnel did not reach a certain length by the end of November, our contract would be given to a different company.

I told Marek that he needed to trust me. "We're close to breaking through," I assured him.

Over the course of a few weeks, however, the looks of pride I got from the rest of the crew started to disappear. So too did their confidence.

On the morning of October 31, 1896, Marek told me I was through. "It's time for you to go back to school, where you belong," he said with no emotion. "Your books and equations have no use to us out here in the real world."

I was devastated.

I couldn't bear the thought of his rejection. I couldn't face the image of walking out of that tunnel, past my family members, as a failure.

"Give me one more chance," I pleaded. "These tests have all been leading to one grand explosion. One breakthrough."

"And are we at that point?" he asked.

"We are very close."

He studied my face before saying, "You have until the end of this shift to get us there."

I was telling the truth when I said the tests had been leading to a single grand explosion, but I thought we needed at least another week to get the mixture right. His declaration meant I had ten hours to complete a week's worth of work.

At my direction, everybody started to drill small holes into the face of the rock in a specific pattern I had designed. I carefully filled the holes with all the explosive powder I had. I worked as fast as I possibly could, knowing Marek would not give me any extra time.

With fifteen minutes to go, the fuse was ready.

"Just one more set of calculations," I said as I reviewed my notes and checked them against the arrangement of explosives.

We had hurried so much in those last hours, and I wanted to make sure I hadn't overlooked anything.

"No more calculations," he said. "Is it ready or not?"

Marek only believed in definitive answers. I could not think, *I had to* know.

"Yes. It's ready."

We all moved into position, and Marek lit the fuse. It was then, after the fuse had been lit, but before the flame reached the explosives, that I realized my mistake. I was so focused on making the explosion strong enough to break through the rock that I hadn't fully considered that the force of a blast that big would need a place to go. Undoubtedly, it would follow the path of the tunnel right back to us.

"Oh no!" I gasped. "What have I done?"

Marek heard me, and our eyes locked. He knew what was coming, and in his face I saw anger and fury like I had never seen.

He went to say something but never got the chance.

The explosion ripped right through the bedrock and shattered it into countless tiny pieces. I had been correct. The mixture was finally strong enough to break through the schist. But the force of that explosion rocketed back toward us. It flung our bodies into the air and slammed them against the hard rock walls. Within seconds, the thirteen of us were littered across the tunnel floor, buried under rock and dirt.

I was dead.

My brothers and cousins were dead.

But, as I learned that day, death, especially sudden death, is not always permanent. My body had no feeling, and there was no oxygen in my lungs, but something still fired in the neurons of my brain. A single thought repeated over and over, like an old phonograph when its needle reached the end of a record.

In my mind, I was a boy back in the infirmary. I could hear my brother repeating the same phrase again and again.

"Blackwells are strong. Blackwells survive. Blackwells are strong. Blackwells survive."

And then the most unexpected thing happened. My fingers began to move.

3

Strangers on a Train

I scanned the faces in the subway station, looking to see if my mother had followed me underground. I'd spotted her two more times on our way to the Procession of the Ghouls, and even though each was just for a moment, I had the strangest sense that she was *letting* me see her. It was like she was trying to send me a message that I didn't understand. Still, I knew she'd be harder to pick out down here, where crowds of people pushed in every direction and the subway lighting played tricks on my eyes.

It also didn't help that the station was filled with the oddest assortment of people I'd ever seen. Halloween on the subway is already pretty weird, but, when the Procession of the Ghouls ends and all of those ghouls have to catch a train for home, Halloween at the Cathedral Parkway station becomes the Super Bowl of Strange.

As Grayson and I waited for the 1 train to arrive, we stood surrounded by people wearing the most elaborately grotesque costumes imaginable. Each devil or demon was spookier than the last. But none was quite as spooky as the man standing on the platform directly across from me.

At first, I thought he was dressed as an undertaker. But, when I noticed that he was doing some sort of card trick, I realized he was supposed to be a magician. (I'm guessing a good stage name for him would be Creep-O the Amazing.) He looked like he hadn't showered in months, and the rare patches of skin that weren't covered in dirt and grime were so pale you could practically see through them.

The spookiest part, though, was the card trick.

He just stared blankly into the distance as he kept flicking his right hand, making the queen of diamonds appear and disappear over and over again. The fact that he was really good at the trick made it that much creepier.

"All right, Mr. Costume Connoisseur," I whispered to Grayson. "What do you make of him? He's dressed like an undertaker, but he's doing a magic trick."

Grayson thought about it for a moment and smiled. "Maybe he's a . . . magician mortician."

"That's catchy," I said. "The Magician Mortician: He makes dead bodies disappear."

Even though we both laughed, there's no way the magician mortician could have possibly heard us or known what we were talking about. The station was way too loud. Despite this, he instantly stopped doing the trick and looked right at me with that same blank stare. He held the look and slowly began to smile until he had a big Cheshire cat grin that gave me chills. Then he started to do the trick again.

Grayson tried to lighten the mood by playing off his superhero costume. "Don't worry about him. Chemistry Man will protect you!"

"Chemistry Man?" I said with a chuckle. "*That*'s your superhero name?"

"You laugh, but only Chemistry Man has . . . the equation for justice."

"Is that so?" I asked. "Well, what scientific superpower would Chemistry Man use on him?"

Grayson studied Creep-O for a moment before answering, "I'm thinking a mixture of sodium . . . potassium . . . and salts of fatty acids."

"What does that make?" I asked. "Some type of explosive?"

"No," he answered. "That makes . . . soap."

We both laughed again, but before the psycho magician could give me another death stare, the train arrived on the track between us and blocked his view. Grayson and I squeezed our way into an overstuffed car, and I breathed a sigh of relief knowing Creep-O the Amazing was waiting for a train headed in the opposite direction.

We found a space to stand at the back of the car, and as the train rattled down the tracks, I stared out the rear window into the black darkness of Dead City. My mind raced back and forth through the events of the night. I thought about the man on the news who had died handcuffed to his subway seat, and I thought about the creepy magician giving me his death stare. But mostly I thought about my mother.

"Are you okay?" asked Grayson.

I nodded and answered with a faint but convincing "Yeah."

"Really?" he said, not letting it go. "Because you don't seem okay."

(Okay, maybe it wasn't as convincing as I thought.)

"I'm just creeped out by the way that guy looked at me," I explained. "That's all."

Grayson thought for a moment, and I could tell that he wasn't sure if he should continue to push or just let it go. He decided to push.

"No, that's not all," he continued. "I'm worried about you. We're all worried about you. You haven't been yourself ever since you fought Marek on the bridge. And that makes total sense. I'm sure it was the worst thing ever. But we don't know how to help you, because you haven't really told us much about what happened up there."

I wouldn't know where to begin, I thought.

He waited for a moment to give me a chance to talk, but I just looked at him and tried to force a smile.

"I understand if you're not ready to talk about it yet," he said, softening. "But when you are, know that I'll be ready to listen."

"That means a lot," I told him. "Believe me, you'll be the first one I tell. But I'm not ready yet."

He nodded and smiled. "Okay."

We kept the conversation light until we reached Times Square, where we both had to switch trains. Even though I was headed home to Queens and he was going to Brooklyn, Grayson walked with me toward my platform.

"If you want, I can ride back with you and keep you company," he offered. "After all, I am Chemistry Man."

"Thanks, but I really am fine," I answered with a laugh. "I'll see you at school."

He flashed a heroic pose and said, "Then I'm off to fight evildoings wherever they may be." He spun around dramatically, making his cape flutter, and then he disappeared into the crowd.

I know a lot of people don't know what to make of Grayson, but I think he's awesome and hilarious. And, despite his geeky persona, he has an odd ability to be reassuring and protective. In fact, a few minutes later I wished that I hadn't been so quick to turn down his offer of company. That's because when I reached the platform for the subway to Queens, I noticed that Creep-O the Amazing was waiting for the same train.

He was talking to a woman dressed in a black leather outfit like a magician's assistant. I began to wonder if he really could do magic because I couldn't figure out how he'd gotten here so fast when he'd been waiting for a train headed in the other direction. They were standing toward the front of the platform, where the first car of the train would stop, so I hung back and waited. When the train arrived I slipped into the back of the car.

I was so focused on trying to keep track of the magician that I didn't notice the woman who sat down next to me.

"How's your hand?" she asked softly.

I looked up and saw that it was my mother. I was speechless. For years, I had imagined what it would be like to talk to her. I'd thought of a million things I wanted to say. But now, through some impossible twist of fate, she was actually talking to me, and I couldn't come up with one.

I was beyond mad and sat silently for a moment before blurting out, "What are you doing here?"

"I had to see if you were all right."

"Well, three bones in my hand are broken," I said, my voice rising. "Oh, and my dead mother's not dead. So no, I'm not all right."

She checked to make sure we weren't attracting any attention and warned, "You need to keep it quiet. If any undead see us together, you'll be in danger."

I gave her a disbelieving look and held up my cast. "In case you hadn't noticed, I already am in danger. I . . . I . . ." I was too angry to form a complete sentence.

"Molly, I know you're upset. . . ."

"Upset? You don't know anything about how I feel," I said, trying to keep my emotions together. "I was at your funeral. I listened to Dad cry himself to sleep. And it was all a lie. You're still alive." I shook my head.

"I don't know how to describe what this is," she said. "But it's not *alive*."

When we reached the next station, she stopped talking and checked out the faces of everyone who got on or off our car. I waited until the train started back up and we reentered the darkness of the subway tunnel before asking, "If it's not alive, then what is it?"

"It's a way to look out for you."

"*You* look out for *me*?" I asked, still disbelieving.

"Yes," she said. "To make sure you're safe."

"If you're so concerned with my safety, then why did you leave me at the top of the George Washington Bridge? I was injured. You know how scared I am of heights. Oh, and I'd just come face-to-face with the mother who'd died two and a half years earlier."

"I wanted to stay, but it was too far from the Manhattan schist," she explained. "I could already feel my body changing. I couldn't have lasted any longer without degenerating into a Level 3. As it was, it's taken me this long just to regain my strength."

Actually, this thought had occurred to me. While we were on the bridge, I'd noticed her weakening. I paused for a moment and asked, "Then when do you look out for me?"

"I watch you go to school. Some days, like today, I follow you when you leave the campus and stay in Manhattan. Just like sometimes I hang out near your dad's fire station so I can see him for a second or two."

I was trying to stay calm, but inside I was freaking out. It was all more than I could handle, and it only got worse once we pulled into the Fifth Avenue station. Over the loudspeaker, the conductor announced that our next stop was Lexington Avenue, which is the last one before the train leaves Manhattan. My mom would have to get off there, or she'd wind up like the guy they'd found on the train that morning in Brooklyn. I could tell that she was thinking the same thing, because she started talking faster.

"How's Beth?" she asked. "I see you at school, and I see Dad at the station. But I don't have any way to know when she's coming in from Queens. I haven't seen her since I was sick at the hospital. How's she doing?"

"Well, she thinks her mother's dead," I said coldly.

Mom sagged, and for the first time in the conversation I felt something other than anger and confusion. I felt bad for her. "She's doing well," I offered. "Really well."

She smiled. "Are you guys getting along?"

I laughed and asked, "Do you want me to tell you the truth or what I think you want to hear?"

Before she could answer, I saw the magician mortician

again. He had made his way back through the train, going from car to car, and now he was in ours. At first, I thought he was looking for me, but then I realized that he was performing magic tricks for the passengers while his assistant held out the top hat for people to give them money. The tricks were actually very good, but the creepy factor and his lack of showering made it so that few people made donations.

"Can you focus for a second?" Mom asked. "Lexington Avenue is next, and that's where I have to get off."

"I can get off with you," I offered hopefully. "We can talk about everything."

She shook her head. "I'd love nothing more, but it wouldn't be safe for you. Just tell me something about you, your father, Beth. Tell me anything."

It's amazing how when you have to think of something on the spot, your mind is a total blank. It took me a moment to come up with any news about the family. "Beth made varsity cheerleading and is thinking about going to NYU. Dad's still dopey as ever. He made lasagna for my birthday; it was delicious. And I'm an Omega. But I guess you already knew that."

She smiled proudly. "Molly, you're not just an Omega," she said. "You're amazing. . . ."

It was right then, just as my mother was about to compliment me on my Omega awesomeness, when I began to realize something was wrong. The magician had now reached our end of the car and stood only a few feet away from us as he did a trick with a pair of handcuffs.

His assistant cuffed him behind his back and then covered them with a black handkerchief. Somehow he managed to slip out of them and escape. It was impressive, and this time a few of the passengers clapped and even tossed money into the hat.

That's when I remembered the news story about the zombie whose body had been discovered that morning. The victim had been handcuffed to the subway seat.

I was still putting it together as we pulled into the Lexington Avenue station and the magician smiled right at me. Unlike earlier, this time he showed his teeth, which were bright yellow and orange. Before I could even react, he'd used his magician's sleight of hand to slip one of the handcuffs around my mother's wrist. . . .

Ω4

I Reconnect with Mom

The magician's plan was simple. He had one handcuff around my mother's wrist and was trying to lock the other onto the frame of her seat. If he succeeded, there was no saving her. She would be trapped on the train, unable to get off before it left Manhattan. Considering she'd already died on me once, I was not about to let it happen again.

My first move was to club him across the face with my cast. I'd accidentally hit myself with it enough times to know it could cause some damage, but I was pleasantly surprised when it completely dislocated his nose. It also dazed him long enough for me to shove him away and break his grip on the handcuffs and my mother.

Just then, the train stopped, the sliding doors opened, and both the magician and his assistant escaped into the Lexington Avenue station, hoping to blend into the crowd. Apparently, they were unaware that freakishly tall, unwashed zombies dressed in magician/mortician costumes do not blend in. Anywhere. Even on Halloween.

My mom and I jumped up and started to follow, but when she stepped onto the platform, she turned around and held up her hand for me to stop. "Stay on the train and get home safely," she said. "I'll take care of this."

There we were, just inches away but worlds apart, my feet on the subway, hers on the platform. I wanted to say something, but I couldn't find the words.

"But there's one thing you need to know," she continued. "Something I should have told you on the bridge."

"What?"

She looked at me with the mom look I'd missed so much and said, "You need to know that I love you, Molly. You need to know that you're my hero."

Okay, technically that was *two* things. But, considering they were the two nicest things anyone has ever said to me, I ignored the mistake.

I also ignored her instructions.

We may have some pretty big issues to work out, but there was no way I was going to let the doors close with us on opposite sides. I slipped through just as they were sliding shut.

"Okay," I said, pumped and ready to go. "Let's go get 'em."

Considering we were in the middle of a chase with two killer zombies, I assumed she would jump into action. Like right at that very moment. But, of course, I forgot who I was dealing with, because my mom decided *this* was the perfect time for a lecture on listening.

"Didn't I tell you to stay on the train?" she asked. "I couldn't have been any clearer. I said, 'Stay on the train and get home safely.' It's just like your birthday party at the Central Park Zoo."

I slumped in total disbelief.

"Can we not do this?" I asked. "Can we please not relive the Central Park Zoo story . . . again? I'm sorry you were so worried, but I was *five years old*. Five-year-olds make mistakes."

"And, apparently, they never learn from them," she said. "Because you still don't listen to a word I say."

It was the same old Mom, like we'd ridden some sort

of subway time machine back to one her countless "teachable moments." And just like she always did, she used her hands a lot when she was trying to make a point. Except now she had a pair of handcuffs attached to one of those hands, and when she gestured, they bounced around in every direction.

"You might want to hide those," I said as I motioned toward a transit cop standing just a few feet away. "They'd be pretty hard to explain."

She nodded and quickly jammed her hand and the cuffs into her coat pocket. Since I really wasn't in the mood to continue the lecture, I just started following the zombies again, and she had no choice but to do the same.

The two of them were headed for the far end of the platform, where they could make a run for the open tunnel and vanish into Dead City. Mom's mini lecture had given them a pretty good head start, but we caught a break when another transit cop stepped out from behind a column in the middle of the platform. There was no way they could get down onto the tracks and into the tunnel with him standing there. He would have arrested them on the spot.

They turned back and saw us coming right at them. Unless one of Creep-O the Amazing's tricks was literally making people disappear, we were about to have them cornered. Out of desperation, they hurried through a maintenance door marked AUTHORIZED PERSONNEL ONLY.

It looked like the door to a storage closet, and when we got there, I was sure we had them trapped. Mom, however, was still in lecture mode. I went to open the door, but she slapped her palm against it and held it shut.

"We still haven't settled the part about you not staying on the train."

"Yeah," I said, nodding. "In fact, there are a lot of things we still haven't settled. But I don't think we have the time to go through them all right now. So unless you really want to stand here and argue, I say we take care of the two zombies who just tried to kill you."

She considered this for a second and gave me a faint smile. "I go first."

"Just be ready for whatever's on the other side of that door," I replied with confidence. "I already had to save you on the train. Don't make me do it again."

"Is that so?" she asked, giving the attitude right back at me. "And who saved who on the bridge?"

"Who saved *whom*," I said, correcting her like she always used to do to me. "Just because we're in the middle of a crisis doesn't mean it's okay to use bad grammar."

We both laughed. Now we were a team. We'd gone from mother and daughter to Omega and Omega. Okay, one was undead and retired and the other suspended, but after all, the saying is *Omega today, Omega forever*.

She checked to make sure neither transit cop was looking our way, and then she opened the door. I think we both expected to find two angry zombies crammed into a storage closet.

We were wrong.

It turns out that the Lexington Avenue station was originally built to be twice its current size. This door opened up onto the other half, which was now an abandoned ghost station, complete with dust-covered platforms and empty tunnels. Instead of a closet, the magician and his assistant had found the perfect escape route.

"It would not be good if they made it back to tell their friends about us," my mother said as we ran after them.

"I don't plan on letting them get away," I replied, turning up the speed.

The two of them were about twenty yards ahead of us, but they'd made a huge mistake. They'd already gotten down onto the track bed, and the gravel made it difficult to run. We stayed up on the platform, where the only thing blocking us was the occasional spiderweb. (Although at one point I did get some web in my mouth, which was beyond gross.)

It took me about two-thirds of the platform to catch up with them. When I did, I jumped off the platform and crashed right on top of Creep-O the Amazing. A few seconds later, I heard Mom tackle his partner.

We rolled around on the gravel for a moment before we were able to get back on our feet. I squared off against him, and my confidence got a huge boost when I saw how badly I'd dislocated his nose with the punch on the train. It was all twisted and turned to the side.

"Wow," I said as I tried to get him worked up. "It's the first time I've ever seen someone who can actually smell his own eye."

"Really?" my mother said as she lined up against his leather-clad assistant. "All those years of Jeet Kune Do and your plan of attack is to taunt him?"

(Is there some rule that says moms can never let you seem cool? Even for a second?)

"Are you going to criticize everything I do?" I asked.

"Nope," she responded as she flashed a smile at me. "Just the things you do wrong."

Both of us turned to face our opponents and unleashed a flurry of attack moves. I'll be honest and admit I was trying to show off a little. I wanted Mom to know I had major skills. But the fight was much harder than I expected. First of all, I'm left-handed, but my left hand was in a cast, so I had to fight the opposite way I normally do. Second, it turns out that the sleight of hand and deception skills magicians use to pull off their tricks also make them difficult to fight.

I kept thinking he was going one way when he was actually going the other. At one point, he even distracted me with that stupid card trick he'd been doing earlier on the train platform. While my attention was momentarily focused on the card as it disappeared and reappeared, he knocked me down with a leg swipe.

I came back at him strong and really thought I had it won when I yanked his arm completely off his body. It was the same thing I'd done to the first zombie I ever fought. Except it turned out that it wasn't a real arm. It was a fake one he used for one of his tricks. Ugh. (So much for demonstrating my impressive skills.)

As I stared in disbelief at what I was holding, he leveled me with a punch that slammed me against the ground. I looked up and wiped the gravel from my face just in time to see my mother whip the handcuffs around her wrists like a weapon and whack him right in the face. She followed it up with a couple of lightning-quick punches that reminded me of her reputation as the ultimate Zeke, which stands for ZK or "zombie killer."

"You still keeping track of who's saving *whom*?" she said, exaggerating the word.

"I am if you are," I answered as I leapt up and saved her right back by cutting off the assistant who was just about to jump her from behind. It was surreal to fight a pair of zombies side by side with my mother. I guess this was our version of playing catch in the backyard. But so much more fun.

At least, it *was* more fun, until the moment where I reared back to throw a punch at the assistant, only to have Creep-O grab my arm from behind. Before I realized what was happening, he'd slapped the other handcuff around my wrist.

Now my mother and I were literally connected to each other like a pair of prisoners. We wound up back to back, trying to fight them with one hand each. And this was when she decided to take another trip down memory lane.

"You remember swing dancing?" she asked.

I couldn't believe she was choosing this moment to revisit another one of our failures. When I was nine, she signed us up for mother-daughter swing dancing classes. It was something she and my sister Beth had done the previous year. They'd loved it and thought it brought them closer together. She wanted to have the same experience with me, except unlike my sister I have no rhythm. I was terrible at it and quickly grew to despise everything about it. I began coming up with all sorts of lame excuses to miss, and eventually, Mom got the hint. It was a sore subject for a while and not something I wanted to reminisce about in the current situation.

"First the Central Park Zoo and now swing dancing," I said. "Are we going to go through every mistake I've ever made?"

"That's not what I meant," she said. "I just wanted to know if you remember the Big Finish."

The Big Finish was what our teacher called the finale of the dance we learned. For the move, we had to stand back to back and lock our arms together. Then Mom leaned forward and flipped me over her head so that I landed face-to-face with her. It was the only thing from swing dancing that I enjoyed.

It was also something we could do even if we were handcuffed together.

"Got it," I said as I locked my arms into hers. "On three."

"One . . . two . . . three," she counted off.

She snapped forward, and I started to flip over her. On the way up, I did a scissors kick and nailed the magician's assistant right under the chin with my foot. On the way back down, I popped Creep-O with a head shot that laid him out.

It took a moment to realize what had just happened. My mother looked at the two of them in amazement. "Unbelievable! You managed to kill two zombies in a single move."

I smiled broadly. "I guess that's why they call it the Big Finish."

We both laughed and tried an awkward high five. (Awkward because we were handcuffed and because of my whole lack of rhythm thing.)

She unlocked the cuffs with a key she dug out of the magician's coat pocket, and we snuck back into the subway station to wait for my train. Whatever issues we'd had before were now, at least for the moment, overshadowed by what we'd just been through.

According to the electronic sign on the wall, the next train was four minutes away. That didn't leave a lot of time for catching up.

"So, is your plan to keep following me around?" I asked.

She nodded. "Pretty much."

"What if I need to get in contact with you? Is there some sort of phone number I can call or a Bat-signal I can flash?"

"No, but you're right. . . . We do need a way for you to reach me." She thought for a moment and smiled. "Your birthday at the Central Park Zoo."

"Again with the zoo story?" I couldn't believe it.

"Relax," she said. "Remember when you got lost, where did I find you?"

"Watching the big clock with the dancing animals."

"Right," she said. "And if you need me, that's where I'll find you again."

"You want me to stand there and wait under the clock?"

"No, just leave a coded message there," she said. "I'll check it every day."

"It's not exactly e-mail," I said. "But I like it."

We stood there, unsure what to say, our conversation frozen by awkwardness. Finally, I spoke up. "They told me you were the greatest Zeke of all time, and now I can see why. You were amazing."

"Me? You killed two zombies with one move. You're the star, Molly. I have no doubt that you'll be the best Omega ever."

"Don't be so sure," I said.

I explained about our team getting suspended and the

343

review hearing scheduled for the next week. She thought about this for a moment.

"If you think they're going to rule against you," she said, "tell them that you have to be reinstated to work on the Baker's Dozen."

"What's the Baker's Dozen?" I asked.

"It's a long-running top secret assignment," she replied. "It supersedes the review panel and the Prime Omega. They have to reinstate you if you get asked to join it by one of the teams that are already part of it."

"What if they figure out that no one really asked us?"

She smiled. "But I just did."

Suddenly, a thought occurred to me. "Are you still part of an Omega team?"

"Maybe," she said with a sly smile.

Then we heard the train approaching the station, and she quickly explained exactly what I needed to say during the review hearing. The train came to a stop, and it was time for me to get on. She gave me a hug, and I melted. I couldn't stay mad at her.

I stepped on and turned back to tell her one last thing.

"I'll figure out a way for you to see Beth. I promise."

The doors closed, and she mouthed the words *thank you* and pressed her hand against her heart.

Triskaidekaphobia

The massive steps in front of the Museum of Natural History were overrun with different groups ready to go inside. The loudest was the mob of elementary students piling off a row of school buses from the Bronx, and the most colorful was the cluster of kids, parents, and grandparents wearing bright pink sweatshirts marked BERGER FAMILY REUNION. But the smallest, and by far the most anxious, was the collection of four people standing at the base of the giant statue of Teddy Roosevelt astride his horse.

It was my Omega team.

Unlike the other groups, we hadn't come to explore the dinosaur exhibits or stare in amazement at the giant blue whale hanging from the ceiling of the Hall of Ocean Life. We'd come for our review hearing, and Natalie wanted to give us some last-minute coaching before we headed inside.

"According to Dr. H, a review panel has never overturned a ruling of the Prime Omega," she said. "But that doesn't mean there can't be a first time. We just need to admit our mistakes, assure them that they won't happen again, and convince everybody that we're worthy of a second chance."

Alex and Grayson both nodded in agreement.

"Actually," I said, "I've got another idea."

Natalie wasn't exactly looking for opposing viewpoints, so she was a bit perturbed as she asked, "What's that?"

I wanted to tell them about the Baker's Dozen. My mom had assured me that it would save our team. But I didn't know how to do it without telling them everything, and I wasn't ready for that. Still, there was no escaping the fact that I had created this problem. That meant I should to be the one to fix it. I'd been mulling it over for days and had come up with only one solution.

"Why don't we tell them the truth?" I suggested. "Tell them that everything was my fault and that you were just trying to protect me. Then they can kick me out of Omega, and you guys can find someone to replace me on the team. That was Dr. H's original verdict, so they can accept it without overruling him."

Alex reached over and put his hand on my shoulder. "You just don't get it, Molly. We're not interested in being a team without you."

"That's right," Grayson added. "We're a package deal. Either they want us all, or they don't want any of us. Got it?"

I looked at Natalie to make sure she agreed. Then I nodded and said, "Got it."

"Good," she replied. "Now, let's go do this."

We went inside and took the elevator to the fourth floor. According to our instructions, we were supposed to wait by the skeleton of the Tyrannosaurus rex. Someone was going to meet us there and take us to the hearing.

Even though I was nervous about everything, just being in the dinosaur hall made me smile. It was one of my favorite places on earth.

"This is where it all started," I said, looking up at the dinosaur's massive jaw.

"What do you mean?" asked Grayson.

"I was five years old, and my dad put me up on his shoulders so I could get a closer look at T. rex here." I closed my eyes as I pictured the memory in my head. "It was love at first sight."

Grayson laughed. "You fell in love with a massive theropod with tiny arms whose name means 'tyrant lizard king'?"

"Head over heels," I said as I looked around the room at all the other dinosaurs. "I fell in love with all of them. That was the day I fell in love with science."

"Well," said Alex, "let's hope our Omega team doesn't join your boyfriend on the extinction list."

"Yes, let's hope," said a voice from behind us.

We turned and saw that it was Dr. Hidalgo. Dr. H was my mom's best friend and colleague at the coroner's office. They'd been a part of the same Omega team when they were in school and he'd become the Prime Omega— or Prime-O—in charge of all the Omega teams. He'd had to step down from that position because we'd been forced to uncover his identity.

As usual, Dr. H was sharply dressed in a perfectly pressed dress shirt and pants and wore a stylish bow tie. He also wore a friendly smile, which was a big departure from the last time we'd seen him. (That would be the day he suspended our team for breaking countless rules and procedures.)

Smile or not, I wasn't sure how he was feeling toward us, and me in particular. I offered a rather faint "Hello, Dr. Hidalgo" and tried to avoid eye contact.

He wasn't having any of that. He placed a firm finger under my chin and lifted it until I was looking him right in the eye. "Molly Bigelow, how long have I known you?"

"My whole life," I said weakly.

"Then act like it."

He held his arms out, and I gave him a hug.

"No matter what happened before and no matter what the panel decides today, nothing changes what you mean to me." He gave me one last squeeze and then turned to the others. "Now follow me."

Dr. Hidalgo had been a family friend for as long as I could remember. One of the things that I had been dreading most about this day was the thought that we were opposing each other. Talking to him now made me feel a whole lot better about everything.

He led us beyond the exhibits, down a maze of hallways, and past a couple of security checkpoints. At each one, he just flashed a badge and the guards waved us through with no questions asked. Finally, we stepped into a giant freight elevator.

"It's big," Grayson said, referring to the size.

"Big enough to hold a dinosaur," Dr. H pointed out as he pressed the button for the basement.

"If we're going to the basement, why did you have us meet you on the fourth floor?" asked Grayson.

He looked back at me over his shoulder and then turned to face the others. "Because it's Molly's favorite place, and I thought it might help calm her nerves."

Natalie gave me a sideways glance and a smile. This was the Dr. H we both knew.

As we rode in the elevator, he gave us a rundown of what to expect.

"It's pretty straightforward," he explained. "I'll go first and tell them why I suspended you. Then you'll make a statement and answer any questions from the review panel."

From the elevator, we went down another hallway until we reached a large lecture hall. The room was built like an auditorium, with steep banks of seating that looked down on the stage.

"This is a sacred room," Dr. H told us. "More than a century ago, this is where the museum's paleontologists presented their initial findings about dinosaurs and prehistoric life. Ever since, this is where some of the true legends of scientific thought have shared their discoveries."

"And this is where our hearing is taking place?" Natalie asked.

"Yes."

"How did we get such an important room?" asked Grayson.

Dr. H smiled. "Let's just say that some of the legends of scientific thought also happen to be Omegas, too."

"Cool," Grayson said, echoing what we were all thinking. "Very cool."

In the middle of the stage were four wooden chairs. Dr. H motioned for us to sit in them, and we each took our place. The lighting was so bright that we couldn't really see what was happening out in the auditorium. If I squinted, I could make out some shapes and shadows but no faces. The identities of the past Omegas had to be kept secret, even from us.

It all happened just like Dr. Hidalgo told us it would in the elevator. He went first and talked about the team and our past accomplishments. He also pointed out that I was the daughter of Rosemary Collins, whom he called "my dearest friend and a legendary Omega." Then he gave a detailed report of all the mistakes we'd made. This included my unauthorized visit to Dead City, when I crashed the flatline party and had to escape underwater in the Old

Croton Aqueduct, as well as our team's trip underground to see Marek Blackwell.

Next, Natalie spoke on behalf of the team, and she was amazing. She talked about successful assignments they'd completed before I was part of the team and how they went about selecting me to join them. She sang all of our praises and went into detail about how I had kept the *Book of Secrets* from falling into the hands of the undead. By the time she was done, I knew they were going to reverse the suspension.

I was wrong.

The questions were relentless. "Why did you go into Dead City when you knew it was against the rules?" The fact that we couldn't see the people asking the questions was disorienting. "Why didn't you alert the Prime-O the moment you found the photographs of the Unlucky 13 along with the *Book of Secrets*?" Voices came from every direction. "What exactly happened with you, Miss Bigelow, and Marek atop the George Washington Bridge?"

After about fifteen minutes, it was obvious things were not going well. My teammates looked defeated, and I had to do something. I leaned toward them.

"I can save us, but you can't ask me how I know," I whispered.

Natalie had a confused look on her face. "What?"

"I know a way to save us," I said a bit louder. "But if I do it, you can't ask me how I know. You just have to accept it."

She shook her head. "If we're a team, we have to trust one another."

"I do trust you," I replied. "But you have to trust me that if I say I can't tell, it's for a good reason."

She thought for a second and nodded. "Just do it."

I looked at the others, and they nodded too.

"Excuse me," an annoyed voice called down to us. "I hate to interrupt your conversation, but we need you to answer our questions."

I looked at the others one more time to make sure, and then I turned toward the unseen woman.

"I apologize," I said. "Can you please repeat your last question?"

"Is there any other reason you can give us that would make us reconsider your suspension?"

"Yes, there is," I said, taking a deep breath. "Our team needs to be reinstated because we've been asked to work on the Baker's Dozen."

Suddenly, things on the other side of the lights got very quiet. My teammates looked at me, wondering what on earth I was talking about. Dr. H considered this for a moment and begrudgingly smiled.

Now a different voice called down to us. It was one we hadn't heard before, a pleasant voice belonging to a man who sounded older than the others.

"Could you please repeat that?" he asked.

"I said we have to be reinstated because we've been asked to help on the Baker's Dozen."

"That's what I thought you said," he replied before pausing and adding, "I'll have to ask everyone except for the Prime-O to leave the room."

Natalie, Alex, Grayson, and I all stood up to exit, but the man chuckled and called down to us again. "You four stay. I was talking to everyone else."

"Good luck," Dr. H said with a wink as he got up and left.

Now my teammates really gave me confused looks, and all I could do was shrug. My mom had told me what to say, but I had no idea what it all meant. We heard the others collect their things and leave, and soon the only noise was the sound of the lights humming. Then the older man had a brief conversation with the woman who had asked the last question. (I guess that means she's the new Prime-O.)

"What's the current status of the Baker's Dozen?" he asked her.

"We're down to two teams," she said. "One current and one made up of past Omegas."

It occurred to me that my mother must be part of the second team, a fact that made me smile.

"I thought we added a new team last month," he said, a bit bewildered.

"We tried, sir," she said, "but they were unable to solve the riddle."

He thought about that for a moment. "Well, then I guess they wouldn't have done too well on this assignment. Were you aware that a new invitation had been given out?"

"No, sir," she said, "but they don't need approval from me to extend one."

Now the man directed his attention toward us. "Molly, can you confirm that you truly have been asked to help on the Baker's Dozen?"

I repeated the response exactly as my mother had told me on the subway platform. "I can confirm that Triskaidekaphobia is the irrational fear of the number thirteen."

"And do you suffer from this phobia?" he asked.

"No," I answered, staying to the script. "Because, like the number thirteen, I am completely rational."

"That's very good to hear," he replied.

We all waited for a moment to see if there was more.

"Does that mean we're reinstated?" asked Natalie.

"Yes," he said to our relief before adding, "with one catch."

We traded nervous looks and then turned our attention back to him.

"What's that?" I asked.

"The Baker's Dozen is a top-secret operation," he explained. "In fact, it's so secretive that we cannot discuss it here."

"Then how do we find out about it?" asked Natalie.

"By solving a puzzle," he said. "If you can figure out this riddle, it will lead you to everything you need to know about the Baker's Dozen."

"And if we can't?" I asked nervously.

"Well, then you're back where you started," he answered. "How do you think the hearing was going?"

"Not well," I answered, stating the obvious.

"No, it wasn't," he said. "So I suggest you solve it."

"What's the riddle?"

"With this iron, you cannot press a shirt, but you can press your luck."

6

Pressing Our Luck

Since Natalie's apartment is only six blocks from the museum, we decided to go there to try solving the riddle. Alex was especially pleased with this decision when he found out that there was still plenty of leftover British Halloween candy. "That will definitely help," he said with a straight face. "British candy's good for thinking."

"And you base that claim on what?" Natalie asked with a raised eyebrow.

"It's a well-known fact," he answered. "How do you think Isaac Newton came up with all the laws of motion? Chocolate."

Considering we had just been reinstated, you'd think everyone would have been in a better mood as we walked along Central Park West. But there was definitely some tension, and I was pretty sure this had to do with the "You can't ask me any questions" requirement I put on saving the team. To their credit, they didn't ask. But they also didn't say much of anything else.

Part of me wanted to blurt it all out and tell them about my mom and what happened on the bridge and the fight with the magician and his assistant. They had proven their friendship and trust to me more times than I could count. But Mom told me it would be dangerous if anyone knew about her. And I kind of worried what they'd think of me if they knew my mother was a zombie. Would they begin to question my loyalty to Omega? I mulled this over for a couple blocks as the cold November wind turned my cheeks a nice bright shade of pink. Finally, I decided to tell them the truth.

Well, sort of.

I told them about my mother approaching me on the subway and telling me what to say about the Baker's Dozen. Only I left out the part about her being my mother. I just said it was a past Omega who wanted our team to work on the project. Technically, it was all true. But I'd left out some important facts.

358

I think Natalie was about to push for some more details, but Grayson saved me by changing the subject. "Do you think it's significant that 'baker's dozen' and 'triskaideka-phobia' both have something to do with the number thirteen?" he asked.

I thought about this for a second and realized I had no idea what he was talking about. "What does 'baker's dozen' have to do with the number thirteen? Aren't there twelve in a dozen?"

"Usually," he said. "But in the Middle Ages, there were strict laws against bakers overcharging. If an order of bread was underweight, the baker could get his hand chopped off as a penalty. So they'd add an extra piece to every order to make sure there was enough."

"Which means if you ordered twelve," I said, under-standing, "you'd get thirteen."

"A baker's dozen."

Only Grayson would be familiar with medieval baking laws. I was truly impressed. "Is there anything you don't know?"

He thought about it for a moment. "Well, I don't know the answer to the riddle."

We all laughed, which finally broke the tension.

For the rest of the walk, we tried to solve the riddle. We

talked about ironing clothes, dry cleaning, and anything else that might relate to an iron. We played around with the phrase "push your luck." But we got nowhere. We were totally stumped. We were also well aware of the fact that the last team that had tried to solve the riddle had failed, which was something we could not afford to do.

By the time we got to Natalie's building, the only thing we knew for sure was that the lobby was nice and warm. My face had already started to thaw as we stepped onto the elevator.

"Here's an example of triskaidekaphobia for you," Natalie said as she pushed the button for the twelfth floor. "There's no thirteen."

"Seriously?" I said.

I looked at the panel and couldn't believe my eyes. Sure enough, the button next to the twelve was fourteen.

"There's no thirteenth floor on this building? Because of a silly phobia?"

"That's true of a lot of the older buildings in New York," Grayson said. "People were so scared of living or working on the thirteenth floor, they would just skip that number. There's no thirteenth floor in the Chrysler Building or at 30 Rock."

Like I said, there was virtually nothing Grayson didn't know.

"Speaking of phobias," I said as the elevator began its climb, "I hope everyone notices that I'm going up to Natalie's apartment. Again. That's the second time this month I've overcome my fear of heights."

"Are you counting Halloween as the first time?" asked Alex.

"Yes!" I said. "Why wouldn't I?"

"I seem to remember you screaming in fear," he joked.

"At the movie . . . and it was just a flinch," I said as I gave him a slug.

"So how have you overcome this fear?" asked Grayson.

I thought about it for a moment before saying, "Once you've been in a fight on top of a bridge six hundred and fifty feet in the air, a twelfth-floor luxury apartment doesn't seem so scary anymore."

"Good point," Natalie said.

The elevator dinged and the doors opened onto Natalie's floor. But when the others started to get off, I motioned for them to stay and said, "Wait."

"She jinxed it," Alex said. "She talked about it and now she's scared of heights again."

"Wrong phobia," I replied, on the verge of a break-through.

"What do you mean?" asked Grayson.

I pointed at the panel of buttons. "Because of triskaidekaphobia, you can't press a button for thirteen."

"Yeah," Natalie replied. "That's kind of what we just said."

"Don't you see? It's just like the riddle," I explained. "You can't press the number thirteen. You can't *press* your luck."

"Oooh," Alex said. "That's good."

The others nodded and for the first time in a while, we felt like an actual Omega team. We went into the apartment and settled in the family room to work on the puzzle. Natalie and Grayson sat at the computer, Alex kicked back in a recliner, happily munching from the bowl of Halloween candy. And I took the chair that was farthest from the window. (I may have been getting better at dealing with heights, but there was no reason to tempt fate and sit by the massive twelfth-story picture window.)

"Let's break down the riddle piece by piece," Grayson said. "With this iron, you cannot press a shirt, but you can press your luck."

"I'm on board with Molly's elevator theory," Alex said midchew. "I'm thinking it's an elevator that has a button for the thirteenth floor."

"But what does that have to do with an iron?" asked Natalie. "And what elevator?"

He thought for a second before answering, "I have no idea."

"Wow! You were right. That chocolate really does make you as smart as Isaac Newton," she said sarcastically.

"What about an elevator made of iron?" I suggested.

"That could be," Grayson said with a nod as he typed in a search and scanned the results. "There's an elevator made out of iron in Brooklyn, but it's a grain elevator, so there wouldn't be buttons for any floor."

"What if the elevator isn't made out of iron?" Alex wondered. "What if it's the building?"

"Can you make a building out of iron?" asked Natalie. "I don't think it's strong enough."

"Maybe not," Grayson said as he looked at the results of another search. "But there are some buildings in SoHo with cast-iron facades."

"Any of them thirteen stories high?" I asked.

He shook his head. "Nope."

"I think we're getting off track," Natalie said. "The riddle said, 'With *this* iron, you cannot press a shirt.' I don't think it's talking about the metal. I think it's talking about one specific iron."

Grayson kept running through search after search on the computer. He called out to us whenever he found something potentially useful. "At the Metropolitan Museum of Art, there's a Degas painting called *A Woman Ironing*."

"Is there anything lucky or unlucky about it?" I asked.

"Other than having to do chores," he said, "not particularly."

"What about this one," Natalie said, looking farther down the same list. "There's also a painting of St. Reparata being tortured with hot irons. That sounds extremely unlucky."

"I got it!" Alex exclaimed.

We all stopped and turned eagerly to him.

"Really?" Natalie said. "You figured it out?"

"Umm . . . no," he said, guiltily holding up a candy bar. "I meant I found the specific type of chocolate bar I was looking for. It has nuts and caramel I had one on Halloween. It's really delicious."

Natalie balled up a piece of paper and threw it at him.

"Here's one at the Museum of Modern Art by the artist Man Ray," Grayson said. "It's a painted flatiron with tacks glued along the bottom."

"Does that even count as art?" Natalie asked, leaning in to get a closer look at the picture.

"Forget the art museums," Alex said. "It's not *Flatiron with Tacks*."

"Wait," I said excitedly. "That's it."

"It *is Flatiron with Tacks*?" asked Alex, confused.

"Not the tacks, just the flatiron," I said. "Look up the Flatiron Building."

Grayson smiled as he typed. A moment later, a picture of the Flatiron Building was on the computer screen. Grayson read the description next to it. "Completed in 1902, the Flatiron Building is considered a pioneering skyscraper of historical significance. The building is shaped like a triangle and gets its name from its resemblance to a similarly shaped clothes iron."

By now, Alex and I had both gotten up and were looking over Grayson's shoulder, reading along with him.

"Does it have a thirteenth floor?" Alex asked anxiously.

Grayson clicked on a couple links and found the answer. "Yes, it does!"

"Well, Molly, it's a good thing you're getting over your fear of heights," Natalie said, "because it looks like we've got an elevator to catch."

Ω 7

The Room That Isn't There

The Flatiron is the only building I know that has its own optical illusion. That's because it's a giant triangle. If you stand at just the right spot and look at the front, you can make it seem like half the building vanishes. The security guard in the lobby, however, was not an illusion. And there was no trick to make him disappear. Too bad, because we needed to get past him in order to reach the elevators.

Our plan was to quickly check the directory on the wall and see which companies had offices on the thirteenth floor. Then we could try to convince the guard that we had an appointment with one of those companies. It was a good plan . . . except for one small problem.

"There are no floor numbers," Alex said as he looked at the list, "just the names of the companies."

Ugh.

There were at least fifty companies listed on the directory, and rather than arranged by floor, they were listed alphabetically. If we'd solved the riddle correctly (and I had a good feeling that we had), one of them held the secret to the Baker's Dozen. But we had no idea which one it was. We also didn't have much time to figure it out. Our sense of desperation must have caught the guard's attention, because after a few moments, he got up from his desk and started walking toward us.

"Stall him," Natalie whispered.

"Yeah," I said in agreement. "Stall him."

She gave me a nudge. "I was talking to you."

"*Me?* How am I supposed to stall him?"

"Be creative."

You've got to love the way Natalie gives advice that has absolutely no actual advice in it. I decided the best thing to do was to start talking to the guard before he got a chance to ask us any questions. That way, at least, I could direct the conversation. So I just asked him the first thing that came to mind.

"Excuse me, but how do you know which side's the front?"

He stopped for a moment and tried to figure out what I was talking about. "I'm sorry, what?"

"Which side of the building is the front?" I asked. "Square buildings have a front, a back, and two sides. But with a triangular building, how can you tell which side is the front?"

He gave me the same look I give my Latin teacher whenever she asks me to conjugate verbs. You know, the look that says, "I should probably know this, but I have absolutely no idea." I decided to keep piling on.

"I mean, the side facing Fifth Avenue looks like the front. But so does the side facing Broadway. Does it have two fronts? Can a building even have two fronts? Is that possible? Or does it just have two sides and no front?"

"Those are all good questions," he said. And while he was busy trying to come up with an answer to any of them, the others kept searching the directory for any hint as to where we needed to go.

The stall was working perfectly until an uninvited guest jumped into the conversation. Apparently, the fact that I was not actually looking for an answer did not matter. A question had been asked, and Encyclopedia Grayson couldn't help himself.

"Fifth Avenue is the front."

He said it like a fact and not like an opinion. And, knowing Grayson, I'm certain he was right. Still, I gave him my angry eyes, hoping he'd get the hint and help out.

"Are you sure?" I asked as I pointed to a photograph of the building that was hanging on the wall. "Both sides look identical. Why isn't Broadway the front?"

"Yeah," wondered the guard. "Why not Broadway?"

"Because the address is 175 Fifth Avenue," he explained. "According to the US Postal Service, the address signifies the front of the building."

"Hey, that makes perfect sense," said the guard. "I could have thought about that all day and never figured it out."

"Yeah, thanks for clearing that up," I added, still staring daggers at Grayson. "I would have hated to waste any more of his time."

By Grayson's reaction, I could see that he finally realized his mistake.

"Sorry," he whispered.

The guard now turned to the others and asked, "So, what brings you all to the Flatiron?"

"Well," Natalie replied, taking the lead. "We have an appointment on the thirteenth floor."

"Great," he said as he moved back toward the desk. "Just come on over, and I'll sign you in."

We all breathed a sigh of relief. This might be easy after all.

"I just need to know who the appointment's with," he continued.

And then again, it might not. We stood quietly for a moment until Natalie stammered a very unconvincing, "You mean who on the thirteenth floor?"

But out of nowhere Alex stepped forward and answered, "Palindrome Games."

The guard handed us the sign-in sheet. "I should have guessed. Are you the game testers?"

Without missing a beat, Alex nodded and said, "Yes. Yes, we are. We're the game testers."

We signed in and walked straight onto the elevator. Sure enough, it had a button for the thirteenth floor.

"Ready to press your luck?" Natalie said as she pushed the gold button.

The moment the doors closed, I slugged Grayson in the arm. "Thanks a lot, Mr. United States Postal Service."

"I said I was sorry," he protested. "I can't help myself. When I know the right answer, I have to say it."

"Speaking of right answers," Natalie said, turning to

Alex. "How'd you come up with Palindrome Games?"

"It was on the directory."

"Yeah," she replied. "But so were about fifty other companies."

"True," Alex said. "But none with 'Omega' hidden in the middle of their names."

Sure enough, the last three letters of "Palindrome" and the first two of "Games" spell "Omega."

"Nice," Grayson said as he gave Alex a fist bump.

I knew that a palindrome is a word like "racecar" or a phrase like "Madam, I'm Adam" that's spelled the same backward or forward. But I had never heard of Palindrome Games. It turns out it's a software company that designs word games that can be played on social media.

When we walked into their office, I thought Grayson was going to faint. It was total compu-geek heaven. There were electronic gadgets everywhere and a handful of programmers working on computers with giant monitors. As far as offices go, it was supercasual. One wall was filled with the latest video game consoles, and there was a massive cappuccino maker in the corner that made the room smell like a coffee shop.

One of the workers wore a vintage concert tee, another had on a Yankees jersey, and a couple sported

Hawaiian shirts. All of them looked like they'd been putting the cappuccino maker to good use and had gone at least twenty-four hours without any sleep.

"I'm home," Grayson said as he soaked it all in. "*This* is where I belong."

The man in the Yankees jersey got up and walked over to us. "You must be the game testers," he said, offering his hand. "I'm Adam."

"Just like the palindrome," I answered. "Madam, I'm Adam."

He smiled as he shook my hand. "Just like the palindrome."

After some quick introductions, he led us into an office filled with even more high-tech stuff.

"We're not really game testers," Natalie admitted after he'd shut the door.

"I know that," he answered. "But there's no reason for the guys in the other room to know it. Let's just keep that between us Omegas."

"You were an Omega?" I asked.

"Still am," he corrected me. "Omega today, Omega forever. I graduated from MIST nine years ago and started this company when I was a senior at Stanford."

"Impressive," Grayson said, looking around at it all.

"Not as impressive as you four figuring out the riddle in less than three hours," he said. "This morning I got word from the Prime-O that you might be coming soon. But we thought it would take at least a couple days for you to make it here."

We each stood up a little straighter and tried to hide how pleased we were with ourselves, but I think our big goofy smiles kind of gave us away.

"Are you going to tell us what the Baker's Dozen is?" Natalie asked.

"I'm going to do better than that," he said with a sly smile. "I'm going to show you. But first we need to take care of security and I need to scan your handprints."

He plugged a scanner the size of a textbook into his computer and had each one of us press our right palm against it. Then he used the palm prints to create security access for us.

"Okay," he said once he was done. "Let's check out the attic."

"What's the attic?" asked Natalie.

"The attic is what you're looking for," he said somewhat cryptically.

He led us back into the hallway and onto the elevator. Then he pushed the button marked 20.

"Originally, this building was twenty stories high," he explained. "But a year after it was completed, they mysteriously decided to add an additional floor. Everyone calls it the attic."

The elevator door opened, and we stepped out onto the twentieth floor. The entire floor was a little strange. First of all, the layout of the offices was odd. Adam said this was due to the shape of a building. "Without nice square walls, it's hard to make nice square offices," he said. Even stranger are the windows. They're high on the wall so that their bottoms only reach down to your shoulders. If you want to get a good look outside, you have to stand on your tiptoes.

"Funky, isn't it," he said. "It gets weirder. Because the attic was added later, the main elevators don't go high enough. The only way to get there is by taking a separate elevator that just connects the twentieth and twenty-first floors."

We stepped into the other elevator, and the button panel had a scanner like the one in Adam's office.

"Try it out," he said to me.

I pushed the button for twenty-one, and nothing happened. But when I pressed my palm against the glass, the elevator instantly came to life and started carrying us to the attic.

"Cool," I said.

"Isn't it?" Adam agreed. "Believe it or not, it gets cooler."

When we reached the twenty-first floor, we stepped out into a tiny hallway.

"Welcome to the attic," Adam said. "It's all Omega."

We traded looks.

"Seriously?" I asked.

"Well, on paper, it all belongs to Palindrome Games," he explained. "This is where we keep our computer servers. But they also function as the electronic hub for the Omegas. For example, every message to or from the Prime-O comes through here. And each door requires a palm scan."

He led us through a series of rooms filled with computer servers.

"Because the building's a triangle, the rooms have an unusual alignment," he explained as we went through them. "As a result, there is one room that virtually nobody knows about. It isn't even in the blueprints, and it can't be detected from outside."

We reached a door that had another palm scanner. Instead of an office number on the nameplate there was simply the symbol "Ω"—Omega.

"Your palm prints will open this door for exactly three

hundred and sixty-five days," he said. "Why don't you give it a try?"

We all traded looks, and then Natalie pressed her hand against the glass. A bright green light traced its outline, and moments later, we heard the door unlock. She reached for the knob, but before she opened the door, she paused and took a deep breath.

"You know that feeling you get on Christmas morning, right before you unwrap your first present?" she asked.

"Yeah."

She flashed a smile and said, "This is way better than that."

She opened the door, and I think each one of us was surprised. So far, everything that we'd seen in the attic was high-tech and ultramodern. The endless rows of servers looked like something out of a science-fiction movie. But this room was strictly old-school. There was a manual typewriter sitting on the end of an oak table and four wooden file cabinets next to a rolltop desk. Knickknacks sat on dusty bookshelves next to outdated encyclopedias and travel guides.

"Apparently, the room's not just a secret from other people," Alex said as we began to poke around. "It's also a secret from the twenty-first century."

Grayson took in a deep breath and added, "It even smells old."

Despite this, there was something undeniably appealing about it. I imagine it's the same vibe you'd get in the office of a brilliant but somewhat offbeat college professor.

"Welcome to the Baker's Dozen," Adam said, addressing us. "For the next year, you're responsible for monitoring the Unlucky 13. These cabinets are filled with more than a hundred years of observations and information about the original thirteen zombies. You must determine their current identities, which are ever changing, and keep close track of their actions to see if there are any changes to the structure or balance of power of Dead City."

"We're not the only team, though, right?" Natalie asked. "They said something about two others."

"That's right," Adam said with a nod. "There's a team of past Omegas who are responsible for support. I'm part of that team, and among other things, we make sure that the room is secure."

Grayson tapped a key on the manual typewriter and asked, "Who makes sure that we have modern office equipment?"

Adam laughed. "Yeah, you're just going to have to get used to that. Think of this room like it's a research library.

Nothing can be taken out. If you generate new reports, they are to be typed on the manual typewriter and not on a computer where they could be hacked."

Natalie gave me a sideways look. "What have you gotten us into, Molly?"

"I'm so sorry," I said.

"Don't be," she replied.

"Yeah," added Alex. "This is awesome."

"Agreed," said Grayson.

"You said there was another current team?" I asked Adam.

"Yeah," he said. "But to be honest, they've been a disappointment. This assignment is not easy. They've struggled to identify the Unlucky 13's current identities, and I haven't seen them in months. That's why we needed to add another team."

"So I guess that means it's up to us," Natalie said.

"You guys solved the riddle in three hours," he reminded us. "I think you'll be up to the challenge. I've got to get back to work. Let me know if there's anything you need."

We said our good-byes, and Adam left us in the room to explore.

We started looking into the different file cabinets. Each one of us took a different one and called out whenever we found something that seemed particularly interesting.

Grayson found an envelope that had photos of eight of the thirteen. They were mostly the same pictures I'd found in the *Book of Secrets*, but this was the first time the others had seen them. He spread them out on the table.

"You were right," Natalie said, pointing at one of them. "That is the guy who died on the subway, Jacob Ellis."

The boys looked and nodded their agreement.

"Check it out," exclaimed Alex a few minutes later. "You know how Adam said this floor was mysteriously added one year after the building was completed?"

"Yeah."

"It gets even more mysterious than that."

He carefully laid a piece of yellowed paper on the desk.

"This is on White House stationery," he announced quickly, getting our undivided attention. "It instructs the builder to add one floor to the top of the Flatiron with enhanced security for the sole exclusive use of the United States Secret Service. It's signed by President Theodore Roosevelt."

"That's strange," I said.

"I think if we look around here some more," Natalie said, "we'll find all kinds of strange and unusual things."

"Like this," Grayson said, holding up an aged ledger.

"This has a section for each of the thirteen. And in that section, it lists sightings, locations, known addresses, and so on."

He flipped through the pages, which were filled with handwritten notations and dates going back to the early 1900s.

"Now, look at this section," he said.

He turned it to the final tab. The name on the top of the page was Milton Blackwell. Everything beneath it was blank.

"How are we supposed to find a guy who nobody's seen for over a hundred years?"

The Three Wise Men

B lackwells are strong. Blackwells survive. Blackwells are strong. Blackwells survive."

The phrase kept repeating in my brain until it was drowned out by a steady throbbing in my ears that distorted all sound. I could tell someone was talking to me, but I couldn't understand the words. Then, after a few moments, I was able to make out a voice calling my name.

"Milton, can you hear me? Milton, are you alive?"

Time seemed to bend as my mind raced back and tried to piece together what had just happened. In one flash of memory, I could see the fuse burning its way toward the explosives.

In another, I caught a glimpse of the blast in slow motion, a million tiny pieces of rock heading right toward us. That's when I realized that I was still in the subway tunnel. I bolted upright and cried out, "Oh no! What have I done?"

And so it happened that the last words I said while I was alive were also the first ones I said once I became undead. The mind is a funny thing, and in trying to make sense of the incomprehensible, it had replayed the last moments before the explosion, trying to undo my mistake.

"You're alive," said the voice. "Thank goodness you're alive!"

I looked over and realized that the voice belonged to my brother Marek, who had also survived.

Or so I thought. So we all thought.

One by one, as my brothers and cousins regained consciousness, they all arrived at the same conclusion. They had cheated death. Each one was sure that he'd been spared by some miraculous twist of fate. But unlike them, I had done the computations and understood the magnitude of the blast. I was certain that fate alone could not explain it.

"That's impossible," I said as I pulled myself up from the rock and debris. "The explosion was too strong. Every law of science dictates that we should be dead."

Marek laughed. "That's the problem with your books and

equations, brother. You believe them more than you believe your own eyes. Look around. We're all alive. And not only that, but do you see what your explosion did to that black devil?"

I turned toward the rock face and could not believe my eyes. The massive bedrock that we had battled for weeks was gone. The impenetrable wall of Manhattan schist had been reduced to a pile of crushed rubble that sparkled with flecks of orange and green.

A momentary wave of relief washed over me.

"I did it?" I asked in stunned amazement. "My explosives broke through the rock?"

"Yes," he said gleefully. "You brought the devil to his knees!"

I turned to embrace Marek and celebrate, but that's when I noticed that something was wrong. His left arm was bent completely behind his back and twisted in an odd corkscrew. It seemed humanly impossible.

"Your arm," I gasped.

I expected him to scream in agony when he realized what had happened. But he didn't seem pained at all. He just looked at it curiously and simply untwisted his arm and snapped it back into its proper place.

"How did you do that?" I asked.

He thought about it for a perplexed moment and answered, "I have no idea."

The tunnel was dark, but what little light there was reflected in glimmers of orange and green along his cheeks. I saw the same phenomenon on my hands, and when I looked closer, I realized that the light was reflecting off of tiny crystal shards of the schist that had imbedded into my skin.

As the thirteen of us congregated and surveyed one another, we quickly discovered other injuries that defied explanation. The jaw of my brother Elias had detached and dangled from the bottom of his face. Still, he was able to pop it back so that it worked perfectly. Several cousins had fractured bones that had broken through the skin yet somehow caused no pain. And my brother Bartlett was able to walk among us despite the fact that a pickax was buried deep into the middle of his chest. In addition to these injuries, all of us were covered with the glistening shards of rock.

Marek asked me if I knew any scientific explanation for what we were experiencing.

I shook my head and said, "No."

I thought back to when I was a child and had been trampled by the horse. Somehow, Marek had instinctively known what to do that day. So I looked to him again. We all did. He was our leader.

"What should we do?" I asked him. "Where do we go?"

Marek had always trusted family above all else. That's how he selected where to carry me when I was near death as a child, and that's what drove his thinking now. He decided that we would go to our grandfather, Augustus Blackwell.

Before we exited the tunnel, we did our best to mend the most obvious injuries so that we wouldn't attract attention. Then, under cover of night, we traveled to what is now known as Roosevelt Island but which at the time still bore our name.

In 1896, Blackwell's Island was no longer farmland belonging to the family, but our grandfather still owned a large portion of it, and he lived in the same two-story house as his father and grandfather had lived in before him.

That night, of course, we had no idea that our continued survival was directly related to our proximity to Manhattan schist. It was simply our good fortune that Blackwell's Island was formed on the same bedrock. Had our grandfather lived in Brooklyn or Queens, we would have all died the moment we crossed the East River.

As it was, one of us was almost killed anyway.

It was a cold, moonless night, and by the time we reached the house, it was nearly three in the morning. Our grandfather was awakened by the alarming sound of thirteen dazed and confused men walking along the old dirt path in the woods behind his home.

Considering Blackwell's Island was also home to a large prison with frequent escape attempts, it is understandable that he was concerned for his safety. He came out onto his back porch, carrying a lantern and a shotgun. When we emerged from the woods, he was startled by our appearance and aimed the gun at the one leading the way, Marek.

"Grandfather, no!" I shouted out to him. But it was too late. He'd already pulled the trigger, and the bullet ripped right through Marek's chest.

When he raised his lantern and looked closer at our faces, he realized what he'd done and rushed to Marek's aid.

"I didn't know it was you," he wailed as he ran to him.

But a funny thing happened when he got there. Marek didn't need any aid.

"Hello, Grandfather," he said matter-of-factly as a trickle of green slime drained from the fresh hole in his chest. "It seems as though we have a problem."

Grandfather fainted right on the spot. We carried him into the house, and when he regained consciousness, we moved into the dining room, where we had eaten so many Thanksgiving and Christmas dinners. There we tried to explain something that simply defied all explanation. The only thing that *made him somewhat open to our wild claims was the fact that Marek had survived the gunshot with no serious injury.*

By sunrise, the man we'd called Grandpa Auggie as children had a plan of action. He wanted us to check into the hospital that was right there on the island.

None of us wanted anything to do with that. Known as the Asylum, the hospital had a notorious reputation for mistreating the mentally ill. Just a few years earlier, the horrors of what happened there had been uncovered in an exposé by a journalist named Nellie Bly, who had posed as a patient.

"We are not crazy," Marek said, his voice rising. "These injuries may defy logic, but they are real, not imagined."

Our grandfather assured us that things had changed dramatically and for the better. The Asylum was now a hospital that treated all patients with top doctors. It was also looking to expand and wanted to purchase family land. Grandpa Auggie told us that he could use this as leverage to get us the best treatment and care.

"You are my blood, and I promise I will protect you to the ends of the earth," he said firmly. "This is where I can make sure that you are treated properly."

Reluctantly, we agreed. That morning the thirteen of us arrived at the main entrance to the hospital, a building known as the Octagon.

Initially, we were given first-class treatment, just as our grandfather had promised. Doctors and specialists ran endless series of tests trying to figure out what had caused our condition. They tried to understand why we had no pulse and felt no pain. They tested our suddenly overdeveloped sense of smell.

They were especially fascinated by the fact that each one of us had an identical scar on our right shoulder. It was purplish blue and in the shape of a crescent moon. It was the only injury consistent among each of us.

But the more tests they ran, the more confused they became. Before long, they seemed to view us not as patients to be treated, but as oddities to be feared. By the third day, we were moved into a large basement ward that was little more than a dungeon with solid rock walls.

The walls, however, were made of Manhattan schist, and the longer we were kept there, the stronger we became. My legs, which had been weak ever since my childhood accident, were suddenly powerful and straight. One time, I saw Marek twist the iron frame of a bed like it was nothing.

The continued exposure also magnified our moods. More than ever, Marek was prone to fits of anger and rage. Many of them were directed at me because he saw me as the cause of the accident.

Eventually, the doctors determined that there was no medical explanation for why we were the way we were and therefore no way to treat us. Instead, a secret panel was created to determine what should be done with us. It was a panel of the so-called "three wise men," who represented the most important sectors of city life. It included the mayor, the Catholic archbishop, and the chief of police, a young man named Teddy Roosevelt, who five years later became president of the United States.

Each one of us was questioned individually by the panel. I spoke with them on three separate occasions and developed an instant kinship with Mr. Roosevelt, who shared my love of science.

It soon became evident, however, that even these wise men didn't know what to do with us. We were beyond explanation and as a result were a threat to society. We began to worry that we'd never be allowed to leave the dungeon. Soon, even our own grandfather stopped visiting us. One day, we heard from a nurse that his construction company had just been awarded a large contract with the city. He had traded our well-being for financial gain.

We felt betrayed and abandoned. And Marek . . . well . . . he just felt empowered.

One day, he stood on top of a table in our dungeon and made an announcement.

"It is time for this to end," he proclaimed. "And for that to happen, I must take charge again. Two times, I have let others tell us what to do. The first was with Milton and his explosives. That mistake is what put us in this condition in the first place."

He paused for a moment, and I felt all eyes beating down on me. I did not run away, but I also did not say anything in my defense.

"The next was when I trusted our grandfather to decide our fate. That mistake is how we wound up where we are. I promise you that I will never let anyone else take control of us again. Trust me and follow me and I will get us out of here and onto a new life."

"How?" asked Elias.

Marek flashed a terrifying smile and signaled the others to come closer. I could not tell if I was still part of the group, so I remained where I was.

Then he told them his deadly plan.

9

Family Time

I love my sister Beth. I really do. My problem is that I just can't stand her. Scientifically speaking, we both have forty-six chromosomes, twenty-three from each parent. But that means there are also twenty-three chromosomes from each parent that we didn't inherit. And while I haven't run our DNA through a gene sequencer or anything, I'm pretty sure Beth and I each took the opposite twenty-three from Mom and Dad. She got all of the cheerleading, popular, "My life is one big teen soap opera" chromosomes, and I took all the, you know, lame ones.

And it's not just that we don't have anything in common. It's that almost every conversation turns into an argument. Anytime one of her possessions is not in the exact location she expects it to be, I get the blame. I mean, just because I borrow her clothes every once in a while doesn't mean I want all of her junk. Still, there she was storming into my room, making an accusation.

"Where's my phone?" she demanded.

At the time, I was trying to figure out why my Internet connection had gone down, so I was too busy to bother turning around. I just kept clicking the reconnect button and answered, "How should I know?"

"Because you took it."

See what I mean? Every time.

"I didn't take your stupid phone," I said, still without giving her the satisfaction of eye contact.

"It was recharging on the counter, and now it's gone," she continued. "If you didn't take it, then what happened to it?"

"I don't know," I replied. "Maybe it got sick of listening to your idiotic conversations and threw itself out the window. Or maybe it died of embarrassment because of that stupid pink case you put on it. But I have no idea where your phone is."

"I'm going to count to ten, and if you don't give it to me, I'm going to I tell Dad."

"All the way up to ten?" I said. "You need help with that math?"

We gave each other dueling stink eyes for a second, and then both of us raced toward the kitchen. In these situations, it's essential for me to reach Dad first, before Beth can start filling his head with misinformation. Unfortunately, she beat me to the door and then butt-blocked me the entire way down the hall. When we got to the kitchen, Dad was getting ready to make dinner.

"Dad," Beth whined. "Molly took my phone and won't tell me where it is."

"Dad," I said at the exact same time. "Beth always accuses me of stuff, and there's never any evidence. It's not fair."

"Time-out," he said, making a *T* with his hands. "Let's settle down. We'll get to the phone and the accusations in a moment . . . but first things first. . . . Is this new apron too frilly? Or am I pulling it off?"

"Dad?!" we both whined in unison.

"Okay, okay, we'll skip my problems and work with yours," he said. "Let me get this straight. Beth, your phone is gone?"

"Yes."

"But if it's gone," he said in his goofy, over-the-top way, "then how will you text anyone?"

Beth completely missed the sarcasm. "That's the problem. I can't."

"O-M-G," he replied.

"Wait a second," she said, finally getting it. "*You* took my phone?"

"Y-E-S."

I folded my arms and gave her my best self-righteous look. "I'll just wait here for my apology."

Instead of an apology, I got attitude. "You know, you'd look more like a victim of unfair accusations if you weren't wearing *my* sweatshirt."

I looked down at what I was wearing and realized I'd been busted. But of course I wasn't going to admit to that. "I thought this was a family sweatshirt," I offered lamely. "For all of us to wear."

"There's no such thing," she said.

Then it occurred to me that if Dad took her phone, then maybe . . .

"Does that mean you have something to do with the Internet being down too?" I asked.

"I don't know," he said. "Would disconnecting the

router and hiding it in the same spot where I hid Beth's phone make the Internet go down?"

I sighed. "Yes, it would."

"Then yes, I had something to do with that, too," he answered. "It sounds like I've been pretty busy. But on the plus side, the three of us now have some free time to hang out. You know . . . like a family."

Beth and I both made identical groans. (Okay, so maybe we have a couple of genes in common.)

"Do we have any choice in this?" Beth asked.

"Of course you do," he said. "I'm not some evil dictator. I'll let you decide what we're going to do."

"What are our options?" I asked.

"Well, we can make dinner together, eat dinner together, and talk to one another during the whole time we're making and eating dinner."

"Or?" Beth asked, clearly unimpressed with option one.

"Or," he said, "we can go to your grandmother's house, and I can show you how to massage her calves and pumice the calluses on her feet. Totally your choice."

Beth almost laughed, but she was trying to prove a point, so she wasn't going to give in that easily. "I should call your bluff and pick Grandma," she said.

Now Dad laughed. "If you don't think I'd go through

with it and make you actually chisel those suckers down, well, then you haven't been paying attention for the last seventeen years."

I needed no more convincing than that. "I vote dinner."

"That's my girl," Dad said. "What about you, Beth? Care to make it unanimous?"

"Okay, but I want to go on record as saying that you, in fact, are nowhere near pulling that off," she said, pointing at his apron.

"That's what I thought," he said as he took it off and handed it to her. "I guess that means you'll have to wear it and take the lead."

"Sucker," I said, pointing at her.

"Normally, I don't condone taunting," he said, giving me a high five, "but she did walk right into that."

That night, Beth and I learned how to make crawfish jambalaya with maple butter cornbread. Of course, you don't just learn a recipe with Dad. There's a whole production that goes into it. In fact, there are a few things that are guaranteed to happen anytime you cook with him.

Most important, you're going to end up with an incredible meal. I'm not just saying this because he's my dad. He's an amazing cook. He can take something simple like spaghetti and turn it into the best meal you've ever had. But along the way you're going to have to put up with goofy accents that are directly related to the food. That means while he's making the life-changing spaghetti, he gives you a lot of "Molly, that's-a not-a da way to make-a da meatball."

Finally, no matter what he's making, there will be one point during the meal when he drops the accent, gets serious, and claims that this one particular food provides the key to understanding the universe. He'll literally say, "You see, Molly, a peanut butter sandwich is just like life," or "Girls, if you can figure out what toppings to put on a pizza, you can figure out how to make the world a better place." (For the record, the peanut butter sandwich is like life because sometimes the simplest things provide the most enjoyment, and pizza toppings teach you the value of diversity, bringing out the best in all of us.)

This night was no exception. The jambalaya was incredibly good, and the ridiculous Cajun accent was incredibly bad. (Funny but bad.) And how is jambalaya like life?

"Look at all the ingredients," he said a few bites in. "It has crawfish, sausage, peppers, onions, rice, all with unique tastes. But if you add just a little bit of hot sauce, the taste of all those things changes. It's amazing how just a little bit of something in the right place can change the world around it."

"That's really deep, Dad," Beth mocked. "Color me amazed."

"Yeah," I added. "You just changed my entire outlook on life."

"You tease, but you know I'm right."

Also amazing was the fact that Beth and I had spent more than two hours together without a single disagreement or accusation. It took her a little while to warm up to the whole cooking idea, and it was a struggle for me to chop okra with a cast on my hand, but we laughed a lot, caught up with one another's lives, and had a really nice time.

When we were done, Dad reached into a drawer and pulled out Beth's phone and the router.

"Before I give these back," he said, dangling them in a tempting manner. "There's a new policy in the Bigelow house."

Beth and I both started to moan, but he cut us off.

"Just hear me out," he said. "You're both busy with school and friends, and that's great. And I work crazy hours, and that's not going to change. But in the old days, Mom used to take care of this. She would plan little day trips for us that we all enjoyed."

"Like the zoo," I said.

"Or the time we went to that corn maze," Beth said with a laugh. "And we got lost in the maze."

"And then again on the drive home," added Dad.

"Those trips were great," I said.

"Yes, they were," Dad agreed. "So, like it is with most things regarding your mother, it's going to take all three of us to accomplish what she did by herself."

"What do you mean?" I asked.

"I want us to make time to do one special thing together every week or so," he said. "It doesn't have to be big or long, but it has to be together. And we'll take turns planning them."

I was game, but I wasn't sure Beth would go for it.

"What qualifies as special?" she asked with a slight hint of attitude.

"Anything I do with the two of you is special to me," he answered, totally melting away her resistance.

"Okay," she said as he gave her phone back to her. "It sounds great."

The Whole Enchilada

Sometimes Omega work can be scary, like when you're locked in hand-to-hand combat with a completely unhinged Level 3 zombie who's intent on killing you. And sometimes it can be nerve-racking, like when you're hiding in an abandoned catacomb and holding your breath so that you don't make a noise and get discovered. But what I never would have imagined is that sometimes Omega work can be really . . . boring. I'm talking mind-numbingly, eye-glazingly, fall-asleep-in-the-middle-of-a-sentence boring. But that's exactly what it was the first two weeks we worked on the Baker's Dozen.

Every day after school, we went to the secret room in the attic of the Flatiron Building and—get ready to be totally jealous—we sorted papers. (I know. You wish you were me right now, don't you?)

Natalie is something of an organization freak, so we sorted through more than a hundred years of notes, newspaper clippings, logbook entries, and other really dull things so that we could create a two-page document she named "The Whole Enchilada." Her idea was that since we weren't allowed to take anything out of the room, we needed to cram the most important information into something small enough to memorize.

"You realize you're ruining one of my favorite foods by calling it this," Alex protested one day. "Now, instead of cheesy deliciousness, the word 'enchilada' makes me think of endless paperwork. I hope that makes you happy."

"Yeah," she said, not missing a beat. "It kind of does."

Grayson had a problem with it too. But it had nothing to do with the name and everything to do with the lack of technology. "This floor is filled with state-of-the-art servers. With that much computing power at our fingertips, we could digitize these files and cross-reference them a million different ways. It would be faster and better."

Natalie held firm.

"The instructions were specific," she replied. "Adam told us we could only use the manual typewriter that came with the room. So that's what we're going to do. Besides, there's something to be said for using the processing power in our heads. By going through the information and analyzing it ourselves, we might find something that a computer would miss."

Grayson gasped at the mere suggestion. "I'll just pretend you didn't say that."

Despite these protests, everyone whose arm wasn't in a cast took turns at the typewriter, and "The Whole Enchilada" began to take shape. An entry was typed for each one of the Unlucky 13. The first three were the easiest, because they were the ones we already knew were dead.

1. **Marek Blackwell**: Deceased

   Occupation: Consultant, NYC Sandhogs Local 147

   Aliases: Marek Bedford, Marek Fulton, Marek
      Linden, Marek Nostrand, Marek Driggs

   Most Recent Home: Lower Manhattan near City Hall

   Role within the 13: Mayor of Dead City

   Last Sighting: Pushed from the top of the George
      Washington Bridge

2. **Cornelius Blackwell**: Deceased

   Occupation: Laborer

   Aliases: Cornelius Hayes, Cornelius Buchanan,

   Cornelius Fillmore

   Most Recent Home: Greenwich Village

   Role within the 13: Marek's enforcer

   Last Sighting: Killed by Molly in the St. Andrew's

   Prep locker room

3. **Jacob Blackwell**: Deceased

   Occupation: Jeweler

   Aliases: Jacob Long, Jacob Staten, Jacob Ellis

   Most Recent Home: Roosevelt Island

   Role within the 13: Unknown

   Last Sighting: Found dead, handcuffed on the

   R train in Brooklyn

Natalie sat at the typewriter and began the next entry. "Ulysses Blackwell, "she said. "What can you tell me about good old Ulysses?"

"He should be rich," I said, looking at a logbook. "He's always worked with money, either at banks or on Wall Street."

4. **Ulysses Blackwell**: Deceased

   Occupation: Banker/Finance

"Occupation: banker slash finance," Nat said as she typed in the information. "What aliases has he used?"

I had the slips right in front of me. "Ulysses *Hudson* worked as a teller for the First Chemical Bank in the 1940s. Ulysses *Cabot* was a trader on Wall Street in the seventies. And Ulysses *Drake* was president of a small bank near Lincoln Center as recently as 2005."

"Look at that: He went from bank teller to bank president, and it only took him sixty-five years," Grayson said. "I guess if you live forever, you really can get ahead in this world."

   Aliases: Ulysses Hudson, Ulysses Cabot,

      Ulysses Drake

Next, she turned to Alex. "Where's the last place we know that he lived?"

Alex was sitting cross-legged on the floor, surrounded by stacks of files that looked totally random but somehow made sense to him. He ran his finger along one of the piles and pulled out a sheet of paper like a magician pulling a rabbit out of a hat.

"According to this . . . nowhere," he said as he double-checked the paper. "The Omegas have never been able to confirm a home for him."

Most Recent Home: Unknown

"However, we do have a picture," Grayson said, holding up a photo. "And judging from the really ugly polyester suit he's wearing, I'm guessing that if he is rich, then he's not spending his money on nice clothes."

"What's it say on the back?" Natalie asked.

Grayson turned the photograph over and read the caption. "May 25, 1977, Ulysses Blackwell wearing an ugly suit in Columbus Circle. Okay, I added the part about the suit, but seriously?" He held it up so I could see.

"I'm with you," I said. "I think calling it ugly is being generous."

Natalie went back to the list. "And his role within the 13?"

"Definitely finance," Grayson said. "He's involved with anything concerning money."

"And last but not least, where was his most recent sighting?"

"Give me a sec, I have that," I said, going back to my slips of paper. I shuffled through them and found what I was looking for. "According to this observation log in 2005, he was followed from his bank until he disappeared into a crowd in Columbus Circle."

Natalie thought about this for a moment. "Interesting . . . If the picture was taken at Columbus Circle, and the last sighting was at Columbus Circle . . . maybe that's where he lives."

"Maybe," Grayson said. "But there's no way to know that from a picture and a sighting twenty-eight years apart."

"Okay," Natalie answered. "I was just thinking out loud."

"Wait," Alex said as he clapped his hands and let out a woot. "He does live in Columbus Circle."

"Did you unearth another piece of paper in that pile of yours?" asked Nat.

"Nope," he said with a big smile.

"But I thought you said no one's ever been able to confirm an address?" Natalie said.

"*I* just confirmed it."

Grayson and I exchanged confused looks.

"And how did you do that?" I wanted to know.

"His aliases: Hudson, Cabot, Drake," he said. "What do those names have in common? Henry Hudson, John Cabot, and Sir Francis Drake. They're all explorers, just like Columbus. Therefore, Ulysses lives in Columbus Circle."

"That's not confirmation," Grayson said. "It's coincidence."

"No, I think it's a pattern," Alex replied. "What about Jacob Blackwell? Where did he live before he got handcuffed to his seat and died in on the subway?"

"Roosevelt Island," said Natalie.

"And his aliases . . . ?"

"Jacob Long, Jacob Staten, and Jacob Ellis." As she read them off, she made the connection and couldn't help but laugh. "They're all islands! Long Island, Staten Island, Ellis Island, Roosevelt Island."

"Okay," Grayson said, getting into it. "That *is* a pattern."

Natalie thought about it for a moment. "So they're all picking aliases based on where they live?"

"Sounds like it," I said. "What are Cornelius's phony names again?"

"Hayes, Buchanan, Fillmore," she said, looking at the list.

It took only a second for Grayson to solve it. "Presidents. All three were presidents."

"For that matter, all three were bad presidents," Alex joked.

"But Cornelius lived in Greenwich Village," said Natalie, bringing our momentum to a halt. "What do presidents have to do with Greenwich Village?"

We all considered this for a moment.

"Nothing," Grayson said.

"And Marek's names are all streets in Brooklyn," I reminded them. "But since he couldn't leave Manhattan, there's no way he lived in Brooklyn."

We were close. We knew the names followed a pattern. We just weren't quite sure what the pattern meant. We all sat there for a moment trying to figure it out.

"Remind me again: Where did Marek live?" asked Grayson.

"In Lower Manhattan," said Natalie. "Near City Hall."

I laughed.

"What's funny about that?"

"It's ironic that he lived near City Hall," I said, "considering he was called 'The Mayor of Dead City.'"

That's when Natalie made her "eureka" face. "That's it," she said. "That's our mistake."

"What's our mistake?" I asked.

"I wasn't aware that we'd made any mistakes," said Alex.

"We're trying to think of places in New York City," she explained. "But the Unlucky 13 don't live in *New York City*."

"No," I said, getting her point. "They live in *Dead City*."

"That's right," she said. "And in Dead City, you're not looking for landmarks aboveground. You're looking for ones that are underground. You're looking for . . ."

". . . subway stations," Grayson said, finishing her sentence before she could. "Columbus Circle and Roosevelt Island aren't just parts of town; they're also the names of subway stations."

Alex made a noise like a game show buzzer signaling a right answer, and we all crowded around Natalie and looked at the list together.

"Okay, so Jacob lived in Greenwich Village," Alex said. "But there is no subway station named Greenwich Village. The main one there is . . . Washington Square."

"Washington, Hayes, Buchanan, and Fillmore," Natalie said, listing them off. "Presidents all."

Grayson and Alex did a celebratory chest bump.

"And what subway station is at City Hall?" I asked as I started to do a little victory dance of my own.

All four of us answered at the same time, "Brooklyn Bridge."

"So the Brooklyn street names make sense!" I concluded as I spiked an imaginary football.

Suddenly our incredibly dull paperwork didn't seem quite so boring anymore. We kept typing up the Whole Enchilada, and the pattern helped us fill in some blanks. There were still some holes, especially concerning Milton Blackwell, but we now had a much better picture of the Unlucky 13.

Natalie laid the two pages on the table, and we all looked them over. As always, we were trying to find patterns.

"Here's something that doesn't make sense to me," Natalie said. "Why do they live so far apart from each other? You'd think they'd want to be closer so they could help each other out. But they're spread all over Manhattan."

"Maybe we can ask them ourselves," Alex joked. "Now that we've got this part figured out, we get to go out into the field and look for them, right?"

"Yes, Alex," she said. "Now you can stop doing paperwork and go back to doing what you love best . . . hunting zombies."

Alex flashed a huge smile. "It's not so much that I love it. It's just that I'm really good at it."

"Speaking of which," said Grayson, "what's our plan for finding these guys? Are we just going to stand in Columbus Circle and look for a banker in a really ugly suit?"

Now it was my turn to smile. "I think it's time for you guys to meet my friend Liberty."

"You mean the crazy, bald whack job who gives speeches about zombie rights at all the flatline parties?" asked Alex.

"I prefer to call him the 'former Omega who saved my life when I was about to get attacked by a mob and knows more about the Unlucky 13 than any of us,' but yes, I mean him," I said.

"Well, it doesn't matter what you call him," Alex said. "We can't ask him for help. We're only allowed to discuss the Baker's Dozen with people who are part of the project."

"About that," I said as I set a paper down in front of them.

"What's this?" Natalie asked.

"It's the observation log about Ulysses Blackwell going from the bank to Columbus Circle. Look at the signature at the bottom."

She looked at it and smiled. "Liberty Tyree. He was part of the Baker's Dozen."

"Cool," Grayson said.

Alex, however, had a concerned look. "Okay, I get that he saved you, and I believe in the whole 'Omega today, Omega forever' thing," he said. "But I'm just going to say what I think, even if it sounds prejudiced. He's a zombie, and I don't think the undead can be trusted. For all we know, he's a Level 2 and doesn't have a soul or a conscience."

"We can trust him," I said firmly.

Alex went to say something else, but he held his tongue.

"How would we even get in touch with him?" asked Grayson.

"Just like Alex said," I answered. "He gives speeches at every flatline party. All we have to do is crash one of them."

"Didn't Liberty have to save you from an angry mob because your cover was blown at a flatline party?" Alex pointed out. "I don't think it's safe for you to go back down there again."

The thought of them going without me was not good. I didn't want to miss it.

"I didn't have you guys to help me with my makeup," I said defensively. "With your help, I can totally blend in."

Grayson went to say something, but Natalie held up a finger to quiet us.

"Do you all want to hear what I think?" Natalie asked in a way that reminded us that she was in charge.

"Yes," said Grayson.

"Of course," said Alex.

"Liberty might be able to give us some valuable information, so I think talking to him is a good idea," she said. "We should be cautious about it, but it's not like we'll be revealing anything. He already knows Molly's an Omega, and he already knows about the Baker's Dozen."

"What about me and the flatline party?" I asked her.

"I'm with Alex on that one, I don't think you should go," she said, bringing a frown to my face.

"But Liberty doesn't know any of us, so he'll probably only help if you're there," she continued. "We'll just have to make it work."

And there's the smile again.

"We'll do the makeup at my place," she said. "My mom's got a couple of wigs you can try."

I went to protest, but I could tell by her expression that she didn't want to hear it.

"A wig sounds nice," I lied.

"Where did you go down last time?" she asked.

413

"J. Hood Wright Park," I told her. "Just like we did when we went underground for my final exam."

"You might get recognized if you go to the park again," she offered. "We should probably try a different approach."

"You thinking subway salsa?" Alex asked.

Natalie and Grayson both nodded their agreement.

"Subway salsa?" I asked. "Is it just me or does that sound like the worst Mexican food ever?"

"Come on," Natalie said, ignoring my question. "We better go try on some wigs."

11

Subway Salsa

Normally, you crash a flatline party by scoping out a group of zombies at a park and then following them into Dead City once they get word of the location. The advantage of this approach is that because the undead are waiting around, they're easier to pick out and follow. But since we were worried I might get recognized at the park, we were piggybacking instead.

"Piggybacking" is when you pick up a group after they're already on the move. To do this, you've got to find an underground location where you can wait around without being noticed but still be in position to move the moment you spot them. That's what brought us to the Times Square subway station.

Not only is it centrally located, but it's also the biggest and busiest station in the entire subway system. That means that no matter where a flatline party is being held, there's a pretty good chance that at least some zombies will have to pass through it on their way. It's also one of the only places in which there are stores actually inside the subway station. This let us stand around without attracting attention. Grayson and Natalie were over at the Smoothie Shack, while Alex and I pretended to browse at a Spanish music shop.

"This place is legendary," Alex said as he flipped through the CDs made by bands I'd never heard of. "It has the best selection of Latin music anywhere."

I looked down and noticed that Alex's feet were moving in perfect rhythm with the music playing throughout the store.

"What's that?" I asked, pointing at his feet.

Judging by his reaction, I think he was unaware that he'd been doing it.

"Salsa dancing," he said sheepishly.

So that's why they call it subway salsa, I thought.

Alex is always full of surprises, but salsa dancing had to rank pretty high on the "I never would have guessed he could do that" list.

"*You* know how to salsa dance?" I asked, still trying to process it.

"It's not too difficult," he said. "You move on the first three beats and pause on the fourth. Like this."

He demonstrated the steps for me, and they seemed as fluid and natural as could be. It was like he was on one of those TV dance shows.

"And you know this . . . how?"

"I have three sisters, and they all take dance," he said. "Who do you think gets to be the partner in all of their living room practice sessions?"

I laughed and realized this was just one item on the endless list of things that made Alex awesome. Of course, I was still going to give him a hard time about it. But before I could do that, Natalie and Grayson appeared at the entrance and signaled us to follow them.

It was piggyback time.

"We've got six on the move," Nat said once we caught up with them. She nodded toward a group about fifteen feet in front of us. We stayed with them but made sure not to get too close or do anything that might attract attention. All of us, that is, except for Grayson, who took a loud slurp from a bright pink smoothie.

We all stopped for a moment and looked at him.

"Seriously?" Alex asked.

"It's Caribbean Delight," answered Grayson with a big smile. "It has coconut, strawberry, and banana. It's delicious."

"It's also distracting," Alex said. "Get rid of it."

"No way," Grayson protested. "Do you know how much this cost?"

"Fine," he replied, "then hurry up and drink it."

"If I hurry," Grayson said. "I'll get brain-freeze."

Before Alex could get too frustrated, Natalie took charge of the situation.

"Let's just focus here," she said. "Grayson, just drink it quietly."

He nodded and took a silent sip as if to demonstrate that he could do just that.

"Perfect," she said.

We followed the group as they moved through the station. It sprawls for blocks in every direction, and they covered a lot of ground before they came to a stop on the southbound platform. There, they blended in with the crowd, and we got in position so that we could board the train a few cars behind them. But when the train pulled up and everyone started to get on, we noticed that they were staying on the platform.

We stopped cold, which of course means we got bumped into a few times, and we fought against the flow of traffic to keep from getting on. There was no way we could have just stood on the platform without attracting their attention, so we tucked in behind a stairwell where they couldn't see us. Luckily, Alex spied a large security mirror set up above the track. Their image was a little distorted by the roundness of the mirror, but we were able to watch them in total silence until . . .

Slurp.

All eyes turned to Grayson again. He swallowed a gulp of smoothie before mouthing the word *sorry*. Alex and Natalie shook their heads and turned their attention back to the mirror.

"Where'd they go?" Alex said. "They're gone!"

I looked up at the mirror, and sure enough, there was no sign of them.

We came out from behind the stairwell and scanned the entire platform. We were all alone.

"How is that even possible?" asked Natalie. "Did they get down onto the track?"

"No way," Alex said. "We would have still been able to see them."

"How do six zombies just disappear?" I asked.

"It was not because of my smoothie," Grayson added defensively.

We walked down to the end of the platform and were surprised to discover a large metal cover in the middle of the concrete floor.

"I don't believe it," Alex said, shaking his head.

"Is that some kind of trapdoor?" I asked.

He nodded. "I think it is."

"If so, we'll have to wait until after the next train to see," Natalie pointed out as another wave of commuters soon filled the platform, making it impossible for us to lift the door without being seen.

I looked across the tracks and noticed something interesting. Normally, the northbound and southbound platforms of a subway are directly across from each other, so there's almost always somebody waiting on one side or the other. But at Times Square, the platforms are staggered a block apart, so when one empties out you get a little privacy before the next crowd comes along.

Sure enough, a few minutes later, everyone but us piled onto the train, and we were all alone for a moment. Alex reached down, flipped up a handle, and pulled.

"It *is* a trapdoor," Grayson said as he peered into the darkness below.

We each entered and went down the small flight of stairs. Alex was the last one through, and he closed the door behind him. We stepped into an abandoned station that was laid out with tracks going east and west instead of north and south like the one above.

"I've never seen this ghost station before," Natalie said as she looked around at our surroundings.

"Me neither," added Grayson. "And I'm kind of wishing I wasn't seeing it now."

The first time I'd crashed a flatline party, it was in an ornate ghost station that had beautiful tile mosaics, brass chandeliers, and stained-glass skylights. This one was not like that at all. It was filled with trash and garbage and had graffiti painted on all the walls and floors. In other words, it was downright scary.

"Hear that?" Alex asked, referring to the thumping beat of house music coming from the darkness. "The party is close by."

Sure enough, we followed the sound and hadn't walked very far before we came across a small crowd of zombies heading for the party. We slipped right in behind them and acted like we belonged. Pretty soon, we were zigzagging through ancient basement hallways until everything slowed down and we realized we were at the end of a line waiting to get in.

"Check it out," Grayson said, pointing to the wall where NEW YORK TIMES was painted on a faded metal sign. "We're still close to Times Square."

I nodded.

"Why is it so backed up?" Alex asked the man standing in front of us.

"Security," he said.

We all exchanged confused looks.

"Security?" I asked.

"You know," the man responded. "They want to make sure no breathers try to get in. There's been a problem with that lately."

Suddenly I felt very nervous.

"Relax," Natalie whispered, sensing my fear. "It's dark, and your wig and makeup both look good. We'll be fine."

This calmed me until we reached the next corner and turned. Ahead of us, we could see the doorway to the party. Two massive Level 3s were standing guard while another two slightly smaller but no less intimidating ones were checking each person's ear before they were allowed to go in.

"Is that what I think it is?" I asked, referring to the small white object each guard was holding.

Alex looked at it for a moment and nodded. "I'm afraid it is."

Relaxing was now out of the question.

The guards were holding ear thermometers like the ones doctors use to check your temperature. But, unlike my pediatrician, they weren't checking to see if anyone had a fever. They were checking to see if anyone had any temperature at all.

The undead have no blood, so they produce no warmth. You'd think the simplest way to tell if someone is living or undead would be to check for body heat. But the problem is that because their sense of touch is so distorted, they can't feel the heat given off by a living person. That's why a zombie can touch you and not know you're still alive. But once those guards put a thermometer into one of our ears, we were bound to be exposed.

My instinct was that we should run. But it was crowded, and there was no way we could without attracting attention. So while I stood there and silently panicked, I gulped. So did Grayson. But his was not so silent.

Slurp.

Natalie snapped her attention toward him, and he cringed.

"Why do you still have that?" Alex asked.

"We got here so quick, I didn't have time to throw it away," he said. "I'll do it now."

He moved to toss his smoothie on the ground with the other trash, but Natalie reached over and stopped him.

"No," she said with a sly smile, reaching for it. "Give it to me instead."

"That's pretty gross," I commented. "You don't know what kind of backwash is in that thing."

"I'm not going to drink it," Natalie said as she looked both ways to make sure no one was looking right at her. "Why don't you guys surround me for a sec?"

We moved in tightly around her to give her as much privacy as we could. Then she put her finger over one end of the straw so that it held some of the smoothie inside as she lifted it out of the cup. Next, she pulled back her hair and put the other end of the straw in her ear. Finally, she released the top of the straw, letting pink goop pour out.

"Okay," I said. "That's even grosser than drinking."

"No, it's not," said Alex. "It's brilliant. You are absolutely brilliant."

Natalie smiled proudly, and I suddenly realized what she was doing. She was lowering the temperature inside her ear. Luckily, it was dark and crowded and we were each able to secretly fill our ears with Caribbean Delight. It felt disgusting and made it hard to hear clearly, but when the guards put the thermometers in our ears they only measured the ice.

Each one of us was waved in.

"So yay me for buying the smoothie," Grayson said once we'd cleared the entrance and were all trying to clean the gunk out of our ears.

Alex shook his head and laughed. "You got lucky on that one."

The party was being held in a cavernous room the size of a football field. It was filled with the hulking remains of printing presses that stood thirty feet tall and were connected by twisting chutes and conveyors.

"This must have been where they used to print the *New York Times*," Grayson said, marveling at the massive machines.

"Very impressive," Natalie commented. "Now they look kind of like . . ."

"Dinosaurs," I said. "They look like giant metal dinosaurs on display at the Museum of Natural History."

She smiled. "That's exactly right. That's just what they look like."

As we looked for Liberty, we couldn't help but notice that this party had a different vibe than the other ones we'd been to.

"Is it me or does this not seem very party-ish?" asked Grayson.

"It's certainly not you," Natalie said. "The music's dark, the lighting's dark . . . everything is dark."

There was something else very different about this one. Normally, the Level 3s stay off to the side and out of the way, but on this night they were everywhere. Because of the giant printing presses, there was no single main area for the party to take place. Instead, it wrapped in between and around them, making it feel like a maze with Level 3s standing guard at almost every turn.

Despite these differences there were still some things that were just like the other parties. Betty's Beauty Balms were on sale in one corner of the room, and Liberty was giving a speech in another. As usual, most of the people were ignoring him, but (also as usual) he didn't seem to mind. Liberty was determined to get his point across even if he had to do it one zombie at a time.

We waited for the speech to end before we walked up to him.

"Molly?"

"Like my wig?" I joked.

"Not particularly," he said. "What are you doing here? Wasn't last time bad enough?"

"I know," I answered. "But we have to ask you some questions. They're important."

He quickly began to look around. "I can't be seen with you all. Did you notice the security? Things are changing down here. If they think I'm talking to breathers, they'll finish me off."

"See, I told you guys this was a bad idea," Alex said. "Let's get out of here."

Natalie shot him a look and turned to Liberty.

"We need to ask you about the Baker's Dozen," she said.

This caught Liberty off guard, and he wasn't sure what to say. "I . . . I just can't talk about that. . . . Not here."

I followed his gaze and saw that he was looking at a pair of Level 3s who were eyeing us suspiciously.

"Then we'll talk somewhere else," I said. "At the waterfall. Meet us there in an hour."

When he had rescued me at the last flatline party, we'd escaped in the aqueduct, all the way to Morningside Park, where there's a waterfall. He thought it over for a moment before answering.

"Two hours," he said. "I'll get there if I can."

He didn't give us a chance to disagree. He just stormed past us, making a point to push Grayson out of the way as he did.

"Hey," Grayson complained, turning toward him. "What was that for?"

"Them," I whispered as I nodded toward the Level 3s who'd been watching us. They seemed satisfied and finally turned away.

"I don't know about you guys," Natalie said. "But I want to get out of here. Right now."

No one disagreed.

12

A Walk in the Park

The question came from out of the blue, but it tells you everything you need to know about Alex.

The four of us were standing on the heights that overlook Morningside Park because, despite my many assurances, he still didn't trust Liberty. It was five minutes before we were supposed to meet him, and Alex was still worried. He wanted us high enough to see the entire area around the waterfall so that we could make sure Liberty was alone when he got there.

"I can't stress how dangerous it is for Omegas to arrive anywhere according to a schedule," he reminded me as he scanned the park. "That's especially true at night in an area surrounded by trees. There are so many potential dangers."

I didn't know how Grayson and Natalie felt about it all, but I was frustrated. And to be honest, I was a little offended. We were the ones who had asked Liberty to help us, and yet I felt like we were treating him like the enemy.

"Liberty doesn't have any friends waiting in the bushes to jump us," I said with some attitude. "I don't even think he has any friends. You know, the fact that someone's a zombie doesn't automatically make them evil. The sooner you realize that, the better."

"Hey . . ." Natalie started to protest.

I instantly regretted what I said, and when I saw the hurt look on Alex's face, I wished I could take it all back. This was a sensitive issue for him. Sometimes we kid him about his attitude toward the undead, but I think he worries that we think he's prejudiced.

"I'm sorry," I said, starting to apologize. "I shouldn't have . . ."

He held his hand up to stop me. That's when he asked me the question.

"If we were a rock band," he said, "who would I be?"

I'm sure the bewildered look on my face hinted that I had absolutely no idea what he was talking about. I looked to Natalie and Grayson, and they seemed equally per-plexed.

"If the four of us were in a rock band," he said, motion-ing to us all, "which band member do you think I'd be?"

"I'm sorry," I said, still confused. "I don't understand the question."

"Natalie's the lead singer," he said with a nod toward her. "She's our leader. She's our voice. The other day at the hearing, she spoke for us, and she was brilliant. That's because she's the one who knows the perfect words to express what we're all about."

"Thank you," Natalie said with a pleased smile.

"And me?" I wondered, a bit worried by what he might say.

"That's easy. You're the lead guitar." He answered this as though he had thought through it more than a few times. "You're the musical prodigy who gives us flair and shreds up the stage. You don't even need words to speak. And every now and then, you're the one who gets the huge solo because, quite frankly, we just can't keep up with you."

I smiled and may have even blushed a little.

"Please don't make me the guy who drives the tour bus," Grayson said, perhaps only half joking.

"No, you're the bass player." At this point he pretended

to play a little air guitar, coolly slapping the strings of an imaginary bass. "People who aren't into music don't get how important the bass is, but it's essential. You're under-rated and stand off to the side, but you give us our rhythm. You provide our moral center."

Now Grayson started slapping an imaginary bass too.

"So I'm guessing that makes you the drummer."

"That's right," Alex said proudly. "I'm the drummer. I'm the one who sits in the back and keeps an eye on every-one else. I don't sing. I don't do solos. My job is to make sure you all stay on course. I make sure that you don't get so caught up in the moment that you lose track of the beat. And when some crazed fan tries to mess with one of you, I'm the one who throws the punch that protects you."

"Hey," I said with mock indignation. "I can throw a punch for myself."

"Sure you can," he answered as he tapped my cast. "And you've got the broken bones to prove it."

That made me laugh.

"We're not up here because I don't trust you," he con-tinued. "And we're not up here because I don't trust Liberty. We're up here because I don't trust *anyone*. I can't risk it. You guys make great music, and it's my job to make sure you get to keep playing."

"Well . . . I really am sorry about what I said," I told him.

"Apology accepted."

"You know, the really good drummers get solos too," Natalie pointed out.

He cracked a smile. "Maybe once in a while."

I looked down at the park and saw Liberty walking toward the waterfall. He wore a hoodie and a leather jacket, but even in the darkness, I could tell it was him.

"And just like I promised, he's all alone," I said with an "I'm so proud of myself" smile that lasted the entire ten seconds it took for me to see the four zombies taking their places and hiding in the bushes.

"I don't believe it," I said, turning toward Alex. "You were right."

But just when I expected Alex to say "I told you so," he did something completely unpredictable. He started to run down the stairs toward the zombies. Instinctively, we chased after him.

Worried that he hadn't seen the others and was running into an ambush, my voice rang through the park as I called out, "Stop! It's a trap!"

By this point, Alex was taking two or three steps at a time, and none of us could come close to catching him.

The stairs go on forever, and we were only halfway down by the time he reached the ground level and started sprinting toward the waterfall. That's when I looked up and realized what Alex had already figured out.

The four zombies weren't *with* Liberty. They were there to hurt him. I was now close enough to recognize that two of them were the Level 3s who'd been watching us after his speech. And when I'd called out to Alex, it had spooked them into action. They moved from their hiding places and surrounded Liberty. He had a nervous look as he saw that bad guys blocked every escape route.

Well, almost every one.

Realizing he had no chance in a four-on-one fight, Liberty turned around and dived right into the water. The pond at the bottom of the waterfall is small, but it was still big enough to buy him a little time.

More important, it gave Alex some time too. He kept sprinting at full speed while the zombies tried to figure out what to do with Liberty. Two of them jumped into the water at opposite sides so that they could force him back out while the other two waited for him on the bank.

Unfortunately for them, the zombies on the bank were so focused on Liberty, they didn't see Alex coming until the last second.

Now, before I get to the next part, which I'll warn you gets a little gross, I want to explain a couple things about martial arts that you may not know. First of all, most martial arts, like judo and karate, come from Asia and are primarily used in sporting competitions. They have rules and long traditions of sportsmanship that celebrate elegance and grace.

But Alex was trained in Krav Maga, which is not used in competitions and has absolutely no rules. It's a type of street fighting developed by the Israeli Defense Forces. And, judging by what I saw over the next thirty seconds, it's really effective.

The first zombie turned just in time to throw a punch at Alex, only to have him intercept the fist and snap his wrist with a violent twist. They traded a couple of lightning-quick punches, and out of nowhere, Alex knocked him unconscious with a head butt.

Meanwhile, now that Liberty realized he was going to get some help, he stopped trying to get away from the two zombies that had dived in after him and started fighting one right there in the water.

Natalie, Grayson, and I reached the scene just after Alex had knocked out the first zombie and had been jumped from behind by the second. This is when the "no rules" thing came into play. The whole point of Krav Maga is to end a fight as quickly as possible, even if it means using methods some people might call fighting dirty.

As zombie number two tried to squeeze the life out of him, Alex reached back and jammed his fingers up his nostrils. Then he literally ripped his nose off his face. Next, he spun around inside the bear hug, jammed two fingers into each side of the zombie's mouth, and did a move he calls "the double fishhook." I don't even know what he did next because I had to turn away to keep from throwing up.

By the time the rotted flesh had settled and the water stopped splashing, two zombies were dead, the other two had run off into the darkness, and Natalie was helping Liberty out of the pond.

Liberty looked at me and shook his head, water dripping everywhere.

"The first time we met, I ended up riding in the Old Croton Aqueduct," Liberty said to me. "And this time, I wind up fighting for my life in the Morningside Pond. You're not exactly a good-luck charm."

"Sorry," I said sheepishly.

Next, Liberty walked over to Alex and shook his hand. "You, on the other hand, couldn't have been better luck. I can't thank you enough for saving me."

"It's my pleasure," Alex replied. "Omega today, Omega forever."

"I've never seen someone fight like that before," Liberty said. "What do you call that?"

"I know," Grayson said before Alex could answer.

We all looked to him.

"What?" asked Liberty.

"That's what you call a drum solo."

The Undead Calendar

Rather than hang out at the park, where there might have been some more undead bad guys lurking in the darkness, we decided to head back up the stairs to Morningside Heights. We walked for a few blocks, which gave Liberty a chance to air dry and let Alex change our course enough times to be satisfied that no one was following us.

Finally, we found a pizza place across the street from Columbia University that was jammed with college students. In addition to being loud, it was filled with the mouthwatering aroma of pizza dough baking in the oven.

This last part was important not only because it smelled yummy, but also because it masked Alex's and Liberty's scents, which might have been picked up during the fight by the two zombies who got away.

In short, this was the perfect place for us to hide in plain sight.

We slid into a booth in the back, with Alex, Grayson, and Natalie taking the side against the wall so they could watch both doors for any unwanted visitors. I sat next to Liberty and quickly realized that it was going to take more than air for him to dry off.

"Sorry," he said as he used a wad of napkins to mop up the pond water dripping off his jacket and onto the seat.

"It's all right," I replied as I grabbed a couple napkins myself and helped out.

At first, everything about the conversation was awkward. Here we were, an Omega team, sitting down for some slices with . . . a zombie. Of course, we were all careful not to use the z-word in front of him, but that was kind of the problem. We were so worried we'd say the wrong thing, we barely said anything at all. That is, until I broke the ice in typical Molly fashion by sticking my foot in my mouth.

It happened when I handed Liberty a menu and it

dawned on me that getting pizza might be a big mistake. Undead taste buds are totally different from living ones. I'd learned this the hard way when I'd crashed my first flatline party and tried a dollop of that brown paste they call food. It was disgusting and made me gag. But here we were asking Liberty to eat something that probably tasted just as disgusting to him.

"I'm so sorry," I said as I began to stumble over my words. "I'm sure you don't like . . . I mean, this is not the right kind of . . . or rather, we don't need to . . ."

"Is she always like this?" he asked the others. "Or does she sometimes actually finish her sentences?"

"Sometimes," Alex said, "but even then they don't always make sense."

While the others had a laugh at my expense, I took a moment to compose myself and tried again. "What I meant to say is that I'm sorry we brought you here. It's pretty insensitive . . . considering the type of food you normally eat."

He laughed loud enough that a couple people at other tables turned to look.

"You really are one of a kind, Molly," he said. "You've almost gotten me killed. Twice. But the thing you're worried about is insulting me by bringing me to a pizza joint."

Now our whole table laughed out loud, including me.

"Well, when you put it that way," I said with a bashful smile.

"Have no fear," he continued. "The pleasures of greasy pizza extend across all taste buds, even those in . . ."—he looked around to make sure no one was listening before he whispered—"my condition."

We placed our orders, and I handled the official introductions. Despite their concerns about him, Liberty quickly won them over with his sense of humor, and the conversation flowed easily once he started talking about his time at MIST. It turns out we had some of the same teachers and many of the same opinions of them.

"What about the principal, Dr. Gootman?" he asked, smiling. "Does he still give the yeast talk on the first day of school?"

"Every year," Natalie said.

"We will eat bread made from this yeast," Alex said, doing his best Dr. Gootman impression. "And in doing so we will continue a meal . . ."

". . . that has included every student and teacher in this school's history," the rest of us said in unison, laughing.

Liberty closed his eyes for a moment and smiled, maybe replaying the memory in his head. When he opened them he pulled a garlic knot from the basket in the middle of the table and held it up with two fingers.

"To Dr. Gootman, to MIST, and to bread," he said.

We each grabbed a knot and joined him in the toast.

"Dr. Gootman, MIST, and bread!" we said as we "clinked" the knots with one another and popped them into our mouths.

"I want to ask you something," Grayson said, "but I'm worried it's rude."

Considering Grayson's total lack of social skills, we were now all worried about his question.

"Okay," Liberty said. "Give it a shot."

"How . . . did you . . . ?"

"Get this big old scar?" Liberty said, tracing his finger along the scar that ran across his bald scalp.

Grayson nodded.

"It was when I undied, as I like to call it."

I would never have asked the question, but I was so glad Grayson had because I desperately wanted to know the answer.

"I was a student right across the street from here," he said, pointing out the window toward the Columbia campus. "And one Friday night I was bored. I didn't feel like doing homework and couldn't find any friends to hang out with. Remembering my days at MIST and the thrill of being an Omega, I thought it might be fun to go to a flatline party. So, like an idiot, I went there alone. I mean, who does that? Right?"

All eyes looked my way.

"What are you looking at me for?" I asked sheepishly, even though I knew the answer. "Go ahead, Liberty, you were saying . . ."

"I was recognized at the party, and someone jumped me from behind and knocked me unconscious," he continued. "The next thing I remember, I was waking up in an abandoned tunnel surrounded by Manhattan schist. I had a big cut across my head, and Marek Blackwell was standing there looking down at me. He said that he was the mayor of Dead City and informed me that I was its newest citizen. He also told me that he wanted to be the one looking at my face when I realized what I had become. When I realized that I would spend the rest of time running from Omegas, just like the undead had run from me when I was one."

The story was chilling.

"That's why you helped me at the flatline party," I said. "You realized the same thing could happen to me."

Liberty smiled and nodded. "I may have seen some of

my stupid self in you that night. Luckily, we got away."

"What did you do next?" Grayson asked, mesmerized by the story. "Did you move underground? Is that what happens? Did you find an abandoned tunnel to live in?"

Liberty laughed. "No, that's not how it works at all. Most undead try to keep the life they were already living. I didn't change much. I tried to act like it never happened."

"You stayed in school?" asked Natalie.

"I was lucky because my dorm room was on the second floor. The undead are usually fine on the bottom three floors as long as we go underground for an hour or so every day to recharge."

"And no one at the college ever suspected anything?" I asked.

"How could they suspect something that they didn't know was possible?"

"What about your parents?" Grayson wondered.

"That's a different story," he said. "I tried to keep it from them, but they seemed to sense that something was wrong. That Thanksgiving we were supposed to visit my grandmother in New Jersey. I kept trying to come up with excuses to miss it, but they said it was a family obligation and that I needed to go. Finally, I had to tell them that I wouldn't survive past the Lincoln Tunnel. It was all very dramatic."

"How did they take it?" Alex asked.

"Not well." He paused for a moment. "It took a while, but my mom eventually came around. Now we spend Saturday mornings together at the farmer's market in Union Square."

"And your dad?" I asked.

Liberty shook his head. "He still won't have anything to do with me."

The look on his face was heartbreaking. We were all quiet for a moment because no one knew what to say.

"But I'm guessing you didn't crash a flatline party just so that you could find out about my family problems," he said, changing the subject. "I believe someone mentioned something about the Baker's Dozen."

Natalie nodded. "Have you ever been to the attic of the Flatiron Building?"

Liberty flashed a big smile. "That would be the attic with the manual typewriter?"

"Yes," she said. "That's the one."

"Yes, I have been there," he said. "Many times."

He sat up a little straighter and looked at each one of us. Then he leaned forward like he was sharing some sort of secret. "I'm guessing you guys have some questions about the Unlucky 13."

Over the next forty-five minutes, we ate pizza (which, by the way, was totally delish), and we got an understanding of Dead City that was more detailed than we had ever known.

"First of all," he said, "you've got to realize that most undead don't live underground. The Level 3s do, but the ones and twos usually find a low-lying place on the surface. And most live pretty regular lives. They try to keep their undeadness to themselves."

"If they don't live there," Alex said, "then why does Dead City even matter?"

"The Manhattan schist, for one thing. You've got to go under every day for at least an hour," he said. "But more than that, Dead City is like Chinatown or Little Italy."

We all exchanged completely confused looks.

"How?" I asked.

"In the old days, when the Italians immigrated to New York, their first stop after Ellis Island was Little Italy. That way, they were around people who understood what they were going through and spoke the same language. And even though most of them settled someplace like Brooklyn or the Bronx, they'd still come back to get that really great Italian food or see old friends. And they'd come back to help new arrivals make the adjustment from the Old Country."

"And that's what happens in Dead City?" asked Alex.

"Yeah," Liberty said. "When you're first undead, you go there just to figure things out and find others who can help you. Eventually, you try to create a normal life aboveground. But you still come back to recharge your energy and keep in touch."

"How do the Unlucky 13 fit in?" I asked.

"Well, you've got to go down somewhere, and every bit of underground is controlled by one of them. They split up the island by subway stations, and whichever one of the Unlucky 13 controls the area around a particular station is called the *stationmaster*."

"And they do this for money?" I asked, trying to make sense of it all.

"That's part of it," he said. "You know that stuff they sell at flatline parties, like Betty's Beauty Balms? Well, for every jar of makeup that Betty sells, a little bit of that money goes to the stationmaster. But mostly, it's about trading something you have that they want. For instance, I studied computers at Columbia. So sometimes I get called to help set up new computer systems. And in exchange . . ."

". . . you get to give your speeches about undead rights."

"That's right," he said, nodding. "I get to give my speeches. And when I go underground to recharge, I don't have to crawl around in some dirty old sewer. There's a place I go to that's nice and has good people there."

"Do the 13 all get along?"

"That's hard to say. Just because they're related doesn't mean they're one big happy family," he continued. "Some get along, and some don't. Some work together, and some like to be left on their own. But there is one thing they all have in common."

"What's that?"

"They're all terrified of Marek," he said. "And that's what keeps them from actually fighting station against station. Marek, as bad as he is, keeps the peace."

The four of us shared confused looks.

"So what's going to happen now that he's dead?" Natalie asked.

Suddenly, Liberty turned very serious. "Marek's dead?" he asked, surprised at the news.

"Hadn't you heard?" I asked, assuming news like that would have spread quickly through Dead City.

"Yeah," Alex said. "Molly killed him."

Liberty turned to me. "You saw his body?"

"I saw him fall off the top of the George Washington Bridge."

Liberty thought about this for a moment and shook his

head. "That may explain why things have been changing."

"What do you mean?" asked Alex.

"Dead City's been getting a little rougher around the edges lately," he said. "Like the party tonight, there were way too many Level 3s taking charge for my taste."

"And why would Marek's death cause that?" I asked.

"If he's not there to keep order, some of the others might be flexing their muscle."

"But you said word hadn't gotten around about that," mentioned Alex.

"Just because it hasn't reached me doesn't mean the Unlucky 13 don't know," he explained. "Besides, it won't become official until he fails to show up for Verify."

"What's Verify?" asked Natalie.

Liberty explained that Dead City follows what's known as the Undead Calendar. Even though the Unlucky 13 control the underground, they rarely come out in public. They let others do all their dirty work for them. But once a year, each one of them has to come out for something called Verify.

"They make an appearance at a large public event so that the general undead population can verify that they're still around and still in charge," he said. "They split up the calendar among them. Twelve months, twelve of them, it works out perfectly."

"But aren't there thirteen of them?" I asked.

"There were thirteen in the explosion," he said, "but only twelve who set up Dead City. Even in the world of the undead, Milton's a total ghost. No one knows what happened to him."

I wondered if we would ever be able to find Milton.

"So what will happen when Marek misses his Verify?" asked Natalie.

"That's a good question," Liberty answered. "My guess is that some of the others already know he's gone and have been trying to get things lined up so that they're in position to take charge."

"How?"

"When it's time for Marek to appear, whoever stands up in his place will be the new mayor of Dead City."

"When's his Verify?" Alex asked.

"New Year's Eve," he said. "In Times Square."

Ω 14

The Night of the Three Screams

There were three screams that night. And even though more than a hundred years have passed, I sometimes still hear them in my sleep. Despite this, my most chilling memory of those events is not a scream but a whisper.

"Milton, can you hear me?"

My cousin Jacob was lying on the floor no more than eight inches from me, but his voice was so faint I could barely make out the words. We were under strict orders not to move or speak, so I knew he was taking a risk simply by communicating with me at all. I nodded ever so slightly.

"No matter what happens, you stay with me," he continued.

"And if I tell you to run, do not look back. Do you understand?"

I nodded again, and no doubt the fear in my eyes confirmed that I understood him perfectly. Jacob was warning me about Marek. The same brother who once saved my life was now looking to end it. Tonight was the night he had picked for our escape. It was the night Marek planned to settle all unfinished business.

In the weeks after the explosion, I'd noticed that the thirteen of us started to form two separate groups with distinct personality traits. Today, the undead refer to these as Level 1 and Level 2, with the primary difference being that Level 1s maintain their souls and their consciences while Level 2s do not. In this way, Level 1s act more like the living while Level 2s are more prone to extreme mood swings and unpredictable behavior.

I have come to believe that the deciding factor as to which level someone becomes is directly related to their emotional state at the moment of death. In the seconds before our accident, I realized the explosion was imminent. My final breathing emotions were guilt and responsibility. Marek, however, was standing next to me and saw my reaction. He also knew the explosion was coming, and as a result, he died angry and filled with hate.

Confined to our so-called ward in the dungeon of the hospital, we were surrounded by walls of Manhattan schist, which only magnified these differences. Marek's anger and hate grew. It was directed at the grandfather who had betrayed us, at the three wise men who had condemned us, but most of all at me.

"You put us here," he sneered at me one day. "But of course I am the one who will have to get us out."

His escape plan was inspired by an unlikely source. Since actual doctors rarely ventured down to see us, we were primarily under the watchful eye of an evil man named Big Bill Turner.

Big Bill had no medical education. In fact, he had no real education at all. His training had come from his days as a street fighter with the Swamp Angels, a notorious gang that terrorized the East River dockyards for decades. His role at the Asylum was not much different, only now he kept order by terrorizing patients with brute force and intimidation.

He loved to brag about his criminal past with the Swamp Angels and one day told us the secret of their success. "We used the sewers," he said with a toothless cackle. "It was genius. We'd rob the ships at night and sneak everything we stole through the sewers so the police couldn't find us."

It was this detail that caught Marek's attention. He wondered *if the same sewers that protected the Swamp Angels might also be able to protect us. Over the next few days, he took advantage of Big Bill's ego and got him to talk more about his "genius."*

With his experience digging tunnels and Big Bill's knowledge of the layout of the New York sewer system, Marek began to envision a life for us beneath Manhattan. One night he laid out his plan for what today is known as Dead City.

"We will make a home out of the underground," he said as he ran his hand along the craggy wall of schist behind him. "The black devil we once feared will now give us power and protection."

"But we're locked in this hospital," Cornelius reminded him. "How will we even make it to the underground?"

"The same way everyone does eventually," Marek said with a laugh. "We'll die."

Two nights later, the nurse brought us our dinner. She was the only person at the hospital who ever treated us with any kindness or compassion. I especially liked that when she brought us our meals, she'd say, "Good evening, gentlemen. It's time to eat." It was the closest anyone came to treating us like we were human.

That night, however, there was no greeting—just the first scream, a horrified shriek followed by the sound of a dinner tray clattering to the floor. Rather than patients, she saw thirteen lifeless bodies strewn across the room. It appeared as if we'd finally succumbed to our mysterious unknown disease.

"Mr. Turner! Mr. Turner! Come quick!"

In keeping with Marek's plan, my eyes remained tightly shut, but I still had a vivid picture in my mind of what it looked like when Big Bill's massive frame filled the doorway and he looked out at the scene that had traumatized the nurse.

"They finally died," he said, no doubt with a smile on his face. "Well, it saves me the trouble of having to kill them."

He walked over and poked at a couple of us with the tip of his muddy boot. Satisfied that we were, in fact, dead, he turned to the nurse and said, "Best go get the doctors."

The brilliance of Marek's plan was that it took advantage of people's prejudices. The doctors were so relieved that we were dead and no longer their problem that it never occurred to them that we could be faking. We had no pulse. We were not breathing. We were dead. They were so happy to be rid of us, they sent us out for burial that night. Our bodies were loaded onto the backs of two horse-drawn wagons, and we slowly pulled away from the hospital.

It was a still night, and for a while the only noises I heard were the sounds of the horses' hooves clopping against the brick road, the creaking of the wooden wagon wheels, and the very unmusical serenades of Big Bill Turner singing Irish drinking songs as he drove one of the wagons. Soon, however, these were drowned out by the evening's second scream.

It was Big Bill.

Marek and Cornelius had risen from the back of the wagon and attacked him. Unlike the other driver who ran away, Big Bill relished the opportunity for a fight.

That was his mistake.

By the time I was out of my wagon, he already lay motionless on the ground. I couldn't tell if he was dead or unconscious, but he was certainly no threat to us.

We knew it would not be long until the other driver made it back to the hospital and raised the alarm about our escape. Search gangs would soon follow. But we had a tremendous advantage. We were Blackwells, and this was Blackwell's Island. We had spent our childhoods visiting our grandfather and playing in the woods around his home. We knew every path and trail by heart.

Even on this moonless night, we could travel at full speed.

"We scatter here and meet up at the dock," Marek said. "If you're late, you'll be left behind on this godforsaken island."

Everyone began to scatter, and I moved to join Jacob, but Marek took me by the shoulder.

"Milton, you come with me," he said.

I tried to hide my fear. "I-I thought the plan was for me to go with Jacob," I stammered.

"The plan has changed," Marek said ominously.

"Then I'll come with you both," Jacob said, coming to my rescue.

Marek glared at him. "He does not need a cousin to protect him when he has a brother."

It was dark, and all I could see of Jacob were the whites of his worried eyes. I knew he wanted to help, but there was nothing left for him to do.

"I'll see you at the dock," I said to him, hoping that it would be true.

"See you there, cousin," he replied as he turned and disappeared into the woods.

Soon, everyone was gone but Marek and me. He was lingering, and I wasn't sure why. I decided to try to win him over with some flattery.

"Your plan worked perfectly," I said. "You are so very smart."

When he laughed, I could see the flash of his white teeth cut through the darkness. "Smart enough to know what you're thinking."

He was standing next to the horse that pulled one of the wagons and ran his palm across his mane. "I remember another horse and wagon," he said.

I nodded. "So do I."

"And do you remember who saved you that day. It wasn't your cousin Jacob."

"No, Marek, it was you."

"Yet you think I would hurt you now," he said, shaking his head.

I couldn't bring myself to say it out loud. Instead, I just nodded.

"Have no fear, Milton. You are still my brother. I am not going to kill you."

I breathed a sigh of relief, although I wasn't completely certain I could believe him.

"But we have work to do, so follow me."

He started walking down one of the paths, but it led in the wrong direction.

"The dock is this way," I said, pointing behind us. "Aren't we going there to meet the others?"

"Eventually," he replied. "But like I said, the plan has changed."

We walked in silence until I heard the alarm sound from the prison.

"Do you think there's a prison escape on the same night?" I asked, amazed at the coincidence.

"No," Marek said. "I'm sure that's for us. The other driver must have alerted them. Now the guards will be searching for us. We must hurry."

We picked up the pace, and I soon realized where we were headed.

"No, Marek," I gasped. "He's our grandfather."

Marek stopped for a moment and turned to me. The hatred in his voice was unmistakable. "He stopped being our grandfather the moment he abandoned us. And tonight he stops being anything to anybody."

"Why bring me along?" I asked. "You know how much I love him. Yet you want me to be part of this?"

"You're not part of this. You are all of this. This is your fault. The reason I am not going to kill you is because I want you to suffer like the rest of us. Your punishment is that you have to live with the guilt of knowing that all of this is your fault. And you'll have to live with the blood of your beloved grandpa Auggie on your hands."

I shook with emotion, and in the distance we heard the bloodhounds of the guards. I didn't know what to do. But I was not going to back down.

"I won't let you hurt him," I said.

He laughed. "In what world do you think you can stop me?"

"In this one," I said.

He looked at me menacingly for a moment and said, "Maybe I spoke too soon about not killing you."

I had no intention of fighting Marek. But I did have a plan. One side effect of our undead state was that I no longer felt the pain of my childhood injuries. My legs had grown stronger, and it turned out that I was fast. So instead of fighting, I began to run.

I bolted toward my grandfather's house as quickly as I could. Marek chased after me, but he could not catch up.

The third scream that night was mine.

"Grandfather! Grandfather!" I screamed as I approached the house and awakened him. "You're in danger!"

Like he did on the day we first arrived, Grandpa Auggie came out on his porch with a gun. This time he fired a couple of shots into the air that attracted the attention of the bloodhounds. They began to howl and move toward us.

I looked back at Marek, about twenty yards behind me. He was angrier than I had ever seen him. But he knew that he would not get his revenge that night.

Just before he disappeared like a ghost into the darkness he yelled to me.

"Don't ever let me see you again!"

I haven't.

15

I Love a Parade …
I Just Don't Like Watching
from the Twelfth Floor

At the risk of sounding like a really bad word problem, I'm going to give you some impressive numbers. This year, more than ten thousand people marched in the Macy's Thanksgiving Day Parade. They sang, danced, and clowned as they waved from twenty-five different floats, performed in twelve different marching bands, and held ropes that kept fifteen giant balloons from floating away. Literally, millions of people stood in forty-five-degree weather to watch it in person. And while most of the people were bundled up and jammed together along the sidewalk, four watched from the comfort of the balcony in Natalie's apartment.

Okay, technically only three watched it from the balcony and one watched on the TV in Natalie's living room, but I could see some of the balloons as they floated by her window, so that should count for something.

"You're missing all the best stuff," Alex said, oohing and ahhing in a lame attempt to lure me out.

"I'm not missing anything," I replied, pointing at the TV. "When you watch in HD, it's like you're really there."

Grayson gave me a look. "But we *are* really there."

I ignored him.

"I thought you were over your whole fear-of-heights thing," Natalie said.

"I'm up here on the twelfth floor, aren't I?" I pointed out. "I don't see any reason to push my luck and dangle from the ledge of the building."

"It's a balcony, not a ledge," Grayson said. "There's kind of a huge difference."

"Just keep looking for Ulysses, okay?" I said.

Ulysses Blackwell was the reason we had gotten up early, fought our way through the crowds on the subway, and met up at Natalie's on a day we should have slept in. According to Liberty, the parade was scheduled to be his Verify. That meant Ulysses was one of the ten thousand participants. So, while the millions of other spectators kept a lookout for their favorite inflatable cartoon characters, we were trying to get a glimpse of an undead banker last photographed wearing an ugly polyester suit in the 1970s.

It was all the more important because Liberty thought there was a good chance that Ulysses might become the next mayor of Dead City. He had a lot of money and power, and that made him a logical choice to replace Marek.

"Would you guys mind sliding that door shut?" I asked as I wrapped a blanket around my shoulders. "It's getting kind of chilly in here."

Their only response was to open it even more.

"Thanks a lot," I said sarcastically.

With its location overlooking Central Park West, Natalie's apartment was in the perfect spot to see the start of the parade. And while the twelfth floor is a little high to see faces clearly, the balcony let us set up a whole viewing station with a telescope, two pairs of binoculars, and a fancy camera on a tripod with a telephoto lens. (And by *us*, of course, I mean the three of them while I offered encouragement from inside.) It looked like the stakeouts you see in detective shows or spy movies. My job was to keep track of the television broadcast and follow parade information that was streaming online.

Plus, I was in charge of making the hot chocolate, so I was contributing.

"There's got to be an easier way to find him," Natalie said, frustrated, as she scanned faces with a pair of binoculars. "The whole point of Verify is to be seen. So the undead must have a way to identify him in the crowd."

"Yeah," Alex said in my direction. "You'd think your buddy Liberty could have helped us out on that."

"He said he didn't know because Ulysses isn't his stationmaster," I reminded him. "Besides, I thought Liberty was your friend now too."

"I like him, but *friend*?" Alex said, half joking, half serious. "It's going to take a little more."

"Let's go over his aliases again," said Grayson, who was working the telescope. "We know he always uses the names of explorers. In the past, he's been Ulysses Hudson, Cabot, and Drake. What other famous explorers are there?"

"It doesn't matter if there's a Ulysses da Gama, a Ulysses de Leon, or even a Ulysses Magellan marching in the parade," Alex said. "The name doesn't help us because there's no list of participants to search through. The only names that are made public are for the different entries, like the floats, marching bands, and balloons."

"Now, if there was a giant Ulysses Magellan balloon,

that would be a pretty big clue," Natalie joked. "There isn't one, is there, Molls?"

I played along and scanned the roster on the computer. "Let's see, we've got Superman and Mickey Mouse, but no Ulysses Magellan."

Then something on the list caught my eye.

"But how about this?" I said, suddenly getting excited. "There is a marching band from Christopher Columbus High School."

They considered this for a moment and nodded.

"That has potential," Alex said. "How soon until they come by?"

"They're the next marching band," I told them as I checked the lineup. "First there's a Mount Rushmore float, then the cast of a Broadway show, and the band is right after that."

Grayson looked down the street to check how close they were. "That should give us about five minutes," he said with a sly smile. "Or, put another way, that should give us plenty of time for One Foot Trivia."

And so began another round of One Foot Trivia, a game invented by, and to date only ever played by, Grayson and Alex, in which they quiz each other while balancing on one foot. According to the rules, the first one to miss a question or lose his balance is declared the loser.

In their boy world, there was no greater challenge. And as pathetic as it is that they get so competitive about trivia, they make it even worse with their nonstop trash-talking.

"You're not worried that the television cameras might catch you losing and broadcast the shame of your defeat across the globe?" Alex taunted.

"No," answered Grayson. "But I am worried they'll get a picture of you crying like a baby."

"Seriously, guys?" I said.

"Name your category," said Alex.

"What else?" Grayson answered. "Macy's Thanksgiving Parade trivia."

Alex flashed his most intimidating look and said, "Gobble, gobble."

They both lifted one foot into the air.

"Let's start at the beginning," said Grayson. "When was the first parade?"

"Too easy, 1924," answered Alex. "Who was the first balloon character?"

"That's what you're going to ask me?" Grayson said as though he were deeply offended. "You think I don't know Felix the Cat?"

"Do you two have to play that on the balcony?" I asked

while trying to mask my nerves. "We're twelve stories high."

They completely ignored me, and Grayson had a little wobble as he asked, "Which character has appeared in the parade the most times?"

"Snoopy," Alex answered, doing some odd sort of flamingo thing with his legs. "By the way, I read that same article you did. I am so in your head. I know your questions before you even ask them."

"I mean it, guys," I said. "Why don't you play Two Foot Trivia instead? It's just as fun and much safer."

"First of all, this is completely safe," Grayson replied. "Second, if we had both feet down, we'd just be asking each other trivia questions."

"Which would be lame," added Alex.

"But isn't that what you're doing now?" I asked.

"No," Grayson said defensively. "Balancing on one foot makes it a sport."

I turned to Natalie. "Can you make them stop?"

"You know my rule about One Foot Trivia," she said as she sipped some hot chocolate and continued to ignore them by looking down at the parade. "I don't get involved in anything that's stupid."

"How many people watch the parade?" Alex asked, resuming the game.

Grayson looked unsure of the answer and took a huge wobble, which I swear was just to get at me. "In person or on TV?"

"In person," Alex said. "Stop stalling."

Grayson thought about it for a moment and answered, "Three and a half million."

"Actually, it's only 3,499,999," Alex said as he pointed toward me. "You know, because Molly's hiding in the living room and doesn't count."

Grayson tried not to laugh, but when he did, he lost his balance and his second foot came down. Alex raised his hands in triumph and started singing some sort of victory song.

"By the way," I protested, "I'm not hiding."

"If you *athletes* aren't too exhausted by your big game, you might want to check out the marching band," Natalie said. "Here they come."

Alex grabbed a pair of binoculars and Grayson used the telescope while Natalie started taking pictures.

"I see band members in furry hats and flag girls," Grayson said, narrating.

"I don't think he's one of the flag girls," Alex said with a laugh.

"Check along the side and in the back for any adults,"

Natalie said. "He might have slipped in with the chaperones."

They scanned all the faces of the people with the band and came up empty.

"What do you see on TV?" asked Grayson.

"Commercials," I said weakly.

He looked over his shoulder at me for a moment. "Just like being there in person. Thanks for all your help."

We completely struck out with the marching band, and after that, we also came up empty with a float called "Age of Discovery," which sounded promising as a name but turned out to be about computers, and a group of Shriners riding in antique cars, including a DeSoto, which is a car named after the first European to explore the Mississippi River but was driven by someone who was most definitely not Ulysses Blackwell.

With just a few more floats to go, we were discouraged.

Grayson came back inside to get another cup of hot chocolate. "Maybe we missed him," he said.

"Or maybe this isn't his Verify," added Alex.

I gave him a look. "If Liberty said it's his Verify, then it is. There are still a couple more entries."

"I only see two," Alex said. "The New York Police Department and Santa Claus."

"Are the police marching or on a float?" I asked.

"Both," he said. "Want to take a look?"

The broadcast was showing another commercial, and despite my fears, I felt like I was in the position of defending Liberty. I took a deep breath and stepped onto the balcony.

"Can I have those binoculars, please?" I asked Alex.

"Get back inside," he said. "You don't have to prove anything. I was just playing with you."

"I'm fine," I lied.

"You're shaking."

"That's because it's cold. Can I have them, please?"

The float was designed to be like the Statue of Liberty's torch, with people standing around the flame and waving to the crowd. I used the binoculars to get a close look at their faces.

"Well, I recognize the chief of police," I said, "but I can't tell with the other people. Most of them are looking the other way."

"What about the marchers?" Natalie called out as she took my spot on the couch. "Anything interesting?"

"No," I said. "They're just high school kids."

Grayson put his hot chocolate down on the counter and rushed back out onto the balcony.

471

"That's it," he said.

Alex and I traded confused looks.

"*What's* it?"

"The kids in high school who volunteer with the police," he said. "They're called *Explorers*."

Suddenly, Natalie was back on her feet, and all four of us were on the balcony.

"Police Department City of New York," Alex said, reading the name from the banner two of the teens were holding. "Law Enforcement Explorer Program."

We all searched the group, looking for Ulysses. Natalie used her telephoto lens to take photos of everyone so we could check them out later. Grayson went back inside to look at the computer and found something online.

"Listen to this," he said, reading an article. "Last month, a donation from a generous benefactor paved the way to break ground on a new learning center for the NYPD's Explorer program. The donor's name is Ulysses Clark."

"Lewis and Clark," said Natalie, identifying the explorer connection.

"Is there a picture with the article?" I asked.

"Yes," said Grayson. "It's small, and he's surrounded by the Explorers, but you can get a good look at him."

Natalie popped back inside for a second and looked at

the picture. "He's definitely one of the guys on the torch."

She went back on the balcony and started snapping pictures of him.

"At least he's dressing better," Alex said, peering through binoculars. "I wonder if he's cleaning up his act so he can become the new mayor of Dead City."

"Yeah," said Grayson. "And it certainly shows off his influence and power that he's hanging out with the chief of police."

Once the float had passed by, we went back into the warmth of the apartment and relaxed. I was sipping some hot chocolate when it occurred to me that Natalie had disappeared into her room for a few minutes. When she came back out, she had changed clothes and was now wearing a dark blue winter coat, a scarf, and a beret.

"Are we going somewhere?" Grayson asked.

"Well, in about an hour, that float is going to reach the end of the parade at Herald Square," she said. "I don't know about you guys, but if there's a chance that he's going to take charge of Dead City, I want more than a picture. I want to follow him and see where he goes from there."

16

The Mysterious M42 and Track 61

The Thanksgiving parade officially travels for two and a half miles before ending in Herald Square, right in front of Macy's department store. But once the performers reach the finish line, they still have to turn onto Thirty-Fourth Street and continue for a few more blocks before they can park the floats and tie down the balloons. Our plan was to be there when Ulysses Blackwell climbed down from the Statue of Liberty float so that we could follow him and see where he went. The problem was that this area was closed to the public. The only way you could get in was if you were wearing a special admission pin that was given to all the parade participants.

"We're going in there," Natalie informed us as she stood on her tiptoes to get a good look at it all. She said it in that superfocused way she gets when she won't take no for an answer. But, considering none of us had a pin, I didn't see how we could say yes. Talking your way past a guard at the Flatiron Building was one thing, but this place was swarming with security and police.

"You know, I'm really looking forward to Thanksgiving dinner," Alex said, "and I don't want to miss it because I'm locked up in parade jail."

Natalie gave him the death stare. "You don't think we should try to get in there?" she asked in disbelief.

"No," he replied, holding his ground. "I don't."

She considered this for a moment before curtly answering, "Fine. I'll just go by myself."

See what I mean? When she gets this way, there's nothing you can say or do to stop her. She disappeared for a while, and we didn't see her again until the NYPD float arrived. Ulysses Blackwell and the chief of police were still on the torch, waving to the crowd, and the high school police Explorers were still marching right in front of them. But there had been a small change, and Alex was the first to spot it.

"Now I've seen everything," he said, shaking his head.

It took me a second, but then I saw it too. It was Natalie, and she was marching right in the middle of the Explorers just like she was one of them. It was only then that I noticed her coat and beret were almost a perfect match for their uniforms.

The moment she got past the security guards and made it inside the restricted area, she split off from the group before anyone had a chance to notice her or question who she was.

The three of us just stood there, stunned.

"She did not just do that," Grayson said.

"Oh, she did," Alex replied. "In fact, I'm pretty sure she's going to—"

He was interrupted by Natalie's ring tone coming from the phone in his pocket.

"Give me a call and tell me all about it."

He answered the phone and listened for a moment before relaying a message: "Natalie says hello and wants everyone to know that she is okay and not in parade jail."

"Hi, Natalie," Grayson and I said into the phone, laughing.

Alex listened some more and slumped before saying, "Seriously?"

Apparently, she *was* serious, because he got down on his hands and knees, placed the phone on the ground in front of him, and bowed repeatedly toward it while saying, "I'm not worthy of you or your Omega awesomeness."

Grayson and I laughed until we had tears in our eyes. Both of us were glad that even though we'd all thought it was a bad idea, only Alex had had the nerve to tell her.

About ten minutes later, Alex's phone rang again, and Natalie told him where we could find her now that she had followed Ulysses back onto the street. When he hung up the phone, he gave me a curious look. "It was loud, and I couldn't hear her perfectly. But I think she said to tell you that we need to be careful because Ulysses is with . . . Big Red and Glass Face? Do those names mean anything to you?"

They absolutely did.

A few months earlier, Natalie and I had gone to the morgue to investigate three mysterious bodies that had been discovered on Roosevelt Island. When we got there, we were surprised to learn that the bodies were not actually dead. They were zombies, and we interrupted them right as they were trying to steal the *Book of Secrets*, which Dr. H had hidden there. Our fight with them was intense, and we barely escaped. At the time, we knew that one of the zombies was

Cornelius Blackwell, but we didn't know the other two, so we nicknamed them Big Red and Glass Face.

I explained this to the boys and told them that when we were looking through the photographs of the Unlucky 13, we had been able to identify both of them. Big Red is actually Edmund Blackwell, and Glass Face is his brother Orville.

I thought back to what we had typed out about them.

5. **Edmund Blackwell**: Deceased

   Occupation: Sandhog

   Aliases: Edmund Vanderbilt, Edmund Stanford,
   Edmund Flagler

   Most Recent Home: Grand Central Terminal

   Role within the 13: "the Butcher"; security for Marek

   Last Sighting: New York City Morgue/Alpha Bakery

6. **Orville Blackwell**: Deceased

   Occupation: Sandhog

   Aliases: Orville Barnard, Orville Pratt, Orville
   Fordham

   Most Recent Home: Hunter College

   Role within the 13: "the Enforcer"; security for Marek

   Last Sighting: New York City Morgue/Alpha Bakery

"If I remember correctly," Alex said, "aren't Edmund and Orville the ones who beat up anyone who got in Marek's way?"

"Yep," I said. "Their nicknames are the Butcher and the Enforcer."

Alex shook his head and commented, "This suddenly sounds much worse than parade jail."

We caught up to Natalie a couple of blocks away and congratulated her on her undercover work.

"Tell me one thing," I said. "Were you already planning on doing that when you picked out your coat and beret?"

She looked offended that I would even ask such a thing. "Of course I was. Have you ever seen me wear a beret before?"

Farther up the street, we saw Ulysses walking with Edmund and Orville. Orville had a serious limp, which was the result of the beat down Natalie had put on him in the morgue. She had kicked his leg so many times it almost fell completely off at the knee.

"Did one of you cause that limp?" asked Grayson.

I looked at Natalie, who smirked and said, "Maybe."

She took some pictures with her phone, and we continued to follow them from a safe distance. We now had new photos of three members of the Unlucky 13. Our work on the Baker's Dozen was off to a great start.

"Here's something I'm wondering," said Grayson. "According to the logbooks, Edmund and Orville always provided protection for Marek."

"Right," said Natalie.

"And now that he's out of the picture," he continued, "it looks like they're bodyguards for Ulysses."

"You think it's a sign that Ulysses is next in line to take charge of Dead City?" asked Alex.

Grayson nodded. "That's exactly what I think."

We followed them for about twenty minutes until they reached Grand Central Terminal. If you've never been there, trust me when I say that it's amazing. It's one of the world's largest train stations, with over forty different platforms and a massive subway station, all of which are underground.

"This is Edmund's home station," Grayson reminded us. "So I'm sure he knows every little twist and turn."

No kidding.

Unlike when they were on the street and kept things nice and leisurely, they picked up the pace once they got inside. This made it harder for us to keep up with them. So did the fact that the station was clogged with tourists who had come into the city to see the parade. I could tell they were tourists because instead of looking where they were going they kept staring up at the chandeliers and the mural of the night sky on the ceiling. At one point, I was hurrying down the grand staircase when I ran smack into someone who had stopped so that he could take a picture of the concourse.

We still managed to keep up and followed the three of them through a hidden door that led to the longest stairwell I'd ever seen. It was cut right into the bedrock, and its rusted steps seemed to descend forever. When we finally reached the bottom, we found a passageway that was part hallway and part cave. The floor was made of cement, but the walls and ceiling were jagged rock.

"Do you think this is still even part of Grand Central?" Alex whispered.

Natalie looked around and tried to get her bearings. "I'm not sure it's still part of New York," she joked while keeping equally quiet.

Since we didn't know which way the three zombies went, Natalie just picked a direction and we followed it. The hallway was curved in a way so that we couldn't see very far ahead of us, which made each step just a wee bit nerve-racking. We never knew what we might be stepping into. Finally, we reached a dead end. It was a massive steel wall with a door that seemed like it belonged on a bank vault. It was old and rusted and looked as if no one had used it in decades.

"Is it locked?" Natalie asked Alex.

He tried to open it but couldn't get it to budge.

"Either locked or rusted shut," he answered. He tried again, but this time we heard an electronic beep.

"What's that?" Alex asked, worried that he'd set off an alarm.

A hand scanner lit up on the wall. It was off to the side, so we hadn't noticed it at first, but it looked just like the ones we used to access the attic in the Flatiron Building.

"Explain this," Grayson said as he examined it. "What is something so high-tech doing down here?"

Natalie studied the door and said, "My guess is that it was installed to protect whatever's on the other side of this."

The nameplate on the door was covered in dirt and grime. Alex wiped it clean with his thumb.

"M42," he said, reading it. "Any ideas what that means?"

We all shook our heads.

"None," I said.

We poked around a little bit more, and Natalie took a picture of the nameplate and a few more of the scanner.

When we didn't find anything else that was interesting, we decided to follow the hallway in the opposite direction. Rather than a dead end, this way led us into a huge open space and a tunnel with a train platform and a single railroad car that was rotted and rusting. A faded sign on the wall read TRACK 61.

"Is this another ghost station?" I asked.

"Well, it's not a subway track," Grayson said, perplexed, as he tried to figure it out.

"And this is certainly not a subway car," Alex said as he climbed up onto its back platform.

As the rest of us walked alongside the car, Grayson reached up and rapped it with a fist. "I think it's made out of armor."

Except for the fact that it was all beat-up, it seemed like something that belonged in a museum. Natalie pointed out an official seal mounted on the side of the car.

"Check it out," she said. "Seal of the president of the United States."

"What is this place, anyway?" I asked as I bent down to tie my shoe. When I did, I looked under the train and saw some rotted wood and a rusted-out panel. And then I noticed something else on the other side.

Feet.

"We're not alone!" was all I was able to get out before the attack began.

There were five zombies in all, although at times it seemed like there were more. They worked as a team and seemed to coordinate their attacks.

The first two came running from the front of the train car and instantly engaged Natalie and Grayson. I had never seen Grayson fight before, and while he wasn't as polished as Natalie or Alex, he had some impressive skills.

I looked back to the rear platform of the train car, where a zombie had jumped Alex from behind and was now crushing him against the railing. I went to help but was caught completely off guard when a hand reached out from beneath the train and grabbed me by the ankle.

I smacked face-first into the ground, and when I turned over, I could see the zombie about to body slam me like they do in professional wrestling. I rolled out of the way just in time and whacked him in the back of the head with my cast.

It was total chaos as the fighting spread across the tunnel and platform.

The fifth and final zombie was none other than Orville Blackwell, who stood on the roof of the train car and barked orders that made no sense to us but seemed to really motivate the undead.

Despite the limp, he moved around pretty well for a guy who was over a hundred years old. At one point, he jumped off the car and landed on his feet as though it was nothing.

"Watch out!" I called over to Natalie, who was now fighting her zombie over by the tunnel wall. "I think he's looking for you."

Sure enough, Orville went straight for her, no doubt wanting revenge for what she had done to him during their fight in the morgue. When he reached her, the other zombie backed away and Orville sized her up for a moment.

Natalie was exhausted and breathing heavily, but this was still Natalie, and she was not about to show the slightest sign of weakness in front of the undead.

"Didn't you learn your lesson the last time?" she asked, trying to get a rise out of Orville. "Here, let me remind you."

She went to kick him in the same leg that she had nearly destroyed in their previous fight. But unlike before, when her foot hit his leg, he didn't crumble.

She did.

She screamed in pain as she fell to the ground and grabbed her foot. Then she looked up at Orville, and he gave her a big toothy grin as he rolled up his pant leg to reveal a thick metal pole that had replaced his damaged leg beneath the knee.

"Now you learn a lesson," he said as he bent down and lifted her by the shoulders. Natalie kicked and squirmed but couldn't break free of his grip as he slammed her against the rock wall again and again.

I felt so helpless. And then Alex came to the rescue.

He came running up from out of nowhere and in a single move managed to rip Natalie free from Orville's grasp and at the same time sucker punch him from behind with three quick jabs. Orville was dazed and turned just in time for Alex to go Krav Maga on his face. He was poking and pulling, and Orville screamed for help. The other zombies instantly stopped fighting the rest of us and rushed to help him.

At one point, it looked like Alex was going to fight all of them single-handedly, but they'd seen enough. Once they'd helped Orville to his feet, they formed a wall around him and ran into the darkness of the tunnel and disappeared.

Grayson and I did the only thing we could think of. We applauded. But Alex was in the moment, and he spun around to check on Natalie.

"Are you okay?"

Natalie was still trying to catch her breath and get up from the ground. She made it to her hands and knees but had to stop there. She looked up at Alex, and I couldn't read her expression. I was worried that she was seriously hurt until she flashed him a big smile. Then she bowed repeatedly and said, "I'm not worthy of you and your Omega awesomeness."

It was dark, so I couldn't tell for sure, but it looked like Alex was blushing.

A Time for Giving Thanks

D o my eyes deceive me, or is my Little Molly Bear wearing makeup?"

Little Molly Bear. Ugh.

Apparently, my grandmother was under the impression that I was still four years old. Of course, I could have straightened this out by telling her that the reason I was wearing a little makeup was because I was trying to hide the cuts and bruises I'd gotten during hand-to-hand combat with a couple of killer zombies in what appeared to be an abandoned top-secret government bunker underneath Grand Central Station. But that probably would've ruined the flow of Thanksgiving dinner conversation.

And it definitely would have gotten me grounded.

So instead, I just smiled and tried to be the best Little Molly Bear I could possibly be. I passed the mashed potatoes and said, "Yes, Grandma, I wanted to look especially nice for you."

We don't have a ton of relatives, but with one set of grandparents, two aunts, an uncle, and three cousins over for Thanksgiving, we more than filled up the apartment with holiday cheer. And when it was time to hold hands and say what we were thankful for, I truly had a lot of things to choose from. There were some I listed out loud, like "great friends and an amazing family," and some I kept to myself, like "surviving this morning's run-in with the zombies and reconnecting with my undead mom."

As for dinner, we had all the Bigelow family's greatest hits. Dad made turkey and stuffing that was so good you could write poetry about them, Aunt Fiona baked not one but two of her famous Texas-style pecan pies, and Grandpa Homer ended the feast the same way he did every year, by patting his ample belly and saying, "Thanks for having us over, Michael, it's the only time I ever get a good meal."

It really was great to see my relatives again, but big family gatherings are kind of hard for me. No matter how many people are there, I still can't help noticing the hole where Mom isn't. That was especially true this year because I knew she was spending Thanksgiving all alone somewhere underneath Manhattan.

That night, after everybody left and Beth and I took care of the dishes (or, put another way: that night after everybody left and because of the cast on my hand Beth washed and dried the dishes while all I did was put them away), we found my father kicked back on the couch with a huge smile on his face and a big piece of pie on the coffee table. He was in heaven . . . but it was not going to last for long.

"What do you think you're doing?" Beth asked.

"Well, let's see," Dad said in his special Dad-pointing-out-the-obvious way. "I'm wearing my Jets jersey. I have a slice of your aunt's amazing pecan pie. And on the television, there's a football game featuring the Jets. . . . Hence the jersey. So I believe I am enjoying Thanksgiving just as the Pilgrims intended it to be enjoyed."

"Umm . . . I don't think so," she said as she picked up the remote and turned off the television. "Or have you already forgotten about family time?"

"Hey, hey, hey," Dad said as he grabbed the remote from her and turned the TV back on. "I'm pretty sure we just had family time. Don't you remember? Your grandpa patted his belly and everything."

"But you said *we* were supposed to have family time," she reminded him. "Just the three of us. Grandpas and cousins don't count. It's my turn to plan it, and I choose tonight."

Dad gave her a suspicious look as he tried to come up with a way to save his night of football. "I know," he suggested. "Why don't we watch the Jets game . . . together? That'd be fun."

"Excuse me," I interrupted. "But how is that family time?"

"I'm glad you asked," he replied, stalling as he tried to come up with an answer. "My Jets jersey . . . was a birthday present from the two of you—family. The pie was baked by your aunt Fiona—family. The TV . . . is owned by . . . you know . . . the family. Family time."

He could tell by our expressions that this was going nowhere and realized that he could not win. He took one last sad look at the game and then turned it off himself.

"Thank you," Beth said.

"My pleasure," Dad replied as though he meant it. "So what did you plan for us to do?"

"You're going to love it," she told him. "We're scrap-booking."

It was almost more than he could bear.

"Scrapbooking?" he asked, trying to make sure he heard her correctly. "You realize that I'm a very masculine member of the Fire Department of New York City, right? Scrapbooking's not exactly . . . my thing. Isn't there some sort of mountain climbing or chopping down of trees that we could do?"

"Molly," she said, turning to me. "Please remind him what he said to us."

"And I quote," I said, trying not to laugh at my dad. "'*Anything* I do with the two of you is special to me.'"

"And tonight," Beth informed him, "*anything* is scrap-booking."

She headed into her room for a moment, and Dad eyed me warily.

"I like that the two of you are working together," he said. "It would be nice if it wasn't in some evil plot to keep me from watching the Jets game, but I do like it."

To be fair, Beth wasn't just messing with Dad. There was a reason she picked scrapbooking and a reason she picked Thanksgiving night. The fact that it also messed with him was just a big bonus in her eyes. She came back out carrying a couple boxes.

"Remember when Mom kept signing us up for activities like mother-daughter yoga?"

"Or mother-daughter swing dancing," I added.

"Right, like swing dancing," she said. "Well, one time she signed us up for scrapbooking, and we started to make this."

She pulled a large scrapbook out of one of the boxes.

"The plan was that it would cover our entire family history," she said. "Except we didn't get too far before she got sick. For the longest time, I couldn't even look at it. So I just kept it under my bed."

She handed it to us, and I started flipping through it with my dad. There were about ten completed pages. They were amazing, with pictures and keepsakes from things I hadn't thought about in years. My dad ran his fingers across some old ticket stubs from a Broadway play, and I thought he was going to cry.

"I had Grandma and Grandpa Collins bring over this box of old photos from their house," she continued. "I thought tonight we could all start working on it together."

Dad was extremely quiet, and I didn't know if maybe it was all too emotional for him. But then he smiled and looked right at Beth.

"You so get what family time is all about!" Then he wrapped her up in a big bear hug.

While she was still in the hug, with her face buried in his shoulder, she decided to go for broke and mumbled, "Does that mean I get the last piece of pecan pie?"

Dad let go and stepped back. "Don't touch my pie!" he said. "I kept close count. I only had one piece. You had three."

Beth just smiled and did her little eyelash thing.

"Okay," he said, melting, "we can split it."

I cleared my throat.

"Three ways," he said, begrudgingly but not really. "We can split it three ways."

It's not an exaggeration to say it was one of the best nights of my life. We told old stories, heard a few new ones, and found some hilarious pictures of Mom and Dad when they were first dating and they looked so young.

"Notice that your mom had big hair and I had a small waist," he said with a chuckle. "Over the years those adjectives somehow managed to trade places."

By eleven o'clock, the entire floor of the living room was covered with photographs and keepsakes and none of us wanted it to end. That's when Dad went into the kitchen and started making hot open-faced turkey and stuffing sandwiches.

Not to keep using it as an excuse, but my cast made

it really hard to cut shapes and designs with those little scrapbook scissors. I had a good eye for layout, and we discovered that Dad had a knack for picking out decorations to go around the pictures and he was especially skilled at curling ribbon. (He said it was because of all his first-aid training with bandages.)

It was almost two in the morning when Dad called it quits.

"I have to get enough sleep before my shift tomorrow," he said as he got up from the floor.

"Are you going to tell your buddies in the station that you watched the football game?" Beth asked. "Or that you cut ribbon and pasted pictures all night?"

He took a deep sleepy breath as he considered the best answer.

"I'm going to tell them that I hung out with the two most beautiful, intelligent, and interesting girls in all of New York," he said as he gave us each a good-night kiss on the forehead. "And I'll tell them that we watched the Jets game together."

He headed off to bed and left Beth and me alone.

I sat there and looked at her for a moment. In some ways, Beth is so easy to underestimate. She's pretty and she's social, and you get jealous and assume that she must be shallow. But she's not. And though I'd never tell her, there are so many ways I want to be just like her.

"What are you looking at, Little Molly Bear?" she taunted.

And so many ways I don't.

"This was pretty incredible," I told her. "You know, there's no way anything I come up with for family time will be as cool."

"No, there isn't," she joked. "But I'm sure whatever you pick will be nice and weird."

"You are so very funny."

She started to clean up, and I took the box from her hand.

"Let me do this," I said. "You had to take care of the dishes. My cast won't get in the way of me picking up."

"You sure?"

"I insist."

"Okay," she said, pleased. "But be careful to keep the pictures organized. You have to put them in the right—"

"Do you want me to do it or not?" I interrupted.

She stopped herself and smiled. "Good night."

She went to her room, and I picked up. The little scraps of ribbon and paper were easy, but the pictures took a while. I couldn't just put them in the box; not only did

I have to organize them according to Beth's system, but I found myself looking at each one, reliving some moments and trying to figure out others. I was getting supersleepy, but didn't want to stop.

I was particularly excited when I found an envelope with pictures that had been taken at MIST. It was odd seeing my mom just a little bit older than me but at the same school I go to. I especially liked a photo of her with some friends on the patio. It was right next to the bench where my Omega team eats lunch every day.

Then I noticed something about the picture that woke me right up. There were two adults talking to her friends and her, and much to my surprise, I recognized both of them.

The first one was Jacob Blackwell. He was the member of the Unlucky 13 who had been killed on Halloween by being handcuffed on the subway car.

I looked at the second one and came to a realization so unexpected that I said it out loud even though I was all alone.

"I think I just found Milton Blackwell."

Ω 18

MIST

As I walked across Roosevelt Island from the subway station to school, I had a flashback to the first time I was there. It was the summer before sixth grade, and I'd come to the Metropolitan Institute of Science and Technology for an admissions interview. Every year, more than a thousand students from across New York City apply to MIST, and of those only about seventy-five are invited to interview for one of the openings. The biggest reason I'd applied was because it's where my mother had gone to school and I wanted to be just like her. But when I caught my first glimpse of the campus, I began to have second thoughts. It was nothing like St. Francis of Assisi, the Catholic school in Queens where I'd gone since kindergarten.

"What do you think?" asked my dad, who was walking beside me.

I stood there for a moment and studied the four gray buildings. They looked cold and ominous, and I couldn't picture ever feeling at home in them.

"I think I hate it," I answered honestly. "St. Francis looks like a school, but this looks like . . ."

". . . a really scary hospital," said a voice from behind me.

I turned around and saw a tall man with wild hair and a friendly smile. He held his hands behind his back as he leaned forward so that he could look me in the eye.

"And you know why it looks that way?" he continued. "Because that's what it was when they built it. I have come to think that buildings must have DNA just like people do, because no matter how many times we paint it or plant pretty flowers around it, the whole place still looks like something you'd see in a horror movie."

He offered me his hand and said, "I'm Dr. Gootman, the principal of this excruciatingly unattractive school."

I couldn't help but laugh. "Nice to meet you, I'm Molly Bigelow."

"That's very interesting," he said as we shook hands. "Because I am supposed to interview a prospective student named Molly Bigelow. So unless this is an amazing coincidence, I'm guessing that's you."

I nodded.

"And considering you've already told your father that you *hate* the school," he added with a humorous expression, "I'm worried that things do not bode well for the interview."

"I'm so sorry, I didn't mean to—"

He cut me off as I tried to apologize.

"There's nothing to be sorry about," he said. "It's a completely reasonable reaction. But before we go inside, I would like to ask you a question or two."

"Okay."

"What did you think the first time you saw a human heart? Not just a picture of one but an actual bloody, pulpy human heart?"

The question caught me completely off guard, and I no doubt made a doofus face as I replayed it in my head to make sure I'd heard him correctly.

"It's not what you expected me to ask, is it?"

"No," I said. "In fact, I think it's a really . . . weird question."

"It's only weird if the answer is that you've never seen one," he replied. "But you seem like someone who *has* seen a human heart before. And if that's the case, then the question might be considered . . . insightful."

And that's where he had me, because I had seen one.

"Okay, I've seen a heart before," I admitted, "but how did you know that?"

"Wouldn't it be fantastic if it was because I had some sort of extrasensory mind-reading capability?" he replied. "But, actually, I know it because in preparation for our interview I reviewed your application. In it you said your mother was a medical examiner and that you liked to help out in her office. This means the odds of you having seen one are pretty good. So I'll ask again. What did you think the first time you saw a human heart?"

This guy was not like any teacher or principal I had ever known. I glanced at my dad for a second, but he just shrugged and tried not to laugh. Then I looked back at Dr. Gootman and answered, "I thought it was really gross."

"That is also a completely reasonable reaction," he said. "In fact, if you had reacted any differently, I'd probably be concerned. But I'm curious what you thought of it when you found out that inside all those gross, disgusting parts occurs a miracle that pumps oxygenated blood throughout the body, making life possible. I want to know what you thought when you were able to look past its appearance and see it for what it truly was."

He may not have been able to read minds, but he sure seemed to know how mine worked, because I specifically remember the day when I came to the same realization and stopped being grossed out by the stuff in my mom's office.

"I thought it was beautiful."

He put his hand on my shoulder and turned me back around so that I faced the school again.

"You will find that a miracle beats inside these gross, disgusting buildings, too. It's the miracle of gifted students and talented teachers coming together. It's the miracle of education," he said. "And seven years from now, when you graduate from this school, I guarantee that you'll no longer see how it looks. You'll only see it for what it is. And I'm willing to bet that you'll think it's beautiful."

"That's . . . pretty hard to believe," I answered, not giving an inch. "But before I can do any of those things, I still have to get past my interview."

"Don't worry about that," he said as he gave me a friendly pat. "You just aced the interview."

That's how I found out that I was accepted to MIST, and nearly a year and a half later, the memory of that day brought a smile to my face as I walked onto the campus. I stopped at the same point where we'd met, and I looked at the school. While I still wouldn't call it beautiful, I had to admit that it was growing on me.

There are four main buildings on the campus, and each one is named after a letter from the Greek alphabet. Alpha is the largest and is home to the Upper School, grades nine through twelve. The Lower School, where I take most of my classes along with the rest of the sixth, seventh, and eighth graders, is in Beta. (Since it was built alongside the East River, Beta has the best daydreaming views when you get bored in class.) The cafeteria and the gym are both in Gamma, which is why the teams at MIST are nicknamed the Gamma Rays. And my favorite building is Delta because it houses most of the science labs as well as the auditorium and library.

The library is where Alex asked the rest of us to meet him during lunch that day. Apparently, my theory about the current identity of Milton Blackwell wasn't the only big revelation of Thanksgiving break. And while I wanted to do a little more research and think mine through before sharing it with the others, Alex said he had news about Track 61 and M42, the mysterious places we'd discovered underneath Grand Central Terminal. (You know it had to be important if Alex was willing to skip a meal.)

I was the last one to arrive because I had the longest walk. I found them in a back corner, away from where Ms. Turley, the media specialist, has her office.

"Can we start now?" asked Natalie, anxious to hear what he had found.

"Yes," Alex said.

He had a stack of three dusty library books that looked like they had never been checked out. He read the title of each one as he set them down on the table in front of us.

"*Techniques for Converting Electricity from AC/DC to Traction Current, Architecture of Grand Central Terminal,*" he said, "and my favorite, *Secret Nazi Plots of World War II.*"

"Tell me that you're not starting a book club and asking us to read these," joked Natalie. "Because I've already read *Techniques for Converting Electricity*, and I found the love story to be completely unrealistic."

"No book club," he said. "But there are a couple of things in them that I'd like to show you."

He started with the book about Grand Central. It was extremely technical and filled with complex drawings, blueprints, and schematics. It showed every detail of the train station. Or so it seemed. Alex pointed out that there was no mention of the long stairway we took or of the deep basement where we'd found M42 and Track 61.

"It's like they don't exist," he said. Then he pointed to a diagram on a different page and said, "Except both of them are listed here."

He laid it out for us to examine. I couldn't make much sense of the blueprints, but Grayson instantly understood what he meant.

"This is all wrong," he said. "They have the room and the platform on the opposite side."

"I know," Alex said. "It's a total fake out. Just like this book."

"How is the book a fake out?" I asked.

"I don't think it's real," he said. "I've searched publishing records, the Library of Congress website, the New York Public Library database; I've searched everywhere, and none of them have a record of this book ever being published."

"But you're holding it," Natalie said, "so someone must have published it."

"I think the government printed a few copies and then smuggled some into Germany during the war," he said. "I think they wanted to confuse Adolf Hitler."

This led us to the next book, *Secret Nazi Plots of World War II*. He said there was an entire chapter devoted to how the Germans wasted months planning an attack on Grand Central.

"They had two targets at the station," Alex said.

"Track 61 and M42?" asked Natalie.

"That's right," Alex answered. "Track 61 was a special platform built for the president for whenever he came to New York. It was hidden for his protection."

"And M42?" I asked.

Now he referenced the book on electricity.

"That's even better," he said. "According to this, M42 was a top-secret room built to hold the equipment that converted electricity into the right type of current to run the trains."

"Why was that such a secret?"

"Because if a Nazi spy was able to get into the room and dump just a single bag of sand into one of the converters," he explained, "it would begin a chain reaction that would stop virtually all train travel on the East Coast of the United States. During the war, trains were responsible for moving food, supplies, military troops—almost everything. To think that you could disable all of that with a bag of sand."

"It's just like crawfish jambalaya," I said, thinking about my dad's cooking lesson. "Just a little hot sauce in the perfect spot can change everything else."

"So now we know what it was," Natalie said. "But what happened to it after the war?"

"Converter technology changed," Alex said. "New equipment was installed in a different location in Grand Central, and M42 was closed for good."

"If it was shut down for good," wondered Natalie, "then when did a super-high-tech biometric palm reader get installed?"

"As for that," said Alex, "I have no idea."

"I do," answered Grayson. "It was installed a little more than six months ago."

All eyes turned to him.

"And how do you know that?" I asked.

"It occurred to me that since the undead can't leave Manhattan, they would have had to purchase it somewhere on the island," Grayson explained. "There aren't too many electronics stores that carry stuff like that, and I buy computer parts from most of them. So I had Natalie e-mail me the pictures of the scanner, and I spent Saturday taking it from store to store to see if anyone recognized it."

"And did they?" asked Alex.

Grayson nodded. "A friend at a place over in Greenwich Village."

Natalie looked excited. "I don't suppose he remembered who bought it."

"Actually, he did," Grayson said. "He said that normally

he wouldn't but that he remembered the name because it was so unusual."

He looked right at me before he continued.

"He said he sold it to a guy named Liberty."

Suddenly, everything got quiet and all eyes turned to me. Once again, I felt like I was being put in a spot to defend Liberty. I didn't know what to say.

"I told you we need to be careful about that guy," Alex said "Zombies simply cannot be trusted."

I went to defend him, but Natalie beat me to it.

"We don't know what it means," she said. "There might be a perfectly good explanation."

Alex snickered and was about to say something, but Natalie cut him off.

"I'm serious," she said. "We don't know what it means, but thanks to you guys, we know where to look. If Liberty installed it, maybe he can help us find out what it's hiding."

I think Alex would have protested more, but the bell rang. Unlike the others, who had to get to class after our lunch period ended, I had a study hall and was able to linger in the library and continue my search for the mysterious Milton Blackwell.

I found the books I was looking for in the special collections room, and since my library card had been suspended because of excessive overdue fines, I quietly slid them into my backpack and slipped out the door.

I left the library and walked along the main path that crossed the campus. As I did, I passed a row of smaller buildings that also have Greek names. Zeta is the greenhouse set up for botany class, and Sigma is the art studio. But the most interesting building in the row is known as Kappa Cottage. Originally, this was where the hospital's chief doctor lived, but now it had been converted into an office and lab for Dr. Gootman.

Dr. Gootman has an open-door policy, and I still had a little time left in my study hall and no desire to actually study, so I decided to drop in for a visit. I stepped inside and had to raise my voice so that I could be heard over the classical music playing on his old record player.

"Dr. Gootman?"

"I'm in the kitchen," he called out to me.

What had once been a kitchen now served as Dr. Gootman's own personal mini-laboratory. He was wearing his white lab coat and safety goggles as he molded a lump of clay into the shape of a volcano on the counter.

"Miss Bigelow, what a pleasant surprise," he said in that cheery voice he always had when he was working on an experiment. "Just fixing up Vesuvius here for the sixth graders."

He tossed me a pair of safety goggles, and I put them on.

"Already time for the baking soda volcano?" I asked, recognizing the project.

"It's an oldie but a goodie," he said.

"Is it as old as the music?"

"This is the *Moonlight* Sonata," he said with reverence. "A deaf man wrote this, believe it or not."

"Actually," I joked, "that's not hard to believe at all."

He leaned forward and gave me the stink eye over the top of his goggles. "Watch yourself, young lady."

I couldn't help but smile. Dr. Gootman is as much a mad scientist as he is a principal, and that's what makes him great at his job. I thought back to the first day I met him and he challenged me to see things not as they appear to be but as they truly are. It's a method I've used countless times since. And it's the method that brought me to his office that day.

I studied him for a moment and looked past the mad scientist/educator exterior and saw him for what he truly was.

I saw him as Milton Blackwell.

Secrets

It's easy to get distracted in the old cottage that serves as Dr. Gootman's office. It seems as though every bookshelf, cabinet, and tabletop is always overflowing with something interesting. But I was determined to keep my attention focused on him so that I could carefully read his reactions.

"To what do I owe the honor of your visit?" he asked as he continued prepping the experiment by pouring some vinegar into a beaker. "Or did you just drop by to mock Beethoven?"

"I'm having trouble with some research I'm doing and

was wondering if you could help me," I said. "Do you know anything about a man named Milton Blackwell?"

I watched his eyes for any hint of recognition, but there was none. Instead, they carefully followed the tiny droplets of red food coloring he was adding to the vinegar.

"Milton Blackwell?" He said it as though it were some foreign language. "I don't recognize the name."

I guess it would've been too easy if he'd just admitted it. After all, he'd kept his identity secret for more than a hundred years. But I knew what I knew, and I came armed with evidence. I opened my backpack and pulled out the picture that had first given me the idea. It was the one I'd found when I was putting away the old photographs of my mother.

"Maybe you'd recognize him from this picture." I held it up for him. "It was taken at MIST."

He studied the picture for a moment and shook his head.

"These goggles don't make it easy, but he's turned away from the camera too much for me to get a good look at his face." Then he added, "It's a nice picture of your mother, though."

That's when I knew I had him.

"Interesting," I said. "And how did you know she's my mother?"

Without missing a beat, he replied, "You look just like her, Molly, right down to the mismatched eyes. After all, heterochromia is genetic."

"That's true. But I think you recognized her because you're the man she's talking to in the picture. The giveaway is how he's holding his hands clasped behind his back as he leans over to look her in those mismatched eyes. You do that."

"I do?"

"Yes, you do."

"Then I guess there are at least two of us who do," he said, "because I wasn't at this school when your mother attended MIST. I've only been here for fifteen years."

"It's true that *Dr. Gootman* has only been here for fifteen years," I said. "I looked it up."

I reached into my backpack and pulled out an old yearbook that I'd taken from the library. I opened it to the faculty section and held it up for him.

"But there was a Mr. Pax who taught chemistry while my mom attended," I said. "This is him."

Once again, he gave no hint of recognition as he looked at the picture.

"He's rather ordinary-looking," he said. "Why are you showing me a photo of Mr. Pax?"

"Because he's you," I said. Then I began to hold up more yearbooks. "And so is Mr. Speranza, who taught physics in 1959, and Mr. Wissenschaft, who was selected Teacher of the Year by the class of 1940. Congratulations on that by the way. I'm sure you deserved it."

One by one, I stacked the yearbooks on the corner of a nearby table.

"The names and the subjects they teach change," I continued, "but aside from a beard here and a mustache there, the face stays the same."

Even confronted with this evidence, Dr. Gootman kept his cool and remained focused on the volcano experiment before him.

"And these pictures of average-looking men who are vaguely similar in appearance to average-looking me somehow lead you to believe that I'm Martin Birdwell?"

"Milton Blackwell," I corrected. "And, actually, the yearbook pictures only tell me that you're undead. By the way, you look great for a guy who must be pushing a hundred and forty. No, I connected you to Milton and the Unlucky 13 with the photograph of my mother."

I held it up for him again.

"The man standing next to you is your cousin Jacob, who passed away on Halloween," I explained. "I recognized him when I saw him on the news. At first, I thought it was because I'd seen his photo as one of the Unlucky 13. But when I came across this picture, I remembered that I'd also seen him here on campus . . . with you. It was about a week before he died."

This time, there was a slight flicker of reaction, a hint of sadness in his eyes.

"I'm really sorry about what happened to him," I added. "It was terrible."

He looked at me as he considered what he was going to say next.

"You need to be careful, Molly." He held a box of baking soda in one hand and the beaker of vinegar in the other. "On their own, baking powder and vinegar are harmless. But if they're mixed . . ."

He poured them both into the volcano, and within seconds, the resulting chemical reaction started spewing out of the top like lava.

". . . they can be volatile. Information is like that too. Some secrets should remain secrets."

"But if I remember the experiment correctly," I said, recalling the demonstration he'd made to my class when I was in sixth grade, "if they're mixed properly, they can help make cookies."

I pointed at the fresh batch of cookies cooling off on the opposite counter. He looked at them and then at me and smiled faintly. "And you're looking to make cookies?"

I reached over and grabbed one from the counter. "I'm certainly not trying to make a volcano."

He picked up one for himself and took a bite as he thought for a moment.

"Jacob wasn't looking to make a volcano either," he said. "That day you saw him, he'd come to warn me because he was worried about me. Protecting me is what got him killed."

He stared at the photograph for a moment, and it dawned on me that he probably didn't have many, if any, pictures of his family.

"If you'd like, you can keep that," I offered.

He looked up at me and seemed genuinely touched. "I'd like that very much."

He walked over and placed it on his desk. Then he took another bite of his cookie as his mind raced in a thousand directions.

"Milton Blackwell." He said it again, only this time he let it slowly roll off his lips. "It's been so long since anyone's called me that, I barely recognize it."

I plopped down in the comfy chair in front of his desk

and rubbed my hands together in anticipation. I had so many questions to ask him about the Unlucky 13, Marek, MIST—everything.

Then the bell rang.

"No," I moaned as I turned to the clock and saw it was time for sixth period. "This can't be. I can't go to Latin. Not now." I turned back to him. "Can you write me a pass for this period?"

"Of course I can," he said with a laugh. "But I won't."

"You won't? But . . ."

"No buts. You need to go to your class and learn Latin, and I need to make a volcano erupt for a bunch of sixth graders."

"But what about my questions?" I pleaded. "I have many, many multiple-part questions."

"I'm sure you do," he said. "But they've waited for more than a hundred years—I think they can wait until after school."

I took a deep breath and tried to compose myself.

"Okay," I said as I reluctantly got up and headed to the door. "I'll see you after school."

"Why don't you bring your friends along?"

"Really?"

"Really," he said. "But let me tell them. I'll make sure

you get the credit for the discovery, but I'd like to be the one to own up to my identity."

"It's a deal."

When I reached the door, I realized he could be pulling a fast one on me. I turned back to him and waved an accusing finger. "You will be here, right? You promise you won't try to get away?"

"You can trust me," he promised. "I'll be here."

The Unwanted

He wasn't there.

I was standing outside Kappa Cottage, cupping my hands over my eyes so that I could look through the window by the door, and there was no sign of anyone—living or undead—inside. Every light was off. Every door was locked. Dr. Gootman had lied to me. I'd uncovered his true identity, and he'd made a run for it.

"I do not believe it," I said, furiously rattling the door-knob to no avail. "I do not believe he isn't here."

"Wow," Alex joked at my expense. "This really is the biggest surprise of the year. Dr. Gootman's door . . . has a lock."

"I never knew that!" Grayson added with mock amazement. "Do you think it's a dead bolt?"

Okay, not only had Dr. Gootman lied to me, but he was making me look stupid in front of my friends. I had texted them to meet me after school at the cottage for an "earth-shattering" surprise. This was supposed to be my moment.

"You don't understand," I said, my frustration level rising. "You just . . . don't . . . understand." I looked back through the window and tried the doorknob again.

"Sure, I understand," Alex said, needling me some more. "You're a little jealous because I found out all the information about M42 and Track 61, and Grayson figured out that Liberty installed the hand scanner, so you wanted to . . ."

"Dr. Gootman is Milton Blackwell."

I couldn't stop myself. I just blurted it out. Actually, I blurted it so fast it was probably more like "Dr.Gootman-isMiltonBlackwell." But you get the point. And, yes, I remember I had promised to let him tell them, but he'd promised not to run away so I figured that deal was off.

"What?" Natalie said in total disbelief, trying to compute it all in her head. "Dr. Gootman?"

Grayson and Alex exchanged stunned looks and then

turned back to me. It was around this time that I realized a school courtyard filled with students was probably not the best place to announce that the principal was living under a false identity. But the genie was already out of the bottle, and I could tell by their expressions that the others wanted to make sure they'd heard me right.

"Dr. Gootman is Milton Blackwell," I said again, but this time slowly and in a whisper only loud enough for the three of them to hear.

"Well, so much for letting me tell them," a perturbed voice responded.

I looked up and quickly had to amend two of my assumptions. First of all, my whisper was apparently loud enough for at least four people to hear. And since the fourth was Dr. Gootman, my runaway pronouncement may have been a bit premature.

"I'm so sorry," I said lamely. "But the door was locked, and I figured that meant you'd . . . you know . . . become a fugitive."

"Really? *Fugitive* was the most likely explanation?" he asked as he nodded down to the large volcano model that filled his arms. "Not that I'd locked up because I'd gone to Beta to do the volcano demonstration for the sixth graders?"

"Well, now that you say it," I responded, "that's also a logical explanation."

I was completely frustrated with myself, and not just because I'd been so impatient. It was mostly because I knew that it probably did have something to do with me being jealous of the boys and wanting to one-up them as quickly as I could.

"Is it true, Dr. Gootman?" Natalie asked him softly. "You're Milton Blackwell?"

He forced a smile and nodded. "Yes. It's true."

We helped him carry the volcano experiment into the cottage, and despite his initial frustration, he didn't seem too mad at me for telling the others. First, we sat around his conference table and he had me show the others my yearbook evidence. Humbled by my earlier mistakes, I toned down my self-congratulatory tone and kept it pretty straightforward. When I was done, Dr. Gootman took over.

"It really is impressive," he said. "Molly is only the third person to ever figure this out."

Okay, I'll be honest. I had assumed I was the first. Humility lesson number two. But it did make me wonder something. "Was one of the others . . . ?"

"Yes," he said before I could finish. "One of the others

was your mother. Apparently, Sherlock Holmesian skills of deduction are just as genetic as heterochromatic eyes."

"If two others figured it out, then how come there's no mention of it in the Baker's Dozen files?" asked Natalie.

"Because those teams did what I am going to ask you to do," he said. "They kept it a secret. They didn't leave any evidence anywhere. Not even with a manual typewriter at the top of the Flatiron Building."

"Why do you need it to be a secret?" Grayson asked. "Because it puts you in danger?"

"No, if it was just me, it wouldn't be such a big deal," he explained. "But the simple truth is that to many of the citizens of Dead City, I am to blame for their condition because I built the explosive that started it all. If word ever got out that I was here, a never-ending stream of Level 2s and 3s would come to MIST looking for revenge. And that would endanger all my students, which is something I cannot let happen. I understand if you feel you can't keep this secret. I do, however, ask that if you're going to share it, you first give me a few days to make arrangements so that I can disappear properly."

"Wait a second," Alex said. "You can't *disappear*. You run the school. You make everything possible."

"That's kind of you to say, but hardly true," he replied.

"Just as Newton's First Law of Motion says of momentum, this school will continue to move in a straight line unless compelled to change that state. There were gaps of five to ten years before the arrivals of Mr. Pax, Mr. Speranza, and Mr. Wissenschaft. The school continued to prosper in my absence in those periods, and it will do so when Dr. Gootman suddenly retires, whether that's in two days or two years."

"But where would you go?" I wondered.

"I'm afraid that is something I cannot share."

"You don't have to worry," I said. "Your secret's safe with us."

"Really?" he said, only half joking. "'Cause you didn't do such a good job keeping it earlier."

I was so embarrassed with myself.

"Really," I said. "That was a one-time-only malfunction."

He looked around the table at the others. "You all feel the same?"

The others nodded and smiled.

"We won't write or mention a thing," Grayson promised.

"Okay, then," he said. "I'll make some popcorn. This could take a while."

First, he showed us some clips from some videotapes he was making that chronicled the entire history of the Blackwells and what happened before and after the subway tunnel explosion. Then he suggested we go for a walk around the island that had been his home for more than a century.

A pathway wraps around Roosevelt Island like a ribbon, and together the five of us walked along it as Dr. Gootman told us about the Unlucky 13. We discussed the explosion in the subway tunnel and the three wise men who had banished them to the dungeon at the Asylum. He also answered some of our nagging questions.

"Why do some people become undead when they die while others do not?" I asked.

"I only know of two ways to become undead," he answered. "It happens if you die a sudden death surrounded by Manhattan schist, which is what happened to the thirteen of us in the tunnel. And it happens if you get infected by exposure to the undead, which is what happened to your friend Liberty."

We stopped walking for a moment when we reached the Blackwell House. It was now a museum, but back in 1896, it still belonged to his family. This was where he had his final confrontation with his brother Marek.

"I had to make a choice," he explained. "I could have gone along with Marek and let him kill our grandfather, or I could have defied him and in the process cut myself off from my brothers and cousins."

"Do you think it was the right choice?" asked Alex.

"I know it was," he said with certainty. Then he looked at the house for a moment and added, "Although it was a very lonely choice, and there are moments of weakness when I wonder how things would have turned out if I'd chosen otherwise."

"And you stayed on the island after that?" Natalie asked.

"I thought I would be safe here. I knew that Marek would never want to come back to this place he liked to call a 'godforsaken island.' In 1896, this was home to the Asylum, the prison, and a smallpox hospital. There were a few scattered homes like my grandfather's, but mostly this was where New York sent its unwanteds. Among those were the children in the smallpox hospital. No teachers would risk going in there for fear that they would catch the disease and die."

Grayson turned to him and smiled. "But you couldn't die."

"That's right," he said. "So I began to teach at the hospital. And I was happy. I thought that it was my calling to help those sick children. But then I started to hear stories about monsters in Manhattan. People with unexplained powers who lived underground and could withstand bullets. Some people claimed they were werewolves or vampires. But I knew it was Marek and the others. And since I couldn't stop them by myself, I decided to train others who could."

Natalie stopped walking and turned to him. "The Omegas? You started the Omegas?"

"Well, first I had to start MIST," he said. "But, yes, I started the Omegas to fix the problems I had created."

Our walk had brought us back to the campus. Knowing what I now knew made it look a little different.

"But how did you just *start* a school?" Alex asked, motioning to the campus full of buildings.

"Fortunately, I wasn't the only one with a guilty conscience. My grandfather owned much of the property on the island. He also owned a construction company. He made much of this possible. And then there was one of the three wise men."

I turned to him. "Theodore Roosevelt?!"

Dr. Gootman laughed. "Quite the interesting fellow."

I got goose bumps when I thought about the idea of Dr. Gootman actually knowing Teddy Roosevelt.

"He helped you?" asked Grayson.

"Very much," he said. "It's amazing what you can accomplish if you have help from the president of the United States."

We were now at the door to the cottage.

"I have one last question," I said. "Actually, I have hundreds of questions, but one last one I want to ask you now."

"What is it?"

"Why did Jacob come to warn you? What had changed things?"

He thought about it for a moment and looked out over the campus to the East River.

"You did, Molly."

"Me? How did I change things?"

"You beat Marek. And when he fell from the top of the George Washington Bridge, everything changed. Ever since our escape back in 1896, Marek has told the others what to do. With him out of the picture, they will all try to take control of Dead City."

"I'm so sorry," I said.

"Don't be," he replied. "Marek came looking for you because he knew you were strong enough to beat him. He thought he could get to you while you were young. But you were already too strong. And so was your team."

He looked at the four of us and shook his head with wonder.

"You four are amazing," he said, giving us quite the morale boost. "Don't ever be sorry for that. You're the reason I created the Omegas. I hoped that one day it would produce people like you. Because, believe me, we're going to need them."

21

Blue Moon

Amazing or not, we were running out of time and needed help. There was less than a month until Marek's Verify on New Year's Eve, and all we knew for sure was that once the crystal ball dropped to signal a new year, someone was going to take control of Dead City. Beyond that we had no idea what was going to happen.

We thought there might be some answers hidden deep below Grand Central Terminal in M42, so we went looking for Liberty. He'd installed the security system, and we hoped he could help us get inside.

Since we'd had a few too many close calls crashing flat-line parties, we decided to try a different method of contacting him this time. We went to the farmer's market in Union Square, where he told us he met his mother every Saturday. Unlike the flatline parties, there was less danger and more snacks. Yum.

"I'm going to go on the record and say that kettle corn is the greatest invention of all time," I proclaimed as I stuffed a fistful of it into my mouth and crunched.

"Even more than, say . . . the computer . . . or the Internet?" offered Grayson.

"Both great inventions," I mumbled as I tried to talk and chew at the same time. "But kettle corn is sweet *and* salty. It's easy to carry, and unlike computers and the Internet . . . it's delicious."

"She makes a compelling argument," Alex added as he reached into my bag and stole a handful for himself.

It was a cool December morning, and we were walking around eating snacks because Alex insisted we watch Liberty from a distance and approach him after his mother left.

"He only has family one morning a week," Alex explained. "Let's not take that from him."

(You see, deep down Alex has a huge heart.)

Liberty's mom left around noon, and we caught up with him in front of a booth where a man was selling homemade pretzels.

"I saw you the second you arrived," Liberty said, shaking his head. "I hope you guys do a better job hiding when you're following the bad guys."

"We weren't trying to hide from you," Natalie said, "just your mom."

He considered this for a moment and smiled. "Thanks for that. I appreciate it."

When we told him about M42, he wasn't impressed.

"*That's* why you came looking for me?" he asked. "Because you found a secret room from World War II?"

"Well, we were hoping you'd tell us what's inside it now," Natalie said.

Liberty seemed totally confused. "How would I know that?"

"Didn't you install the biometric hand scanner that controls the door?" Alex said.

"No . . . although, now that you mention it, I do remember setting one up for Winston. But I don't know where he installed it. I gave it to him in his office."

I knew from our research into the Unlucky 13 that Winston Blackwell was in charge of the portion of Dead

City directly beneath us. His home station was Union Square, and he was Liberty's stationmaster.

7. **Winston Blackwell**: Deceased

   Occupation: Businessman

   Aliases: Winston Grant, Winston McClellan, Winston Burnside

   Most Recent Home: Union Square

   Role within the 13: Organization and Logistics

   Last Sighting: Greenwich Village

"If you didn't know anything about it," Alex said, somewhat suspicious, "why did he ask you to set it up for him?"

"Like I told you guys before. Every now and then I do some computer work for them, and in exchange, I get to give my little speeches and move around Dead City without getting hassled too much," he answered. "It was just one of those times. There was nothing special about it. Winston told me that he was going to take care of the installation. He just needed me to buy a new scanner and fix it."

"If it was new," I wondered aloud, "why did it need to be fixed?"

"Palm scanners measure all the different aspects of your

hand and turn them into a geometric equation," he explained. "They're great for security . . . unless you're undead."

"Why?" I asked.

"Body heat," Grayson said, figuring out the problem. "They're triggered by body heat."

"That's exactly right. I had to reprogram the scanner so that it would recognize hands like mine," he said, wiggling his fingers for emphasis. "Winston also had me create security profiles for the whole group."

"What group?" asked Natalie.

"The Unlucky 13," he said. "They get pretty secretive about who's doing what with whom. So Winston had me build a separate profile for each one of them. That way, I wouldn't know who it was really for. All he had to do was bring it to the ones he wanted and scan their palms into the profiles I'd built."

We mulled this over for a moment.

"So the only way to open the door to M42 is to have one of the Unlucky 13 with you," Natalie said. "That should be . . . impossible."

She looked defeated, but Grayson smiled as he had a brainstorm. "Wait a second," he said excitedly. "You don't technically need one of them. You only need one of their hands."

"Okay, ewwww," said Natalie. "I'm not sure where you're going with this, but let me stress, ewwww."

"Jacob Blackwell was one of the Unlucky 13 before he was killed on the subway," he pointed out. "Can't we dig him up and get his hand?"

Natalie shook her head. "You're kind of freaking me out, Grayson. I don't expect stuff like this from you—Alex maybe, but not you."

"Hey, what's that supposed to mean?" Alex protested.

"You know what it means," Natalie said. "It means . . ."

Before this could escalate into an argument, Liberty jumped back into the conversation. "You know, there is an easier way that doesn't require any grave robbing or dismemberment."

Suddenly, everybody stopped talking, and all eyes turned to him.

"You remember the part where I said I programmed it to recognize hands like mine?" He held his hand up and wiggled his fingers again. "I did that by actually programming it to recognize my hand."

Natalie looked at his hand and smiled. "I like this plan better," she said. "No ewwww."

Thirty minutes later, we were at Grand Central, walking down the seemingly endless series of stairwells that according to the blueprints did not exist. Along the way, we told Liberty all about our last visit, when Orville Blackwell and his thugs attacked us at the hidden train platform.

"You survived an attack from Orville?" he asked Natalie, obviously impressed. "Not many people can say that. You know, there's a reason they call him the Enforcer down here."

"Well, I don't know if there is much to brag about. He pretty much redecorated the wall with my body," she replied while she rubbed a sore spot on the back of her head. "Luckily, Alex was there to rescue me."

"I guess we have that in common," Liberty said, "because I can say the same thing about Alex being there to rescue me in Morningside Park."

"Our hero," Natalie said.

"Yes, he definitely is our hero," Liberty added.

"Can we focus here?" Alex asked, embarrassed by the praise. "Or I might not save you next time."

When we reached the bottom, Liberty ran his fingers along the jagged rock that made up the walls of the hallway. "You weren't kidding when you said it was creepy down here."

"That's saying something coming from a guy who spends a good bit of his time in Dead City," Grayson said with a laugh.

We started walking along the curved hallway toward M42, and with memories of the Orville ambush still fresh in our minds, we did our best to keep quiet and stay alert. At one point, we stopped cold when we heard a noise just around the curve heading our way. It was too close for us to retreat, so we got into fighting positions. The noise got closer and closer until we finally saw our enemy . . . a giant rat scurrying along the wall. We each breathed a sigh of relief. (Okay, so Liberty didn't actually "breathe" in the classic sense, but you get my meaning.)

"I don't know about you guys," I said, "but it's a little troubling that we've reached a point in our lives when coming across a hideously large sewer rat is a reason to be relieved."

The others laughed, and we continued until we got to the door.

"Don't touch the scanner," Liberty instructed us as he moved to the front of the group to examine it. He squatted down and looked at it as closely as he could without making contact.

"This is definitely the one I set up for Winston," he said quietly. "And the good news is that it doesn't look like it's been used in the last twelve hours."

He stood up and now used his regular speaking voice.

"Hopefully, that means that there isn't anyone inside there."

"How can you tell that?" asked Grayson.

"It's in a deep sleep mode to save battery power," he replied. "If it had been used more recently than that, there'd still be a little red light blinking on and off."

"All right, then," Natalie said with a sly smile. "Let's take a look inside."

Liberty pressed his palm against the scanner, and a green laser instantly began tracing the outline of his hand. After a few seconds, we heard a loud click come from inside the door.

"We're in," Liberty said with a touch of evil genius to his voice.

Alex opened the door to reveal a massive room. There were hard metal edges and old-school electronics everywhere you looked. I'm sure when they built it, everything seemed modern and futuristic, but now it just looked like an outdated museum exhibit about early computers. The floor was a combination of cement and metal grates, while endless ducts of wiring ran along the ceiling.

"Should we be concerned that the lights are already on?" I whispered nervously.

Natalie nodded. "I know I am," she replied. "Let's make sure we're alone."

It was all much bigger than I'd expected. In addition to the main room, there were doorways to several other rooms along the far wall, and a hallway that disappeared into darkness. We silently poked around until we were satisfied that no one else was there.

"Is it just me, or does this place look like it's from one of those old spy movies?" Grayson asked. "You know, like when James Bond makes it into the supervillain's master control room?"

"That's exactly what I was thinking," Liberty answered. "I thought I knew a lot about computers, but I don't recognize any of these electronics."

"These are the converters that turned the electricity into traction current for the trains," Alex said, pointing toward a bank of tall gray machines with big dials and gauges. "They worked with these turbines." He gestured toward a row of massive fans that ran down the middle of the room.

"I don't think the Unlucky 13 are coming down here to convert electricity to run trains," Natalie said. "So let's look around and see if we can figure out why this place was worth adding the high-tech security."

We started snooping around, and I came across an old metal cabinet and managed to wiggle its door open.

Everything inside of it was covered in a thick layer of dust. There were office supplies, like pens and paper clips, which I expected, but there was also a calendar that seemed out of place.

I called over to Alex, who was checking out one of the turbines. "You said this was closed right after World War II, right?"

"In 1946, according to the book," answered Alex.

"Then why do they have a calendar from 1967?" I asked. I held up the calendar for him to see.

Alex just shrugged. "That makes no sense to me."

"Hey," Grayson said as he stepped out of an office. "I think you guys might want to check this out."

We hurried over, and when we reached the room, it was obvious why he'd called us. It looked like it had been decorated by a demolition team. Everything was either bent or broken. There was a metal desk and three filing cabinets. Each drawer had been pried open, and there were broken padlocks scattered on the floor.

"Did you do this?" Natalie jokingly asked Grayson.

"Yes," he deadpanned. "I broke all of these thick metal locks with the superhuman strength I've been hiding from you the last few years."

Alex looked closely at one of the file cabinets and shook

his head in disbelief. "Whoever did this was strong, and I mean really strong," he said. "It looks like it was broken off with a sledgehammer. It's a clean break, which means it only took a couple hits at most."

"Well, I'm guessing that whatever they wanted was in here," Natalie said.

"Did you use your superdetective Spidey sense to come up with that?" Alex joked.

"Let's just figure out what these files are," she said.

I couldn't help but think it was a lot like when we started on the Baker's Dozen and went into the attic of the Flatiron Building for the first time. Once again we were digging through old file cabinets. What we found inside them began to paint a picture of M42 and what took place there.

Apparently, the fact that M42 was so far underground and secret made it too valuable to the government for it to just go to waste. When it was no longer needed to convert electricity for the trains at Grand Central, it was turned into a top-secret shelter for government spies. Immediately following World War II, the US government was worried about communists trying to infiltrate or attack New York City. M42 was repurposed to make sure that didn't happen.

"Listen to this," Alex said, reading from one file. "In case of an emergency, the agents were supposed to come here, where they could survive for up to three months. It can be completely sealed off from the outside world and has a kitchen, a communication center, and down the hall there's supposed to be a medical center with an operating room."

"What type of emergency were they worried about?" Natalie wondered.

"All sorts of them, going by what I've got over here," Grayson said from behind a stack of files. "These are all different plots or strategies that the government was worried the Russians might use."

"Do you think the Unlucky 13 might try one of them now?" I asked.

"I don't see how," he said. "They all seem useless."

"Why?" asked Alex.

"Most of them rely on technology that no longer exists," he said. "Like this one called 'Operation Alexander Graham Bell.'"

He held up a file folder.

"It explains how the Russians could knock out communication by disabling the switchboards at all the major office buildings in town, but nobody uses phones like that anymore. Cell phones are completely different."

He picked up another file.

"Or this one, which wonders how many communists you would need in New York City before it began to change public opinion in favor of the Soviet Union." He looked up at the rest of us. "The Soviet Union fell apart decades ago."

Something written on the cover of that file, however, caught Liberty's attention. "Wait a second," he said, turning his head to try to read it. "What's the name of that one?"

"Well, it was originally called 'Operation Red Tide,'" Grayson said. "But someone changed the name to 'Operation Blue Moon.'"

Liberty considered this for a moment.

"That's it," he said, suddenly anxious. "Blue Moon is why they put the scanner on the door. Read the first page."

Grayson didn't see the point, but Liberty was adamant, so he went along with it and started to read the report out loud. "'Although there is widespread distrust of the Soviet Union throughout the country, social scientists predict that if as few as ten to fifteen percent of the people in a big city such as New York were to change their opinion, it could start a ripple effect that would eventually grow into a majority.'"

Grayson looked right at Liberty.

"It's not going to happen," he said. "The Soviet Union doesn't even exist anymore. And if it did, ten to fifteen percent of the population of New York is about a million people. You can't turn a million New Yorkers into communists."

Liberty had a panicked look on his face, and it dawned on me why.

"No," I said, suddenly short of breath, "but maybe you could turn them into zombies."

22

Scars

A million people turned into zombies. Just the thought of it sent a chill up my spine. I sat there for a moment contemplating the mass zombiefi-cation of New York City when it dawned on me that I'd used the z-word in front of Liberty.

"I'm so sorry," I apologized. "I should never have said that."

"It's okay," he told me. "It's a terrifying thought, no matter what word you use."

Natalie considered it for a moment and asked, "Do you really think it's possible? Do you really think they could make a million people undead?"

"No way," Alex answered.

"Maybe not," agreed Liberty. "But that doesn't mean they wouldn't try to turn as many as they could. How many undead in New York would it take for acceptance to begin? That's what they're after most of all. Ever since the three wise men sentenced them to the dungeon, the undead have been looking to come up from the underground and gain acceptance among the living. They call it the Rise of the Undead."

And there goes another chill up my spine.

Grayson reached the end of the file and handed it to Natalie. "I don't know if this is important or not, but the last couple pages have been ripped out. The conclusions are missing."

"And by 'conclusions,' you mean . . . ?"

". . . all the ways the government came up with to stop the plan," he answered.

"Too bad," Natalie replied. "Those might have been helpful."

"Suddenly, this is sounding kind of ominous," I said.

Natalie looked at the torn pages in the back of the file, and then she turned to the cover, where someone had crossed out the original name and written in a new one. "What's significant about Blue Moon? What does it mean?"

"It's just an astronomical phenomenon," answered Grayson. "It refers to the second full moon of a calendar month."

"Or it can be a saying," I added. "Something that's rare only happens 'once in a blue moon.'"

Natalie shook her head and looked right at Liberty. "But it means something different to you, doesn't it? The instant you heard it, you were convinced that the Unlucky 13 were involved. Why?"

He hesitated for a moment, unsure whether or not he should share something with us. Then he took off his jacket, revealing a T-shirt with a Columbia University logo on it. He paused again and then pulled up his right sleeve.

"This is what 'blue moon' means to the undead." On his shoulder, there was a purplish blue scar about the size of a nickel and in the shape of a crescent moon.

"How'd you get that?" I asked.

He shook his head. "Nobody knows where it comes from. All we know is that everybody who's undead has one."

"Everyone?" I asked.

He nodded, and for the first time since I'd met him, Liberty seemed vulnerable. He quickly covered it up and put his jacket back on. We were all quiet for a moment as we considered what we'd discovered.

The thought that the undead might be planning something like Operation Blue Moon was chilling, but what we found next literally gave me nightmares. We ventured farther down the hall and came across the operating room that had been set up to care for the spies in case of an attack.

"Not exactly state-of-the-art," said Grayson as we surveyed the contents of the room. There was a rusty old examination table and medical equipment that was so outdated, it looked more like something you'd find in a horror movie than in a hospital. But in the corner of the room, there were two modern additions—a small refrigerator and a long freezer. Both were plugged in and we could hear their motors whirring.

Even though we all wondered what was inside them, none of us made a move to open either one. After a few moments, Natalie stepped forward. "Fine," she said. "Don't everyone be in such a rush to be brave."

I cringed as she reached for the refrigerator. She took a deep breath and opened the door to reveal three shelves of plastic bags like the ones doctors use to hold blood for transfusions. Only these didn't have blood in them. Natalie reached in and pulled one out. She held it up to the light of the refrigerator, and we could see that it held some sort of green goop. She offered it to Liberty.

"Know what this is?"

"We call it zombie juice," he answered as he took it from her.

"Hey, watch the z-word," I joked.

"I can say it," he answered with a smile. "You can't."

He examined the bag for a moment and added, "I've never seen it stored like this."

She put it back in the refrigerator and closed the door. Next she moved over to the freezer and put her hand on the lid.

"Call me crazy, but I have a feeling we're not going to like what we see in here."

(We'll call this an understatement.)

The instant she lifted the lid the light from inside the freezer flooded the room. It was closely followed by a hideous odor I recognized from my many days at the morgue. When I'm there, I also carry vanilla to fight the smell. . . . Unfortunately, I didn't have any on me now.

Natalie fought back the gag reflex and took a look inside. She leaned over and started to list off the contents. "Let's see. One arm, one lower leg, and a hand."

"Don't forget the finger," Liberty said, pointing into the freezer.

"Sorry about that," she said. "And one finger."

I stepped closer and peeked in. For some reason, this all seemed more upsetting than anything I'd seen in the morgue. Everything there felt hygienic and scientific. Here it was just gross. It didn't help to see the body parts resting in a mixture of ice and rock. I reached in and pulled out a piece of it.

"Manhattan schist?" I asked.

Liberty nodded.

Unlike Natalie and me, the boys didn't have morgue experience, and they were turning green.

"You wanna shut that?" Alex suggested.

Natalie started to close the lid, but I reached over to stop her.

"Wait," I said. "Check the shoulder."

She gave me a confused look for a second and then smiled when she realized what I meant. She bent over to get a close look at the shoulder.

"Yep," she said. "Blue moon."

"So we know that it belonged to someone who was already undead."

"Seriously," Grayson said, trying to talk and hold his breath at the same time. "Can you please shut that?"

Natalie let the lid fall shut with a thud. She was just about to make a joke when we heard a noise. Someone was activating the scanner to open the main door to M42.

In a flash, Natalie took charge and motioned us to follow her two doors down, where there was an empty office. We slipped inside and shut the door so that it was barely cracked open.

We heard the main door open and shut, followed by the noise of a squeaky wheel turning again and again. It reminded me of someone pushing an old shopping cart. We weren't sure how many people were out there, but we could hear at least two talking.

"You left the lights on again," the first voice said.

The second voice replied in the broken English that some of the undead use. It didn't make sense to me, but it must have to the first guy, because he laughed.

"If everyone knew how scared you are of the dark, they'd stop calling you the Enforcer."

Orville.

Orville was the Enforcer, and knowing he was out there made me try that much harder to remain perfectly still. We could only see a small sliver of the hall through the crack in the doorway, and when they walked past, we could see that the other person was Edmund. As if we hadn't already had enough fun with Big Red and Glass Face.

Luckily, they were too busy to notice us. They were

pushing an old hospital bed loaded with supplies that, unlike the ones in the room, were brand-new. Just enough light came in for me to see the worried expression on Natalie's face.

My pulse was racing, and it felt like my heart was beating all the way up in my throat. They wheeled the bed into the operating room, and the instant we heard the door slam shut behind them, Natalie bolted into action.

"Let's go now!" she said more as a command than a suggestion.

"What about them?" Alex asked. "Orville? Edmund? The operating room? Shouldn't we see what they're doing?"

She was determined. "No way! We're getting out of here before anyone else arrives."

She poked her head out the doorway and made sure everything was clear, then she motioned for all of us to follow her. We moved as quickly and quietly as possible down the hall and through M42, toward the main door.

"Can't we just go take a peek?" Alex asked, not giving up.

"The space is too confined," she said. "We'll get caught."

Alex shrugged. "So what? There are five of us and two of them. I like our odds."

"First of all, there are four of us," she said. "We've already asked a lot of Liberty to help us this far. He's a part of Dead City, and we can't ask him to fight the Unlucky 13. And second, we don't know how many more are on their way."

Alex was frustrated and went to say something, but she didn't want to hear it. She just cut him off and said, "This is not a debate. I'm in charge, and we're leaving. Now!"

I'd never seen the two of them so much at odds with each other. And I'd have to say it wasn't the ideal location for this to happen. Still, Natalie was not backing down, and after a few deep breaths, Alex relented. The mood stayed pretty tense as we snuck out of the shelter and then during the long climb back up the stairs. No one really talked until we reached Grand Central, where all the arms and legs we saw were actually attached to living, breathing people.

"Can I talk now without you pulling rank on me?" Alex asked, more than a little peeved.

"Sure," Nat snapped back at him.

"I don't understand what happened down there," he complained. "The Unlucky 13 is setting up a secret operating room a couple hundred feet underground. There are mysterious body parts in a freezer. There are new medical supplies being brought in. That sounds exactly like the kind of thing that we should investigate."

Natalie thought for a moment before responding, and I couldn't tell if she was regretting her decision or was just angry at Alex. Maybe it was both.

"I didn't think it was safe," she said. "There was only one door in and out of there, and we had no idea how many people were coming behind them. There was too much of a chance that we'd get trapped."

"What happened to Danger Girl?" he said, shaking his head in disbelief. "Normally, I'm the one trying to get you to be more careful. Didn't you risk getting arrested by marching in the Thanksgiving Day Parade just to sneak up to Ulysses Blackwell?"

"I did," she said, her voice rising. "And do you remember how that day turned out? I got slammed against a rock wall a couple times. Maybe it knocked some sense into me, because I will not let that happen to anyone else."

Suddenly, it made sense why she was being more cautious than usual.

"I'm sorry," Alex said. "I should have been more sensitive to that."

"It's okay," she replied, her mood calming down. "I just want us to be careful."

"I want that too," he said softly. "You made the right call."

There was an awkward silence, and I decided to break the tension, or at least try to, with a little humor. Not always my strong suit, but I'm getting better.

"Are we done fighting? Because I haven't had anything to eat since that kettle corn, and it's making me cranky. Oh, and so is the thought that the Unlucky 13 might be planning to unleash the zombie apocalypse on Manhattan."

"There's that word again," kidded Liberty. "Remember, I can say it and you can't."

"I'm so sorry," I said. "Do you guys see what the hunger is doing to me? It's making me insensitive."

Luckily, there was a cinnamon pretzel stand nearby, and I was able to calm the rumbling in my stomach long enough for us to say our farewells. Mostly, I wanted to make sure that Alex and Natalie were all patched up and that Liberty knew how much we appreciated his help.

"I promise we won't keep popping up unannounced," Natalie said to him.

"Good," he said. "But I'm more worried about Blue Moon. What are you all going to do about it? You're on the Baker's Dozen. You've got to take charge."

"The problem is that we don't really know what it is," Natalie responded. She turned to Grayson. "Any chance your big old computer can find a copy of that file without the final pages ripped out?"

Grayson smiled. "If it's out there, Zeus can find it."

"Zeus?" Liberty said, confused.

"He thinks his computer's a person," Nat explained.

Grayson went to deny this, but then stopped himself. "I kind of do."

We all laughed, and that helped improve the mood.

"I'll start him searching tonight," he continued. "But CIA documents are usually encrypted, so it could take a while for him to find what we're looking for."

"Don't take too long," Liberty said as we were about to leave. "I've been thinking about Marek missing his Verify. That's going to be huge. And it's going to happen at midnight on New Year's Eve, when a million people come to Times Square."

"A million people," I said, making the connection. "Sounds like the perfect time to try out Operation Blue Moon."

23

Time Management

One of the real drawbacks of being an Omega is that in addition to finding random body parts and uncovering plots for the zombie apocalypse, you also have to make time for regular life stuff like doing chores and finishing your homework. I caught a break (literally) when I fractured my hand and got out of some chores for six weeks. But the day the doctor removed my cast (or as my sister liked to call it, "the neon purple excuse machine"), Beth greeted me at the front door with a sponge and a dish towel and simply said, "You're it." Apparently, I'm now on dish duty for the rest of my life.

As far as homework goes, I returned from our terrifying adventure into M42 and was still coping with the above-mentioned "parts and plots" when I got another shocker. I glanced in my planner and realized that I had only one day to cram for a major math test, build a shoebox diorama of Edgar Allan Poe's "The Tell-Tale Heart," and write a three-page research paper about the War of 1812.

The last thing I needed was a couple of bad grades just as winter break was about to begin. Nothing says "home for the holidays" quite like being grounded the week of Christmas and New Year's. So I woke up Sunday morning determined to focus on nothing but schoolwork.

I started off by creating special playlists designed to provide the perfect mood music as I worked on each one of my assignments. Sure, this took a little while, but I was certain it would come in handy down the line.

Next, in order to relax both physically and mentally, I walked over to Astoria Park and shot baskets until I was able to make ten free throws in a row. This way I knew my mind and body were in perfect harmony with each other and therefore in the ideal state to do my best work.

Finally, I headed over to Grayson's to hang out . . . I mean, I headed over to Grayson's to use his computer for help on my research paper. Zeus really is the most amazing computer I've ever seen, and the fact that Grayson pretty much built it from scratch gives you an idea of how talented he is. The fact that after an hour of using it, I'd only written a paragraph and a half of my term paper gives you an idea of how disinterested I was in doing homework.

Everything made my mind wander. I was reading about the British Army invading Washington, DC, but I could only think about the undead invading New York. I was trying to compose the perfect topic sentence when I got distracted by an amazing aroma.

"What is that?" I asked. "It smells delicious."

"Latkes."

I crinkled up my nose as I tried to figure out what a latke was. "What are they?"

"Potato pancakes," he said. "My mom makes them every year for the first day of Hanukkah. They're delicious."

Grayson's family is Jewish, it was the first day of Hanukkah, and I was in the way. How very Molly of me.

"I'm sorry," I said. "Am I interrupting some special family time?"

"That's not until dinner," Grayson said. "How's your paper coming along?"

I looked up at him and smiled sheepishly. "Can't we just talk about the latkes and forget the paper?"

"That bad, huh?"

"I'm just having trouble building enthusiasm for the War of 1812," I answered. "It seems kind of insignificant in light of the impending zombie apocalypse scheduled for New Year's Eve. Speaking of which, has Zeus had any success in his search for the missing pages of Operation Blue Moon?"

(See what I mean? Easily distracted.)

"He had it narrowed down to two hundred million potential documents the last time I checked," Grayson said with a shrug. "As soon as he finds the right one, he'll e-mail it to me."

Something about the way he said it made me laugh. "You know, you really do treat Zeus like a person."

Grayson rolled his eyes.

"It's cool," I said. "Why don't you have him e-mail me, too? Or if he'd rather, he can just give me a call." I held my fingers up next to my face like a phone.

"You guys joke, but with his voice recognition software, he's totally capable of doing that," he boasted. "So don't be surprised one day when the phone rings and it's him. Let me show you."

Even though it meant postponing my homework, I slid over and let Grayson use the keyboard. He typed a quick command and started speaking to the computer.

"Zeus, notify Molly when Blue Moon search results are complete."

The computer answered in a perfectly human-sounding voice, "By text or e-mail?"

Grayson looked at me for the answer.

"Text is fine," I said with a laugh.

"Confirmed," said Zeus.

"Doesn't he need my number?" I joked.

"He already has all your contact information," Grayson said, pleased with himself and his computer.

"Maybe we should just have him solve our New Year's dilemma," I added. I turned to the computer and said, "Zeus, what are the Unlucky 13 planning to do about Blue Moon on New Year's Eve?"

Okay, so I was kidding, but Zeus didn't know that.

"Initiating search," he replied.

"Yikes," I said. "How do I tell him I was joking?"

"You don't," he said. "Zeus does not have a sense of humor. If he doesn't know the answer, he'll search for anything that has all of those keywords in it."

Before I could say anything else, the computer made a beeping noise and spoke once again. "One result."

We looked up at the main monitor and saw a freeze frame from a podcast. The funny thing is that we both recognized the person in the picture.

"Isn't that . . . ?"

". . . Action News reporter Brock Hampton," I said when Grayson couldn't place the name.

It was the same newscaster we'd eavesdropped on when he was reporting about the dead bodies discovered on Roosevelt Island and also the same one we'd seen on the Halloween broadcast talking about Jacob Blackwell's death on the subway. He was cheesy and over-the-top, which made him infinitely more interesting than the War of 1812.

"Click play," I said.

"Don't you have a ton of homework to do?" Grayson asked.

"I promise I'll get back to it in one minute and fifty-eight seconds," I said as I checked the time bar at the bottom of the video clip.

"Okay," he said.

The report wasn't really news. It was a list of special things Brock recommended to celebrate the holidays in New York. Most of it was obvious stuff like ice skating in Rockefeller Center or seeing the Christmas Spectacular at

Radio City Music Hall. But the one that caught our attention, and the one that had made it turn up in Zeus's search, was what he said about New Year's Eve.

"And what better way to celebrate the end of one year and the beginning of another than to spend New Year's Eve in Times Square," he said. "This year, I'll be there with live updates all night long, and there will be a special treat as it will be a rare blue moon. Don't be one of the unlucky ones to miss a blue moon in Times Square. It will be a night you'll never forget."

It stopped and we looked at each other.

"There's a blue moon on New Year's Eve?" I asked. "Is that weird?"

Grayson made a funny face as he thought about it. "A blue moon is just the second full moon in a month," he said. "It's almost always going to be the last day or two of the month, so that makes sense. But his phrasing at the end was really weird. Even for Brock Hampton."

He dragged the cursor back, and we watched the end again.

"Don't be one of the unlucky ones to miss a blue moon in Times Square. It will be a night you'll never forget."

"Didn't he say something about being unlucky when Jacob Blackwell's body was discovered?" Grayson asked.

I thought back and realized that's how I'd made the connection between Jacob and the Unlucky 13.

"He did. We thought it was strange then, too."

Grayson smiled, and then he started to laugh.

"What?"

"Check this out," he said. "Zeus, search Action News . . . Brock Hampton . . . unlucky."

A minute later, there were about a dozen podcast clips on the screen dating back to the beginning of the year.

Grayson smiled, and I had no idea what he was so excited about.

"This is how the undead find out," he tried to explain. "This is how they learn when and where to show up for Verify or get any other news about the Unlucky 13. They watch Brock Hampton."

We played through all of the clips, and in each one Brock used the word "unlucky" and reported on a public event. Some we already knew for sure involved the Unlucky 13. In addition to the report on the bodies discovered on Roosevelt Island and Jacob Blackwell's death on the subway, we found a story about Ulysses Blackwell's float in the Thanksgiving Parade.

"Brock's probably undead too," Grayson said. "What a perfect scam. We just think he's inept, but he's really sending secret messages to everyone in Dead City."

"Do you know what this means?" I asked.

"That we can track the Unlucky 13?" he said with a goofy smile on his face.

"Yes," I answered. "But I think it also means the undead really are planning on launching Operation Blue Moon on New Year's Eve."

Suddenly, his smile disappeared.

"You know, I think you're right."

Grayson dragged the cursor along the end of the time bar again, and we listened to Brock Hampton's final sentence one more time.

"It will be a night you'll never forget."

24

All Hands on Deck

We called Natalie and Alex and told them what we'd learned about Brock Hampton. Then it was time for Grayson to celebrate Hanukkah with his family and for me to stop talking about doing my homework and actually start doing it. I went home, shut myself in my room, and somehow managed to get it all done. It wasn't exactly my best work, but at least it didn't inflict any permanent damage to my grades. In fact, the only real harm done was to the night of sleep that got ruined by "The Tell-Tale Heart."

The story is about a murderer who hides his victim's

heart under the floorboards of his house. He then imagines that the heart comes back to life and beats so loudly that it drives him insane. It's not exactly the kind of thing you want to read just before you go to bed, right? So imagine reading it the day after you've looked into a deep freezer containing several random body parts. Needless to say, I wound up having various nightmares in which the hand, arm, leg, and finger we discovered all came back to life.

But here's the funny part: My sleeping brain was able to make a connection that my wide-awake brain totally missed. At some point during the night, it must have figured out where the body parts came from, because when I woke up, I just knew. I had suddenly put it together that Jacob Blackwell was missing an arm when his body was discovered on the subway, that Orville Blackwell lost the lower part of his leg because of the beat down Natalie gave him when we fought in the morgue, and that I chopped off Cornelius Blackwell's hand during that same fight. (The finger had fallen off it earlier.)

Theoretically, they could have been an entirely different arm, leg, hand, and finger, but I'm not a big fan of coincidence, and that seemed unlikely. The part that didn't make any sense to me, though, was why they were being preserved in the freezer. Jacob and Cornelius were both dead and would no longer have any use for their missing pieces, and Orville seemed to have transitioned quite well onto his artificial leg.

The lack of sleep caught up with me the next day, and by third period, I was dragging my way through school. I even nodded off during lunch. Lucky for me, Natalie snuck up from behind and poked me in the ribs, startling me so bad, I literally jumped out of my seat and screamed. Lucky because there might have still been a few kids left at school who weren't totally convinced I was a freak show.

"What'd you do that for?" I asked once I managed to catch my breath and regain my ability to form words.

"Sorry," she said. "It was just too perfect to pass up."

Alex and Grayson plopped down on the other side of the table and tried not to laugh too hard. Judging by the fact that everyone in the cafeteria was staring, it must have been pretty loud.

"How bad was it?" I asked.

"Not too bad," Alex said.

"No," added Grayson. "I think it's what you'd call . . . a *flinch*."

The reference to my flinch/scream on Halloween brought more laughter from the three of them. They all started digging into their lunches, and rather than defend my honor, I just laid my head back down and tried to use my backpack as a pillow.

"You've got to wake up, girl," Natalie said, poking me. Again. "Do you have your vanilla extract with you?"

"Why?" I asked. "You want to pour it on my head as a prank when I fall back asleep?"

"Tempting, but no," she answered. "I think we should save it for after school, when we're all going to the morgue."

Suddenly, I was wide awake and happy. I know that most people would think it's weird that I love going to the morgue so much. But I guess *most people* will just have to deal with the fact that the city's death house also happens to be my happy place. Go figure. The same could not be said for Grayson.

"The morgue?" he moaned. "Haven't we seen enough body parts this week?"

"You know, for a boy who likes to make fun of my flinching, you're a pretty big scaredy-cat," I teased. "The morgue's nothing. I've been hanging out there since I was seven years old."

"Yeah," said Alex. "And look how normal she turned out."

Okay, even I laughed at that one.

"Why are we going to the morgue?" Grayson asked.

"Because I contacted the Prime-O about Blue Moon and Times Square, and she wants us to go there and tell

Dr. H everything we know about it." She took a big bite out of her apple and added, "I think she's considering an all-Omega alert asking every Omega, old and new, to be in Times Square, ready to fight."

Just the thought of that was hard to fathom.

"How many Omegas would that be?" I asked.

"Maybe a hundred, a hundred and fifty," she guessed. "The Prime-O is the only one who really knows."

The addition of the morgue to my schedule and the possibility of an all-Omega alert gave me the boost of energy I needed to stay awake the rest of the school day. In fact, I was in such a good mood when we left the campus, I was willing to ride the Roosevelt Island tram. Normally, I avoid it, because, you know, it dangles from a cable above the East River. But I'd been trying to conquer my fear of heights, so when they all headed toward the subway station, I suggested, "Why don't we take the tram instead?"

They stopped in their tracks.

"The tram?" Alex asked. "The tram that runs from Roosevelt Island to Manhattan?"

"Yes," I said. "The tram."

"The tram that hangs two hundred and fifty feet in the air?" added Grayson.

"Listen, do you guys want to take it or not?" I asked as I started walking in that direction. "It'll be faster, and I know you like the view."

"You don't have to prove anything to us," Natalie said. "We can ride the subway."

"I told you guys that I'm working on my fear of heights," I said. "Besides, I have a new system."

"Does that system include an onboard anesthesiologist who is going to knock you unconscious?" Alex asked.

"You know, you really should try stand-up comedy if the whole science thing doesn't work out," I said.

"All joking aside," said Grayson. "What's your system?"

"If you must know," I admitted somewhat reluctantly, "I'm using . . . 'Endless Love.'"

Now they were really confused.

"'Endless Love' as in the eternal emotion of devotion and affection?" Grayson wondered aloud.

"No, 'Endless Love' as in the overly sappy and romantic love song from the 1980s." I told them I had come across it the day before when I was making my new playlists.

"You know how couples have a song?" I continued. "Well, 'Endless Love' was my parents' song. They danced to it on their first date and at their wedding."

Alex was trying to make sense of this. "And that somehow

makes it so you're no longer scared to dangle above the East River?"

"No, that's just an interesting part of the backstory," I said. "The reason it helps me is because it's exactly four minutes and twenty-six seconds long. That's precisely the same length as one ride on the tram."

"I'm sorry," said Alex as we reached the turnstiles. "It still doesn't make any sense to me."

"That's okay," I said, sliding my Metrocard through the reader. "It only has to make sense to me."

The big red tram car holds about one hundred people, and it was pretty full for our ride. We found a spot toward the back, and I grabbed hold of the strap that hung from the ceiling. The others were staring at me, curious as to how I was going to respond, but I was cautiously optimistic that it would work. Technically, it was just a theory. This was my first actual attempt.

"The one drawback is that I'm going to have to tune out of the conversation for the duration of the ride," I said.

I slipped my headphones on, and the instant I felt the floor beneath me rumble to life, I pressed play and cranked up the volume all the way. While everybody else was looking out the window at the approaching Manhattan skyline or down at the river below, I was in another world, listening to Lionel Richie and Diana Ross sing a duet and imagining my mom and dad slow dancing at their wedding. This way I had an idea of how far across we were without having to look. When the last note faded, I opened my eyes just as we touched down in Manhattan.

"Brilliant," said Alex, who was staring right at me.

I couldn't help myself when I responded, "I know I am, but what are you?"

Part of the reason I was so excited to go back to the morgue was that I hadn't been since the day we'd gotten suspended. I hung out there so much with my mom growing up, it felt like home and not seeing it for a few months was just odd.

My good buddy Jamaican Bob was working the guard's desk, and he flashed me a huge, toothy grin the moment he saw us. "Molly, Molly, in come free," he said playfully. "Long time no see. Wagwan?"

"That's Jamaican slang for 'What's going on?'" I explained to Grayson and Alex.

"Nothing much, just heading to an appointment with Dr. H," I answered as I put my backpack on the X-ray machine. "What's going on with you?"

"Well, now that I see you and Miss Natalie, my day is picking up," he said as he and Nat did their special six-step ritual handshake greeting.

"I don't think we introduced our two friends the last time we were here," Natalie said. "This is Alex and Grayson."

"Nice to meet you boys," he said. "Welcome to the morgue. You can call me Bob."

"Nice to meet you, Bob," Alex and Grayson said.

"And do you know what to call the dead bodies?" he asked them.

The exchanged a curious look with each other and then turned back to Bob.

"Corpses?" answered Grayson.

"No," said Bob. "You don't call them anything. They're dead, and they can't hear you anymore."

Natalie, Bob, and I all burst out laughing while Alex and Grayson shook their heads.

"It wouldn't be a trip to the morgue without one of Bob's bad jokes," I said to them as we all walked through the metal detector.

We took the elevator down to the bottom level and went to Dr. Hidalgo's lab. Right before we stepped inside, Natalie and I each swiped some vanilla extract under our noses to counteract the smell of the bodies. I offered some to the boys, and unlike our first visit they were smart enough to take me up on it.

"Is that your mom?" Grayson asked, noticing a picture on the wall.

"Yes," I said. "They put that up right after her funeral."

It was a nicely framed photograph of her in her lab coat. Underneath was a little plaque that read ROSEMARY COLLINS, FOREVER IN OUR HEARTS.

We told Dr. Hidalgo everything we knew about Blue Moon and the documents we found in M42. We even told him about the body parts in the freezer. We didn't think these were part of the same plan, but we knew that it would interest the coroner in him.

"They were stored in a mixture of ice and schist?" he said. "Fascinating."

Then we all moved over to his computer and watched some of Brock Hampton's news reports. By the time we were done, Dr. H was convinced.

"Well, looking at all of this, there are two things that I know for sure," he said.

"What?" asked Alex.

"First of all, the undead have something big planned for New Year's Eve, and we have to prepare for a worst-case scenario."

"And the other?" asked Grayson.

He looked at the four of us for a moment. "Whoever

picked you guys to work on the Baker's Dozen was pretty smart. What you've done is amazing."

Suddenly, even Grayson didn't mind being in the morgue so much. We talked a little longer, and Dr. H wrote down some notes to share with the Prime-O. He said that he'd get in touch with us once they came up with a strategy for New Year's Eve.

My lack of sleep had caught back up with me, but even though I was exhausted, I had one more thing I needed to take care of. I said good-bye to the others and took the subway up to Central Park. I walked by the zoo where I'd had my birthday party when I was five and stopped at the big clock with the dancing animals, where my mom had found me when I got lost. I had to reach her about something, and this is where she'd told me to leave her any messages.

I wrote it out on a piece of masking tape and stuck it right along the archway beneath the clock. It was written in the basic Omega code, which uses the periodic table of elements and read, "Mg/Cr O:Zn 53,58 16,19,85,68 4,90."

It wasn't about the undead. And it wasn't about the Omegas. I had promised to find a way for her to see my sister in person, and this was my plan.

Decoded, the message read, "12/24 8:30 Ice Skater Beth."

I knew Mom would know what it meant.

25

(A Not Particularly) Silent Night

Every Christmas Eve, Beth and I help my father with two projects at his station house. First of all, we're the servers for the big holiday feast he makes for all the firefighters who are on duty. We've known most of them forever, and it's like we're one big Italian-Irish-Polish-African-American family. They love to give Dad a hard time about anything and everything and are always looking for new ammunition. Beth gave them plenty when she told them about his mad scrapbooking skills.

"You should see how he makes the little ribbons," she said. "They're so delicate and pretty." Dad's captain, a giant man we've always called Uncle Rick, laughed so hard, he almost spit out his mashed potatoes.

Moments later, Dad walked in wearing his favorite apron—which says FIRE CHEF instead of FIRE CHIEF—and carrying a plate of turkey. Things got quiet, and all eyes turned to him.

"What's wrong?" he asked.

"I was wondering if you could help me with something," Uncle Rick said.

"Of course," he answered.

"I've been studying for my recertification test, and there's one thing I can never get straight."

"What is it?" asked Dad.

"Are you supposed to glue the pictures directly onto the scrapbook? Or should you use double-sided tape instead?"

The entire table erupted into laughter, and Dad turned two shades of red. He laughed too but quickly tried to change the subject. "So, did you catch that Jets game on Sunday? It was unbelievable, wasn't it?"

After the feast was done and all the leftovers were labeled and loaded into the refrigerator, we picked up the final donations to the station's toy drive to take them to a nearby homeless shelter.

"Michael, we left those last toys unwrapped," Uncle

Rick said to my dad. "'Cause we know you like to do the ribbon."

There were more laughs, and Dad gave Beth the stink eye as we headed out the door to go to the shelter.

It was my turn to choose family time, and since we were already going to be in the neighborhood, I decided on a night in Manhattan. The plan was to start with ice skating in Rockefeller Center and then to cross the street and go to midnight mass at St. Patrick's Cathedral.

This worked for me in so many ways. First of all, Midtown is beautiful during the holidays. There are lights and decorations everywhere, and I can't think of a better way to spend Christmas Eve.

Second, we'd learned from one of Brock Hampton's newscasts that midnight mass was going to be this year's Verify for Elias Blackwell. As my Omega team's lone Catholic member, I'd told the others that I would take care of getting a picture.

8. **Elias Blackwell**: Deceased

   Occupation: Lawyer

   Aliases: Elias Wollman, Elias Belvedere,

   Elias Olmsted

   Most Recent Home: Central Park

Role within the 13: Legal

Last Sighting: Fifth Avenue

Most important, though, I thought both of these activities gave me the perfect opportunity to include Mom as part of our holiday plans. There were plenty of places where she could watch us skate, and it would be easy for her to hide among the packed congregation in the cathedral. It wasn't exactly the same as being together, but it was as close as I could come up with.

As far as ice skating goes, the family falls into varying levels of ability. Beth is by far the most graceful. She's long and lean and took figure skating lessons when she was little. Dad played hockey in high school. He's the fastest, although it's not particularly pretty to look at. He also has a tendency to slam into people—and by "people," I mean me—like he's playing for the Stanley Cup. Meanwhile, I'm the worst. (I know, shocker!) I do what Dad calls "the Molly shuffle" and never stray more than a few inches from the safety of the side rail that wraps around the rink. Despite this lack of skill, I really enjoy going once or twice a year. I especially love skating at Rockefeller Center, where you're outside, surrounded by the city, and right beneath the massive seventy-five-foot-tall Christmas tree.

After going around for a few laps without spotting Mom, I began to worry that she didn't see my message. I was scanning faces in the crowd when Dad came to a hockey stop right in front of me. But because I was looking up instead of where I was going, I slammed right into him, and we had to scramble to keep our balance.

"Dad?!" I said, exasperated. "You almost tackled me."

"Tackling is football," he said. "In hockey, they call it 'checking.'"

"Well, I'll make sure to use the right term when I try to explain to the doctor how I broke my hand . . . again."

"Besides, you were the one who wasn't watching where you were going," he said. "Who are you looking for?"

Busted.

I stammered for a moment, trying to come up with an answer. "Hockey scouts," I said. "You know, from the Rangers or the Islanders, in case they're looking for a middle-aged player with good paramedic skills."

He smiled and waved a finger at me. "Don't forget the Devils," he said. "I could handle a commute into Jersey to play professional hockey."

We skated around together for a little bit and talked about nothing in particular. It was nice and relaxed. We both looked over at Beth, who was gliding effortlessly across the middle of the rink. Her bright pink jacket made it impossible to miss her. If Mom was up there somewhere, I'm sure she was glued to her every move.

"I want you to be honest with me about something," he said.

"Of course," I answered, nervous about where this could go.

"Did the thing about scrapbooking just slip out? Or did she sell me out on purpose?"

I laughed. "You know the answer to that one."

"That's what I figured," he said as he focused in on her. "I think it's time for a little revenge."

"You're not going to tackle her, are you?"

He gave me a frustrated look. "It's *check*, not tackle. How many times do I have to go over that? And of course not. I'm going to do something much worse than that. I'm going to embarrass her in front of those boys she's flirting with."

Sure enough, there were a group of high school boys watching her closely. She wasn't exactly skating with them, but she was staying close and maintaining just enough eye contact to keep them in her orbit, not unlike Jupiter does with its many moons.

Of course, Jupiter gets by with gravity and doesn't have to worry about a dad getting in the way. Ours skated right up and did his hockey-stop thing and almost knocked one of the boys to the ground. Then he started giving her encouragement.

"Looking good, Beth!" he said loud enough so I could easily hear him all the way on the edge. "You're burnin' so bright, you're going to melt the ice."

As if that weren't cringe-worthy enough, he turned to the boys and said, "I'm her dad. I used to play hockey in school, and I'm thinking about getting back into it. You know any leagues around here for guys my age?"

They were gone before he finished his question.

"Guess that's a no," he said, turning toward Beth. "It's just you and me now."

"All right, I shouldn't have mentioned the scrapbooking," she said. "I apologize."

"Good. Consider this your first Christmas present, a little gift I like to call sweet revenge," he said. "And, fitting for this weather, it's a dish best served cold."

The ice skating rink is located on the lower plaza of Rockefeller Center so that if you're on the street level, you look down on it. That's where I finally spied Mom on my next lap. She had tucked herself into a little spot near the Christmas tree and blended right in with the crowd. We locked eyes long enough so that she'd know that I'd seen her, and then she flashed me a smile that was the best present I could ask for.

As far as skating goes, I was starting to get the hang of it and actually went about fifteen feet without holding on to anything when I got slammed into the rail. Again.

"C'mon, Dad," I said, a little frustrated. "I get the point. It's called a *check*, not a tackle."

Except, when I turned around, it wasn't my dad.

She was a big, orange-and-yellow-toothed Level 3 zombie. She squeezed my forearm so tight, my fingers tingled, and she pressed me against the rail long enough so that she could sniff me like an animal and get my scent. I looked up to where I'd seen my mother, and she was already gone, no doubt on her way to rescue me.

Instinctively, I tried a Jeet Kune Do move, not thinking about the fact that they weren't exactly designed with ice skates in mind. Instead of kicking Zelda Zombie, I wound up slamming butt-first into the ice.

I looked up at her and considered my situation, which was quickly spinning out of control. I had to defeat a zombie . . . on ice skates . . . without attracting the attention of my father and sister . . . and without them seeing my undead mother. There was simply no way this could get worse.

Then it got worse.

As I struggled to get back up onto my skates, I saw none other than Natalie skating right toward me. And she was angry.

I braced to be slammed into the railing one more time. But Natalie being Natalie, she of course stopped with the precision of an Olympic ice dancer inches from my face.

"Who are you sending messages to?"

I didn't know who to deal with first: Natalie or the zombie. I checked to see that my dad and Beth were busy, so that was good, but I still had no idea where my mom was.

"What are you talking about?" I asked her.

Just then, Zelda Zombie took a wild swipe at me, and I had to duck to miss it, which almost made me fall again.

"I mean, haven't your secrets already gotten us in enough trouble?" Natalie asked.

"I still don't know what you're talking about, and I'm kind of in the middle of something here," I said as I scrambled to keep my balance. "So, either you can be more specific, or you can help me fight this girl without my dad and sister finding out."

"I saw the coded message in Central Park," she said. "It led me here to you. Who was it written for?"

While she was talking, Zelda grabbed me by the

shoulders and pushed. With skates on, I had no way to stop, and I just slid in reverse and braced to slam into either the ice or the railing. But someone caught me from behind and lifted me just as I was about to hit the ice. I looked up and saw her face.

"Mom," I said out loud before I realized it.

"Mom?" Natalie asked, looking at me and then at her.

With me in her arms, my mother had nowhere to go. She looked up at Natalie and smiled. "Hi."

Zelda, of course, was still determined to take me out, and as I looked back, I saw that my father and sister were about to turn the corner and come right at us.

"Beth, Dad, zombie," I said to the two of them, hoping they could do the math on their own.

Natalie thought for a second and nodded.

"Got it."

She did an axel or spin or whatever you call it and clipped Zelda in the backs of her thighs with her skate, knocking her right into my mother's arm. Mom spun around, taking Zelda with her, and by the time Dad and Beth got to me, everything appeared normal.

"We should probably head over to mass," Dad said. "It's going to get pretty crowded in there."

"Great idea," I answered.

I shuffled off with them, and neither had any idea that they were just a few feet from Mom. I'd just have to trust that she and Natalie could take care of Zelda and figure out a way to deal with Natalie knowing about Mom.

As far as church goes, I don't really love going to services all that much. I think my time in Catholic school kind of burned me out. But I've always loved midnight mass, especially singing all the carols. It started with "O Come All Ye Faithful" and ended with "Joy to the World," two of my favorites.

I managed to use my phone to sneak a couple of pictures of Elias Blackwell, who was actually one of the readers. He spent much of the mass sitting with the archbishop, and I couldn't figure out how he managed to get such a prominent spot. I later learned that he's a big donor to the church and often provides free legal services for some of its charities.

Apparently, Natalie and Mom were able to take care of everything, because halfway through the service, I got a text from Natalie that simply read, "All good." (I also got a dirty look from my dad for checking a message during church.) And as I was walking from my seat to communion, I saw my mother in the crowd. I was able to pick a line that went right by her, and as I did, I put my hand on the pew in front of her. She put her hand on mine and said, "Merry Christmas, Molly."

"Merry Christmas, Mom," I said as I held her hand for an instant longer.

She was crying, but I'm pretty sure they were tears of joy.

26

Countdown (We Return to Where the Story Began)

T he week between Christmas and New Year's was surprisingly quiet. Once I got the pictures of Elias Blackwell at St. Patrick's, there wasn't really anything else for us to do Baker's Dozen–wise. And as for Blue Moon and New Year's Eve, we were still waiting for instructions to come from the Prime-O.

Christmas Day started in Queens with Beth and Dad; moved on to Brooklyn, where Grandma and Grandpa Collins called me Little Molly Bear about a thousand times; and ended in northern New Jersey, where we had dinner and opened presents with Grandma and Grandpa

Bigelow and slept in the same house where my dad grew up. That night, it snowed, and we spent the next morning sledding down a hill on cookie sheets. It was a total blast.

A couple days later, I was finally able to meet up with Natalie and talk about my mom. Her parents were having some sort of ritzy dinner party so she snuck out and met me at a pizza place close to her house.

"I'm guessing your big secret is that your mother is undead," she said.

I nodded, unsure what her mood was like, but I was relieved when she smiled.

"That certainly explains a lot. When did you find out?"

"On the bridge with Marek," I said. "She saved my life."

"Wow," Natalie said, taking it all in. "Just wow."

I could tell she was running through the time line of events in her head. "Was she the one who picked us for Baker's Dozen?"

"Yep."

"I can understand why you didn't tell us."

I was ready for there to be a "but," some kind of angry admonition, but there wasn't. She just said, "Well, you don't have to worry about me telling anyone. Your secret's certainly safe with me."

Then the most unexpected thing happened. Natalie started to cry. She really didn't want to, but the more she tried to stop it, the worse it got.

"What's the matter?" I asked.

At first she said it was nothing. But I pushed and after she thought about it for a long while she said, "I'm going to tell you a story that I've never told anyone."

"I think we're beyond the point of keeping secrets from each other."

She smiled and nodded her agreement as she still tried to keep her emotions under control.

"A few years ago, we were at the country club, and I was horseback riding while my parents played golf. It's something we'd done a million times. Just a normal Saturday. Except this time, I got thrown from my horse and was knocked unconscious."

"Oh no," I said.

"It was terrifying. Everything turned out okay, but for about an hour it was bad. I've never been so scared in my life. And the thing that helped me through it, the thing that gave me strength, was the look of concern on my father's face as he checked to make sure I wasn't having any side effects from the concussion. I'll never forget that look. I remember thinking it must be the same look he gives his patients before he operates. It just made me feel safe and cared for."

"That's . . . really nice," I said.

"I'm not finished," she said, trying to keep from crying more. "Later, as we rode back into the city, I found the scorecard from their game . . . and when I looked at it . . . I realized that they finished playing their round before they came to check on me."

I couldn't believe this was possibly true. I stared in stunned amazement for a moment. "You don't know that," I said, hoping I was right. "They might have already been done by the time they found out you'd gotten hurt."

"No," she said, the tears falling again. "I asked them, and they admitted it. They weren't even embarrassed by it. They said that they knew I was in good hands and explained that Dad was having one of the best rounds of his life. So they played the last two holes, and *then* they came to check on me."

She looked right into my eyes, and her expression broke my heart. I didn't know what to say.

"Your mother literally came back from the dead to help you, and my parents couldn't even be bothered to interrupt a golf game."

We sat quietly for a while until the server brought our

pizza. We hung out for a few hours, and by the time I left her, she was actually laughing and having a good time. But it still broke my heart, and I would never have guessed that the girl with the luxury life on Central Park West would envy anything about my cramped Queens existence?

Our New Year's Eve assignment came on December 30. We were told that there was an all-Omega alert due to a credible threat from the undead against the living.

Even though we knew it was coming, there was something about reading it that took my breath away. There was no telling how big this could get. Our team was assigned to the Rockefeller Center subway station and told to separate and follow any Level 2s heading for Times Square.

That's how I wound up tailing the hipster couple I told you about at the beginning of the story. Now it's about an hour and a half before midnight, and I'm still barricaded in right behind them. I've thought back through everything that's happened since Halloween, but it still seems like there's a missing piece that I'm just not seeing.

I'm not exactly sure where the other members of my team are, but we have been texting back and forth, trying to lighten the mood with some humor.

According to Liberty, Marek's Verify won't officially begin until the stroke of midnight. Once he doesn't show, however, there's no telling what will happen. The real fear is that when everyone starts counting down the final sixty seconds of the year and the crystal ball goes down the flagpole, it might also be signaling the beginning of an all-out war with the undead. At that point, one of the other Unlucky 13—my money's still on Ulysses—could step forward and claim control of Dead City. Then, in his first act as mayor, he could order Operation Blue Moon into full effect.

My phone buzzes, and I check to see which teammate is sending me a text. I laugh out loud when I read that it's not from any of them. Believe it or not, it's from Zeus. Grayson had instructed his computer to alert me when it finished its search of the CIA database, and it's doing just that.

"Hi, Molly. Here is the report. Zeus."

Okay, there aren't any abbreviations or emoticons, so it doesn't feel like an text from an actual person, but it's still pretty impressive. The band that's currently onstage isn't particularly good, so I decide to go ahead and read the file.

According to the CIA, the mission's original plan was to see how many New Yorkers would have to be converted to communism in order to change public opinion of the Soviet Union. Our worry is that the undead are using the same strategy, except rather than converting people to communism, they're planning on changing them into zombies. Now Zeus has sent me the CIA's conclusions, which had been ripped out of the file.

I start to read them, and they aren't at all what I expected. Apparently, the experts concluded that it would be completely impractical to convert so many people to anything. This makes me smile. Hopefully, the undead reached the same conclusion, and we're all just out here with nothing to worry about.

But as I continue to read, I come across a passage that's alarming. The experts also concluded that it would be much easier to reach the same goal by simply converting a few powerful people who could help shape public opinion.

If the Unlucky 13 wanted to do something like that, they would have to infect community leaders and turn them into zombies. I mull this over for a while. I think back to the first Verify, when we saw Ulysses Blackwell riding in the Thanksgiving Day parade. He spent hours standing next to the chief of police. Then I consider the most recent Verify at St. Patrick's. Elias Blackwell spent the entire mass sitting with the archbishop. Suddenly, it starts to make sense.

I pull a folded sheet of paper out of my pocket and

look at the schedule of events for the night. At midnight, the ball is going to drop when the mayor of New York pushes a plunger on the stage.

I finally see the puzzle pieces that I've been missing.

The chief of police. The archbishop. The mayor.

The undead aren't infecting a million New Yorkers; they're getting revenge against the three wise men. The actual men are different, but their positions are still just as powerful today as they were in 1896. If those three men become undead, the Unlucky 13 will be able to start building the power it has always craved. I start to hyperventilate.

At midnight, one of the Unlucky 13 will appear on the stage with the mayor of New York. When he's there, he'll become the new leader of Dead City and will infect one of the most powerful people in the country.

Unless I can stop him first.

27

Two Zombie Mayors

As soon as I figure out what's happening, I send a text to the rest of my team and tell them that we need to have an emergency meeting in front of the New York Public Library. I pick the library because we need to find one another as fast as possible, and it's the closest landmark I can think of that might not be overrun by tourists. I also send a quick text alerting Dr. H so he can pass the info along to the Prime-O. I'm not going to make the same mistakes I've made before. I don't have time to give many details, but I want them to know that we're on the move.

Getting out of my spot in the crowd turns out to be harder than I expect. Luckily, I'm small enough that I'm able to push and squeeze and crawl around and under all of the people and barricades until I finally break free of the mob. As soon as I do, I start sprinting toward the library. Even though the temperature has dipped into the thirties, I'm running so hard that I start sweating inside my jacket.

When I get there, I find Alex anxiously pacing back and forth between the two lion statues that stand in front of the library's entrance. He hurries down the flight of stairs and comes right up to me. His eyes are full of frustration as he says, "You know we've lost our spots, right?"

"Yes, I know," I answer, trying to calm him like it's no big deal.

"I was right in the middle of the crowd next to some mean-looking Level 2s, and I had a good view of the stage," he continues. "Now that place is gone for good. I can't get back there."

"It's okay," I assure him. "That's not where we need to be."

"Really? Because I thought the whole plan was for all the Omegas to be spread throughout the crowd in Times Square so that we can fight back once the zombies start to attack."

"They're not going to attack the crowd," I tell him, hoping that I've got this figured out correctly. "They're only going to attack one person."

Before I can elaborate, Natalie comes up from the corner of Fifth and Forty-Second, taking long angry strides, with Grayson a few yards behind her, trying to keep up.

"What's the emergency?" she demands, her mood mirroring Alex's. "Because I was in a good position to take out four Level 2s. Four of them. And now they're all alone, with no one to stop them when they get the order to attack."

Oddly, in the middle of all this, it dawns on me that even though they're mad about it, they still came. All of them came. They trust me that much, and that trust means everything to me. Of course, now I have to prove that I deserve it.

"Stop complaining and listen to me!" I exclaim, hoping a little intensity will quiet them for a moment. "We need to change the plan because the undead aren't going to attack the people in the crowd."

"And why do you say that?"

I hold up my phone with the text from Zeus. It's not like they can read it with me waving it around, but it's the only prop I have.

"Because Operation Blue Moon isn't about infecting

as many people as possible," I try to explain. "It's about infecting a small but important group of people. Three, to be exact."

"Three?" says Alex. He's confused, but he's starting to listen. "Why three instead of a million?"

"It started back at Thanksgiving," I say. "That's when they infected the chief of police. Then on Christmas Eve, they infected the archbishop. Tonight, they're planning to infect . . ."

". . . the mayor!" Grayson says, putting it all together.

I point directly at him. "That's exactly right. Tonight they want to infect the mayor." (I admit that having someone else reach the same conclusion makes me feel a whole lot more confident.)

"But why?" Natalie asks, shaking her head. "What does that give them?"

"It gives them power and revenge," I answer.

"What revenge?"

"Revenge against the three wise men," I say. "Revenge against the men who ruined their lives."

"But the three wise men are long dead," Alex responds.

"Maybe so, but the positions that they held are still important and powerful," I remind him.

"And if the current people in those positions are

undead," Grayson continues, "it will bring that power and influence to the Unlucky 13. Both above- and below-ground."

"Think about it," I say. "Think about what it would be like if there are two zombie mayors. One for New York and one for Dead City."

Just the concept of that quiets us for a moment as we contemplate the dangers that could result from such a situation.

"That would be very, very bad," Natalie says, coming around. "But what can we do? It's already after eleven. That means we've got less than an hour to warn the mayor, who happens to be surrounded by a million screaming people at the biggest party in the world."

"Do we have any idea where he is?" I ask. "Has anyone seen him tonight?"

"I did," Alex says. "He was already on the stage, doing a television interview."

The stage was built right at One Times Square, the old skyscraper that used to be home to the *New York Times*. This is where the crystal ball has dropped every year since the newspaper started the tradition in 1907.

"And that's where he'll be at midnight when he presses the plunger to make the ball fall," Grayson adds.

"Is there any way we can charge the stage?" I ask, even though I'm pretty sure I know the answer.

"No," Alex replies with a chuckle. "In addition to the million people in the crowd, there are also police everywhere. We'd never get within a hundred feet."

"We've got to think outside the box," Natalie says as she starts to pace. "We've got to be creative."

"I know," offers Grayson. "Let's play One Foot Trivia."

Natalie looks at him and frowns. "That's not what I meant," she moans. "This is serious."

"I *am* being serious," he says as he lifts one foot in the air and begins to balance. "We always answer the hard questions when we play One Foot Trivia. Maybe it will help us find the right answer if we play now. Who's with me?"

"Not me," says Alex, shaking his head. "Games aren't going to help us any."

I go to shoot down the idea too, but then I think about the fact that everyone trusted me when it seemed like an unwise thing to do. I figure the least I can do for Grayson is return the favor.

"I'll play," I say to him. "I'll try anything that might help."

"Thanks," he says. "The category is Times Square."

I lift my left foot and look him right in the eye. "Go."

"How do you get to One Times Square without actually going through Times Square?" he asks.

I wobble for a moment and start brainstorming. "Helicopter?"

"Won't work," he replies. "We couldn't get one, and even if we could, we wouldn't be able to navigate through all the buildings and land there."

"Come on, guys," Natalie says frustrated. "You're wasting time."

"I don't see you coming up with any answers on two feet," Grayson says defensively. "Keep trying, Molly."

Natalie and Alex have had enough. They turn away and start pacing again, but I'm sticking with it. As I try to keep my balance, I wobble some more and almost put my second foot down. I have to bend over to keep from falling, and when I do, I get a glimpse of a newspaper vending machine. Something about it catches my attention. It's the *New York Times*. Suddenly, my brain races back to the last flatline party we crashed, and much to my surprise, I come up with the answer.

"You go underground and enter through the giant room with all the old printing presses left over by the *New York Times*!" I practically shout, thrilled with the realization. "Just like we did when we crashed the flatline party."

The others all turn to me with amazed expressions.

"That would work," says Alex. "That would absolutely work!"

Natalie goes over to Grayson and gives him three quick high fives. "I take it all back. I freaking love One Foot Trivia."

"I know," he says, beaming. "It's amazing. There's nothing it can't do."

When we crashed the flatline party, we got there by using the trapdoor inside of the Times Square subway station. But Alex points out a problem. "Times Square station is closed on New Year's."

"That's right," says Natalie. "I forgot about that."

Grayson smiles.

"But Bryant Park is open," he says. "We can go underground there and sneak over to Times Square through the walkway that connects the stations. And since the station's closed, there won't be any people on the platform when we want to use the trapdoor."

No one says another word. There's no time. We just start racing toward the Bryant Park subway station.

"What time is it?" I ask between heavy breaths as we reach the entrance.

"Eleven eleven," Natalie answers without breaking stride. "We've got forty-nine minutes."

The Power of the Press

There are a couple of transit cops we have to avoid, but since they're watching a small television broadcasting the New Year's celebration, we're able to slip by them and move unnoticed into the Times Square station. We hurry past the darkened Spanish music shop and down two flights of stairs before we make it to the southbound platform. Just as Grayson predicted, there's not a person in sight. Alex lifts the trapdoor, and we silently disappear down into Dead City.

"I forgot how ugly this place is," Natalie says as she scans the abandoned tunnels that run beneath the station. There's trash and graffiti everywhere. And lots of rats. I can't see them, but I can hear them scurrying along by my feet.

I try to block the image of the megarodents out of my mind and ask, "Does anyone remember the way?"

"We followed the music from the party," Alex says. "Unfortunately, there's not a flatline party again tonight."

"No," Natalie says with a grin. "But there *is* music. Listen."

We listen for a moment, and sure enough, we can make out the faint echoes of a rock-and-roll song playing in the distance. It's coming from the band performing live on the stage in Times Square. All we have to do is follow it, and it will lead us right where we want to go.

"Remember, we're not the only ones who'll be coming this way," Alex reminds us. "Any zombies coming from Dead City are going to take this same route."

We try to move quickly while still being careful, but it's not easy because the tunnel is so dark. We all hold our phones out so that they cast some light ahead of us, and we keep following the music, which gets louder as we get closer.

"There it is," Grayson says, pointing toward a doorway ahead of us. "I remember that sign."

Sure enough, there's an old metal sign with faded lettering that reads NEW YORK TIMES.

"I remember it too," I say. "We're almost there."

Once we reach the door, we pick up the pace and hurry through a series of hallways as the music continues to get louder and louder until we step out into the massive printing press room.

"Found it!" I say with a proud swagger as Natalie and I share a fist bump.

The room is two levels high, and even though there are security lights hanging from the ceiling, they're barely bright enough to illuminate such a large area. The lights sway back and forth and cast twisted shadows across the hulking presses.

"Eleven thirty-five," Natalie says, checking the time on her phone. "We've only got twenty-five minutes to get up to the stage and warn the mayor."

"Yeah . . . about that," a voice says from in front of us. "I think we're going to have to say . . . no on warning anybody."

Just then a bank of much brighter lights turns on and floods the area. I have to blink a few times for my eyes to adjust, but when they finally focus, I see none other than Ulysses Blackwell standing in our way. The banker who once wore ugly polyester suits is now dressed for success in an expensive business suit, a red power tie, and a thick charcoal gray overcoat.

"It looks like someone's running for mayor of Dead City," I whisper to the others.

It would be one thing if Ulysses was alone, but he's flanked by a rather imposing collection of Level 2 thugs, including his bodyguard cousins Orville and Edmund.

"Eleven," Alex says, giving us a quick headcount.

"Which is much more than four," Ulysses interjects. "You see, I work with numbers, so I can tell you that the math doesn't really work in your favor. That puts you in a bit of a rough spot."

"He's right," I say to the others. "Any suggestions?"

Alex barely moves his lips as he whispers a one-word answer. "Stall."

At first I don't get it, but then I realize what he's thinking. If we can keep Ulysses busy past midnight, we can keep him from appearing at Verify and taking over Dead City. I think back to when I had to stall the security guard at the Flatiron Building. Like it or not, it turns out that I'm the team's "staller." The trick is to talk first and talk fast to try to control the conversation.

"You know, we've never formally met," I say, stepping forward. "You're Ulysses, right?"

"Nice try, but I don't really have time for chitchat." He turns to his cousin. "Orville, you want to take care of this?"

Orville flashes a terrifying grin of crooked orange-and-yellow teeth, many of which are broken in half. He starts to limp my way. But he's not really coming at me. Instead, he's focused on Natalie behind me. He no doubt wants to finish what he started the last time they fought. I know that if that happens, Alex will jump in, and there'll be no stopping the battle from playing out. With eleven against four, we'll be finished in minutes, and Ulysses will have plenty of time to get to Verify.

I decide to try option number two.

"And you're Orville," I say, trying to intercept him. "You know, we don't need to fight. There's no reason why the living and the undead cannot work together. All we have to do is . . ."

Orville doesn't even wait for me to finish. He just reaches down, picks me up, and throws me against a rusted old printing press. My body makes a pair of loud thud noises. The first is when I hit the press, and the second is when I crumple to the floor.

As much as I'd like to lie on the floor and moan, I see Alex start to make a move toward him, and I bounce back on my feet.

"No!" I call out forcefully, trying to keep the fight from beginning. "Orville and I are just negotiating. I made a suggestion, and he rejected it. Now I'm going to make a counteroffer."

I'm more than a little woozy, but I somehow manage to stagger toward him. I check my watch, there are still twenty-two minutes left until midnight. I don't know how many times I can take getting thrown through the air. But at the current rate we're going, that would take a lot more *thuds*.

"Seriously," I say, offering Orville a handshake. "We can do this peacefully."

Once again, Orville picks me up and holds me high in the air. Then, just as he's about to throw me for a second time, a woman's voice calls down from above.

"I would suggest putting her down . . . gently," she says. "Consider that a warning."

All eyes move to the metal catwalk that winds through the printing presses on the upper level.

"Is that who I think it is?" gasps Grayson.

"Yep," I call to him. "It's my mom."

"But how . . . ?"

"It's kind of a long story," I say, cutting off the questions for now.

"I'm sorry," Ulysses interrupts, turning to my mother. "My cousin Orville's not much of a talker, but I'm curious:

What kind of warning are you giving us?"

"A simple one so you'll be sure to understand it with your tiny zombie brains," she says with badass confidence. "If you mess with my daughter, you mess with me."

Ulysses laughs and goes to say something else, but she cuts him off and continues talking.

"And if you mess with her team, you mess with mine."

Suddenly, a host of past Omegas start to step out from the shadows and behind the printing presses. I don't know if it's my mother's actual team or just people she pulled together from all the Omegas in the crowd, but there are eight or nine in total. I recognize some of the faces, like Dr. H and Liberty, but am totally surprised by others like Jamaican Bob, the security guard from the morgue. None, however, is more surprising than the man who walks right up to Orville: a man who hasn't left Roosevelt Island in decades.

"Dr. Gootman?!" I say, surprised.

"Actually," he replies, "for tonight, I prefer Milton."

Orville drops me to the floor (thud number three, but still a welcome development), and he turns to face the cousin he hasn't seen in more than a century.

"Hello, Orville," Milton says. "Edmund, Ulysses. It's been a long time."

"You have no business being here," Ulysses thunders as he storms over to him.

"Well," Milton replies, refusing to back down, "you have no business trying to hurt these children."

The two of them stand face-to-face for a brief but tense moment until Alex walks over and interrupts by tapping Ulysses on the shoulder.

"By the way," he says, "when you add in the new people, the math turns out to be pretty good for us."

Without hesitation, Alex throws a punch that sends Ulysses sprawling across the floor and then moves right at Orville.

"You're pretty good at beating up girls," he says. "But how are you with guys closer to your own size?"

Orville and Alex grab each other, and within seconds, the entire room bursts into a rumble. It's like nothing I've ever seen before as little pockets of action erupt all around me. I see my mom leap down from the catwalk and start throwing punches at Edmund while Liberty joins Alex in fighting Orville.

Ulysses gets up from the floor, and the moment he realizes that he's lost control of the situation, he tries to make a run for it toward Times Square. He's cut off by Grayson and Jamaican Bob, who make a rather unique pair. Neither of them is actually fighting much, but they still manage to trap Ulysses in between two printing presses.

I'm so swept up in the action that's unfolding in front of me that I don't notice the zombie who comes up from behind and knocks me into the printing press. (That's one thud too many.)

"You got lucky there," I say, rubbing my jaw as I get up. "But that luck's about to change."

I charge at him and pull out some of my best Jeet Kune Do moves. He has no idea how to fight back and after three fake outs, he leaves me an opening, and I land a punch that knocks him out cold. I'm about to go in for the kill when I hear it.

The scream belongs to Natalie, and it's bloodcurdling.

I leave the zombie and race over to where she is. I find her unconscious on the floor, one trail of blood trickling from her nose and another from her mouth.

"Natalie!" I cry out.

I look and see that Edmund is the one who had done this. He's sneering down at the two of us, his red hair wild and his eyes burning orange. I get up to fight him, but I never get the chance. Instead, Alex swoops in from out of nowhere and dismantles him with the most furious attack I've ever seen. It could be a commercial for

Krav Maga. Edmund never even gets a single punch off.

When the flurry ends, Alex steps back, and Edmund's dead body falls to the floor in a heap.

Both of us rush back to help Natalie, but Dr. H and my mother are already tending to her. They're both excellent doctors, so that's a relief, but I can't tell how serious her injuries are. She keeps opening and closing her eyes, trying to focus.

"What time?" she asks.

It seems like an odd question, but I look at my watch and answer, "Eleven fifty."

Finally, her eyes find me and open wide. She's fading in and out but manages to say two words: "Verify . . . Milton."

It takes me a moment to put it together, but when I realize what she means, I begin to nod. "That's brilliant, Natalie. That is brilliant."

"What?" asks Mom.

I look around and see that most of the zombies, including Orville and Ulysses, have run into the darkness of Dead City. With Edmund dead, the only member of the Unlucky 13 left is Milton.

"If we can get Milton to Verify," I say to her, "he'll take charge of Dead City. He'll become the new mayor."

Realizing that I've gotten the message, Natalie flashes a blood-smeared smile and passes out.

"Is she okay?"

"Yes," Dr. H assures me. "She just needs to rest."

"You take him," Mom says to me. "Get Milton on the stage."

I look down at my best friend, bleeding and unconscious. I think about her parents playing golf when she was injured. "I can't leave her," I say. "Someone else can take him."

"We're doctors, Molly, we'll take care of her." I realize she's right.

"Dr. Goot—I mean, Milton—we better hurry." I turn to the boys. "Come on, we might need some help."

The four of us race out of the printing press room and then out of One Times Square. The stage is right in front of us, and as we're heading there, I try to figure out a plan of attack.

"How do we do this?" I ask. "How do we make sure people see him?"

We scan the stage and are almost blinded by the lights of a row of television cameras.

"Action News reporter Brock Hampton," says Grayson. "He's the one who confirms all the Verifies. He said he'd be up here broadcasting all night long. Even a reporter as bad as he is will jump at the chance to have the first-ever interview with Milton Blackwell."

"Perfect," I say. "Let's find him."

There are only a couple of minutes left before midnight, and the crowd is buzzing with excitement.

"There he is!" Alex calls out, pointing toward one of the reporters doing an interview. "He's interviewing the mayor."

I try to give Milton instructions as we hurry across the stage. "All right, you've got to do an interview with Brock Hampton."

"But the undead don't know who I am," he says, raising his voice so that he can be heard over the all the noise.

"They don't know what you look like," I reply. "But they *definitely* know who you are. Just look into the camera and tell everyone that your name's Milton Blackwell and see what happens from there."

We reach the interview site right as Brock is finishing with the mayor.

"It's really going to be an amazing year," the mayor says. "And so much of the credit belongs to my good friend here."

The mayor motions to someone off to his side and asks

him to join him on camera. The man moves awkwardly, as though he's not fully coordinated. The mayor puts his arm around him and talks directly into the camera. "Here's someone that you're really going to hear from in the upcoming year. He's amazing, and his name is Marek Blackwell."

As he steps into the light from the camera, I see that it really is Marek. He seems bent and broken, but there's no denying that it's him. The blood drains from my face, and I feel like I might faint.

"Now, I've got to take care of some business," the mayor says with a laugh as he walks off camera.

There's less than a minute until midnight, and the entire crowd is counting down the final seconds of the year. Alex, Grayson, and Milton all look to me, and I have no answer. I have no idea how Marek is standing before us.

"Do you have anything you want to say?" Brock asks him as he puts the microphone in front of him.

"I will in a few seconds," Marek replies as the countdown reaches ten.

He turns our way and seems genuinely surprised that we're there. He smiles a wicked grin, and I see that his teeth have yellowed even more.

Then I notice his left hand. It's missing the ring finger,

just like his brother Cornelius. I see that he has trouble using the hand, and it dawns on me that it isn't just like Cornelius's hand. It actually *is* Cornelius's hand. As the countdown reaches five, he tries to pose for the camera, and I can tell that his leg is bent in an unnatural direction.

I think about the body parts we discovered in the freezer and realize what's happened. He has Cornelius's hand . . . and Orville's leg . . . and Jacob's arm. I turn to the others.

"They've rebuilt him," I say, trying to be heard over the crowd. I look right at Milton and shake my head. "They've rebuilt him with the body parts of your brothers and cousins."

The countdown reaches zero, and a million people scream, blow horns, cheer, and make noise.

Calmly on the stage, Marek looks right at me and winks. Then he turns to the camera and says, "Happy New Year," verifying his still-strong hold on the world of the undead.

DARK DAYS

For Fiona,
who heard Molly's voice right from the start

Acknowledgments

I am forever indebted to the people who have helped bring the Dead City books to life. It is a debt that I will try to repay with everything from cupcakes to friendship. First on the list are the amazing people at Simon & Schuster. There is the dynamic duo of Fiona Simpson and Mara Anastas, and their Omega team of Nigel Quarless, Kayley Hoffman, Jessica Handelman, Karina Granda, Kara Reilly, Emma Sector, Carolyn Swerdloff, Teresa Ronquillo, Michelle Leo, Candace Green, Anthony Parisi, Kelsey Dickinson, Sara Jane Abbott, and the remarkable Lauren Forte. (Go Mets!)

Those of you who think Molly Bigelow is too good to be true have obviously never met my agent, Rosemary Stimola. Like Molly, ro stimo is straight out of Queens and possesses the perfect blend of tough and tender, brilliant and brave. I'm just glad she decided to rep authors instead of fighting zombies. (Although I wouldn't be surprised if she does that on the side.)

I also want to thank the people who take the time to read the books and share them. They are teachers, librarians, and readers like Brady, Bayla, and Peyton, who stay up late at night because they just have to know what happens next. You are my rock stars.

And finally there is my family, who makes everything possible. They inspire and encourage. They read and edit. They live and breathe on every page. The love that exists between the characters in the books is a reflection of the love they give me every day.

Ωmega Today! Ωmega Forever!

You're Probably Wondering
What I'm Doing in Jail ...

My dad says you should always look on the bright side of things, and normally that's great advice. Like when I had to have my tonsils out, but I also got to eat as much ice cream as I wanted. Or when our weekend on the Jersey shore got canceled, but we ended up going to a Yankees–Red Sox game instead.

I was even able to find a bright side on the first day of school when a maniac zombie attacked me in the Roosevelt Island subway station. (It led to a group of amazing friends and a secret life watching over the world of the undead.) But lately the bright sides in my life have been harder to find.

I mean, what's good about the evil lord of the zombies—you know the one I was totally sure I helped kill—surprising everyone by reappearing even more powerful than ever? Or how about Omega, the secret society I'm a member of, the one that's responsible for maintaining the balance of power and peace between the living and the undead, having to suspend all activity because our security has broken down and the lives of everyone I care about have been endangered?

Then there's my current situation.

Right now I'm sitting on a bench in the middle of Central Park, which sounds kind of bright side-y until you realize the bench is in a holding cell in the Central Park precinct of the New York Police Department.

That's right. I, Molly Bigelow, Little Miss Goody-Two shoes who's never gotten so much as an after-school detention, am in jail. If you can think of anything positive about this, I'd love to hear it; because when my dad gets here, I'm pretty sure he's going to focus on the *getting arrested* part.

I can already hear the conversation: *Gee, Molly, when you said you were going to the Central Park Zoo, I assumed the animals would be the only ones behind bars. You're grounded for life!*

I was charged with disturbing the peace because I jumped

into the water at the sea lion exhibit. I did it in a moment of desperation, and while it seemed like a good idea at the time, I now realize it was a flawed plan.

First of all, the water was way colder than I expected. I'm talking like-a-brain-freeze-but-all-over-your-body cold. And secondly, I didn't think about the fact that I'd be stuck in wet clothes for the rest of the day. Being arrested is bad enough, but being arrested in waterlogged jeans, wet underwear, and sneakers that squish every time you take a step is even worse.

The officer who arrested me was actually pretty nice about it. Her name is Strickland, and instead of putting me in handcuffs, she just led me to her squad car, no doubt confident that if I made a run for it she could easily track me down by following the wet shoe prints.

Once we got to the precinct I was fingerprinted and had my mug shots taken. (By the way, remind me not to jump fully clothed into a pool right before next year's yearbook pictures. The wet look and I are not a good match.) Next I got to use my one phone call to let my father know where I was. That was pleasant. I'll skip the specifics, but the conversation quickly went from "Are you all right?" to *"Are you insane?"* Then I put him on with Officer Strickland.

They talked for a minute or two, and at one point she

even laughed. Afterward she told me that she had some good news and some bad news. The good was that once my father arrived I was going to be released with a warning.

"Although," she added, "if you ever want to go back to the Central Park Zoo, you owe them about fifty hours of volunteer work."

"I guess that's fair," I replied.

"It will probably involve a shovel and animal poop."

The thought of that made me cringe. "Is the animal poop the bad news?"

"No," she laughed. "That's still part of the good. The bad news is that your dad can't pick you up until his shift is over, so you're going to have to spend a few hours in the holding cell."

That's where I am right now, sitting on a wooden bench in the holding cell with a small puddle of water around my feet. The cell is about twice the size of my bedroom, and, for the moment at least, I'm alone. I guess that's technically a bright side; but I think when the bright side is that your jail situation could be worse, then things are still pretty bad.

So why did I do it? Why did I climb up on the rail and cannonball into the freezing water? Was I escaping a crazed zombie? Was I protesting the treatment of animals held in captivity? Was I just being . . . *stupid*?

No, no, and no. Although, the stupid one is debatable. The truth is that I was *trying* to get arrested, and not just anywhere. I needed to get arrested in Central Park so that I would wind up in this precinct, in this holding cell. In that sense I was successful. I just should have figured out how to get here without the wet underwear. (And without the whole shoveling of animal poop thing.)

If the rest of my plan works—and judging by my recent success rate, that's iffy at best—things are going to get a little crazy before I walk out of here. (Actually, if the plan works I won't be *walking* out, but I'll save that part of the story for later.) And if it doesn't work, well, then I'll have a lot of explaining to do when my father arrives. Either way, I'm not going anywhere for a while, so I might as well try to explain how it all happened. Who knows, maybe I'll notice something I missed the first time around. Something that will help me pull this off, because if I don't, New York might have front row seats for the zombie apocalypse.

It all started just a few blocks from here on a January morning when I was too stubborn to come in out of the snow. . . .

The Hamlet Suite

The biggest lie perpetrated by the Christmas card industry has nothing to do with flying reindeer and everything to do with snow. Greeting card snow is festive and fun, but real snow is just cold and annoying. That's why all the people on the sidewalk were hurrying to get out of it. Well, all of them except for me.

"You know we could always wait inside," Grayson said, pointing toward the lobby with his head so he didn't have to take his hands out of his pockets. "I hear they've got electricity and heat."

"If we go in the lobby, Hector will send us up to the

apartment; and I don't want to go to the apartment without Alex," I replied. "I want us all to go together. Like a team."

Hector was the doorman in Natalie's building, and like all good doormen on the Upper West Side he didn't let you just hang out in his lobby. He kept you moving, especially when the weather was bad. That meant we had two options: stand in the snow and wait for Alex, or go up to Natalie's apartment and start without him.

"Let's just give him five more minutes," I said. "If he isn't here by then, we'll go anyway."

It was the first time we were visiting Natalie since she'd been released from the hospital. The first time the four of us were going to be alone since the epic failure that was New Year's Eve, when Marek Blackwell came back from the dead and Natalie wound up in intensive care.

Even though I was excited to see her, a part of me was dreading it. I felt responsible for everything that happened and wouldn't have been surprised if she blamed me too. I was worried that our friendship, which meant everything to me, was about to come to a sudden end. That's why I wanted to wait for Alex. I needed all the friendly faces I could get.

"Is everything all right?"

A police officer was asking us. He was tall, over six feet,

and had broad shoulders. His name tag said PELL and he was curious as to why Grayson and I didn't have enough sense to get out of the snow.

"We're fine, officer," I replied. "We're just waiting for a friend."

"Well, don't wait too long or you'll catch cold," he said. "Or even worse, your ears might freeze off."

"That would be bad," I said with a laugh. "I like my ears right where they are."

He gave me a strange look and replied with sudden seriousness, "I'm not joking. Do you have any idea what that looks like?"

I traded a bewildered glance with Grayson before I asked, "Do I have any idea what what looks like?"

"What it looks like when your ears freeze off?" he said. "It's terrible. Let me show you."

With no further warning, Officer Pell reached up and peeled his left ear off the side of his head. A pulpy green membrane hung from it as he dangled it in front of my face and started laughing. That's when I noticed his orange and yellow teeth and realized that in addition to being one of New York's Finest, he was also one of New York's Deadest. He was a Level 2 zombie with a twisted sense of humor.

I let out a scream and that only made him laugh harder.

Between the snow, the traffic, and everybody rushing along the sidewalk, no one even noticed. You gotta love New York.

"Let this be a warning," he said as he waved it by the lobe, pieces of zombie ear goop flinging past our faces. "We've got our eyes on you."

He thought for a second and chuckled before adding, "And now I guess . . . we've got our ears on you too." With that, he flicked the ear right at me and it stuck to my jacket.

I did a hand flap dance for a couple seconds until I knocked it off, and by the time the ear hit the ground, Officer Pell had disappeared into the crowd.

Grayson stared at me in stunned silence before stammering, "Did that really just happen? Did that really just happen?"

I nodded rather than answer, worried that if I opened my mouth my lunch might spew all over the sidewalk.

The encounter was disturbing, and not just because his ear stuck to me. (Although, by no means do I want to diminish how disturbing that particular detail was.) Looking back, it seemed as though he'd been waiting for us, like he knew we were coming. There was also the ominous threat that we were being watched. But worst of all was the idea that there was a Level 2 zombie on the police force.

An L2 has no conscience, no sense of right and wrong. Combine that with the power of an NYPD badge and it's a terrifying mix.

Alex was oblivious to all of this when he finally arrived a couple minutes later. He gave us a funny look and asked, "What's wrong with you two? You don't look so good."

I still felt sick to my stomach, so I signaled Grayson to answer instead. He filled Alex in on what happened and by the time he was wrapping up the ear throwing portion of the story, I'd finally calmed down enough to talk.

"Are you sure he was a cop?" Alex asked. "And not just a security guard in a similar uniform?"

"Positive," I said. "He was NYPD."

"What does he look like?"

"Let's see, he's tall and spooky and . . . oh, yeah . . . he only has one ear," I snapped, even though Alex didn't deserve it. "Imagine Van Gogh but in a police uniform."

Alex ignored my attitude and kept asking questions. It's the type of focus that makes him a great Omega. He wanted to run through everything while it was still fresh in our minds. "Did he have a precinct number on his collar? A name tag under his badge?"

"I didn't notice any number," Grayson said. "But he did have a name tag. His name is Pell."

"That's good," Alex replied. "That's real good."

That's when I remembered another detail. "He also had a patch on his left shoulder. I noticed it when he turned to rip his ear off his head."

"What did the patch look like?"

I closed my eyes and tried to picture it fully in my mind. "It was red and had a dog on it, maybe more than one dog. I'm not sure. I got kind of distracted when he started peeling off his ear."

"A lot of the squads have their own patches," Alex said. "He could be with one of the K-9 units. I'll check with my uncle Paul to see if he can help."

Uncle Paul was a longtime police officer and a real father figure for Alex, whose actual father had almost no involvement in his life.

"Now for the most important question," Alex continued. "Are you two going to be okay?"

To be honest I wasn't sure. I took a deep breath, and despite my typical dislike of snow, the flakes falling on my face were cool and soothing. I just stood like that for a moment and then I said, "Yes, I'm okay."

"Me too," added Grayson.

"Good, because we're about to visit someone who's recovering from a serious zombie attack, and I don't want to get her worked up about another one. You saw her in the hospital. She's nowhere near full strength."

"You're right," I said.

"Should we even tell her about it?" asked Grayson.

Alex thought about this for a moment. "We'll see. For now let's just play it by ear."

It took me a second to get the joke.

"Oh . . . *by ear* . . . that's so funny," I said sarcastically.

Alex tried to keep from laughing as he said, "Just checking to make sure you still have your sense of humor."

Although Natalie lived on the twelfth floor, her family had temporarily moved downstairs so their apartment could be remodeled. Considering it was already the nicest apartment I'd ever seen, I couldn't imagine how they were improving it. But as someone who hates heights I was more than happy with the change. We took the stairs to the second floor and knocked on the door to 2-B.

"Check it out," Grayson said, pointing to the number. "Hamlet."

Alex gave him a curious look. "What do you mean Hamlet?"

"2-B," he said, as if this were obvious. "'*To be* or not *to be*, that is the question.' It's, like, the most famous line in the play."

"Have I ever told you that you're weird?" Alex asked.

"Yes," replied Grayson. "Frequently."

Natalie opened the door, but only part way, and peered out at us. Her face was pale and she had a confused, almost sleepy look in her eyes.

"Hey, Natalie, it's so great to see you up and out of the hospital bed," said Alex.

She cocked her head to the side and squinted as she studied him more closely. "Do I know you?"

It was devastating.

"Of course you do," he said. "I'm Alex. We've been friends for years. This is Grayson and Molly."

She studied our faces but didn't seem to recognize any of us. I was heartbroken. I think we'd assumed that since she'd been released from the hospital, she was doing better. Now we just stood there silently as we tried to think of what to say.

That's when she laughed.

"You guys are such suckers. You should see your expressions," she said as she finally opened the door all the way. "Welcome to the Hamlet Suite."

"That's not funny," Alex bellowed. "That's not funny at all."

"Ooooh," I mocked. "All of a sudden it's Mr. Comedian who doesn't have a sense of humor."

"By the way, did you hear what she called the apartment?" Grayson asked as he gave Alex a little poke in the shoulder. "The *Hamlet* Suite."

"That only proves that you're both weird," he replied.

I think it was the first time I'd laughed in weeks.

Once she stopped pretending she had amnesia, Natalie seemed more like her normal self, although her voice was still weak. We had gourmet hot chocolate that her mom special ordered from a café on the Upper West Side (It was ridiculously fancy, with shaved peppermint bark and marshmallow chunks, but it was beyond delicious) and we sat down in a family room that looked oddly familiar.

"Why do I feel like I've been here before?" Grayson asked, looking around.

"Because you kind of have," she said. "This apartment is ten floors directly below my apartment, so the layout is identical. My parents had everything brought down and put in the exact same place. Every room, every wall, every everything looks the same. Well, everything except for my room."

"Why's that?" I asked.

"It looks a little less bedroom and a little more intensive care unit," she said. "I guess it's an advantage of having surgeons as parents. They have access to lots of medical equipment."

She tried to play it off as a joke, but I could tell that it bothered her. In a weird way, though, it made me happy. Natalie's parents rarely made time for her in their busy lives. Maybe now, when she needed them most, they were finally coming through.

"Speaking of your parents," Alex said, "are they around?"

"Nope. Dad had to go to the hospital to check on a patient, and Mom is running some errands," she replied. "We've got about thirty minutes until she gets back, so let's start talking."

That gave us just enough time to talk all things Omega. It also let me tell them what I'd wanted to say since the stroke of midnight on New Year's Eve.

"Before we talk about anything else, there's something I need to say."

I took a deep breath and just tried to blurt it all out at once.

"I'm so sorry. I'm so breathtakingly sorry. Everything's my fault. I didn't just think Marek was dead, I was certain of it. I saw him fall from the top of the George Washington Bridge. There was no doubt in my mind. You all believed me . . . and I was wrong."

"Yeah," said Natalie. "About that. How did he survive the fall?"

"They rebuilt him," replied Alex. "They used body parts from his brother and cousins to make him whole again."

"Okay," Natalie said. "There goes my appetite for the rest of the day."

Then she looked right at me.

"So how is that *your fault*?"

It turned out she didn't blame me. None of them did. I don't know why. I mean, I still blamed myself, but it was an incredible relief.

Once I'd gotten my apology out of the way, we tried to fill in the blanks for Natalie about what happened that night. Not surprisingly, her memory was incomplete.

"How much do you remember?" asked Alex.

"Let's see," she said, straightening her posture. "I remember Molly calling us all to the steps in front of the library. And I remember the showdown in the old printing press room. There were a lot of bad guys and not so many good guys until Molly's mom and her Omega team arrived. Then there was a big fight, and that's where it starts to get fuzzy."

Grayson asked, "Do you remember who you were fighting?"

Natalie nodded. "I think it was the big redhead, right? Edmund."

"That's right," I said. "It was Edmund."

"So what happened to him after he was done with me?" she asked.

We exchanged glances for a moment before Grayson answered.

"Alex happened to him," he said.

"It was unbelievable," I added. "Edmund didn't even get to throw a punch. Alex saw what he did to you, and he unleashed the wrath of krav maga and killed him on the spot. And when the others saw what he did, they all pretty much ran away."

The memory of this quieted us all for a moment, until Natalie looked over at Alex and said, "Always my hero."

"That's funny, because a few minutes ago you didn't even recognize my face," he joked. They shared a look and it was pretty great. It was a look of total trust and friendship. During their time in Omega they had each saved the other too many times to count.

"So what's the plan?" she asked, breaking the moment.

"What do you mean?" I replied.

"Marek's back and Dead City is more dangerous than ever," she said. "How is Omega responding?"

The boys and I shared a nervous look, and then I turned back to Natalie.

"We're not," I said. "Omega has terminated all activity."

Through the Looking Glass

At first Natalie couldn't believe what she was hearing. She scanned our faces, looking for any glimmer of a smile or some other hint that we might be joking.

We weren't.

"Omega has terminated all activity?" She said it like it was some foreign phrase. "What does that even mean?"

"Exactly what it sounds like," Alex replied. "Everything and everybody is shut down."

"For how long?"

He shrugged. "Indefinitely."

We told her about an emergency team meeting we had with Dr. Hidalgo, during which he informed us that Omega had been too exposed. All Omegas past and present were in danger, and as a result the Prime O and the executive council had no other option but to enact what he called a "lockdown."

"He said there's even a chance it might never come back," added Alex.

"You had a team meeting?" she asked. "Without me? The team captain?"

"You weren't exactly in condition to meet," Alex reminded her. "Besides, you were sort of there."

"Yeah," I said with a half laugh, remembering how it all transpired. "We had to have it in the hallway right outside your room."

"And why is that?" she asked, still perturbed.

I looked at Grayson to see if he wanted to tell her, but he avoided eye contact, so I explained it instead. "Because Grayson refused to leave the hospital until you regained consciousness."

"Dr. H was not happy about it," Alex added in a total understatement. "He wanted a more private setting, but Grayson would not budge. G said he'd quit Omega before he'd leave. He stayed in that lobby for thirty-seven hours."

Natalie went to say something, but she stopped herself. This bit of information caught her completely off guard, and all the anger building up inside her drained in an instant. When she still couldn't think of the right words, she stood up silently, walked across the room to Grayson, and buried him in a hug.

I didn't always know where I fit in; but, with regard to the rest of my Omega team, Natalie was the brain, Alex was the muscle, and Grayson was always the heart.

That was the end of our Omega conversation. For the rest of our visit we just hung out and talked about less stressful things, like the foods Natalie planned to devour once her doctors cleared her to eat whatever she wanted. Spicy noodles and pepperoni pizza were high on the list. We made a list of where we wanted to go together. It was nice.

By the time we left, Nat looked worn-out and I worried that we'd stayed too long. On my way to the door, though, she pulled me aside for a private conversation.

"Any word from your mother?"

"Not since that night," I replied.

"Have you looked at the clock by the zoo?" she asked.

My mother and I had a secret spot near the Central Park Zoo where we left emergency messages for each other. Natalie had discovered it just before Christmas.

"I check every day," I answered. "But there hasn't been anything there."

Natalie thought this over and said, "Keep looking. I'm sure she'll reach out to you soon."

I nodded as though I agreed, but in truth I was more hopeful than confident.

"And when you do see her," Natalie continued, "tell her I said thanks. I don't remember much about New Year's Eve. But I remember her taking care of me. I'm pretty sure she saved my life."

"I'll tell her," I said. "Now you better get some rest."

I gave her an awkward hug, awkward because I still felt guilty about everything. The fact that my mother saved her life was a reminder that I had a hand in endangering it in the first place.

Alex, Grayson, and I walked to the subway station together. Or rather, Grayson and I walked together while Alex followed a few feet behind us, keeping an eye out for any evil one-eared police officers.

"Be safe," Alex instructed us when we split up to head to different platforms—he was going uptown toward the Bronx, while Grayson and I were riding toward Midtown.

"We will," I said. "I promise."

Grayson had been particularly quiet during our visit, and as we rode the C train I tried to figure out what was bothering him.

"So are you going to tell me what's the matter? Or am I going to have to guess?" I asked. "I think Natalie looked good."

He nodded. "Yeah. She did. Better than I expected."

"Then why do you seem so disappointed? That should make you happy."

"It does make me happy, but . . ." He hesitated for a moment before saying, "With that cop today. Did you see what I did when he ripped off his ear and threatened us?"

"No," I said. "What did you do?"

"Exactly," he replied. "I didn't do anything. I just stood there. Frozen."

"What are you talking about?" I said. "Neither of us did anything."

"Alex would have," he said. "It's just like Natalie said, he's always the hero. I don't know. I guess it's not in my DNA. I just don't have the . . . heroic gene or whatever it is."

"Did you miss the part where she hugged you and cried because she thought *you* were a hero?"

Grayson sighed and shook his head. "I'm loyal . . . but

Alex is brave. There's a huge difference. One you admire and one you depend on."

"No," I said. "You're not just loyal, you're also crazy. Because only a crazy person could draw that conclusion."

He shrugged.

We were almost to Thirty-Fourth Street, where I had to switch trains, so I didn't have much time to straighten out his thinking. That's when I remembered something Natalie told me right after I'd been attacked in the Roosevelt Island subway station.

"The very first day you and I met, when that L2 attacked me, do you know what Natalie said about you?"

"That I was good with computers?" he said lamely.

"No. She warned me not to underestimate you. She said that you were amazing, and she was right. So don't underestimate yourself. You're a total rock star, Grayson. Natalie knows it. Alex knows it. And I certainly know it. You should know it too."

He gave me a begrudging smile, although I couldn't tell if I had really solved the problem or just softened it for a moment.

The subway doors opened and I gave him one last look before I got off the train.

"Say it with me," I told him. "Rock star."

He laughed. "Go catch your train."

"Rock star," I said again as I exited onto the platform.

I lingered there to watch him pull away. I felt bad he thought that way, but I guess it wasn't that different than me blaming myself.

Ten minutes later I caught the train going to Queens. Except, I didn't ride it all the way home. Instead, I got off at Fifth Avenue so I could check for a message from my mother.

I had downplayed it when I was talking to Natalie, because I figured she had enough to worry about, but I was really nervous about my mom. The moment Marek returned, Mom was in danger. She should have run away right then, but she stayed with Natalie until the ambulance arrived. That gave the undead plenty of time to set a trap for her somewhere underground. Every day that had gone by without a message made me worry a little more that she hadn't been able to escape them.

Luckily, it had stopped snowing and the afternoon sun was peeking out from an otherwise gloomy sky. That meant there were people walking around the park, and I didn't stand out as much.

The Delacorte Clock is just past the entrance to the

zoo. It sits on a row of archways, and features sculptures of animals playing musical instruments. (My favorite is the penguin drummer.) Every hour and half hour the animals dance around as a nursery rhyme chimes.

It was twelve thirty and the clock was playing "Row, Row, Row Your Boat" when I slipped in alongside a group of tourists who had stopped to admire it.

I breathed a huge sigh of relief the moment I saw the message. It was a series of numbers written on a piece of masking tape stuck to the middle arch. If you weren't looking for it, you'd never notice it. And, even if you did see it, it wouldn't make sense unless you knew the basic Omega Code, which uses numbers that correspond with the periodic table of elements. They were:

13/53/58 49 74/8/60/68/57/60 8/10/61

Since (unlike my friends and me) you probably haven't memorized the periodic table inside out, I'll translate. The numbers correspond to the following elements: aluminum, iodine, cerium, indium, tungsten, oxygen, neodymium, erbium, lanthanum, neodymium again, oxygen again, neon, and promethium. If you write out all of their elemental symbols you get:

Al/I/Ce In W/O/Nd/Er/La/Nd O/Ne Pm

Alice's Adventures in Wonderland was one of my mother's favorite books. She used to read it to me at bedtime when I was little, and sometimes we'd visit the sculpture of Alice right there in Central Park. I was certain that's where Mom would be waiting for me at one p.m.

That was thirty minutes away, which gave me just enough time to take a couple of false turns and backtracks to make sure no one was following me. Considering my run-in with Officer Pell, I wanted to be extra careful.

It's funny how something you haven't thought about in ages will unexpectedly come back to you as clearly as if it happened yesterday. That's what happened as I was cutting back along a pathway and suddenly remembered my mother's favorite line from the book.

"It's no use going back to yesterday, because I was a different person then."

She loved that line and liked to quote it to me. She thought it was so smart, but at the time I didn't really understand why. Now, though, it made total sense. As much as I sometimes wish that I could go back and erase the mistakes I've made, I really am a different person now than I was just a few weeks ago. And I'm a very different person than I was before I became an Omega.

The sculpture of Alice is bronze and about twice the size of an actual person. It features her sitting on a giant mushroom, surrounded by the White Rabbit, the Cheshire cat, the Dormouse, and the Mad Hatter. One thing I've always loved about it is that you're allowed to climb up onto the mushroom and sit next to her.

I walked up to the sculpture, leaned against it, and waited. About five minutes later I saw my mother walking toward me. She wore black jeans, a black leather jacket, and a Yankees cap. She crossed the ground quickly, taking long, fast strides.

"Are you okay?" she asked with urgency as she neared me.

I nodded and she gave me a huge hug.

"I'm so sorry about what happened on New Year's," I said near tears.

"It wasn't your fault, baby. I thought he was dead too."

I started to cry. Not big tears, but tears. I was over-whelmed by everything that had happened. Right then, she wasn't a zombie killer, she was just my mom.

"What about you?" I said, clearing my throat. "Are you okay?"

"Yeah," she said. "There were a couple close calls, but I'm fine."

For a moment I just sat there and looked at her. Finally I asked, "Why did you put up the message?"

She gave me a perplexed look and asked, "What message?"

"On the Delacorte Clock. The message to meet here, right now."

Her expression changed as she considered this.

"I thought *you* put that message up," she replied, a sense of uneasiness taking over us both. We were being set up by someone who knew our code. Our eyes widened and we started to run away, but it was too late.

Marek Blackwell was walking right toward us.

Row, Row, Row Your Boat

My mom's first instinct was to shield me from Marek. She stepped forward to move directly between us, and subtly adjusted her stance so that her knees were bent and she was up on the balls of her feet, ready to fight.

"Now, now, there's no need for that," he said, holding up his hands in mini surrender. "This is a peaceful meeting."

One thing about Marek that always surprises me is his wardrobe. He doesn't dress like you'd expect an evil dark lord of the underground to dress. He wears sharp clothes like a successful businessman. This was a snowy Saturday afternoon, and while most of the people in the park were bundled up in jeans, sweaters, jackets, and knit caps, Marek wore a dress shirt, a black tie, and a dark burgundy overcoat with a fur collar. He even had on a fedora. If you randomly saw him in a crowd, he'd be the first person you'd trust. Let that be another reminder that you really can't judge a book by its cover.

"I have no desire to hurt either one of you," he continued.

He moved pretty well for a guy who'd been rebuilt with body parts from dead relatives, although he still had the limp I'd noticed on New Year's Eve.

"What if we want to hurt you?" asked my mother.

He stopped walking and looked right at her. "Well, then that's when these gentlemen would get involved."

He motioned to a group of four policemen who had taken strategic positions nearby. Each one wore the same red shoulder patch that Officer Pell had worn earlier in the day. This new partnership between Marek and the New York Police Department was troubling.

"I may not be at full strength," he said as he exaggerated his limp for a couple steps, "but these young men are a different story."

He stopped a few feet from us, maintaining a safe distance.

"Then what do you want?" asked my mom.

"What? No pleasantries? No hello? No 'So glad to see you didn't die when I threw you off the George Washington Bridge'?"

"You mean when you were trying to kill my daughter?"

He flashed a politician's smile. "You make a good point. I probably deserved that."

"I'll ask again," she said, agitation in her voice. "What do you want?"

"Peace," he answered. "I want peace. For more than a century the Omegas have hunted my friends and me, and I want that to end. Actually, let me rephrase that. I *insist* that it end. Don't let my current physical condition mislead you. If there's one thing New Year's should have demonstrated, it's that we are stronger than ever. I am building a better life for my people, and that can't happen as long as you continue to attack and harass us."

"You're forgetting something," said Mom. "You and I have been doing this for a long time. We have a history together and I know you can't be trusted."

"We have been doing it for a while," he said. "And I think we've both suffered greatly as a result. That's why I wanted to make this offer directly to you. If you and I can come to peace with each other, everyone else should be able to do the same. I think it's time we lead by example."

"So what's your offer?"

"We go our separate ways. It's as simple as that. My people will hurt none of yours and your people will leave us alone. All I'm asking is that you make your *lockdown* permanent."

I didn't like the fact that he used the same term, "lockdown," that we used in our private meetings. Somehow he was getting information from inside Omega.

"And what do we get in return?" Mom asked.

"You get to live normal lives," he said. "You get to be with your husband and your daughters. You no longer have to hide out in abandoned sewers and send secret messages with codes on clocks. My brother Milton can even go back to teaching children about science instead of training them to kill the undead."

"The brother you vowed to kill no matter what?" said Mom.

Marek thought about this for a moment. "That was more than a century ago," he said. "I'd like to think that our family could get past our differences and reunite."

Mom did not look like she believed any of this. "And if we don't accept your offer?"

"That would be a shame," he said. "Because from this point on any Omega activity will be considered an act of aggression, and we will respond with all-out war. War like you've never seen. Trust me when I say you don't want to face an undead army. Think about this: We knew you were coming to Times Square. We know about the lockdown. We even know the code you use to talk with your daughter."

He motioned toward the Alice sculpture and smiled.

"If you try to plan anything to get in our way, I'll know about that, too," he added. "And then it will be just like the Queen of Hearts . . . Off with your heads."

Rather than wait for a response, he turned and walked away. I noticed his limp didn't seem as bad as before, and I wondered how much of it had been an act. The policemen joined him and escorted him down the path away from us.

My mother watched silently until they were out of sight, and then she turned to me. I could tell she was thinking through everything.

"What are we going to do?" I asked.

"Exactly what he told us to do," she said. "They know too much about us and we have no idea what they're up to. We have no choice but to remain on lockdown."

"Undead army," I said, repeating the two words that had most caught my attention.

"How terrifying is that?" she said.

I looked up at my mom and studied her face for a moment. "Do you think he meant it?"

"Meant what?"

"That we could go back to normal? That our family could be together? Because . . . that would be incredible."

She closed her eyes for a moment before answering. "That *would* be incredible. But he'll never let it happen. He's planning something. Something huge. I don't know what it is. But I know he's not planning on us being happy. And I guarantee you that he won't be satisfied until I'm dead."

"If he wants you dead, then why didn't he just attack you here and now? They had us outnumbered."

"That's a good question," she said. "I think it's because there's someone he hates even more than me."

It took me a second to figure out whom she was talking about. "His brother! He hates Milton. So you don't think he meant it when he said they could go back to being brothers?"

"No, I don't. I think this meeting had two purposes. He wanted to deliver his threat, but more importantly he wanted to have someone follow me to see if I'll lead him to Milton's hiding place."

"You think there's someone here in the park watching us?" I asked.

"I don't think it," she said. "I know it."

"Wait," I said. "Don't tell me yet. Let me see if I can figure it out."

I tried to be inconspicuous as I scanned the people in the park, looking for anyone who might be spying on us. It took me about a minute.

"I see him," I said. "Red jacket on the bench, reading a book."

"Very good," she replied. "How do you know?"

"I recognize him from earlier," I explained. "He was sitting on a bench by the clock when I found the message."

"I don't think he's alone, though," she said. "Check out the woman pushing the baby stroller. She's already walked by twice. She never checks on her baby, but she makes eye contact with the man on the bench every minute or two."

"So what's our plan?"

"They want to find a secret underground passageway," she said. "Let's make them think that's where we're going."

My mother started walking and I followed right behind her. We walked right past the man on the bench, and I'll tell you this, he was cool. He didn't look up or move. He just read his book like he was totally engrossed.

I was careful not to make eye contact, so I looked down

at his feet as we passed him. He was wearing dark blue running shoes with mud stains at the toes.

"You can't tell anyone what I'm about to show you," Mom said to me in a whisper that was just loud enough for him to overhear. "It's a new entrance to the underground." That's when I noticed the man flinch ever so slightly. She'd baited the hook perfectly.

"How do you get there?" I asked.

She waited until we were out of his earshot, and she answered quietly, "I'm still working on that. We need someplace secluded where we can turn the tables on them."

Here's a fun fact. It turns out that I have a habit of humming whenever I get nervous. (Of course, I never noticed this until one day when Alex pointed it out, and now I can never *not* notice it!) So I started humming the last song I'd heard: "Row, Row, Row Your Boat."

Mom stopped for a second and looked right at me. "Molly, that's a great idea."

I was glad I helped; I just wished I knew what I'd done. "*What's* a great idea?"

"Row Your Boat," she said. "We'll lead them to the boathouse."

There's a lake in the middle of Central Park called The Lake. (Really clever name, huh?) And a popular activity is for people to go out on it in rowboats they rent at Loeb Boathouse, which sits at the end of a long dock next to a restaurant. But it was winter and the lake was frozen.

"I don't think the boathouse is open," I said.

Mom picked up the pace ever so slightly. "That's what makes it perfect."

The boathouse is a square wooden building that looks like a garage with a weather vane on the top. It extends out over the water so that you can literally row in and park your boat. Now that the lake was frozen, there was a gap about three feet high that separated the bottom of the boathouse from the ice.

This gap was how Mom planned to get inside.

"Wait until I'm all the way in before you follow me," she said. "We're still pretty early in the winter, and I want to make sure the ice is strong enough to hold us."

The mere thought of crashing through the ice was enough to slow me down. Mom walked to the edge and put one foot out onto the slippery surface, whispering a near silent prayer, "Please don't break."

It didn't.

Once she knew it was strong enough, she quickly slid under the bottom and climbed up into the building. She made it look easy and I followed her.

"Good job," she said when I popped up inside next to her.

I sat there for a moment, my feet dangling over the edge of the slip where the boats pulled in. The inside of the building looked a lot like my grandparents' attic. There was stuff crammed everywhere, long wooden oars, dingy orange life jackets, and a pair of overturned rowboats.

"Get under there and hide," she said, pointing at one of the boats.

"Why am I hiding?"

"Because I want them to think that we've gone underground. They'll look through that window before they come in, and if they see us in here, they'll know we're on to them."

She lifted up the edge of the boat and I reluctantly crawled under it. When she set it back down, I was plunged into darkness. The combination of dark and damp, frozen and slippery made it the least comfortable place I'd ever been.

"Don't come out unless I call your name," she said.

"Seriously?"

"I mean it," she said. "We play by my rules."

"All right," I whined.

Because the edge of the boat was curved, I could peek out from the bottom. (Although I had to press my cheek

663

against the frozen floorboards to do it.) It took about thirty seconds or so for my eyes to adjust to the darkness, but I was able to see a reflection of the room in a row of silver paint cans along the wall. The round shape of the cans distorted everything like one of those mirrors you see at a carnival, but at least I had some idea what was going on. I could see my mom squeeze into a narrow area between a cabinet and the rear wall. The distortion made her look super skinny and about eight feet tall.

For the next few minutes everything in the boathouse was silent and still, except for the sound of wind racing across the ice and whistling through the slats in the floor. I was cold and shivering like I was in some bad ghost story. First we heard the approaching footsteps, and next there was talking outside. Then someone started to push the door.

They were coming in.

Ice Breakers

I kept perfectly still in my hiding place beneath the row-boat, my pulse quickening as they tried to force their way in. Rather than coming in from underneath the boathouse like we did, they were trying to break through the main door. After about fifteen seconds of grunting and straining, there was a loud pop and the door burst open. A shaft of sunlight cut across the room for as long as it took the two of them to enter and close the door behind them. Once they did, every-thing returned to darkness and my eyes had to readjust.

"Check for any access that leads underground," the man told his partner. "I overheard her say it was a new entrance."

I squinted to make out their reflections in the paint cans as they rifled through all the clutter. He was poking around a pile of life jackets and she was pulling back a large canvas cover, when someone new joined the conversation.

"You're not going to find what you're looking for."

The voice belonged to my mother, and it had the same startling effect on them that it had had on me when I was eight years old and trying to see if there were any Christmas presents hidden under her bed.

"If either of you wants to make it out of here," she said, "I recommend you start talking and tell me what Marek's planning."

I had a good view of Mom as she stepped in front of the doorway and blocked their escape. She had a long metal tool with a hook at the end that she held like a weapon.

"Do you honestly think you can handle the two of us by yourself?" asked the man, who had apparently forgotten that my mom was not alone when she entered the boat-house. I'll be honest. I was offended.

"Oh, I can handle you two," Mom said confidently. "I'm just trying to figure out if a worse punishment might be to let you both live. That way you can go back and tell Marek that you ruined his one chance of finding Milton. How do you think he'll react to that?"

That got him angry and he charged her, slamming her against the wall. She pushed back with the metal tool and spun it around so that the hook cut right into his gut. She jerked it up and down before she pulled it out of him.

You'd think that would've finished him off, but it didn't. He flashed a wicked grin and was completely unfazed by the purple goo oozing from his stomach. Just seeing it in the reflection was gross enough. I'm pretty sure if I saw it up close it would've made me want to hurl.

They traded a couple punches before the woman called out. "Wait a second. What about the girl she was with?"

Finally, somebody noticed I wasn't there.

I could tell by her voice that she was right next to the boat I was hiding under. Since my element of surprise was about to disappear, I decided to be bold.

I rolled over onto my back and tucked my knees all the way up to my chest. Then I pushed up with my legs as hard as I could against the boat so that it flipped over and hit her. She staggered back and tried to get her balance, but there was a problem. She was on the edge of the slip, so when she stepped back there was no floor. She fell and slammed right onto the frozen lake.

"I'm pretty sure I told you to wait until I called your name," Mom said angrily. "You never listen."

Would it have killed her to say, "What a cool move that was, Molly?"

I was about to say something snarky right back at her, when I saw the look of horror on her face. I ducked just as a long wooden oar swung right by my head and missed me by no more than an inch or two. The man laughed as he took another swing at me, but this time I was able to deflect it with an oar that I had just picked up.

It looked like we were about to have a swordfight with the oars, but then I felt a tug at my ankle. It was the woman reaching up and grabbing me. She jerked hard and I came crashing down on her and the ice.

That's when I heard the terrifying sound of ice cracking. I couldn't see where it was and I had no idea how long it would be before it broke. I wasn't planning on waiting around to learn the answer.

I scrambled up onto my feet, and after slipping a couple times, managed to reach up to the edge of the deck. I started to pull myself up, but she grabbed me and pulled me back onto the ice.

She squeezed me tight and whispered in my ear, "I hope you're a good swimmer." For the record, you'd think it'd be scarier when zombies yelled and moaned at you, but my personal experience is that it's far worse when they whisper.

I tried to break free, but she spun me around and landed an elbow into my jaw that sent me sprawling across the ice.

I looked up and saw my mom. She wanted to help, but she had a problem of her own. Despite all the purple ooze coming out of his stomach, the man was still putting up a good fight.

"It's been fun and all," said Mom, "but we're going to wrap this up."

She picked up one of the cans of paint and slammed it up into his chin. He tried to say something, but instead of words there were just some brief gurgling noises before black liquid started pouring from his mouth. A second later his body dropped right in front of her. He was dead.

Meanwhile, I'd managed to get back to my feet, but the woman was still blocking my way back up off the ice, which was cracking even more.

"A little help!" I called out.

"Pulley!" shouted my mom.

I looked up and saw that there was a pulley directly above me. Normally it was used to help lift boats out of the water, but now it was my escape route.

I jumped straight up and grabbed onto it. Then, as the woman charged at me to pull me back down I did a double scissor kick and hit her in the head with each foot. She collapsed to the ice, dazed but not dead. That is, not until my mother pushed a rather large anchor over the edge of the slip and directly onto her. First the anchor smashed through the zombie, and then it broke through the ice as both of them sank down into the freezing water.

I hung there for a moment, my sneakers dangling less than a foot above the icy lake as I tried to catch my breath.

"Can you make it?" asked my mom as she reached out for me.

I swung my body back and forth a couple times until I got close enough for her grab my legs and pull me to safety.

We both plopped down onto the floor.

"You okay?" she asked.

I smiled. "I'm better than okay. How about you?"

"Well, you know how much I love it when we get to share these mother-daughter moments."

We both laughed.

"It may not be a normal family," I said, "but it's our family. This is what we do. This is who we are."

"You got that right," said Mom.

She turned her attention to the man and rolled him over onto his back. The massive stomach wound was actually more disgusting than I imagined, but I was too tired to get sick.

"Let's see what clues you have for us," she said as she

started checking the pockets of his coat and pants. She pulled out a phone, a wallet, and the paperback that he'd been reading.

She handed me the book and started digging through his wallet.

"Defending Manhattan," I said, looking at the cover. "New York City during the Revolutionary War. Sounds boring."

"We have a name," Mom said as she pulled out his ID. "Herman Prothro. West Eighty-Eighth Street."

She looked up at me. "That's a nice neighborhood."

"So he's a rich zombie," I said. "Any idea what Herman Prothro does? I mean, other than read boring books and attack Omegas."

She pulled out a business card and held it up to the light to read it better. "It says that he's the vice president of the Empire State Tungsten Company."

We shared a confused look for a moment before I asked, "What's the Empire State Tungsten Company?"

"I don't know," she answered as she flashed a grin. "But I think they need a new vice president."

She rolled him off of the wooden floor and he splashed through the hole in the ice. There was another gurgling, not unlike the one he made when he died, and then some bubbles as his body disappeared into the darkness.

We exited through the door they had busted open and walked in the park together for about forty-five minutes, until Mom felt confident that there were no other zombies following us.

Our walk ended up behind the Metropolitan Museum of Art looking out over the Great Lawn. Because of the cold weather there was hardly anyone on it, but during spring and summer the Great Lawn becomes the ultimate New York picnic destination.

"Do you remember when we used to come out here?" she asked. "Those amazing lunches that your dad made?"

"Of course I do," I said. "Those are some of my favorite memories ever."

"Mine too," said Mom. "I want those to be the memories you have of me. Not images of me killing zombies in some freezing boathouse. I want you to remember me as a mother sitting on that blanket, reading stories to you."

"Like Alice in Wonderland?" I said.

"Exactly. Remember me as the mom who read Alice in Wonderland to you."

"It's no use going back to yesterday, because I was a different person then," I said, quoting her favorite line.

She smiled. "You still remember that too?"

"I'll always remember that. And now I finally understand it. I can't go back to being that girl on the blanket. I was a different person then."

"I guess you were," she replied. "I guess we all were different people."

She hugged me tight and I lingered in her arms.

"I don't know how long it's going to be until we see each other again," she said, sadness in her voice. "I'm going to have to hide deep."

"I know," I said. "What should we do about Omega?"

"Nothing. Nothing unless you hear different directly from me. Until then Omega is done."

I nodded.

"I mean it, Molly. It can't be like the boathouse, where you're supposed to wait for me but you don't."

"Okay," I said. "But that was a pretty cool move, wasn't it?"

She laughed.

"It was the coolest move I ever saw. But I still mean it."

"I know."

"I love you, Molly Koala," she said, calling me by the nickname I hadn't heard in ages.

"I love you, Mom."

La Traviata

Opera? Are you serious?"

We were less than fifteen seconds into family night, and my sister Beth was already protesting the music that filled the apartment.

"Show some respect for your heritage," Dad said as he handed her some bell peppers and a cutting board. "And chop these while you're at it."

"We're only a quarter Italian," she replied. "What about the parts of our heritage that made music, I don't know, in the last century?"

"You may only be a quarter Italian, but Molly's a quarter too and I'm half," he said. "Two quarters and a half, what does that add up to, Molls?"

"One whole Italian," I said, playing along with Dad's logic.

"There you go. There's an entire Italian person in this kitchen, so be polite," he said with a cheesy Italian accent. "Besides, you know the rules. Tonight's my night and I get to pick."

The rules of family night are simple but firm. Every month we each get one evening to plan. It can be anything, as long as we're all together. And to encourage fresh ideas, we're supposed to be open to new things . . . like opera.

When Dad's in charge of family night we often end up in the kitchen. I think he likes it for a couple reasons. First of all, he's a great cook and wants to make sure Beth and I learn the basics. But more importantly, he likes the way it squishes us all into a small space and forces us to talk and share as we literally bump into each other.

That night we were making kitchen sink spaghetti, which has nothing to do with the sink and gets its name from the fact that Dad puts "everything but the kitchen sink" into the sauce. He thought opera was the perfect addition. But rules or not, he didn't want Beth to be miserable, so he gave her a possible escape.

"How about this?" he said. "I'm going to tell you a story about this opera and once I'm done, if you still want me to turn it off, I will."

"Why don't you save yourself the trouble and turn it off now?" she said with a sly smile. "Because I guarantee my opinion's not going to change."

"Maybe, but that's not the deal," he said. "I get to tell my story first. Then you decide."

She was suspicious, but didn't really have much choice. "Okay, fine."

"You have to keep cooking, though," he said. "Both of you."

We had specific jobs to do so that everything would come together perfectly. Beth was chopping vegetables, and I was stirring and seasoning the tomato sauce while Dad sautéed some Italian sausage. The combination of the sizzle and the smell was incredible.

"We're cooking," Beth said. "Start talking."

"Okay, your mom and I had been dating for about two and a half months . . ."

I knew then and there that Dad was going to win this argument.

". . . and one day she told me she was planning to see *La Traviata* at the Met." He turned from the stove for a

676

second to explain to Natalie. "'The Met' is what we cultured people call the Metropolitan Opera House at Lincoln Center."

She didn't miss a beat and came right back at him. "'The Met' is also what you call the Metropolitan Museum of Art. You'd think for cultured people you'd be able to come up with different nicknames for different places."

"That's funny. I never noticed that." Dad said laughing. "Anyway, your mother was going to go with her sister, Fiona, no doubt because she assumed I was a caveman unable to enjoy something as sophisticated as opera. Now, I couldn't let her think that, so I told her that it was too bad she was going with someone else, because I loved opera."

"Was that true?" I asked.

"No. I didn't know anything about opera except what I'd learned from Bugs Bunny. But I didn't want her to know that. Then she threw me a curve. She said that Fiona didn't really want to go and asked if I wanted to go with her instead."

"Uh-oh."

"No kidding. Of course I said yes, but I was in full panic mode. I was worried I wouldn't understand anything because it's all sung in Italian. I was worried that I was going to prove that I was, in fact, an uncultured caveman.

So I spent three weeks studying everything there was to know about *La Traviata*. I memorized the characters, the plot, famous performances . . . I even knew the English translations of all the song titles. My plan was simple. I was going to dazzle her. But I had a problem."

"What?" I asked.

"I was so focused on studying that I didn't realize I was scheduled to work that night. I had to swap with someone at the last minute just so I could go on the date. I ended up working back-to-back shifts, and by the time we got to the Met I was already pretty tired."

Although her back was turned toward Dad as she chopped, I noticed that Beth was now closely following the story.

"Don't tell me you fell asleep," I said. "Did you snore?"

"I didn't snore . . . but I may have nodded off a little during the first act," he said with a smile. "I was just going to close my eyes for a second, but the next thing I know, there was applause. That woke me right up. It was intermission and I was worried that she was onto me so I just jumped right into my analysis. I talked about everything that I had studied. I could tell she was impressed.

I did a better job staying awake in the second act, and when it was over I picked up right where I left off. She couldn't believe how emotional I got as I talked about the tragic ending. I will never forget the look she gave me, hanging on every word I said. Even I almost believed that I was smart and cultured. We were right there next to the big fountain in Lincoln Center, surrounded by all those people in tuxedos and gowns and I had pulled it off . . . until I saw it."

"What?" asked Beth, now fully engrossed.

"A giant banner advertising that night's performance of . . . *Il Trovatore*."

We all started laughing, Dad loudest of all.

"You did not?" I squealed.

"Oh, I did. I totally learned the wrong opera. *Il Trovatore*, *La Traviata*, the names sound so much alike and they're both by Verdi. Everything I said had been wrong and your mother just went along with it. She knew what I'd done the second I started talking at intermission, and she just would not embarrass me. I should have known better than to think that I could put one over on her."

Now Beth turned from the counter to face him, a wide smile on her face. "So how did she respond once the truth was out there?"

"Not like I would have expected," he said. "She figured that if I tried that hard, it must mean that I really cared about her. And I realized that if she was going to go along with it just so she wouldn't embarrass me, well, that's when I knew I was in love. And seven months later when I proposed, I did it right at that fountain."

He let the story simmer for a moment as he brushed a little garlic onto the sausage. Then he gave her a sly look over his shoulder and said, "But we can always turn it off."

Beth just shook her head. "It's fine. We can keep listening."

I had never heard that story before and I loved it. It had been more than two months since that day with Mom in the boathouse. I thought about what she said afterward, about how she wanted me to remember her. She wanted me to think of her as a mother reading stories on a picnic blanket. And here was another memory, of a young woman falling in love. I'm sure this is how my dad pictures her.

Needless to say, the spaghetti was delicious and the dinner was great fun. Beth told us about a job she was applying for to work as a counselor at a drama camp run by the parks department.

"That sounds great," said Dad.

"If I get it," she said, "we'll put on three different plays during the summer."

"No operas?"

"No operas." She laughed.

"That reminds me," Dad said, turning to me. "Have you thought about what play you want to see for your birthday? I want to make sure we get good tickets."

For years we'd celebrated my birthday by going out to dinner and a Broadway show. It was great, and something I really loved. But the truth is, one of the reasons it became a tradition was because I never had enough friends to have a party. This year, though, things were different.

"Actually," I said, a little worried about how he might react. "I was thinking of having a party instead."

"I thought you loved Broadway."

"I do. It's just that I'd kind of like to do something with Alex, Grayson, and Natalie."

Right then the opera music hit a particularly dramatic moment, and Dad pretended to be the character as he lip-synched for a few seconds. "He's so sad because his daughters are leaving him for drama camp and parties with friends."

Beth and I both rolled our eyes.

"Just kidding," he said. "What kind of party do you want to have?"

This is where I was stumped. I knew I wanted to have one, I just didn't have any experience as to what one might be like.

"I don't know. Do you have any ideas?"

"We can get a clown or a magician. If you want I can get you all a tour of the fire house and you can slide down the pole."

"Yes, Dad," Beth said, exasperated. "She's turning six and she's wants a clown and a magician. Or better yet, we can get her a fairy princess."

"I'm sensing sarcasm," Dad joked. "Do you have any suggestions, Beth?"

"Yeah," I said eagerly. "You've got a lot more experience with . . . you know, being with people who are having a good time."

Beth absently twirled a forkful of spaghetti on her plate as she thought it over. "You want something fun but easy. Good for guys and girls. With low social pressure that will provide lasting memories."

"Yes, yes, and yes," I said. "I want a party that's all those things. And I especially like the fact that there isn't any clown or magician. Although, sliding down the pole in the fire house actually did sound kind of fun."

"As fun as Coney Island?"

Coney Island is awesome. It's a collection of amusement parks, roller coasters, and attractions all along the boardwalk in Brooklyn. It was the perfect party suggestion.

"That's it," I said. "That's exactly what I want to do."

"I like it too," Dad said. "It's been a couple years since I rode the Cyclone."

Beth and I both gave him a look, and he took the hint.

"Of course, you were probably thinking of just the kids riding the rides."

"I'll ride with you, Dad," said Beth. "And after that we can listen to some of *my* music."

"Gee," he said in his goofy dad voice, "I wonder which will make me dizzier."

It wasn't until later, after we'd finished putting away the dishes, that I saw the envelope. It had arrived in the mail that day and was addressed to me. I couldn't remember the last time I'd gotten an actual letter, so I was excited.

I opened it in my room, but rather than a letter there was a folded piece of paper and a small article clipped from a newspaper. The article was dated a week earlier and was about our favorite evil lord of the undead, Marek Blackwell.

It said Marek and the mayor had negotiated a deal for him to take control of some of the city's abandoned subway stations. His plan was to turn these ghost stations into underground entertainment complexes with restaurants, shops, and even some apartments. He called it RUNY, Reinventing Underground New York.

In the article it was hailed as a vision for the future, turning unused space into something good. But I knew something else. Underground and surrounded by Manhattan schist, these entertainment complexes would be the ultimate destination for zombies.

In a way it was kind of genius. Marek said he was trying to build a better life for the undead. This actually did that. As I considered this, I looked at the paper and saw a single question written with blue felt tip pen in block letters. It said:

WHERE IS HE GETTING THE MONEY TO DO THIS?

The Equinox

One of the great things about having a dad who's an amazing cook is that the leftovers that make their way into your lunch tend to be much better than those of your classmates. So, unlike the other kids who'd brown-bagged it and brought PB and Js or tuna fish sandwiches, I was savoring every bite of a rosemary chicken panini. Dad even packed a sweet and spicy dipping sauce with it. It was the kind of lunch that could inspire jealousy. At least, it could have if I hadn't been eating alone.

You see, of the roughly five hundred students at the Metropolitan Institute of Science and Technology, I was the only one who thought it was a good day to eat outside. MIST is a science magnet school that draws kids from all over New York City. They're really smart, certainly smart enough to know that you don't sit outside when it's almost freezing. And though the gothic buildings that make up the campus look like they belong in a horror movie, the view from the picnic tables is nice enough that I was willing to ignore the temperature.

I was nibbling on my sandwich and watching a red-and-white tugboat push a barge up the East River, when I heard footsteps approach from behind. I didn't even have to look to see who it was. Grayson's walk is distinctive: He goes fast until he's almost there, then nearly comes to a full stop and takes a breath before taking the final few steps at regular speed. It's like he's always in a hurry but never wants you to know it.

"Hey, G," I said as I took another bite and kept watching the tug do its job.

"Hey, Molly," he said warily. "How are you doing?"

"Fantastic," I replied, maybe a bit more enthusiastically than the situation warranted. "I've got a great lunch. I've got a great view. What more could I want?" I turned and looked right at him, trying my best to punctuate my enthusiasm with a convincing smile.

"You do realize that it's . . ."

"Check the calendar," I said, cutting him off. "Today is March twentieth, the first day of spring. Spring. As in no longer winter. As in it's totally appropriate to eat on the patio."

"Yeah, but if you check a thermometer," he replied, "it's like . . . forty-seven degrees."

I'll admit that I was being a bit irrational, but it had been more than two months since the boathouse. Sixty-four days, to be exact. And despite some occasional fun moments like family night, they had been sixty-four frustrating days.

There hadn't been any contact from my mother or the slightest hint that Omega might get called back into action. Even worse, there were signs that my friend group was having problems, and, as if all that wasn't enough, it had also been the coldest and snowiest winter in more than two decades.

There was nothing I could do about the first two, and my total lack of social skills left me clueless as to how to fix the third. So I figured the least I could do was celebrate the end of winter. Even if, meteorologically speaking, Mother Nature wasn't cooperating.

"I really am fine, Grayson," I said. "I just . . . can't spend another lunch period in that cafeteria. I guess I need fresh air more than I need heat."

He set his lunch on the table and sat down right next to me. "Works for me."

This is what makes Grayson such a great friend. He was willing to sit out in the cold not because it made sense, but because it made sense to me. And on this day that was just the kind of friend I needed most.

I took a bite of my panini and said, "Thank you."

He shrugged as if to say it was no big deal.

But it was a big deal. Everything about my friends was. I'd never had a group of friends before this school year, and part of me had always worried that I might never have one. But then Omega found me, and suddenly I had three amazing people whom I could literally trust with my life.

At first glance our foursome seemed like an unlikely grouping. There was glamorous and beautiful Natalie with her chic apartment on the Upper West Side, quiet and athletic Alex whose accent and swagger were straight out of the Bronx, Grayson the megabrain computer geek who lived with his professor parents in a Brooklyn brownstone, and good old awkward me, that weird Bigelow girl from Astoria, Queens.

I'm sure some people wondered why we hung out together. But that's because they couldn't possibly know the big thing we all had in common. It was our job to police and protect the zombies of New York. We were the ones who maintained the peace between the living and the undead. Omega made all of our differences insignificant.

And that was the problem.

Now that Omega was on lockdown, our group had begun to drift apart. We didn't have a case to work on or a problem to solve. We didn't have a reason to be together. And on top of that, Natalie's recovery was going slowly. At first she only came back to school for half days, which meant we rarely saw her. And when she finally did return full-time, she had so much make-up work to do she usually skipped lunch and went straight to the library.

I knew these were all good reasons, but part of me felt like she was avoiding us, or more specifically, avoiding me. Since I didn't have much experience in social situations, I tried to come up with ways to reassure myself that it was all in my imagination. My birthday party was going to be one of them.

"Hey, my birthday's in a couple weeks and I was thinking of having a little party out at Coney Island. Do you think you could come?"

Grayson was midchew so he had to swallow a bite of his no doubt inferior sandwich before answering, "Sure, that'd be great."

I looked back toward the river and asked, "You think she'll come?"

He could read my uncertainty and knew exactly what I was talking about.

"I think she's struggling," he said. "She's used to being the smartest and the strongest, and this is all new to her. But I do think she'll come. You're her good friend, Molly."

I just kept looking off into the distance and nodded. I thought about telling him about the newspaper article that had come in the mail, but before I could decide, someone else joined us.

"Hey, you guys realize that it's cold out here, right?" Alex said as he sat across the table from me.

"Really?" I joked. "I hadn't noticed."

"Vernal equinox," Grayson said, using the scientific term for the first day of spring. "We're celebrating."

Alex laughed.

"Speaking of celebrating, we were just talking about my birthday party. It's in a couple weeks. We're going to Coney Island. Interested?"

"In hot dogs and roller coasters? Always."

I felt a little stupid. I had worried that we were drifting apart, but neither one of them hesitated before saying they wanted to come to my party. I think I sometimes (okay, maybe always) make stuff like this harder than it should be.

"And guess what," he added. "I've got an early birthday

present." He unzipped his backpack and pulled out a small catalog. "My uncle Paul brought this over last night, and I thought you might want to look at it."

He handed it to me.

"It's the uniform catalog for the NYPD," he continued. "It's got everything from shirts and jackets to special belts that hold all their gear. In the back is a section with all the different squad patches. You can look to see if you recognize the one the psycho cop who ripped off his ear was wearing."

I hesitated. "We're not supposed to do anything Omega," I said, unsure if this counted.

"I don't think this is Omega," he said. "Some guy threatened you two and we want to know a little more about him. We're not on a case and we're not going to do anything about it. We're just trying to protect ourselves, which is the point of the lockdown in the first place."

I turned to Grayson, who added, "I think he's right."

"Okay," I said as I started flipping through the pages. The patches were located in the back, and there were more than I would have guessed. There was a fire truck for the emergency squad and an antique car for the auto crime division. My favorite was the patch for the mounted division, which had a horse on it.

I remembered that the patch I saw that day had a dog on it, but I wasn't sure if it was one dog or more than one. There was a picture of a German shepherd on the K-9 unit patch and a Labrador retriever on the bomb squad patch, but neither was like the one I had seen.

Then I turned the page and realized why I had been confused about the number. It's because the patch had one dog with three heads.

"That's it," I said, pointing and turning the catalog so that they both could see. "The red one with the three-headed dog."

Grayson recognized it instantly. "That's Cerberus."

I had no idea what he was talking about. "Who or what is Cerberus?"

"He's from Greek mythology," Grayson said. "Cerberus is the hellhound who guards the entrance to the underworld. He craves living flesh, so only the dead can get past him."

"Not exactly one of those feel-good myths, is it?" I said.

"Hardly any of them are," he replied.

Alex took the catalog and looked at it. "It says here that the patch is for the Departmental Emergency Action Deployment Squadron. Sounds like some sort of quick response unit for disasters and emergencies."

Grayson practically jumped out of his chair as he figured

something out. "That's what it sounds like," he said. "Unless you only look at the initials. D-E-A-D. It's the Dead Squad."

We were all quiet for a moment while we thought about this one.

"And their symbol is the evil creature that protects the underworld from the living," added Alex. "That's disturbing."

"That would explain so much," I said. "Remember when I told you about Marek surprising me and Mom?"

"You mean when you killed those two Level 2s in the boathouse?" asked Grayson. "It would be pretty hard to forget."

"Well, the cops that were with him had the same patch. What if there's a whole Dead Squad made up of zombie cops?"

I can't describe the feeling that I had at that moment. We were discussing zombies on the police force, which was terrible. But the conversation was thrilling. This is what we'd been missing. It was the first time I'd felt that kind of excitement since New Year's.

"How could Marek possibly pull that off?" asked Grayson. "This is not some secret underground group roaming around abandoned tunnels beneath the city. We're talking about a squadron within the New York City Police Department. It's a huge public organization."

It did seem far-fetched, and I wondered if maybe we

were jumping to conclusions because we wanted there to be some secret we could solve. We wanted it to be thrilling. But then Alex remembered something.

"Blue Moon," he said. "Operation Blue Moon had very specific goals. The undead wanted to infect the mayor, the archbishop and . . ."

". . . the chief of police," Grayson and I both said.

Alex nodded. "If they turned the chief of police into a zombie, he could easily set up a squadron and handpick who was placed on it."

The three of us were quiet as we considered the magnitude of what this might mean. My mom was right. Marek was up to something big, and we had no idea what it was.

Our little puzzle solving session was exhilarating, but it ended with a dull thud. There was nothing we could do about it. There was no one we could tell. I couldn't even try to get word to my mother, because Marek knew about our secret code on the Delacorte Clock. It did, however, give me something new to talk to Natalie about.

After school I looked for her among the crowd of students heading toward the Roosevelt Island Tram, which was her typical route home. But she wasn't with them. Instead I caught a glimpse of her a block away, heading toward the subway station.

I hurried to catch up, but just when I was close enough to call out her name, I saw the strangest thing. While she waited to cross the street, a man in a red hoodie walked right up behind her and slipped a folded piece of blue paper into a pocket on her backpack. Then he kept walking in a different direction.

It was lightning fast and I wouldn't have noticed it if I hadn't been focused right on her. Even still I might have doubted my own eyes if the man hadn't turned for a second, giving me a look at his face.

It was Liberty.

There was no way that was a coincidence.

Liberty was a friend, but he was more than that. He was an Omega and he was undead. More than anyone we knew, he lived in both worlds. On New Year's Eve he'd been part of my mother's team, the ones who rescued us. But he also was a part of the undead community, known for giving speeches about zombies' rights at flatline parties.

He was being secretive, which made me think he was reaching out to her on Omega business. That made sense, because she was our captain. I was excited, thinking it meant we were being called into action. But then I saw her meet up with a girl I'd never seen before. It was obvious that the girl had been waiting for her.

They entered the subway station together, and I followed from a safe distance. As she rode down the escalator, Natalie pulled out the piece of paper and read it. Then she showed it to the other girl.

If it was a communication about Omega, then she only would have shown it to another Omega.

That's when I figured out what was happening. There was only one explanation that made sense. Omega was no longer in a lockdown. I was just locked out. Natalie had already moved on to a new team. That would explain why she never had time to meet up after school. I wondered if Grayson and Alex were part of her new team as well, or if they'd been left behind like me.

I stayed on the upper level of the station and spied on them as they blended in with the crowd on the platform. When everybody else boarded the subway, they lingered behind.

I stepped behind a pillar so they couldn't see me. Once they thought the coast was clear, they hopped down by the tracks and started walking into the tunnel toward Manhattan.

I just stood there and watched, tears forming in my eyes as they disappeared into the darkness. Not only was I losing a friend, but I was also losing Omega.

The Hollow Men

The MIST library is a two-story stone building that sits on the quad between the Upper and Lower Schools. It looks like a little church, which is why most students call it "the chapel." I found Natalie sitting in the back at a big wooden table strewn with papers and books.

"That looks like a lot of work," I said.

"It is." Natalie seemed genuinely happy to see me. "Do you know anything about the poetry of T. S. Eliot?"

"No."

"That makes two of us," she replied as she started digging through the piles of paper. "Unfortunately, one of us has a critical analysis of it due on in Ms. Brewer's class on Thursday. And now I can't find the paper I need."

It had been approximately twenty-one hours since I saw her disappear into the subway tunnel, and I was full of conflicting emotions. Part of me was hurt because I thought she'd dumped me from the Omega team, but part was also hopeful that it was all a big misunderstanding.

"There's some theory about his work that I'm supposed to analyze, and I don't even remotely understand it," she said.

"That's amazing," I replied. "Because I thought you understood everything."

She laughed. "If you think that, then you've been fooled."

"Well, I have a theory that you might be interested in," I said.

"Is it about poetry?"

"Nope."

"I like it already," she joked.

"It's about a squad of zombies on the police force," I said with just a dash of mystery.

She stopped her search and looked right at me. "That does sound interesting."

I told her what the guys and I had come up with about

the Dead Squad. She seemed really into it and at one point even jotted down the full name of the squad. With her interest fully piqued I tried to use it as an opening to talk about Omega. I asked if she thought we might get back into action soon, and suddenly her whole attitude changed.

"I have no idea," she said. "Honestly, I've been so busy with make-up work I haven't had time to think about Dead City or Omega."

Her smile was sincere, but I knew this was a lie. After all I had seen her enter Dead City the day before. I'm sure my reaction gave me away, because she could tell something was bothering me.

"What's wrong?"

I couldn't exactly say that I had spied on her, so I decided to tell her the other thing that I wanted to talk about. (And also had me nervous.)

"It's just that my birthday is coming up and I was wondering if you'd like to celebrate with us."

She laughed. "Judging by your expression I thought it was going to be something bad. Of course I want to celebrate your birthday. I wouldn't miss it."

That response. Her eagerness, made everything else melt away. "Really?"

"Dinner and a musical, right?" she asked, referring to

my traditional celebration. "Which one are we going to see?"

"Actually, this year we're having a party," I told her. "We're going to Coney Island."

Her expression changed instantly and at first I assumed it was because she thought Coney Island was a silly way to celebrate your birthday.

"What's wrong with Coney Island?" I asked. "Too kiddie?"

She paused for a moment at a loss for words. Then she said, "No, it's just that I'll have to check with my doctors. I'm not sure I'm allowed to go on roller coasters yet."

It had never occurred to me that she might not be able to ride the rides. I apologized and she told me it was no big deal. But I still felt like a total dork.

I tried to change the subject and be a better friend. "What's the paper you're looking for?" I asked. "Let me help."

"'The Hollow Men'," she said.

"Is that one of Eliot's poems?"

She nodded. "A really depressing one."

I started sorting through a different stack of papers.

"I know there's a copy in another book," she said, getting up. "I'll try to find it in the stacks."

"I'll keep looking here," I replied.

I want to be totally honest. I was absolutely one hundred percent looking for the poem. No matter what was going on with Omega, her friendship is what mattered more. But then I noticed that her backpack was open, and I could see a piece of blue paper in the pocket where Liberty had passed her the note. It had to be the same one.

I knew it was the wrong thing to do, but I couldn't stop myself. I looked over my shoulder and saw that Natalie was still looking for the book on the shelf. I had a window of about ten to fifteen seconds.

I reached in with the tip of my fingers and pulled out the note. The message was brief and written in Omega code.

It read: 107/8/92/34 6/15/18/19

Which translates to: BhOUSe CpArK.

I wasn't sure what that meant. I wondered if it was "B House C Park." Unfortunately, I didn't have time to think it through before she came back. I quickly folded the paper and slid it into her backpack.

"Did you find it?"

I looked up and saw her right there. Then I realized she was asking about the poem.

"No," I said. "I don't see it anywhere."

"That's all right. I know it's in here." She sat down and

started flipping through the book to find the other copy.

"Why are the men 'hollow'?" I asked her, referring to the title of the poem.

"I think it has something to do with soldiers feeling empty after the end of World War One," she said. "But it makes me think of the Unlucky 13, left hollow by the explosion in the subway tunnel and wandering the underground, not really living and not really dead."

"That's pretty deep," I said. "Too bad you can't right about that for your paper."

"Comparing and contrasting the poems of T. S. Eliot with the undead of New York City," she said with a laugh. "That would really catch Ms. Brewer's attention."

"You've got a lot of work to do," I said. "I should head to lunch and let you get back to it."

"Thanks for looking," she said. "Maybe we can get together this weekend and do something fun, like pizza."

"That would be great," I replied.

After seeing her I was even more confused than I had been when the day started. I kept replaying the conversation in my head trying to analyze every word and expression as I rode the B train from Rockefeller Center to Cathedral Parkway. Ultimately, I realized I had no idea what to make of it. That's why I was headed uptown.

It took a while to figure out the coded message. I knew that "C Park" probably stood for Central Park. But I had to do an Internet search to find B House. The Blockhouse is an old fort. It's located in the northwest corner of the park right on the border of Harlem.

I read about it online as I rode the subway. It's officially known as Blockhouse #1, and two facts about it instantly caught my attention.

First of all, it was built during the Revolutionary War, interesting because the zombie we killed in the boathouse was reading a book about defending Manhattan during the Revolutionary War. If Natalie was investigating something for Omega, that might have been the reason she went there.

Secondly, not only was the fort made mostly out of Manhattan schist, but it was also built on a giant mound of schist. Schist is the rock formation that gives the undead their power. That meant for a zombie, going inside the fort would be an energy boost.

My relationship with Natalie wasn't the only thing that had me conflicted. My mother had been firm when she told me not to do anything Omega unless she got word to me. This was a close call. If I'd had to go underground, I wouldn't have done it. But the Blockhouse was not in

Dead City. It was just in Central Park; that made it okay.

At least that's what I told myself.

Even though the fort is close to the Cathedral Parkway station, it took me about fifteen minutes to find it because it's hidden in a wooded area. My guess is that hundreds of thousands of people walk by it every day with no idea that a piece of history is right there.

In addition to being hidden, the fort is also pretty boring. It's about the size of a small house and has four square walls about twelve feet high that make it look like a gray stone cube.

I wasn't sure what I was looking for, just that it had something to do with Natalie and Omega. I hoped that it would be obvious and I would be able to figure out what it was when I saw it.

I walked up a small flight of stairs to a gate in the wall. There was a chain on the gate, but when I got up close I realized that it wasn't actually locked. The chain was draped to make it look like it was, but all you had to do was reach through the bars and slide a latch to open it.

The gate made a loud creaking noise as I entered. It should have signaled something creepy, but the inside of the Blockhouse was just as boring as the out. There was a small square area surrounded by thick walls of Manhattan schist. Each wall had a pair of holes that Revolutionary soldiers could use to stick their rifles through and shoot out during an attack. There was also a flagpole right in the middle.

"Underwhelming," I muttered to myself as I tried to figure out what might have brought Natalie here.

I began to wonder if I was just wrong about the clue. Maybe "B house C Park" referred to something completely different. Maybe (hopefully) I was wrong about everything. That was when I noticed a piece of paper that had blown into the far corner.

I walked over and knelt down to check it out. It was blank on the side facing me, but when I turned it over I saw that it was a poem.

"The Hollow Men" by T. S. Eliot.

I slumped as I realized what this meant. This was where Natalie lost the poem. That meant she had come here because an Omega (Liberty) had told her to. I folded up the poem and slid it into my pocket. As I stood up, I heard the creaking of the gate closing behind me.

My first thought was that it was Natalie. I figured she had seen me digging around her backpack and followed me here to confront me about it.

"Listen, I'm sorry that I . . ."

That's as far as I got. When I turned all the way, I realized that it was most definitely *not* Natalie.

"What's that?" the man said, cupping his hand to the side of his head where his ear should be. "I couldn't hear you."

He cackled at his joke as he let the moment of surprise have its full effect. It was Officer Pell, my favorite one-eared member of the Dead Squad. He looked pleased to see me.

"Hello, Molly, what brings you here?"

The Blockhead and the Blockhouse

Pell was big and he filled the doorway, making it impossible to escape. When I didn't answer right away, he asked me again.

"I said, Hello, Molly, what brings you here?"

"Homework," I said, trying to sound calm. "I'm doing a school project on the Revolutionary War and I came here to check out the Blockhouse."

"Really? Is that the best you can do? You and I both know why you're here."

Unfortunately, I really didn't know. I was hoping to find something that made sense to me, but this was a fishing expedition. So, I decided to keep fishing.

"Okay, then why do you think I'm here?"

"You want to see where we supercharge," he said. "Watch this, I'll show you."

He smiled and pressed his back against the wall of Manhattan schist. He sucked in a deep breath of air, and it seemed like he got even bigger.

"I don't know what you're talking about," I said. "But I would like to go now."

He chuckled. "You can't go, Molly. Marek told you to stop messing around in the world of the undead. But you didn't stop, and now you're going to have to pay a penalty."

He took a step toward me and cracked his neck to both sides, loosening up for a fight.

"They tell me you're tougher than you look," he said with a grin. "I hope that's true. Because I want a little challenge."

As a place of interest, Blockhouse #1 was boring. As a place to fight a supercharged Level 2 zombie, it was a total nightmare. The four walls kept me penned in like a boxing ring. I decided that the key to my survival would be the flagpole. I tried to keep it between him and me, hoping that if he had to chase me around, he might leave an opening that let me get to the gate and escape.

"I don't know what you think Marek said, but this has nothing to do with Omega. I really am just working on a class assignment. Here, let me prove it to you." I started reciting the information I had learned during the subway ride. "Blockhouse Number One, which is the official name, was built during the Revolutionary War as part of George Washington's defense of Manhattan."

He didn't wait for more. He charged right at me, and I dropped down to the ground and did a leg sweep that surprised him and knocked him over. I jumped up and threw two quick punches into the side of his head right where his ear once was. My knuckle cracked through the scar tissue and a small trickle of black liquid dripped out.

He seemed dazed, which was the chance I was looking for. I started for the gate, but while I was sliding the lock open he grabbed me from behind. He wrapped me up in a giant bear hug and lifted me so my feet were off the ground.

"You are a better fighter than I expected," he said gleefully. "This is kind of fun. Let me demonstrate how well the supercharge works."

While he still held me in the bear hug, he walked over and pressed his back against the wall again. The schist instantly made him stronger, which kept making his grip tighter and tighter. I kicked and squirmed as I felt him forcing the air out of me.

"Any last words?" he whispered into my ear.

Again with the whispering. I hate the way these zombies whisper. Although, this whisper did help me out. It let me know exactly where his head was.

"Sure," I gasped. "Heads up."

I slammed my head back into his face, which slammed his head right into the rock wall. His grip loosened and I was able to break free.

I had a sudden brainstorm. When I was studying jeet kune do, I went to a martial arts demonstration and a man showed us how to walk up a pole. It's tricky but possible. You keep your arms straight as you grab it, and then you tuck your legs up toward your chest and sort of walk up.

I had never actually done it, but I decided this might be the time to try. Pell was giving himself a little recharge on the wall by the gate, which gave me just enough time.

He had no idea what I was doing until it was too late. By the time he got to the pole, I was up beyond his reach. Even so, I climbed a little bit higher just to be safe. He jumped a couple times but couldn't touch me. Still, it was obvious he felt in control of the situation.

"What's your plan, Molly?" he taunted from below.

"Your arms are going to get tired really soon. And when they do, you're going to have to come down."

He had a point there, but climbing the pole gave me a chance to think. I was high enough that I could see over the wall. If someone walked by I could yell for help. The only problem was that out here in the wooded section of the park there was only a small path nearby. I didn't see anybody walking on it.

Then it dawned on me. I could see over the wall, but he couldn't. He had no idea what was out there. That's when I crossed my fingers and hoped that Beth hadn't gotten all of the family's acting genes.

"Hello," I called to a make-believe rescuer. "Hello! I need your help."

Suddenly, Pell was concerned, although he tried to cover it.

"No one's going to help you, Molly. Remember I'm a police officer."

I looked down. "Yeah. But so is he, and he's going to wonder why you're harassing a twelve-year-old girl. He might even wonder what someone in the Departmental Emergency Action Deployment Squad is doing in Blockhouse Number One. It's not exactly your beat, is it?"

Now he was really nervous. "Molly, stop it."

"Officer, I need your help!" I called out. "Yes. Yes. I'm over here. Thank you so much."

There was something about the thought of an outside police officer getting involved that worried Pell, which is exactly what I was hoping for. He frantically tried to climb up the flagpole to grab at my feet. And, while he didn't get very high, he got just high enough for the next step in my plan.

I didn't need my dad to take me to a firehouse in order to slide down a pole. I loosened my grip and slid down right into him. I jammed my heel into the top of his head and we both slammed hard into the rocky ground, although he broke my fall and I landed on top of him.

His walkie-talkie fell off of his belt and I picked it up and used it like a weapon, slamming it against his head a few times. There was more black liquid dripping out.

He was unconscious, but I don't think he was dead. I didn't care. I just wanted to get out of there. I charged through the gate and sprinted through the park as fast as I could. I didn't stop to catch my breath until I was on the subway heading home.

I plopped down into the seat and breathed a sigh of relief. Then I heard a voice crackle and say.

"Pell. Pell."

It startled me until I realized that it was coming over the walkie-talkie. I hasn't noticed that I still had it.

"Someone better let the chief know that Pell's not responding," the voice said. "We're going to go look for him."

It occurred to me that a walkie-talkie that could listen to transmissions of the Dead Squad might come in handy. But for the moment, I didn't need to attract any attention. I turned it off and slipped it into my backpack.

There was no one in the apartment when I got home, which was a relief. I was messy from the fight and wanted to clean up before my father or sister saw me.

I had a couple of small cuts and bruises, and there was some of the black fluid on me. I was careful to make sure none of it got near the cuts, and then after I got it all off, I dug out some rubbing alcohol and cleaned it some more.

Finally I staggered into my room and lay down on the bed. I felt the crinkle of paper in my back pocket, and I reached in and pulled out the poem that I had found in the Blockhouse. I scanned it for a moment, and the last two lines caught my eye.

> *This is the way the world ends*
> *Not with a bang but a whimper.*

I thought about the fact that my world almost ended with a whimper in the Blockhouse. I was lucky to have made it out in one piece. It was so stupid. I wasn't even doing anything for Omega; I was just snooping around trying to figure out what was up with Natalie. I made two decisions.

Decision one: I would actually do what my mother said and avoid anything remotely related to Omega. I couldn't risk getting hurt and, even worse, I couldn't risk starting the all-out war that Marek had threatened. Those two words he said, "undead army," still gave me panic attacks.

Decision two: I should give up trying to figure out what was going on with Natalie. If and when she felt like she could tell me, she would. Until then, I was determined to be the best friend that I could possibly be.

I felt good about both decisions and was about to take a nap when I saw that another envelope had arrived. Either Beth or my dad had left it on my dresser.

Like the first one, it was addressed to me with no name above the return address. I opened it and it contained a folded map of Manhattan. On the front was a picture of George Washington.

I unfolded it and saw that the map was made for visitors by the National Park Service and that it laid out a tour of places with some connection to the first President.

Just as there was with the first envelope, there was a piece of paper with a single sentence written in block letters with a blue felt tip pen. It said:

RESERVE A PLACE IN HISTORY

9

Thirteen Candles

The only reason I'm letting you get away with that out-fit is because it's your birthday."

Beth was talking. But she was also texting. In fact, she was texting so intently I assumed she was just saying the words as she typed them, like movie subtitles but in reverse. That's why I didn't respond at first.

"Are you talking to me?"

"No, I'm talking to the total stranger standing over there in white shorts, black socks, and red sandals," she said, shaking her head as she continued texting. "Of course I'm talking to you. It is *your* birthday, isn't it?"

We were in Brooklyn at the corner of Stillwell and Surf Avenues. I have no idea how she could simultaneously talk, text, and keep track of peripheral fashion violations, but I was impressed. Unlike the man in the socks and sandals, however, I had actually put some thought and consideration into what I was wearing.

"What's wrong with my outfit?" I asked.

"You mean other than the fact that those shorts and that top belong to me?"

Busted again. I thought I could get away with it because I found them in that sad box of clothes she hangs onto in case old trends come back into fashion.

"I figured when they go into the box, it means . . ."

She looked up from the phone for the first time in our conversation. "Just because I haven't worn them in a while, doesn't mean they're forgotten."

"I just wanted to look . . ."

". . . like a teenager," she said, completing my thought. "I get it. That's why I'm classifying it as borrowing and not theft. No penalty."

"Really?" I said, grateful. "Does that mean you might let me borrow them *permanently*?"

She considered this for a second and then shook her head.

"Not after seeing how good they look together," she said. "I never wore them as an outfit. I think they may get promoted back into the closet. Not for school, but for weekend wear."

As much as I wanted to keep the clothes, I kind of loved the fact that Beth was willing to wear an outfit that I had put together. Mark that as a first.

"You know, if you're interested," she continued, "we can look for some new clothes during spring break. I know a couple places in the Village where you can get something cute without spending too much money."

"That would be incredible," I said. "I absolutely would love to do that."

Even though she immediately went back to texting, I considered it a total teenage sister bonding moment.

I had only been thirteen for half a day, but so far it was great. It began when my dad surprised me with my favorite breakfast—bacon pancakes. (That's right, they're pancakes with bacon mixed right into the batter so you get both tastes in every bite!) Now Beth was volunteering to take me to Greenwich Village to find cool clothes. And my friends and I were about to spend the day having fun at Coney Island.

"I've got wristbands and tickets," my dad said as he

approached, and waved them in the air for me to see. "The wristbands give you unlimited rides on everything but the Cyclone. And the tickets are for the Cyclone. It's going to be great. I'm so glad I thought of this."

My sister didn't say a word. She just raised her eyebrow and he instantly corrected himself.

"I mean I'm so glad Beth thought of this."

She smiled and continued texting.

He gave me a map of all the rides and attractions and I started plotting the day's activities. The plan was for Alex, Grayson, Natalie, and I to ride the rides for a few hours while Dad went back home and did his miracle work in the kitchen to make dinner and a cake. Beth was going to hang out nearby with some friends on the beach in case we needed anything. The thought that we were going to be on our own made thirteen feel even cooler.

A few minutes later Alex and Grayson arrived.

Alex inhaled deeply before letting out an exaggerated breath. "Is that the best smell in the world, or what?"

"The salt air coming off the ocean?" asked Grayson.

Alex shook his head.

"Salt air's nice, but seventy-one percent of the earth is covered by ocean," he said. "No, I was referring to the singular place on the planet where you can breathe in the awesomeness that is the original Nathan's Famous hot dogs."

The "famous" in Nathan's Famous is legit. It's legendary. It's a hot dog stand that fills an entire block and hosts the world championships of hot dog eating every Fourth of July. We were standing right in front of it.

"Happy birthday," Alex said as he handed me a present.

Even though it was wrapped, the shape and feel kind of gave it away.

"I'm guessing . . . baseball cap."

"That's a good guess," he said. "But do you know the team?"

For this there could only be one answer. "It better be the Yankees."

He shrugged his shoulders. "Maybe it is. Maybe it isn't. You'll have to unwrap it to know for sure."

With my lack of birthday party experience, I wasn't sure if I was supposed to open it then or wait until later. I looked to Dad for guidance.

"Go ahead and open it," he said. "I want to know which team it is too."

I tore it open expecting to see the classic Yankee design of navy hat with an *NY* logo, but instead it was a lighter blue and had a white *B* on the front. I didn't recognize it.

"The Dodgers," said Alex.

"Then why is there a *B*?" I asked. "The Dodgers play in Los Angeles."

"They do now," he said. "But they used to play right here in Brooklyn. And it was on this date, your birthday, in 1947, that Jackie Robinson became the first African American to play in the major leagues. He's my hero and was incredibly brave . . . just like you."

Every now and then I'm reminded that Alex is totally awesome and thoughtful. I slipped on the cap and it fit perfectly.

"I love it."

"And this is from me," Grayson said as he handed me a card.

I opened it to find a pair of tickets to the new space show at the Hayden Planetarium.

"Greatness!" I exclaimed. "I want to see this so bad."

Like I said, thirteen was off to a great start. Which is not to say that everything went exactly as I hoped. A couple minutes later I got a call from Natalie that dampened the mood a little. I knew there was a chance she wasn't going to come, but in my heart I thought she'd make it.

I was wrong.

She called and apologized, saying that her doctors and

parents wouldn't let her. I understood, but I was still disappointed. I also felt bad because my dad bought four wristbands and it turned out we only needed three.

"Do you think you can get your money back?" I asked him. "For the extra wristband?"

"What extra wristband?" Beth said, taking the last one from my father.

"I thought you were going to meet your friends at the beach?" I asked.

Beth whipped out her phone and sent a lightning quick text.

"Done," she said. "Now, are we going to have fun or are we just going to stand around and talk?"

It's amazing how much of a difference one person can make. If it had only been Alex, Grayson, and me, I don't think it would have felt as much like a party. But four was the perfect number. When we went on the go-karts, we raced boys against the girls. When we rode the roller coasters, no one ended up sitting alone. It was also cool because it was the first time Alex and Grayson got to hang out with her.

She told them about her plans to work at drama camp that summer and amazed them with her ability to do different accents. She could switch from Bronx to

Queens to Long Island in the middle of a sentence.

The Cyclone was fun for everyone else, but with my dislike for heights I'm not really a big roller coaster fan. I was much more into the bumper cars because they have lots of excitement but stay close to the ground. And also because Beth turned it into a challenge.

"I have a secret mission for you two," she said to the boys, using an exaggerated Eastern European accent. "Do everything you can to make sure Molly does not make it all the way around the track."

"Hey!" I complained. "That's not fair."

"Let me finish," she said, turning to me. "If you can complete an entire lap, you can keep the clothes."

"That's a deal," I said, giddy with excitement. "Challenge accepted."

I hopped into the car and strapped on my safety belt nice and tight. The cars sparked to life and the battle began. The three of them chased me in circles, slammed me with their bumpers, and hounded me all around.

They had me pretty good until I realized that I should stop thinking of it as an amusement park ride and instead consider it a physics experiment. Bumper cars are a perfect demonstration of Newton's laws of motion. Rather than go head to head, where I was losing out, I decided to change direction ever so slightly, which diverted their energy and let me escape from the pack.

It was a bold and exciting move but I soon learned that Newton's laws of motion are nothing compared to Beth's law's of fashion. She was not about to let me get those clothes, and somehow she managed to drive backward and trap me in a corner until the time ran out.

"You put up a good fight," she said as she reached down to help me out of the car. "You even worked up a sweat."

For a second I thought she was going to give me the outfit anyway.

"Make sure you take the clothes to the dry cleaners before you put them back in my closet."

I was so busy having a great time that I didn't really think much about Natalie being a no-show. At least not until after dinner and cake. (The cake, by the way, was out-of-control amazing. It had cream cheese frosting and a layer of raspberry filling. I thought Alex was going to faint when he took his first taste.) I know she had a good excuse, but it still made me wonder about our friendship. And since I was now a teenager, I decided the mature thing would be to talk to her about it. That's why I headed over to see her the next morning.

I spent the entire subway ride trying to come up

with the right way to say what I was feeling.

Natalie, I want to talk to you about our friendship.

Natalie, I want you to be honest with me.

Natalie, is there something you want to tell me?

Each line sounded more and more ridiculous. I didn't want to be emotional or dramatic, just honest. By the time I stepped into the elevator, I realized I was getting worked up and needed to relax. Luckily, I had all the way to the twelfth floor to take a couple of deep breaths and calm down. Rather than blurt it out, I decided the best approach would be to say that I was in the neighborhood and wanted to stop by to see how she was doing. I'd let the conversation flow from there.

I knocked on the door and panicked as I realized that it was a terrible excuse. Her neighborhood was nowhere near mine. It didn't make sense for me to be there. I was still trying to come up with a better reason when the door opened.

"Can I help you?"

I went to talk and then I saw that it wasn't Natalie or her mother. It was some random woman who I'd never seen before. I wondered if she was one of the doctors working with her.

"I'm sorry," I said confused. "I'm looking for my friend Natalie Allen."

The woman smiled. "The Allens are downstairs in apartment 2B."

"Sorry, I totally forgot."

In my moment of full diva drama I'd forgotten that Natalie and her family had moved downstairs. Now I had another elevator ride to come up with a better excuse. But as I started down toward the second floor I realized something. Natalie and her family had moved so their apartment could be renovated. But it wasn't being renovated. An entirely different family was living in it.

That made no sense.

Why had a temporary move become permanent? Why would Natalie's family move ten flights downstairs to a less exclusive apartment? That didn't seem like them at all. Her parents were so proud of their view of Central Park. They also seemed to have an endless supply of money and loved to show it off.

When I got to the second floor, I knocked on the door for 2B. And it was then, while I was waiting for someone to answer, that I figured out a possible answer to my question. It was an answer that was totally ridiculous, yet somehow explained everything that had been going on with Natalie lately. It was an answer that took my breath away.

She had moved from the twelfth floor to the second.

She had gone down into Dead City with someone I had never seen before. She'd gone into the Blockhouse where the undead go to recharge. She said she wanted to come to my party when she thought it was going to be dinner and a musical in Manhattan, but canceled when she learned it was Coney Island in Brooklyn.

What if none of this had anything to do with our friendship or Omega and instead was all about Manhattan schist?

What if Natalie was undead?

The Scientific Method as Applied to Potential Zombies

I t would have been nice if I'd had this brainstorm *before* I knocked on the door. That would have given me a chance to think through my theory and figure out if it was a stroke of genius or just plain crazy. But that's not what happened. Instead this was the order of events as they unfolded in the hallway outside of Apartment 2B: Knock first. Crazy idea second. Awkward moment when Natalie opens the door and I stand there with my mouth wide open third.

"Hey, Molls, what's up?"

I was pretty sure I was making some sort of "I just

figured out you might be a zombie but don't want you to know" face, so I tried to fake a smile.

"Nothing much," I said as casually as I could. "I was just in the neighborhood and wanted to see how you're doing."

"I'm good, thanks," she said. "Come on in."

We walked into the front room, and as we sat down she asked, "What were you doing on the Upper West Side on a Sunday morning?"

I'm a lousy liar and normally freeze at these moments, but I actually came up with a believable excuse. "I'm going to see the new space show at the Hayden Planetarium," I explained. "Grayson got me tickets for my birthday."

The planetarium is part of the Museum of Natural History and is a short walk from Natalie's building.

"My parents went to the grand opening," she replied. "They said it was amazing."

And just as suddenly as it came, my newfound ability to think fast and say clever things disappeared. I couldn't think of any follow-up. My mind just kept racing as I looked at her, trying to figure out if it was possibly true. Luckily, after a brief but awkward silence, she took over the conversation.

"Listen, I want to apologize about yesterday."

With my mind still scrambling through variations of her potential state of undeadness, I had no idea what she was talking about.

"What about yesterday?" I asked.

"Missing your birthday," she said. "I'm so sorry I didn't make it to your party. I really wanted to go."

Two minutes earlier this subject had been so important I had to rush over to confront her about it. It was the topic I wanted to analyze in minute detail so we could figure out what it said about our friendship. Now it was so insignificant I was able to resolve it in two sentences.

"I'm sorry you missed it too. We had a lot of fun."

One problem was over, but the other was just beginning. The thought that she might be undead may have been a crazy idea, but that didn't mean it was wrong. I had to figure out the truth.

"I just remembered something," she said, getting up. "I've got a birthday present for you. I was going to bring it to school tomorrow, but now you don't have to wait. It's in my room."

I remembered that when we came over before, she said her room was filled with medical equipment. I wondered if seeing it might help me figure things out. I stood up to go with her.

"Nope, you wait here," she said. "I've got to wrap it."

"You don't need to go to all that trouble," I said.

She tapped the couch for me to sit back down. "It will only take a second."

The whole thing was surreal. My mouth was having a normal conversation while my brain was spinning wild conspiracy theories about her possible zombie conversion. When she went to her room, it gave me a moment to think things through. Faced with an unproven theory, I did exactly what they taught us to do at MIST. I employed the scientific method:

Observation
Hypothesis
Test
Analysis

My observations went back to the fight on New Year's Eve. First I considered the two ways a person can become undead. One is when the dead flesh of a zombie contaminates an open wound, leading to infection and disease. (This is what happened to my mother.) The other is when someone dies suddenly in an underground area where Manhattan schist is plentiful. (This is what happened to the Unlucky

13 in the subway tunnel explosion that started all of this.)

Either scenario could have happened to Natalie. Her fight with Edmund was intense, and I remember that she was bleeding when it was over. She could have easily been infected. Also, even though we were in an abandoned pressroom, we were underground and there was schist all around us.

The more important observations, though, dealt with her behavior after getting hurt. Going underground, visiting Blockhouse #1, and changing apartments from the twelfth to the second floor were all consistent with someone trying to be closer to Manhattan schist.

I also couldn't think of a single time she'd left Manhattan since she got hurt. A trip to see her grandparents in New Jersey was canceled, and once when we were going to have lunch at Grayson's in Brooklyn, Nat had a sudden craving for Shake Shack and we ended up getting burgers in Madison Square Park instead.

None of this was conclusive, but it was strong enough for me to build my hypothesis, which was that Natalie had been turned into a zombie during or soon after our fight on New Year's Eve. Since I was not about to poke her and see if purple goo oozed out of her skin, my test would have to be more creative.

"I hope you like it," she said when she came back into

the room, holding my present. "When I saw it I instantly thought of you."

She handed me a small, perfectly wrapped box. I felt guilty taking it, considering what I was thinking about her at the moment. I felt even guiltier because when she handed it to me, I pressed my fingers against her hand, trying to gauge her body temperature.

"I'm sure I'll love it," I said.

I unwrapped it and opened the lid to reveal a silver bracelet with a charm on it. I held it up to get a good look at it. The charm looked like an old-style New York subway token.

"Remember the Omega necklace you wore on the first day of school?" she asked.

"You mean the one that made an evil zombie attack me in the subway station?" (I worried that I shouldn't have used the Z word, but it didn't seem to bother her.)

"That's the one," she said. "I thought this might be a good substitute. You can wear it, but the bad guys won't know that it has anything to do with Omega."

I put it on my wrist. "I love it, Natalie. It's perfect."

She smiled and added, "Now we're twins."

She held up her wrist so that I could see she was wearing an identical bracelet. I was truly touched by the sentiment.

I reminded myself that Natalie was my friend, and whether or not she was undead shouldn't matter. After all, my own mother was undead. I thought back to that day when I was attacked. Natalie was the one who saved me.

I looked at her for a moment and decided that I should at least be straight with her. "Can I ask you something?"

"Of course," she said.

"Are you . . . ?" It just hung there while I tried to think of a way to say it.

"Am I what?"

I realized I couldn't just blurt out *Are you a zombie?* If I was wrong she'd never forgive me, and if I was right, well, she probably wouldn't forgive me for that, either.

". . . busy this afternoon? I feel bad about having a party that you couldn't come to, so I thought you might like to catch the show with me at the planetarium. Grayson gave me two tickets."

"Actually," she said, "I am busy. My parents and I are having lunch at the club."

This was fantastic news. Natalie's family belongs to a country club where they like to go on the weekends so her parents can play golf and she can ride her horse, Copernicus. The reason this was such great news is because the club is on Long Island. If she could go there, it meant that she wasn't undead after all. I considered this to be a test result that proved my hypothesis wrong.

"That sounds great," I said. "Are you going to ride Copernicus when you're there? Or do your doctors want you to wait longer?"

"Not that club," she said. "We're going to my dad's university club. There's some sort of special Sunday brunch thing."

I remembered that her dad went to Yale, but I had no idea where the club was located. "Where's that?"

"Midtown," she said. "Right by Grand Central."

"Oh," I said, trying to hide my disappointment. She wasn't leaving Manhattan, but that didn't mean she couldn't. My test was still inconclusive, so I decided to push just a little bit more.

"When are you going to go visit Copernicus next?" I asked.

She looked pained by the question and sighed before answering. "Actually, we ended up selling him. It's expensive to take care of a horse, and with my injuries and all the schoolwork, I've had less and less time to ride."

Natalie loved Copernicus more than anything. The only way she'd let her parents sell him was if there was no way for her to ride him again. I was heartbroken for her.

"I'm so sorry to hear that."

It took all my concentration to keep from crying. We were quiet for what seemed like a minute, and I wondered if she was going to just break down and tell me on the spot. But she didn't say anything.

"I really love the bracelet," I said as I stood up to leave. "I better get over to the planetarium. The show starts soon."

"Thanks for stopping by," she said.

"Thanks for the present."

Just like I had when I visited her right after she got out of the hospital, I hugged Natalie at the door. Only this time, there was nothing awkward about it. I knew she needed friends now more than ever.

I was in a daze when I got to the sidewalk. At first I headed for the planetarium. Even though it started out as a phony excuse, I thought the show might cheer me up. But, as I got closer, I realized I wasn't in the mood. I was too sad.

Instead I wandered through Central Park and thought about everything Natalie must have been going through. Technically, my test results didn't prove my hypothesis, but I had no doubt.

My walk ended up right at the Delacorte Clock and the entrance to the Central Park Zoo. One of the great things about the zoo is that even if you don't go in, the walkway through the park is close enough for you to see some of the animal exhibits.

I stopped and watched the sea lions playing in their pool as my mind ran through everything. I wondered if my mother knew about Natalie. I wished that I could talk to her about it. I turned around and stared at the clock.

My mom and I couldn't use it anymore as a secret message board. We'd lost that the moment Marek Blackwell discovered it.

When the clock struck noon, the animal sculptures came to life and started playing "Row, Row, Row Your Boat," just like they had that last time I saw her.

I thought back to that day and one question kept going through my mind. *How in the world did Marek find out that my mother and I used the clock?*

After all, no one else knew about it.

That's when I got a sick feeling in my stomach. I realized there was one other person who knew about it.

Natalie. She had discovered it before Christmas.

Suddenly I remembered that on the day that Marek surprised my mother and me, Natalie had asked me about the clock and said I should I go check for a message.

The sick feeling got worse.

If it was possible that Natalie was a zombie, then it was possible that she was a Level 2. That would mean she'd have no conscience or sense of right and wrong.

I sat down on a bench and slumped under the weight of it all. I looked at the charm on my bracelet as it glistened in the sunlight.

Was it possible that the person who gave me one of the sweetest gifts I'd ever received was also the person giving Marek Blackwell inside information about the Omegas?

My second day as a teenager was nowhere near as good as my first.

Hogwarts in Harlem

Molly, is something wrong?"

Grayson was probably wondering why I was just staring blankly at my open locker.

"No," I said as I snapped out of it and shut the door. "Just tired. I didn't sleep well last night."

That was true, I hadn't slept well. In fact, I hadn't slept well all week. But that's not why I was dazed and confused. The lack of sleep hadn't put me in the funk, but the funk was keeping me up at night. It had been that way ever since I first suspected Natalie might be undead. I'd tossed and turned each night as I tried to figure out what I should do.

I thought about telling Alex and Grayson, but decided against it. There'd be no way to undo the damage if I was wrong.

"Are you sure that's all it is?" he said.

I smiled and lied. "I'm sure."

Before he could dig any deeper, the warning bell rang, signaling one minute until the next period began. We said our quick see-you-laters and hurried down the hall in opposite directions. I was just about to go into my English class, when I noticed a flyer posted next to the door.

According to the flyer, a professor at City College was going to give an "in-depth visual presentation about the birds of Central Park." That's a nice way of saying he was going to spend two hours showing pictures of mute swans, downy woodpeckers, and who knows how many of the other more than two hundred species that inhabit the park. I couldn't imagine a single one of my classmates wanting to sit through it.

It sounded boring to *me*, and I'm actually interested in birds. My mother convinced me to join the New York Audubon Society's Junior Birder program when I was eight, and as a result I can now identify most of the birds that are common in the city. I even know the difference between red-tailed hawks, which like to nest along Fifth Avenue, and red-shouldered hawks, which sometimes fly over the park but won't nest there.

Across the top of the flyer were pictures of five birds: a warbler, a swan, a starling, a heron, and a pigeon. It was the pigeon that caught my attention. New York is overrun with pigeons. They're everywhere. But the pigeon in this picture isn't the type you'd find in Central Park. It's the kind you'd find in Central Africa. It's even called the African pigeon.

If Professor Michael Stimola, PhD was actually a leading bird expert, how could he possibly make that mistake? I was trying to figure this out when Ms. White tapped me on the shoulder.

"Molly, will you be joining us?" she asked.

I shrugged. "Probably not. It sounds really boring."

When I saw her expression, I realized she wasn't talking about the lecture. The tardy bell had rung and she was about to close the door and start class.

"Wait a second, you meant English class, didn't you?"

"That is why they pay me."

"Of course I'll be joining you," I said sheepishly. "And, for the record, I'm sure it won't be boring at all."

"Better answer," she replied.

We were discussing *A Wrinkle in Time*, a science-fiction

book about a girl who travels through time, searching for her lost father.

It's my favorite of the books we've read for class. I especially like Meg, the main character. She's geeky, socially awkward, and desperate to reunite with a missing parent. In other words, she's a lot like the girl I see in the mirror every morning. Despite this connection, I was having trouble staying interested in the class discussion.

The mistake on the flyer just bothered me too much. So rather than take notes that might come in handy on our upcoming test, I doodled the names of the five birds down the side of my paper and stared at them.

Warbler
Swan
Starling
Heron
Pigeon

I'll admit that I may have been making a big deal over nothing more than a simple mistake. I have been known to do that. I even have a history of overreacting to geographically misplaced birds.

My dad loves to tell the story about when I was six years old and we visited a neighborhood that was decorated for Christmas. We were walking through a yard that was made to look like Santa's workshop at the North Pole. I started laughing because there were giant plastic penguins in Santa hats. I didn't mean to be rude. I thought it was a joke and that you were supposed to laugh, because *everybody* knows that penguins only live in the Southern Hemisphere, not the Northern.

Well, apparently not everybody.

It turns out it wasn't a joke and the people who lived there were offended. I apologized and later my parents explained that you don't always need to point out mistakes that others make. I usually do a good job of remembering that, but this was different. This was a bird expert giving a lecture at a top college.

I kept doodling and filled in the formal names of the different species.

orange-crowned warbler
mute swan
European starling
great blue heron
African pigeon

It took me about thirty seconds to see it, but when I did I let out a hoot that made Ms. White stop in the middle of a sentence.

"Is there something you'd like to add to the discussion, Molly?"

All eyes trained on me. "Just . . . that it's a . . . really good book."

"That's all?" she asked, shooting me a look.

I nodded. "Pretty much."

"Let's hope your book report goes into greater detail."

"It will," I promised.

The instant she went back to talking, I looked back at my paper and smiled. My funk was over and my heart was racing as I drew a circle around the first letter in each name like I was playing a word search puzzle.

It spelled out "Omega."

It had to be a message from my mother. She's the one who made me join the Junior Birders, and she'd know I'd be the only student who could decipher the code. I don't know how she got it posted next to the door to my English class, but I was certain she was trying to tell me something. I wanted to get a hall pass so I could go back and look for more clues on the flyer, but I figured I'd already caused enough distractions in this class for one day, so I waited until the bell rang.

The lecture was scheduled for Saturday at noon. I couldn't wait to tell the others. But then I noticed something else on the bottom. There were pictures of five more birds: an albatross, a loon, an owl, a nighthawk, and an eagle. Using the same coding method, I realized the first letter of each spelled out the word "alone."

I guess my mother didn't want the others to come with me. Maybe it had to do with Natalie. If Mom knew she was undead, she might not trust her to be part of the team.

That Saturday I took the train to 137th Street and walked the last couple blocks to the CCNY campus. (CCNY is the abbreviation for City College of New York.) Part of me felt like the time travelers in the book I was reading, because one moment I was walking in modern day New York, and then I passed through a giant archway and found myself in a secret world of tree-lined paths and gothic buildings. It was like Hogwarts in Harlem.

The campus was built at the same time many of the city's subway tunnels were being dug, and as a result the buildings were constructed out of the leftover rock. That's right, it's an entire campus made out of Manhattan schist. The first thought that went through my mind was that Natalie should think about going to college here where she would be surrounded by it. (That is, if Natalie turned out to be a zombie, which I was still hoping wouldn't be the case.)

The largest building on campus is Shepard Hall, which looks like a medieval cathedral. It's even decorated with gargoyles and grotesque statues on the walls and archways. The presentation was scheduled for a lecture hall on the third floor, and even though I got there right before the noon start time, the room was entirely empty. Apparently, I wasn't the only person who thought it sounded boring.

I took a seat in the middle of the third row. Moments later a giant bell in the building's main tower struck twelve times, and I heard someone enter the room behind me and close the door.

I turned to see a man with a friendly face and a close-cropped white beard. He wore jeans and a sport coat along with a black beret that gave him the air of professorial creativity.

"Hello, I'm Dr. Stimola, and I'd like to welcome you to the City College Lecture Series," he announced, starting right up while he was still in the back of the room fumbling with some equipment. "I'm an ornithologist, and if any of you are unfamiliar with that term, 'ornithology,' it's the study of birds."

Any of us? I looked around the room to make sure that I was still the only other person there. I was.

The lights dimmed, and a picture of a green-headed duck was projected on a screen at the front of the room.

"I'd like for us to get started with some of the more common birds in the park," he continued. "This is *Anas platyrhynchos*, better known as the Mallard or the wild duck."

I was totally confused. He was acting like there was a room full of students, and I was worried that I'd misread the clue and was now stuck in a two-hour lecture about birds given by a man even more socially awkward than I am. He continued to drone on about the mallard, and I was trying to figure out a way to excuse myself when a tap on my shoulder startled me. I almost leapt out of my seat.

"Shh," he whispered.

I turned to see that it was the professor. At some point when he was setting up, he'd stopped talking and was instead playing a prerecorded version of the lecture.

"Hello, Molly. Your mother wanted me to tell you that the Gingerbread House was entirely your fault."

I was totally confused for a moment, and then I made the connection. Once, when we were on a vacation to Pennsylvania, I picked a place for us to eat lunch. It was called the Gingerbread House and it was terrible. Everyone blamed me for the lousy meal and I was banned from picking restaurants from that point on. I thought this was completely unfair for one simple reason.

"I was five years old," I said, shaking my head in disbelief.

"You know who else was five years old?" he asked.

I thought about it for a moment and answered, "Mozart, when he started composing music."

It was a running joke between my mother and me. She said that if Mozart was old enough to compose music, I was old enough to take the blame for the Gingerbread House.

"Is that why you wanted me to come here today?" I asked. "So you could blame me for something I did when I was five?"

"No," he said with a nice smile. "I'm blaming you so you'll know that your mother sent me and that it's safe to come with me."

"Come with you where?" I asked.

"I'll let her tell you when we get there."

"I'm going to see my Mom?"

He nodded. "And she's not alone."

The Catacombs of CCNY

The presentation continued on autopilot as the pre-recorded lecture played and pictures of birds were projected onto the screen. Meanwhile, I followed the professor into an office that was located at the front of the lecture hall, and he signaled me to be quiet until we were inside and he shut the door.

"We've got a lot to do and not a lot of time," he added. "So please give me your backpack."

"Why?" I asked as I handed it to him.

"I'm pretty sure that's where they hid it."

"Hid what?" I asked.

"It's easier if I just show it to you," he said as he started digging through my backpack. The shelves in his office were filled with books about birds and beautiful black-and-white photos of the city.

"Cool shot," I said, admiring one of the Chrysler Building.

"Thanks," he said as he kept digging. "I started off taking pictures of birds, and then I became fascinated with the city and its architecture."

I already knew that I liked him.

We could hear the lecture continue in the other room. "The northern cardinal has a wingspan of twenty-five to thirty-one centimeters . . ."

"By the way, my real class discussions are much more interesting. This one was intentionally designed to keep people away."

I laughed. "It seems to have worked, but why go to all of the trouble of having a recording."

"I locked the door and put up a 'do not interrupt' sign, but just in case any of Marek's men come and put an ear up to the door, I want them to overhear the most boring lecture in the history of mankind. It should get rid of them pretty quickly."

"I don't think anyone was following me," I said. "I was careful."

"They don't need to follow you," he said as he turned a pocket of my backpack inside out. "They have this." He pointed at a small silver and glass capsule that was hidden in one of the seams.

"What is that?" I asked in total disbelief.

"An RFID chip," he explained. "Radio-frequency identification. It's what they put in pet collars so you can find your dog if he gets lost."

I was stunned. "Does that mean they've been listening to me?"

"No, it's not a microphone," he said. "They can't hear anything. They can't even track where you are all the time. That would burn through the battery too quickly. But whenever they want to find you, they can send a signal and they'll get a reply on a map."

"I can't believe it," I said. "So you're destroying it?"

"I'm doing no such thing," he said. "If we destroyed it they'd know you found it and they'd come up with another way to track you. Let them think they've got you fooled. Just don't ever forget it's in there. For now, though, we're going to leave it behind."

He placed the backpack on his desk.

"If they look for you in the next two hours, they'll think you're here," he said. "Which is good, because we don't want them to know where you'll really be."

He opened a closet door and pulled on a shelf to reveal a hidden door and a spiral staircase running through the building.

"Cool, isn't it?" he said when he saw my reaction.

"Amazing," I said. "Where's it go?"

He flashed a big smile. "Have you ever heard of the catacombs of CCNY?"

"No?"

"That's good," he said as he started making his way down the stairs. "We like to keep them a secret."

The staircase was the color of tarnished brass and seemed to descend forever as I followed the professor all the way to the bottom. There we reached a long narrow tunnel cut into the Manhattan schist. The walls were close enough so I could reach out and touch both sides at the same time. It's a good thing I'm only scared of heights, because if I were claustrophobic I might have passed out.

"Stay close," he said as he motioned for me to follow. "The lighting's bad and you do not want to get lost down here."

"You got that right," I replied as I hurried to keep up with his pace.

As far as freaky scary elements go, the tunnel had plenty. The lights were dim and spaced far enough apart so that you had to walk through pools of total darkness every twenty feet or so. But that was nothing compared to the otherworldly rumbling and hissing noises that passed overhead at regular intervals. The professor assured me that although they sounded like a phantom army of disembodied souls coming to attack us, they were actually caused by something much more mundane.

"Steam pipes," he explained, pointing toward the ceiling. "They heat up the buildings on campus."

"They do a good job on the tunnel, too," I replied, wiping the sweat from my forehead. "It's like a rainforest down here."

Soon we veered into a mazelike series of brick passageways. I tried to memorize the turns but quickly lost track. I was hopelessly confused by the time we dead-ended into a wall with three large pipes running along it. Each pipe had a valve control that looked like a steering wheel, and hanging from each wheel was a metal sign reading, CAUTION—EXTREME HEAT.

"This is where it gets tricky," he said ominously.

I nodded back toward the path we just traveled. "You mean all of that wasn't tricky?"

He laughed.

"Okay, this is where it gets *trickier*. Two of these are release valves. If you turn either one, it will let off a steam blast that can be as hot as four hundred degrees."

"So I'm guessing we don't want to turn those," I said.

"No we don't," he said. "But if any of Marek's men ever made it this far and they were trying to locate what I'm about to show you . . ."

"They wouldn't be able to tell which one wasn't real," I said, finishing his sentence. "Because they can't feel the heat on the pipes."

"That's right," he said. "You're good at this."

He turned the middle wheel and I reflexively braced for a blast of steam, but instead there was only the sound of a door opening. The wheel was actually a giant doorknob, and when he pushed on it, that portion of the brick wall opened to reveal a large laboratory.

"Welcome to the *Workshop*," he said with dramatic flair.

The lab looked like something out of an old Frankenstein movie but modern. It was as if someone had taken the scientific equipment of a century ago and partially updated it so that it seemed both antique and new at the same time. Across the room two scientists were working on an experiment. They wore thick white lab coats and aviator-style safety goggles with blue lenses. It took me a moment to recognize that one of them was my mother.

"Molly!" she said as she took off the goggles. "I knew you'd figure out the clue."

She hurried over and wrapped me up in a huge hug. For a moment I closed my eyes and ignored our surroundings. It was just my mother and me, and I needed this more than anything.

"What is this place?" I asked, admiring at it all.

"We call it the Workshop," she said. "It's where we do research and planning. I guess you could say that it's Omega's headquarters."

As her lab partner approached and took off his goggles, I realized that it was Dr. Gootman, or rather the man I knew as Dr. Gootman when he was principal at MIST. I later learned he was actually Milton Blackwell, one of the so-called Unlucky 13, the original zombies who became undead when an explosion killed the crew digging the city's first subway tunnel. He founded Omega to keep his brother Marek and the other eleven from getting out of control.

"Hi, Dr. Gootman . . . or should I call you Mr. Blackwell . . . or is it Dr. Blackwell?"

"Let's go with Milton."

"Okay," I said, feeling both cool and awkward at the same time. "Milton."

"You're the first one to arrive," Mom said. "So why don't I show you around while we wait for the others?"

"There are others coming?" I asked, surprised. "The code on the flyer said you wanted me to come alone."

"We did want you to come alone," she said. "If all of you were together, your trackers would have set off an alarm."

"What do you mean?"

"The radio frequency ID tags they put on you and the rest of your team," she said. "They're not only designed so that Marek's men can find you but also to let them know if you are working together. If any three of the trackers are in the same location other than at school, it sets off an alarm."

"That's why we sent each of you a separate message to lead you to different starting points across the city," said Milton. "It took a lot of planning, but it was necessary, because we can't let Marek find out about this lab. We still have too much work to do."

I looked up at him and suddenly felt panicked.

"Does that mean you invited Natalie? Here?"

Mom gave me a confused look. "Of course we did. We

invited your whole team so we can give you all your new assignment."

This was bad news. If I was right and Natalie was a Level 2, then her learning the location of Mom and Milton's hideout would be a disaster.

"I don't know if that's a good idea," I said.

"Why not?" asked Mom.

Before I could explain, the door opened and Natalie entered with Liberty, who had been her guide like Dr. Stimola was mine. They, of course, had no idea I was just questioning her invitation, so they were all friendly smiles when they came through the door.

"Okay," Natalie said, marveling at the lab. "This may be the coolest place on earth."

"Thank you," said Milton. "I'm pretty fond of it myself."

All of my worlds were colliding, and I was desperately trying to keep calm about it. Somehow I had to tell Mom about my suspicions. She'd know what to do. I turned to talk to her, but Liberty intercepted me and gave me a big hug.

"Hey, Molly, happy belated birthday."

"Thanks," I said.

"Thirteen, right?" he said.

"Let's just hope it's not unlucky thirteen."

I tried to break free from the little conversation, but before I could, Natalie had come over to my mother.

"Where are we exactly?" she asked her. "I tried to keep track of where Liberty was leading me, but I got it all turned around in my head."

Natalie didn't know our exact location and that was good. I didn't give Mom a chance to tell her. Instead, I interrupted and changed the subject.

"What was your clue?" I asked Natalie. "I'm supposedly at a lecture on the birds of Central Park at CCNY."

The sudden change of subject caught her off guard, but one of the advantages of being socially awkward (which I am times a thousand) is that people are used to odd transitions. Rather than wait for an answer to her question, she answered mine.

"I'm at a lecture too," she replied. "It's at the Museum of Natural History, where I'm listening to excruciatingly in-depth analysis of STS-135, the final mission of the space shuttle."

I gave her a confused look. "That was a clue?"

"Since it was the shuttle's last flight, the mission logo was an Omega symbol," she explained.

"And you knew that?"

She smiled sheepishly. "Doesn't everyone?"

Like I said, my worlds were colliding. Here she was, my best friend, a total genius, and I was trying to figure out whether or not she was the enemy.

"So why are we here?" Natalie asked with anticipation. "Are we getting a new assignment?"

"Yes," my mom said. "We want you to—"

"Wait," I said, interrupting again. "We should wait for Grayson and Alex to get here before we talk about anything. That way we'll make sure we all have the same information and there won't be any confusion. And while we're waiting, Mom, I thought you and I might talk for a second . . . alone."

As I moved toward Mom, Natalie looked over at the collection of test tubes and beakers where Milton and my mother had been working.

"What kind of experiments are you working on?" she asked him.

I started to interrupt again, but I didn't really have anything to say. Natalie was frustrated. She started to ask, "Is there a reason you don't want me to . . ." and then she stopped midsentence as she figured it out. The whole room got quiet, and she looked me right in the eyes.

"You know, don't you?" she asked.

"Know what?" I said, trying to play dumb.

"You know exactly what I mean," she said.

I nodded. "Yes," I said softly, "I know."

"When did you figure it out?"

"The day after my birthday, when I came to visit you," I said.

"But you didn't ask me about it."

I shrugged. "I tried to, but I couldn't do it. I kept hoping you would tell me."

She was quiet for a moment, thinking back to that day.

"I almost did," she said. "But I was worried about how you'd take it. I don't mean you specifically, but the three of you. I was especially worried about Alex."

I hate to say it, but I was worried about Alex too. More than any of us, he's distrustful of the undead. It took him way longer to warm up to Liberty than it did the rest of us, and I wasn't sure how he'd respond to finding out about Natalie.

"I would have kept your secret," I said. "In fact, I did keep it. I haven't told anyone. Not even Mom."

"It wasn't a secret to her."

I looked over at my mother.

"The three of us have known since New Year's," she said, nodding toward Milton and Liberty. "We've been working with her and trying to help her adjust to her new life. It's hard, but she's been doing great. I'm really proud of her."

I had only seen my mother once since New Year's and Natalie had seen her multiple times. I'd be lying if I said it didn't hurt my feelings. I understand that Natalie was in an incredibly difficult situation and needed help, but I needed help too. I wanted her to be proud of me, too.

"We thought she should be the one to decide when it was the right time to tell you guys," said Liberty. "I know first hand how difficult that can be."

"That makes sense," I said.

"But I don't understand why you don't want them to tell me where we are or what they're working on, just because I'm undead," she said. "Everyone in this room is, except for you. It shouldn't be a problem."

I didn't know what to say, so I just kept quiet and looked right at her.

"Unless you think I'm a Level 2."

I didn't say yes, but I didn't say no either. I just kept looking at her and watched her face fill with sadness.

"That's it, isn't it?" she asked. "You think I'm an L2."

All eyes were on me, but too much was at stake to do anything but tell the truth.

"Yes, I do."

RUNY

It was terrible. I had just completely devastated my best friend, and I did it right in front of the people who mattered the most to us both. I'd accused her of being a Level 2 zombie. Which is another way of saying I'd accused her of being the enemy. She didn't respond. She just looked like she was about to cry.

"Why would you think that?" asked Mom.

First I hadn't liked the fact that Mom and Natalie had been working together. Now I didn't like that it seemed like she was taking Natalie's side.

"Somebody told Marek about our secret code," I said

pointedly. "Somebody told him that we left messages for each other on the Delacorte Clock. It wasn't me and it wasn't you. Natalie was the only other person who knew."

"You think I told Marek?" Natalie asked, even more shocked than before. "You do realize he's the reason I'm in the condition I'm in? And that I've spent the last three years fighting him?"

"I'm confused," said Milton. "What's this about a code and a clock?"

"The clock by the Central Park Zoo," I told him. "It's where Mom and I agreed to leave messages for each other. Last Christmas Eve, I left one telling her to come to the ice skating rink at Rockefeller Center. Natalie discovered it and surprised us there. That's when she first found out that Mom was undead."

I turned back to Natalie.

"And that's the only time we ever used the clock," I said. "The next time, it was actually Marek using it to lure us. You remember, he did it the same day you told me you were certain that Mom would leave me a message sometime soon. The day you told me to go check it."

"So now you think I'm helping him set a trap for you?" she asked. "After all that we've been through. Don't you remember that I'm the one who asked you to join Omega in the first place? That I'm the one who oversaw your training?"

"I remember all of it, including the part where you said that I should always be careful and assume that anyone who's undead is a Level 2 until they prove otherwise. That it's better to hurt the feelings of a zombie than it is to endanger the lives of your team."

"I would think you'd make an exception for your best friend. After all, I'm not just a zombie. I'm also part of that team you're protecting."

I didn't know how to reply, so things were quiet for a moment. It sounds weird, but the thing that caught my attention was that she considered herself my best friend. Hearing that out loud made my feel even worse about it all.

"By the way, I wasn't the only one who showed up at the skating rink that night," she said. "There was also the zombie who attacked you on the ice. The one who your mother and I had to get rid of. The one who I killed to protect you."

It had never occurred to me that the zombie had seen the message too. I had assumed she just saw me there at the rink and attacked. But it made total sense that she might have uncovered the code just like Natalie had. My mind was racing in reverse.

"Ahh, now you remember," she said, reading my reaction.

"She must have passed the word along to Marek, because I certainly didn't."

It was like a punch to gut. I was suddenly short of breath as I thought through her explanation.

"I'm so sorry," I said. "I forgot all about her."

Natalie went to say something, but my mother interrupted.

"Grayson and Alex are about to get here," she said, pointing at a pair of security monitors that showed them both approaching the lab. "Is this a discussion you want to continue in front of them?"

Natalie looked at me for a moment, then shook her head. "No. It's not."

"Okay," she said. "Molly, knowing what you know now, do you have anything you want to say to Natalie?"

"I really am sorry," I told Natalie. "I was just trying to be careful, and I ended up being stupid."

She seemed unsatisfied with my apology, but with the boys almost to the door she didn't have many options.

"Fine," she said curtly. "Forget about it."

"Good," said my mother. "Because we've got a lot of information to go over."

Moments later Grayson and Alex arrived, and I tried to act like things were normal between us all. Mom and

Milton showed us around the lab, and as they did I noticed Natalie kept her distance from me. Every now and then I caught her glaring my way. I couldn't blame her. I just hoped that the excitement of a new assignment would help distract her from it and make her focus on the work we had to do.

My mother gathered us all around a large wooden table in the corner of the lab and laid out a map of Manhattan.

"Let's talk about RUNY, that's R-U-N-Y," she said. "It stands for Reinventing Underground New York, and it's Marek's big idea. Through his connections with the mayor's office he has taken control of five abandoned subway stations."

She marked them on the map. Three were near each other in Lower Manhattan, another was in Midtown, and the last was on the Upper West Side.

"He is converting them into public areas with restaurants and stores and turning them into underground parks," she continued. "This one even has a playground."

She showed us an architect's rendering of one of the projects. It reminded me of the High Line, which is in the Lower West Side and is about a mile long. Once, it was an abandoned elevated train track, but now it's a public park thirty feet above the ground. Marek was using the same concept, except he was building below the street instead of above.

"It's like he's taking everything about a flatline party and making it permanent," said Alex.

"That's exactly what it is," she replied.

The undead have to go underground for about an hour a day in order to recharge their energy from the Manhattan schist. They often do this at flatline parties, which are held in abandoned sewers and tunnels.

Grayson looked at the drawing and then at all of us. "I know it's Marek and he's evil and all, but this actually sounds like something good. The flatline parties can be scary and dangerous, and this will be much better for everyone. Right?"

"Yes," said Milton. "It's pure genius. He's taking abandoned property that no one else wants and turning it into something useful. And, if all he's doing is making them safe places for the undead, then we're not going to get in his way. But knowing Marek we have to consider that it may be part of something bigger and more sinister. And if that's the case, we have to be prepared to react."

"So what's our assignment?" asked Natalie.

"You're going to find out if RUNY is what he says it is, or if it is what we worry it might be," said Mom.

"Actually," I said, "someone sent me an anonymous letter about this very thing."

Everyone looked at me.

"Who?" asked Grayson.

I gave him a look. "I have no idea. That's why I said it was anonymous."

"And you kept this a *secret*?" Natalie asked. "What's the matter? Didn't you trust us?"

"We weren't supposed to do anything Omega related, so I just kept the letters in my dresser drawer."

"Letters?" she replied. "I thought you said there was *an* anonymous letter. As in one. Now there are letters, plural."

Despite her accusatory tone, I tried to keep my emotions balanced.

"I received two letters," I said. "But only one was about RUNY."

"What did it say?" asked my mother, cutting off our little back and forth drama.

"There was a newspaper clipping about Marek and the ghost stations," I replied. "And a single question written on a piece of paper. 'How is he paying for this?'"

Mom and Milton looked at each other and nodded. "I don't know who sent it," said Mom, "but that's the two-hundred-million-dollar question, because we know he's spent at least that much money so far."

We were all stunned by this number.

"Two hundred million dollars," I said, shaking my head. "Where could he possibly get that much money?"

"That's the key to everything," said Milton. "If we can figure out how he's coming up with the money, then we'll have a better understanding of what he's up to."

"In addition to converting the ghost stations, he's also been doing some other unusual things that appear to be completely random and unrelated," said Mom. "But with Marek, nothing is really ever random. It just looks that way until later on when you see the big picture."

"What types of things?" asked Natalie.

"Out of the blue he donated a lot of money to support the research of one of my colleagues at CCNY," said Professor Stimola. "She's a historian who specializes in the American Revolution."

I instantly thought of the man who attacked my mother and me. I turned to Mom and said, "The guy in the boathouse. He was reading a book about the Revolutionary War."

"It gets better," she replied as she picked up the book off of a nearby table and handed it to me. "This is the book he was carrying."

"*Defending Manhattan: New York City During the Revolutionary War*, by Denise Hendricks," I said, reading from the cover.

"Denise Hendricks is the professor who Marek is suddenly funding," said the professor.

"That does seem like a big coincidence," said Grayson.

"Does she have any particular expertise about George Washington?" I asked.

The professor nodded. "She does. In fact she's writing a biography of him right now. Why do you ask?"

"That was the second anonymous letter," I explained. "It had a map of Manhattan locations that related to Washington, and a note that told me to 'Reserve a place in history.'"

"Any other letters or secrets we should know about?" asked Natalie.

I shook my head. "No. That's it."

I couldn't tell if Grayson and Alex noticed the tension between Natalie and me, but they were probably too excited about the new mission to pay any attention to it.

"What else has been going on with Marek?" asked Grayson.

"There's a company we want to find out about," said Milton. "The Empire State Tungsten Company."

"Back to the man in the boathouse," I said to Mom. "According to his business card he was their vice president."

"That's right," she said. "The company has come up a few

more times in relation to Marek and the Unlucky 13. For example, they just sponsored a fundraiser for the NYPD's brand-new Departmental Emergency Action Deployment Squadron."

"The Dead Squad," said Alex.

"Another amazing coincidence," she replied. "We think these things are all related. We just haven't been able to figure out how, and recent developments have made it almost impossible for us to go above ground to look for answers."

I was trying to figure out what "recent developments" meant when Milton explained.

"She's referring to my brother's current medical state," he said.

We all exchanged confused looks.

"How do you mean?" asked Alex.

"Marek's doctors were able to rebuild him using body parts from my cousins and from my brother Cornelius," he said. "It's quite remarkable, actually. But apparently his body is beginning to reject those parts that came from cousins, while those that came from Cornelius are working perfectly. It seems as though he needs a closer genetic match to make the repairs permanent."

Grayson was the first one of us to really understand what he was implying.

"Do you mean he wants your body parts?" he asked.

"That is *exactly* what I mean," replied Milton.

"As a result, Milton has to keep an extra-low profile," Mom added. "The Dead Squad is looking everywhere for him. They're also on the lookout for me, because they think I'm the way to reach him. That's why we need your help. You can cover more ground than us. You can solve this."

"I've got a plan," said Natalie. "We can only be together as a group at school or else the trackers will go off, right?"

"That's right," said Mom.

"Okay, each one of us will take a specific area," Natalie said, turning to the Alex, Grayson, and me. "Then we'll rotate working in pairs and help each other out. That way we'll follow all the possible leads but also be more likely to see how they come together."

Alex looked to Milton and Mom. "Now you see why we made her the captain."

Mom laughed. "Good choice."

Natalie smiled but otherwise ignored the compliment. She was doing what she did best.

"Grayson, you're going to find out everything there is to know about the Empire State Tungsten Company. Get Zeus on it and start hacking away at every computer database you can find that may be able to help."

"Got it," he said.

"Alex, you know more about the NYPD than all the rest of us combined. Try to figure out as much as you can about the Dead Squad, how they work, and how they're trying to find Milton and Molly's mom."

"My uncle Paul should be able to help with that," he said.

Too much was riding on this, so I decided I had to speak up. "Actually," I said guiltily, "there is something else that I forgot to mention that might be a big help with that."

Everyone looked at me, curious as to what it could be.

"What is it?" asked Natalie. "Another anonymous letter? I thought there were only two."

"No," I responded, more than a little wounded. "I have one of their walkie-talkies. It's set specifically on the band the Dead Squad uses to communicate."

"Seriously?" said Alex. "How did you get it?"

His was not the only expectant look.

"Officer Pell, the one-eared cop who threatened us. Well, the other day he attacked me in Central Park."

That was all I had to say for my mom to respond. "Molly, what did I tell you about—"

"I wasn't doing anything Omega related," I said. "He

just saw an opportunity and he attacked me. I had my back-pack with me; he must have been tracking me at the time."

"Where were you exactly?" asked Mom.

I took a deep breath. "The Blockhouse up in the north-west corner of the park. It was quiet and secluded and we were all alone."

Now the most intense look came from Natalie. The Blockhouse didn't mean anything to the others the way it did to her.

"What were you doing at the Blockhouse?" she asked.

"I was just out exploring. I read about it in a book and wanted to check it out firsthand."

Judging by her expression she didn't necessarily believe this explanation, but the others had no reason to suspect anything so I just kept going.

"Anyway, he attacked me and I beat him back. I don't think I killed him, but I may have. I used the walkie-talkie as a weapon and took it without even realizing I had it with me."

"And what did you do with it after that?" asked my mother. "Have you been eavesdropping on them?"

"No. I turned it off and stuck it in my closet," I said. "I haven't touched it since then. I only kept it because I thought it might be useful in case something like this came along."

"That was good thinking," said Alex. "I'll come by and pick it up later today. If I can listen in on their communication, I can really find out a lot about them. That's huge, Molly."

"Great," I said. I turned back to Natalie and asked, "What's my assignment? Are you and I going to split up the ghost stations?"

"No, I'll take all of those," she said. "I want you to figure out how the Revolutionary War and a history professor fit in to all of this."

I'm going to be honest. My assignment sounded completely boring. I couldn't help but think that Natalie had given it to me as some sort of punishment. But I didn't complain.

We talked for a little bit more about our assignments, and then Grayson asked Milton the same question that Natalie had asked earlier.

"What experiments are you working on?"

He thought about it for a moment before answering. "In a way it's the same experiment I've been working on for the past hundred years. I'm still trying to identify what it is about Manhattan schist that makes all of this possible. How the minerals within a rock keep the undead from dying."

Soon it was time for us to go back. Just as when we'd

arrived, we left with our guides one at a time. Natalie made sure she was the first to leave. My guess is that she didn't want to continue our conversation, and I can't say that I was disappointed. Even though I knew it was unlikely, part of me was hoping that the problem would just go away.

I was the last to leave, which gave me a few minutes to talk to Mom.

"I was just trying to be cautious," I told her once we were all alone.

"I know, sweetie," she replied. "You just have to understand how it sounded to her. She's scared. Her whole world is turned upside down, and now her best friend says that she can't be trusted. It's hard."

I nodded. "I know."

There wasn't really anything else to say about it, so she switched topics. "How's the family?" she asked. "What's going on at home?"

"They're great," I said. "Beth just got a job working in a drama camp this summer. And Dad is, well, he's Dad. He makes it all work out. He told us this great story about when you two were dating and went to the opera."

Mom laughed. "When he confused *La Traviata* and *Il Trovatore*?"

"That's the one."

"That was the night that I knew I loved him," she said.

That comment made me smile. "That's funny, because he said it was the night he knew he loved you, too."

Neither of us said anything for a moment, and then I said, "They miss you so much. I wish they could see you. Like I've gotten to."

She thought about this before replying. "I just don't see how that's possible. I don't see how we can bring them into this world and upend their lives that way. I feel bad enough that it's happened to you."

"I don't feel bad about it at all," I said. "I feel lucky that we have this to share."

Dr. Stimola told me that it was time for us to go, so I said good-bye, and a few minutes later he was leading me back through the catacombs, up the spiral staircase, and into his office. All I could think about was Natalie. Even though I already suspected that she was undead, having it confirmed was intense. I felt terrible for her.

When the professor and I entered the lecture hall, I heard the end of his prerecorded talk.

"Which brings us to the red-tailed hawk," said the voice. "This particular one is named Pale Male. When he was young, he tried to build a nest in a tree in the park but was driven away by a murder of crows. That's right, a group of crows is called a murder. But Pale Male adapted and found a new home on the ledge of a building on Fifth Avenue. He was the first hawk to nest on a building, and with this adaptation he began a dynasty of hawks in Central Park. Today they soar above the park, and like all birds of prey, look for their victims below."

I had heard the story of Pale Male before when I was with the Junior Birders, but this time it made me think of the undead. Just like the hawks, they were driven away from the good parts of the city and forced to adapt. Pale Male chose the ledge of a building, and they picked the underground. And now they had become like birds of prey, keeping their distance and watching potential victims, waiting for just the right moment to strike. I was reminded of this when the lecture ended and I left the building. As I stepped out onto St. Nicholas Terrace, I saw him standing across the street, watching.

He was a cop, a member of the Dead Squad, and it was obvious that he'd been waiting for me. Checking to make sure I was where my transmitter said I was. Circling above, like a red-tailed hawk looking for prey.

14

Teamwork

The next six weeks reminded me a lot of the training I went through when I first joined Omega. Just like then, I was paired with different teammates on different days. Only now, instead of them teaching me how to break codes and fight zombies, we worked together trying to unravel the mysteries of RUNY. (The other big difference was that now there was an unmistakable sense of tension I had to work through with Natalie as I tried to regain her trust.)

Alex was a total rock star as he figured out the inner workings of the Dead Squad. He used the walkie-talkie I took from Officer Pell and rigged it so that he could hide it in his backpack and listen in on all their communications with a pair of earbuds. He sat in the park every day, and to anyone who happened to notice him, he just looked like a regular teenager listening to music.

"Sometimes I even hear them talking about watching me, while they're watching me," he told me. "It's surreal."

After a couple weeks he was able to determine that there were a dozen officers on the squad and that they had two basic jobs. They were either on Omega detail, which meant they followed us around and searched for Milton and Mom, or they were on protection duty guarding Marek.

Alex's favorite place to eavesdrop on them was at Belvedere Castle in the middle of Central Park. It was designed to look like a castle but is actually home to a nature center and the weather service. Alex liked it because the reception on the top floor observation deck was crystal clear.

"It's so good because the Dead Squad is headquartered in the Central Park precinct of the NYPD," he explained one day when I was with him.

"I wonder why they chose Central Park as their home base?" I asked.

"It took a little research to figure out," he told me.

"But it turns out the Central Park precinct house is made entirely out of Manhattan schist. That way they can be on duty and recharge at the same time."

It was the perfect place for a squad of zombies to work.

Sometimes I joined Alex up on the observation deck and the two of us would plug in and listen together. Usually I could only understand about half of what was being said, because they used a mix of regular English, police terminology, and code words. Like this exchange we overheard:

"Advise, what is Coyote's 10-20?"

"CPW and 70."

It didn't make any sense to me, but Alex leaned over and whispered, "Natalie must be walking home."

"Why do you say that?"

"Coyote's 10-20, that mean's Coyote's location," he said. "Natalie is Coyote, and CPW and 70 is Central Park West and West Seventieth. My guess is she's walking home."

"Natalie is *Coyote*?" I said. "We have code names?"

At first he smiled, but then he cringed and muttered, "Well, yeah."

"What's my code name?" I asked.

"It's not important," he said. "The names don't have

any real meaning. They're just randomly assigned words. Nothing special."

"What is it?" I demanded.

He hesitated before finally giving in. "Gopher."

"*Gopher?* Are you serious?" It took everything I had not to scream at the top of my lungs. "Why am I Gopher?"

"Gophers are really good at digging and tunneling," he said. "You're really good at going underground and finding your way through tunnels. I think it's meant as a compliment."

"A compliment? A gopher is a *rodent*. With huge teeth!" Instinctively I reached up and felt my two front teeth. "Are my teeth oversized?"

"Of course not," he said. "They're perfectly-sized."

"Natalie's Coyote, which is majestic, and I'm Gopher, which is . . . the opposite of majestic. I think I want to file a complaint. What's your code name?"

"You don't want to know," he said.

"Oh, I *want* to know."

He tried not to smile as he said it. "Wolverine."

"Totally unfair. That is the coolest code name in the world."

"Isn't it? I think because I'm such a good fighter." He let out a little growl and did what I can only suspect is a wolverine fighting motion with his hands. (Or should I say paws?)

I know it's ridiculous, but I was offended. I would have kept going on about it, but another transmission caught our attention.

"Advise, what is Eagle's 10-20?"

"Who's Eagle?" I asked. "So help me if that's Grayson's code name . . ."

"No, Eagle is Marek."

Over the radio we heard the response, *"He's home at M42."*

Alex and I both turned and looked at each other at the same time.

"Did he say *home* and *M42*?" I asked.

"He sure did."

This was huge. M42 is a secret bunker located deep below Grand Central Terminal. It was once a CIA safe house but had been taken over by the Unlucky 13. It's where Marek's doctors rebuilt him, and if we heard right, it was also now where Marek lived.

"It makes sense, considering his health," Alex said. "They have everything set up there for treatments and transplants. His doctors can monitor him."

Not once since Omega began in the early 1900s had

we been able to identify an actual home for Marek. It had always been a mystery. But now we thought we had, and after a week of follow up Alex was able to confirm that we were right.

While Alex was having great success with his research into the Dead Squad, Grayson was having a more difficult time learning about the Empire State Tungsten Company. Unfortunately, there was no walkie-talkie-like piece of equipment to help him. He did have Zeus, the most amazing computer I've ever seen, but so far every time he thought he might be on the verge of a breakthrough, he ran into a dead end.

Before I could be any help to him, he had to give me a crash course on the importance of tungsten. He explained that it's a hard metal used in lightbulbs and X-ray machines.

"Does Marek have anything to do with either lightbulbs or X-rays?" I asked.

"Not that I can find," he replied. "But the truth is, I can't find out much about the company, either. They seem to buy a lot of tungsten, but there isn't any record of what they do with it once they get it."

Grayson is out of control smart and great at solving puzzles, and I don't think I had ever seen him so frustrated. Once, he told me he'd spent an entire week working on it without figuring out a single new piece of information. Then one day he asked me to meet him at Leonardo's, a pizza place in Midtown. We ordered a couple slices and ate them as we walked up Lexington Avenue.

"Very good," he said after his first bite. "Sweet and tangy sauce, good firm crust."

Grayson considers himself a pizza expert and is in constant search of the perfect slice. After he took a few more bites, he jotted down some ratings in a little notebook he always carries. Later these would be entered into his pizza database for further referencing. He's designing an app called Perfect Pizza π, but says it's still too early in the development stage for him to share any details with the rest of us.

"Is that why we came here?" I asked. "So you could try out a new slice?"

"No, the slice is my reward for finally making a breakthrough. We're here because of this . . ."

We'd reached the corner of Forty-second and Lex, and he pointed up at the Chrysler Building, which was across the street from where we were standing.

". . . and this."

He pointed to Grand Central Terminal, which was a block away.

"You and Alex discovered that our good friend Marek Blackwell lives deep below Grand Central."

"Right."

"And I was able to identify the headquarters of the elusive Empire State Tungsten Company right there on the fifth floor of the Chrysler Building."

"Interesting," I said. "So you can put Marek within a block of the company."

Grayson smiled. "I can do better than that. After searching through the endless records of companies that own other companies that own other companies, I have finally discovered who actually owns the Empire State Tungsten Company."

"Who is it?" I asked eagerly.

"Ulysses Clark."

Bombshell.

"As in the alias of Ulysses Blackwell? Marek's cousin and financier?"

"The one and only."

We'd always suspected that Ulysses was Marek's second in charge. Not only that, he was also the one who infected the chief of police at last year's Thanksgiving Day Parade. That particular connection might explain why his company was raising money for the chief's Dead Squad.

"So we know for sure that they're connected," I said. "If Ulysses owns the company, that means Marek really owns it. But why is he buying up tungsten? Is he using it as part of his construction at the ghost stations?"

Grayson shrugged. "That's what I'll be trying to figure out as soon as I finish this slice of pizza. I said that I'd made a *little* headway. I still have a long way to go before I can solve it."

It was great to be back in action, but the situation with Natalie was massively frustrating. My hope that the problem would just kind of take care of itself turned out to be wishful thinking. That was obvious the second week when I met her on the sidewalk in front of her apartment building. According to the schedule I was supposed to help her scope out the RUNY construction site at the Worth Street ghost station, but she told me that she was going without me.

"What do you mean?" I asked. "I thought we were going to check it out together."

"I know," she said, "but I just think this would be better considering . . . my situation."

"What situation?"

"The fact that I'm undead," she said. "You remember that, don't you?"

(See what I mean about frustrating?)

"I said I was sorry and I'll tell you I'm sorry as many times as you want," I answered. "I know I was wrong, but I want to make up for it. I was just trying to be careful."

"And that's all I'm doing right now," she replied. "I'm trying to be careful."

"How is going into Dead City by yourself being careful?" I asked.

"I'm not going by myself," she said. "I'm just going *without you*. I have to go underground and recharge anyway, and there's a spot close to Worth Street where I can blend in with the other zombies. I can't do that if you're with me."

As much as it hurt my feelings, this actually made sense. She could dig around much better without me in the way.

"Will Liberty be there?" I asked. "You should have someone from Omega nearby."

"Why? Because Omegas are so trustworthy and reliable? Because an Omega would not hurt me or let me get hurt?"

That was my breaking point, so I just stormed off. Natalie must have realized that she'd pushed too hard, because she ran up and put a hand on my shoulder to stop me. She didn't apologize, but she did soften her tone.

"Liberty will be there," she said.

"Good," I answered. "Be safe."

This pattern of her investigating the construction sites without me continued over the next few weeks. We only worked together as a pair when she was helping me explore Revolutionary War locations. She may have been upset with me, but she still put Omega first and she knew that I needed help.

I was struggling because although there were plenty of places in the city that played a role in the Revolution, I couldn't see what any of them had anything remotely to do with Marek or RUNY.

That's what the two of us were trying to figure out one day up in Washington Heights. At one point during the war the British thought they'd cornered the Continental Army in Brooklyn, but General Washington led a daring escape across the East and Hudson Rivers. If it hadn't been successful, the British might have won the war right then and there. We were trying to follow the route they took across Manhattan to see if it might somehow be useful to Marek today.

We were standing in front of a church, checking a map, when I noticed that Natalie kept clenching her jaw and straining the muscles in her neck.

"Is something wrong?" I asked her.

"Why do you ask?"

"Because you're doing that thing with your neck and jaw."

She gave me a confused look. "What thing."

"Clenching and straining."

She obviously had no idea what I was talking about.

"It's just your imagination," she said.

"No it's not," I said. "You just did it again."

She still had no idea what I was talking and was about to say something snarky, when she made a sudden convulsion and started to cough. She tried to talk again but then there was another convulsion. Finally, she looked right at me with a pained, almost helpless expression and managed to get a sentence out.

"What's happening to me?"

That's when the black liquid started to trickle out of the corner of her mouth.

Help Needed

I was in total panic mode. Natalie had just convulsed twice and a small trail of black liquid had started to come out of the corner of her mouth. The first thing I thought of was the man my mother killed in the boathouse. Black liquid came out of his mouth right before he died.

"Have you been underground to recharge today?"

She tried to talk but she couldn't. Instead she just shook her head.

"What about yesterday?" I asked.

She shook her head again.

"We need to get you recharged right now," I said urgently

as I tried to think of where we could go. I remembered how the Blockhouse worked as a supercharger. It would be perfect, but we were at the corner of Fort Washington Avenue and West 181st Street, and that was at least five miles away.

"Let's get you to the subway station," I said, pointing toward a metro sign just up the street.

She had another convulsion as we walked. I put my arm around her and steadied her by holding her shoulder with one hand and her arm with the other.

"You can make it," I said, trying to convince myself as much as I was trying to convince her. "You are the toughest, strongest person I know, and you can make it."

She was getting weaker, and for the last few steps she staggered and almost fell. Just as we got to the entrance, I realized where we were.

"I've got a better idea," I said. "You just have to make it one more block to Bennett Park."

She gave me a desperate look and managed to force out a single word.

"Under . . . ground."

I thought about the subway station and how hard it would be to get down the stairs to a good location. I was certain I had a better plan.

"This will be better," I said looking deep into her eyes. "Trust me."

She coughed again, and I worried that she might not be able to make it any farther, but she nodded.

"I . . . trust . . . you."

It didn't help that Bennett Park has the highest elevation in all of Manhattan. We had to work our way uphill every step, and over the last fifty yards I was practically carrying her. Luckily, my father had taught me the fireman's carry he learned as a paramedic. I didn't quite have her all the way up on my back, but it was close.

I'm sure she thought I was crazy. But then we made it to the park and my thinking became obvious. The reason Bennett Park is the highest point on the island is because the entire park is built on an outcropping of Manhattan schist that was forced upward during the Ice Age.

We staggered into the park and I gently helped her lie down on the rock formation. An old man was walking his dog and looked over at us to see if we needed any help.

"She's just feeling sick and needs to rest," I said.

He gave us a suspicious look, but his dog was pulling him in a different direction, so he left the two of us alone. I held her head in my lap and talked to her as calmly as I could.

"You're going to be fine," I told her. "We'll stay here for as long as you need."

Her skin was pale, but her eyes looked sharp and I considered that a huge plus. She kept eye contact and I smiled at her.

"I know you're still mad at me and I understand that," I said. "If it helps, you should know that I'm pretty mad at myself too."

She closed her eyes for a moment and I panicked, but when she opened them back up she smiled. "It helps a little," she said in a faint voice.

"Don't talk," I told her. "Just rest."

After about twenty minutes she was strong enough to sit up and talk, and after an hour she regained almost all of her strength.

"You can't do that," I said. "You can't go a whole day without going underground. That's not an option."

"I know," she said. "Although, when I wanted to go underground, you took me here to the highest spot on the island."

We both laughed.

"Well, as you've pointed out, I stick out like a sore thumb down there and I knew this rock would help out."

"You and the parks," she said with a chuckle. "You know them so well."

"Well, this isn't just any park," I told her. "This was the site of Fort Washington, where the father of our country tried to save New York."

"Just like you saved me," she said. "You're my George Washington."

I laughed. It's amazing how much that lifted the guilt I had been carrying around.

"Considering how many times you've saved my life, I figured it was the least I could do."

She reached over and squeezed my hand. "Thank you, Molly."

I still felt guilty about accusing her of being a Level 2, but from that moment on, things were good between Natalie and me.

The next day we were at lunch, telling Alex about Washington's escape across Manhattan (and leaving out the part about Natalie's near death experience), when Grayson showed up excited about something.

"What's up with you?" asked Natalie. "Did some new comic book come out today?"

He gave her a look. "Today is Tuesday. Comic books come out on Wednesdays. If you're going to make sarcastic comments about someone's legitimate interests, you should get your basic facts right."

We all laughed, Natalie loudest of all. "You don't know how much I truly love you, Grayson. You are one of a kind."

"Well, you're about to love me more," he said, "because I think we may have gotten the break we've been looking for."

"What is it?" she asked.

"Empire State Tungsten needs help."

"What do you mean?" asked Alex.

"I found a 'help wanted' listing that they are looking to hire a new data entry person," he said. "That would get us inside the office. That would get us access to data. I'd be able to find out what they're doing with all of the tungsten they're buying."

The three of us exchanged confused looks. "Are you saying that one of us should apply for the job?"

"Yes," he said.

"You get the part that Ulysses Blackwell runs the company," I said. "That's the same Ulysses Blackwell who we fought against in hand to hand combat on New Year's Eve. I'm pretty sure he'd recognize any one of us."

This snag frustrated him.

"I get that," he said. "I'm not saying that we should just walk right in there. But we can put on a disguise and some makeup. We've snuck into flatline parties before. How is this different?"

"For one, it's not a darkened tunnel filled with people trying to get away from a world that despises them," Natalie said.

I hated to think that's how she saw her condition.

"And if you remember, we barely made it out of a couple of those parties as it is. Now you're talking about going into a professional situation at a time when the undead are ready to launch a war against us if they get the slightest hint we're causing problems. When it comes to acting, we're not that good."

He slumped as he realized she was right. He was so close to reaching something that had eluded him for weeks. But it was still out of reach.

Or was it?

"You know who is that good at acting?" Alex asked.

Grayson thought about it for a moment and smiled. "You're absolutely right."

"Who?" asked Natalie.

"Molly's sister," said Alex.

"Beth?" I asked. "Now you guys really have gone nuts."

"Have we?" asked Grayson. "She's super talented. Remember all those voices she did at your party. She'd be amazing."

"And, Ulysses doesn't know her at all. None of the

undead know her. They can't recognize somebody they've never seen before."

Natalie and I exchanged a look. "And the part about her not being an Omega," I said. "What's your solution for that?"

"I don't know," said Grayson. "But Milton said it himself. If we can figure out how Marek's paying for this, then we have a good chance of figuring out why he's doing what he's doing. I've tried everything I can to find out what this company is up to, and I've come up dry. This may be our only real chance."

"You want *my* sister to get a job at Empire State Tungsten?"

"I don't want her to get the job," he said. "I just want her to apply for it. That way she can go in there and get a look around. The smallest piece of information might be all we need."

It seemed utterly impossible, but I also knew that he might be right about one thing. It might be the only way for us to find what we were looking for. So even though the idea was totally bananas, that night I knocked on the door of Beth's room.

"Come in," she said.

She was at her desk, doing homework, when she looked up at me.

"I have a question I want to ask you," I said.

"It must be important if you knocked," she said. "You never knock."

"It is important," I said. "But it's also . . . confusing."

Beth laughed. "Sometimes you really are strange, you know that?"

"You have no idea how strange. Anyway, I want to ask you for a favor, but I can't explain *why* I need the favor. You just have to trust me that it really is important."

I expected her to kick me out right then, but she didn't. Instead she turned in her seat and looked right at me, a curious look on her face.

"Does this have something to do with Omega?"

The Job Interview

I stared at Beth, totally astounded. "You know about Omega?"

She smiled. "I guess I do. At least sort of. About a month before Mom died, I was hanging out with her at the hospital. I forget where you and Dad were, but it was just the two of us. And ice cream. Even though she wasn't supposed to have any, she'd smuggled a quart of Rocky Road into her room and said we had to 'destroy all the evidence before the nurses came back.' So we just sat there with two spoons and ate it right out of the carton while we talked."

"What did you talk about?" I asked.

"Boys . . . college . . . you name it. She wanted to cover as many topics as possible, all the things we wouldn't get the chance to talk about later. She told me some great stories, some embarrassing ones, and gave me advice, a lot of which I'll pass on to you when the time is right. It was the most perfect hour of my life. In a year filled with so many terrible memories, it's the only great one."

"So what does that have to do with Omega?"

"We were laughing about something, and then from out of the blue she said that one day you might come to me asking for a favor that didn't make much sense. Apparently she knew what she was talking about because that's just what you did. And she said that even if it sounded really strange, before I said no I should ask you if it had to do with Omega."

"And if it did?" I asked.

"Then she told me I should do it, no questions asked."

I couldn't believe it. That is so like my mother to foresee this situation, and even more like Beth to go along with it.

"Well she was right," I said. "This favor is for Omega."

"Then I'm in," she replied. "Just tell me what you need."

"That's it? You really aren't going to ask me why?"

"I gave my word, little sister," she said. "If we lose faith and trust, then we've lost everything."

It sounded just like something Mom would say. It's funny. People always think that I'm like her because I love science and because I inherited her mismatched eyes. As far as I'm concerned, it's the biggest compliment in the world. But the truth is, I think that Beth is the one who's more like her. They both have a blend of confidence and compassion that I could never hope to pull off. I walked over and gave her a hug.

"Thank you."

"I told her I'd do it," she said.

"Not about that," I replied. "Thank you for being such a great sister."

She hugged me back, and it took me a moment before I could move on. Finally I let go and we both wiped some tears from our eyes.

"All right," she said. "Tell me what I have to do for this favor."

"You have to do what you do best," I said. "You have to act."

I gave her the basics about the job opening, and the next day after school Grayson came over and filled her in on some specifics. He wanted her to look for anything she could find out about what was happening to the tungsten the company was buying. He also said it would be great if she could get the names of any of the employees.

Beth scheduled an interview for the following day. Unfortunately, the only time they had open was at three thirty. Since we didn't get out of school until three, that didn't leave us much time to get there and be close by if she needed any help.

Alex, Grayson, Natalie, and I practically sprinted the moment the bell rang. We didn't have time to come up with an elaborate plan for our trackers, so we just split into pairs and kept away from each other.

Alex and I took the subway and went to Leonardo's, the pizza place a block from the Chrysler Building. Meanwhile, Grayson and Natalie rode the Roosevelt Island tram across the river and then took a cab to Grand Central. All of us were close by, but hopefully we weren't close enough to each other to set off any alarms with the Dead Squad.

Five minutes before her interview was scheduled Beth and I exchanged texts.

> **BETH:** *Getting on the elevator. Feeling very employable.*
> **MOLLY:** *Good luck! Text the moment you're done.*

And that was it.

As nerve-wracking as it is to go undercover or do any

kind of secret surveillance, it's far worse when you have to sit and wait while someone else does it. Everything is out of your control, and all you can do is worry. What made this especially bad was that it was all new to Beth and she didn't really know what she was getting into.

"Relax," Alex said when he noticed that I was nervously twisting the straw from my soda. "She's going to do fine."

"What are they saying?" I asked, motioning to the walkie-talkie in his backpack.

"Nothing unusual," he said, trying to reassure me. "Everything is okay."

In the course of the next five minutes, I must have checked my watch about forty times. I already regretted putting her in this position.

"Would you like to listen in?" Alex asked, hoping it might calm my nerves if I had something to do.

"Yeah. That would be good," I said.

I moved to the other side of the table and sat next to him in the booth. He only had one pair of earbuds, so we had to sit close together and share, each of us using one from the same set. Their conversations were filled with police lingo, so I didn't understand a whole lot of what was being said, but there was no sense of urgency or alarm. I took that as a good sign.

When I checked my phone again, it was 3:55. I figured she would be done at any moment. Then I heard a call on the radio.

"Advise. Eagle is on the move with full detail."

"Eagle's Marek, right?" I asked, even though I knew the answer. It was just nervous chatter.

"That's right, and full detail refers to all the cops that protect him. He normally only travels with all of them if something big is happening."

The message continued. *"There is a change of schedule. Rather than WSS, he is headed to Test C."*

"What are WSS and Test C?" I asked.

"WSS is Worth Street station, it's one of the RUNY construction sites," he said. "But I don't know what Test C is. I've never heard that one before."

I took another bite of my slice of pizza and checked my phone again. It was now 3:57. I had to calm my nerves. I closed my eyes and took a deep breath. It was an exercise we'd learned in jeet kune do. Real masters could do it and significantly lower their heart rate. It also helps clear your mind, and it must have worked because once I tried it I only needed about twenty seconds to figure out what Test C was code for.

"Beth!" I said as I bolted from the table toward the

door. I'd forgotten that I had the earbud in, and when I started running it popped out of my ear and flew back at Alex, flicking him in the face. I was halfway to the Chrysler Building before he caught up to me on the sidewalk.

"What's going on?" Alex asked as he ran with me stride for stride.

"Test C," I said, picking up speed. "It stands for The Empire State Tungsten Company. Marek just changed his plans to go there. They must have figured out who Beth really is."

Eagle's Nest

I sprinted full speed until we reached the entrance of the Chrysler Building. That's when I decided I should at least try to blend in. After all, it's a workplace and we didn't want to attract any extra attention. I took a deep breath and calmly walked through the revolving door. When I got inside, I was surprised to see Grayson and Natalie in the lobby. They could tell I was upset.

"Marek is heading to the office," I explained.

"We know," Natalie said. "We saw him walk through Grand Central with his police escort. We followed him outside to see where he was going, and when he went into the building we put two and two together."

"We called to tell you," Grayson said. "But you didn't answer."

I must not have heard my phone ring as I ran down the street. I beelined straight for the elevators, and the others were right behind me.

"We'll bust in if we have to. I can't let them hurt my sister," I said. "I should never have asked her to do this. This is all my fault."

We got on an elevator and I jabbed the button for five a few times, rapid fire.

"You've got to calm down, Molly," Alex said. "No matter what is happening, keeping calm is our best approach."

I closed my eyes and waited for the ding to signal that we'd reached the fifth floor. Until then I practiced my jeet kune do breathing exercise so I could focus all my energy and anger. By the time the elevator stopped, I was ready to take on an undead army all by myself if I had to.

The bell rang and I opened my eyes just as the doors opened onto the fifth floor. I was prepared to storm into battle, but then I saw something that made me stop cold. My sister was standing there waiting to take the elevator back down to the lobby.

"What are you doing here?" she asked confused. "I

thought I was supposed to meet you at the pizza place."

My mind spun rapidly, trying to figure out what was going on.

"Beth?"

"Actually, today I am playing the role of Sabrina, aspiring data entry specialist. I think the interview went really well."

I still couldn't make sense of it all.

"But what about Marek? Didn't he come into the office?"

"You mean Mr. Big Shot with the bodyguards," she said. "Oh, he came in all right. Everyone got very excited and rushed into a back room. Some big deal is about to go down. It was perfect, because they just kind of left me there unattended and I was able to get this."

She held up a flash drive.

"What's that?" asked Grayson.

"Only everything you ever wanted to know about the Empire State Tungsten Company, and more."

It's amazing how quickly the mood changed from panic to joy. Beth stepped on the elevator and we were all ready to high-five. She had executed the plan better than we could have hoped, and our anxiety had all been a mistake.

"Seriously," I said catching my breath, "that's amazing. You're amazing."

"Let's get out of here," Natalie said as she reached down to press the button for the lobby.

"Stop!" Alex reached out and grabbed her arm. He was listening in on the walkie-talkie, and something made him grimace. "They know we're here."

"What do you mean?" asked Grayson.

"The four of us are together in one place," he explained. "We set off the alarm."

In our panic, we had all completely forgotten about the trackers.

"Then we better hurry up," said Natalie.

"It's too late. Since Marek's in the building, there are already some Dead Squad members in the lobby," he replied. "We have to go up."

He pressed the button for sixty-one, and the elevator came to life and started climbing.

I looked up at the numbers changing on the display above the doors and felt a new sense of panic. "Are you sure we need to go that high?" I asked.

"I'm sorry, Molly, but you're just going to have to deal with your fear of heights," said Alex. "This is an emergency. They're going to outnumber us, so we need to get high enough to really weaken them."

Actually, it wasn't my fear of heights that had me concerned. I was worried about Natalie. Going that high would weaken her, too. I tried to check her reaction without drawing attention to what I was doing. I could tell she was nervous. Neither of us wanted a repeat of what happened in Washington Heights. The vision of her spitting out black liquid was already haunting me. I figured we could stay up there for about fifteen minutes at the most before the height would begin to affect her. That didn't leave me much time.

"Why the sixty-first floor?" asked Grayson. "That seems kind of random."

"It's not," said Alex. "Whenever we're going into an operation I try to work out escape plans in case something goes wrong. I researched the building last night and discovered that the sixty-first floor used to have an observation deck, but now it's closed and abandoned, which makes it an ideal place for us to hide and wait them out."

"Wait them out?" I asked. "Is that our plan?"

"Unless you've got a better one," he said.

I didn't, but I knew that one wouldn't work because waiting was exactly what Natalie couldn't do. "What do you think?" I asked her. "Do you have a different plan?"

It was the first time I ever saw her at a loss for words. She didn't say anything, which the others probably took as her agreeing to the idea. Instead of Natalie, the next person who talked was my sister.

"I know I told you guys that I'd do the favor no questions asked," she said. "But since the favor part's over, would someone mind telling me what the heck is going on?"

I was a mental mess. I still hadn't recovered from the thought that Marek was going to attack Beth. I was worried about taking Natalie up to a dangerous height. And a team of zombies was about to come and attack. I didn't really have any room in my brain to come up with a good explanation, so I just blurted out the truth.

"Omega is a secret society that protects the city from the undead. Marek is their leader and now they're coming to fight us."

For a moment the only sounds in the elevator were the whirring of the motor and the lame music playing over the speaker. The five of us were silent until the bell dinged and the doors opened.

"You mean zombies?" she said, incredulous.

"Actually, they hate being called the Z word," Alex said as he got off and held the doors for the rest of us. "But that's exactly what she means."

I thought back to when they first told me about Omega. We were at Grayson's house, and I was ready to storm out because I thought they were making fun of me. But Beth's reaction was . . . *different*.

She smiled as she considered it and tried to read our expressions. "You know, I almost believe you guys."

"Well, in a couple minutes I think you're going to be convinced," Alex replied. He unplugged his earbuds from the walkie-talkie and turned it up so that we all could hear.

"*Affirmative, Home Base, Eagle is secure. Omega is between the fifty-eighth and sixty-third floors, and we are sending up a team to isolate. We are go to engage Omega.*"

"We caught a break there," Alex said.

"How is that a break?" asked Grayson. "They're coming up to *isolate* us. That doesn't sound like a break."

"But they don't know the exact floor we're on," he said. "The trackers are designed to show where you are on a map, not how high you are in the air. That should buy us an extra minute or two to get ready."

He led us down the hall and forced open a door to reveal a big room that was in the middle of a remodeling project. It was filled with scaffolding, tools, and giant plastic sheets hanging from the ceiling. There were also picture windows that looked out over a terrace and toward downtown. Even for someone normally terrified of heights, I had to admit that it was an amazing view of the city.

"I read about it last night," Alex said. "They're turning it into a restaurant called the Eagle's Nest."

"Not eagle because of Marek's code name?" I asked.

"No," he said. "Because of them."

He pointed out toward the terrace. At each corner there was a giant silver eagle-gargoyle.

"They're beautiful," Grayson said. "I've always wanted to see them up close."

"Gargoyles are supposed to scare off bad spirits," Alex said. "Let's hope they scare off zombies, too."

In my desperation I came up with a plan to get Natalie downstairs.

"I think we need to get the flash drive to safety," I said. "Let's give it to Natalie and she can take the stairs. That way the information will be protected."

"They've probably stationed someone in each stairwell," Grayson said.

"Maybe," I said. "Even so, Natalie can handle one zombie by herself, and once she does it's all clear sailing."

"That's not a bad idea," Alex said, much to my relief. "But we can't afford to lose Natalie, she's too good a fighter. We should send Beth. No one on the Dead Squad knows who she is."

"You don't know me either," Beth said to Alex. "Not

if you think I'd leave my sister in this situation. If there's going to be a fight, I'm going to be part of it."

"It's not like in the movies," Grayson said. "These are what we call Level 2s. They're aggressive, determined, and . . . really disgusting,"

Beth smiled. "You just described all the boys at my school. I'll be fine."

I loved Beth's attitude, but I had to keep my focus on Natalie and getting her downstairs. "We need to get the flash drive out of here," I said forcefully. "And it has to be Natalie!"

"What is going on with you about this?" Grayson asked. "We need Natalie with us because some very scary creatures are about to come here looking for us."

"They're not creatures!" I snapped. "And they're not zombies! They're people. They're undead, but they're still people."

Natalie smiled. "It's okay. I know what he means."

"We are almost out of time here," Alex said. "So if you two want to explain whatever is going on here, it would be great."

Natalie took a deep breath and turned to the boys.

"I'm undead."

Before they could even respond, the elevators chimed in the hallway. Someone was coming for us.

61 Stories

I watched their faces as they reacted to the news. Grayson looked sad, but Alex seemed angry. This was what Natalie and I had been so worried about. Neither one of us knew how he would take the news.

"Take it back!" he demanded. "You cannot be undead. Take it back."

"I can't," Natalie replied softly. "Because I am."

Alex started taking deep breaths, trying to keep his emotions under control while Grayson went over to her and gave her a hug, just like I expected he would.

"I'm so sorry," Grayson said to her. "I'm so sorry."

Natalie rested her head on his shoulder for a moment, but before there could be any real emotion between the two of them we were interrupted by a transmission over the walkie-talkie.

"I'm getting a reading on the sixty-first floor," said the voice. "I'll check for visual confirmation."

This development snapped us out of the moment. Well, all of us except for Alex. He couldn't have cared less about the Dead Squadder in the hallway. He was too focused on Natalie.

"How is this possible?" he asked. "How did it happen?"

"It was during the fight on New Year's," she said.

"No, that's not what I mean," he said. "I mean, how did it happen to *you*? I've gone through this a thousand times in my head and every time it's the same. It's supposed to be me."

We were all confused by this.

"What's supposed to be you?" asked Natalie.

"It's simple mathematics," he said. "When you consider the number of times we get into these situations, the odds are that one of us would become undead. But that's why I always go first. That's why I always keep a lookout. It's to skew those odds toward me. My job is to protect you. If it's going to happen, it's supposed to happen to me."

"It's not your job to protect me," she said. "It's our job to look out for each other."

He was totally devastated, and I had no idea what he was going to do next.

"The reading on sixty-one is very hot," came an announcement on the walkie-talkie.

"Let us know the moment you have visual confirmation?" came the reply. *"If you do, we will send a team immediately."*

"Alex," said Grayson, pointing at the walkie-talkie. "We're about to have company."

"I'm a little busy dealing with something Grayson," Alex said, perturbed. "I need a second, all right?"

"I don't know if we have a second."

We could hear the zombie in the hallway as he checked doors to see if they were unlocked. He was getting closer.

We all looked at Alex, trying to figure out his next move.

"Fine," he said, totally annoyed. He took a deep breath and marched right out toward the hallway.

"What are you doing?" asked Natalie.

He didn't answer. Instead he just walked out the door, and we heard the following over the walkie-talkie.

"I hear a door opening and . . . wait . . . I have visu—" and then static as the transmission went dead.

Seconds later Alex came back through the door. In

one hand he held a walkie-talkie, and with the other he dragged the body of the dead zombie.

"Here's an extra walkie," he said, tossing it to Grayson. "Beth, this is what a zombie looks like. When they attack, go for the head."

The speed with which he took care of the situation was amazing, but while we were all stunned, Alex just picked up the conversation where he left off as if nothing had happened.

"How could you not tell me?" he asked Natalie.

She looked at him for a moment, trying not to get emotional.

"I know what you think of them . . . ," she said, motioning to the dead zombie on the floor. ". . . I mean, what you think of *us*. . . . I'm one of them now."

"You are not one of *them*," he said, his voice rising. "You're one of *us*! *We* are a team. It doesn't matter if you are living or undead, you will always be one of us. Omega today, Omega forever!"

Natalie blinked a couple times, and when she opened her eyes all the way, a tear streamed down her face. It was black, but it was a tear.

"Does that mean you still want me on your team?" she said, looking Alex in the eye.

He wiped the tear off her cheek with his thumb.

"Always," he said. "No matter what."

She hugged him tightly.

We heard an elevator ding in the hallway and the sounds of a group of people stepping out.

"It's really great that you have this whole 'them and us' thing figured out," Grayson said. "But that noise you hear out there? That really is *them*, and they are coming for us. So we have to get ready."

Alex and Natalie redirected their attention from each other and looked to us. We were out of time and we needed to brainstorm.

"You're the one who came up with this escape plan," I said to Alex. "What do we do?"

"Natalie's situation changes everything," he said. "We've got to get her downstairs fast."

"Easier said than done," I said, looking out toward the hall filled with zombies. "How do we do that?"

"I've got it," said Grayson, excited. "I actually think I've got it. They're looking for four of us. But we've got an extra person. Beth can become Natalie."

I didn't understand what he was getting at, but Alex was right with him.

"That's brilliant," he said. "If Natalie gives Beth her jacket and if Beth pulls her hair back like Natalie's, it just might fool them. At least long enough for what we need."

Natalie was wearing a light denim jacket, which she quickly handed to Beth. Beth slipped it on and pulled her hair back in a ponytail.

"Nat, you hide in here and we'll go out on the terrace," Alex said. "They'll be looking for four people, so when they see us they'll head out there and walk right by you. That should give you plenty of time to escape. Once they realize it's really Beth, you'll be long gone."

"That's not fair to Beth," she said. "I can make it about fifteen minutes before there's a problem. They're in the same situation as I am. Whatever happens is going to be fast and like you said, I'm a good fighter."

"There's no time to debate," he said. "They're here and you're going!"

Sure enough, we could hear them trying to open the door. Reluctantly Natalie ducked behind some of the construction equipment, and the rest of us went out on to the terrace.

"Just act like we're enjoying the view," said Alex.

We lined up along the railing and looked out over the city. I was terrified for so many reasons, I couldn't really worry about the height. Although it was awfully high. We heard a voice crackle over Alex's walkie-talkie.

"We have visual confirmation. All four of them are on the terrace on the sixty-first floor. Repeat: All four of them are on the terrace on the sixty-first floor. Everyone engage."

"Part one worked," Alex said. "They think we're all out here. Are you guys ready for part two?"

"Definitely," I said.

"Me too," said Grayson.

"I'll guess we'll find out," added Beth.

Moments later the doors to the terrace opened and we could hear the Dead Squad come outside behind us. We tried to stay cool and kept looking out over the city.

"Don't turn around until you have to," I whispered to Beth. "I will protect you no matter what."

"What seems to be the problem, officer?" Alex said, turning and engaging the leader of the group.

"You know what the problem is," he said. "Marek was clear that the four of you are not supposed to get together. He told you there'd be war. You have been warned, so what happens next is entirely your fault."

Grayson and I both turned, but Beth kept looking out toward downtown. There were eight of them in total. Three, including the one in charge, were dressed in NYPD uniforms. The others were your typical Level 2 lowlifes. They were big, especially the cops, but I thought we could handle them.

"Actually," I said interrupting. "Marek said we cannot engage in Omega activity . . . and we're not. We're just up here enjoying the view. It really is amazing."

The man evaluated the situation for a moment and then turned his attention toward Beth.

"What about you, Coyote?" he said, using Natalie's code name. "You just enjoying the view."

Beth dragged it out for as long as she could before she turned around. When she did, his face filled with rage.

"Who are you?" he demanded.

"I guess I'm Coyote," she said. Then for fun she made a little howling noise.

He was not amused. He turned to the others and said, "Coyote's not here."

He grabbed his walkie-talkie and started to make a transmission. "Coyote is—"

That's as far as he got. Alex kicked the walkie-talkie out of his hand, and our chance for a peaceful encounter was over.

They outnumbered us, so it was important to strike quickly. I did a full roundhouse kick that took out the zombie nearest me, instantly bringing their number down to seven. Next I double-punched another in the stomach, dropping him to his knees, but before I could deliver the knockout shot, I was blindsided by one of the cops.

He was big and smelled disgusting. He slammed me into the railing so that I hit it with my stomach, which bent me over and gave me a dizzying view of the ground more than 650 feet below me. Pain radiated from my gut, and the angle made me a little dizzy as I tried to fight back. Then he added insult to injury when he put his lips right next to my ear and said, "Ready to see if gophers can fly?"

That did it. I really hate that code name.

I slammed my head directly back into him and snapped my body upright so that it pushed him away. I spun around and delivered a punch right to his chest.

"I want a new code name!" I said as I added a flurry of punches, which he deflected.

He was tough and seemed to relish the challenge as he charged right back at me. He was just about to hit me, when I got help from an unlikely source. Out of nowhere Beth came in and took him out with a devastating flurry of kicks to his shins and forearms before dropping him with a punch right to the middle of his forehead. It was a blistering attack that left me momentarily speechless.

"You know krav maga?" I asked stunned.

"I do, but that was actually muay thai," she said. "It's easy to confuse the two, because they use a lot of the same elements."

I was flabbergasted. Here I thought I had been living with a cheerleader all these years, and it turned out she was a lethal weapon. She enjoyed my sense of astonishment and just smiled and winked at me.

"What?" she said. "You thought that only you and Mom had secrets?"

This was a game changer.

Beth and I had taken out two, and when I looked over at Alex I saw one dead zombie on the floor while he fought another one. The odds were evening out, but there were still five of them, and Grayson was struggling with one. The cop had him wrapped up from behind in a full chest hold and was lifting him up in the air.

"Kick him, Grayson," I yelled.

He tried to kick backward with his heel, but he was at an awkward angle and he couldn't get any power into it.

I moved to help, but I was grabbed from behind and slammed down onto the terrace floor. A tall L2 loomed over me and tried to hold me down by shoving his boot into my stomach, which was still sore from getting folded over the railing. I saw that both Alex and Beth were busy, which meant that none of us could help Grayson.

The zombie had lifted him completely into the air, and despite Grayson's flailing he had no problem carrying him.

In a flash I thought back to Grayson's frustrations that Alex was always the hero and that he was never any good in these fights. I'm sure that frustration was only making the situation worse for him. Then I realized what the zombie was planning to do. He was carrying him over to the edge and was going to throw him off of the building.

"Grayson!" I screamed.

I tried to get up, but the zombie still held me down, his boot digging deep into my stomach. I reached up and twisted his knee until it dislocated, green slime shooting out where the bone punctured the skin. Then I punched the other knee from the side so that he fell. Unfortunately, he landed directly on top of me, which kept me from jumping right up to help.

I could see the panic in Grayson's face as the zombie neared the edge.

"Use the railing!" I yelled to him. "Push back off of the railing."

Grayson did exactly what I said. He pushed back off of the railing and drove his body into the zombie, knocking him back. It was a good move, but the zombie was big and bad and it only slowed him down for a second. I scrambled to get back on my feet, but I was too far away to help. So were Beth and Alex.

"No!" I screamed as they neared the edge.

They say that time slows down in your head at moments of great stress, and I've had that feeling. But this was the opposite, it seemed like everything was moving too fast for me to do anything about it. That's why it was such a surprise when a punch came out of nowhere and connected to the back of the zombie's head.

Natalie.

She had come back to help. She delivered a quick series of blows to his lower back, and the zombie loosened his grip, allowing Grayson to break free. She continued her vicious attack, as did we all. Within less than a minute, all of the zombies lay dead on the floor.

"What are you doing here?" Alex demanded. "I thought I told you to go downstairs and be safe."

"Really? Because I thought you told me that we were always a team no matter what," she replied. "Something like 'Omega today, Omega forever'."

She looked around at all of the dead bodies and smiled.

"Besides, I'm still the captain of this team," she added. "You don't tell me what to do. I tell you what to do."

She laughed, and it was by far the happiest I'd seen her since New Year's. For the first time since that day, we were truly a team again.

"We better get you out quickly," Alex said. "They'll send another team right away."

She shook her head. "I don't think so. At least not for a while."

She grabbed the walkie-talkie and turned up the volume so we could all hear.

"All units, trackers report that all four Omegas have left the building and are now walking north on Lexington."

We all gave Natalie a confused look. "Why do they think we're walking down Lex?"

"While you guys were fighting, I collected all the trackers and slipped them into the pocket of a pizza delivery guy on the elevator."

Alex laughed. "Seriously?"

"Totally," she said. "It should buy us some time."

"Advise all units, I'm on Lexington and do not see them. This must be a mistake. Does anyone have a visual on the Omegas?"

Beth reached down and picked up the walkie-talkie. We had no idea what she was doing, but she pressed the talk button and responded. Only, she didn't sound like Beth Bigelow, she used one of the accents she'd demonstrated for the boys at my birthday party.

"That's affirmative," she said, sounding just like a cop

from Brooklyn. "I have eyes on Coyote right now. She is entering a pizzeria."

"His shirt said Leonardo's," whispered Natalie.

"Roger that," Beth added, now switching over to a Bronx accent. "I see her too. She's entering Leonardo's Pizzeria. Repeat, Leonardo's Pizza."

We all marveled at what she was doing. Alex got her attention and pointed at each one of us as he told her our code names.

"Wolverine, Jayhawk, and Gopher."

She gave me a raised eyebrow look and whispered, "Gopher?"

"It's not like I picked it."

"Coyote is with Wolverine, Jayhawk, and Gopher," she said with yet another accent. "All four of them have entered the pizzeria."

"Roger that. All units advance to Leonardo's Pizzeria at Forty-third and Lexington."

She looked up at us and smiled.

"That should give you a few minutes to get out of the building before they figure out you're not in the pizzeria."

We took the elevator down to the third floor. Then we went down the rest of the way by the stairs on the opposite side of the building. By the time we reached the subway station we were equal parts exhausted, ecstatic, and relieved. Grayson took the flash drive, and Alex insisted on escorting Natalie home.

We all exchanged hugs on the platform, even Beth.

Once everyone had gone, Beth and I just stood there looking at each other. So much of the afternoon had been about surviving the attack and the boys learning about Natalie. I hadn't gotten the chance to check on how Beth was handling all of this.

"Let's head home," she said. "You have some explaining to do."

I thought about it for a second. "I'll explain, but first I need to show you something."

We took the subway north to City College and were quiet for most of the ride.

"When did you learn krav maga and . . . what was it?"

"Muay thai," she said.

"That," I said. "When did you learn martial arts?"

"Mom insisted that I do it when I was a kid, and I always kept with it," she replied. "I kind of kept it hidden because I didn't want to catch any flack from the girls in the building or at school."

That's when it dawned on me that Mom might have trained Beth for Omega just like she trained me.

"Did she make you learn the periodic table, too?" I asked.

"Yeah," she said. "How'd you know that?"

I shook my head, disbelieving.

"She was preparing you in case you became an Omega," I said. "She did the same thing with me. The periodic table is the key to our code."

We got off the subway and started walking to the college.

"If I was trained like you, then why didn't I become an Omega?" she asked. "Am I not good enough?"

"Hardly. You'd be awesome at it," I said. "What you did up there was amazing."

"Then why?" she asked.

"It's because you have to go to MIST."

"Oh," she said, a look of disappointment on her face. "I guess I screwed that up."

"What do you mean?"

"It's what Mom wanted, and I wouldn't do it," she explained. "She asked me to apply, but I told her I didn't want to go there. That must have really disappointed her."

"You can't think that," I said. "You never disappointed Mom. She was always proud of you."

Beth sighed. "I guess we'll never really know for sure."

And this is where I had her. She followed me as we snuck down into the catacombs below CCNY. I couldn't remember all of the turns by heart, but I quickly realized that the pipes would help me find my way. The pipes ran along the ceiling but came down the wall by the secret entrance.

Beth hardly asked any questions, no doubt overwhelmed by everything from the zombie attack to our discussion of Mom. Finally, I found the wall and made sure to remind myself which pipe was the right one.

I turned the wheel and the hidden door unlocked. Just as I went to pull it open, I turned to Beth and said, "If you don't believe me when I say you never disappointed her, you can just ask her yourself."

I opened the door to reveal the hidden lab. Milton and my mother were working on an experiment and looked up, surprised by the interruption. Then Mom saw my sister and took off her safety glasses.

"My dear, sweet Elizabeth," she said, shaking her head.

I looked at my sister as tears streamed down her face. "Mom?"

19

George Washington Walked Here

I t had been two weeks since our adventure at the Chrysler Building, and the results had been both emotional (Beth and Mom's tearful reunion) and educational (all the information Grayson had retrieved from the files of the Empire State Tungsten Company). But so far they hadn't been dangerous. Marek had yet to deliver on his threat to start an all-out war between the undead and Omega, and that had us worried.

Not that you could tell from the oh-so-enlightening conversation the boys were having as Grayson, Alex, and I looked across the harbor at the Statue of Liberty.

"Did you ever notice that the Statue of Liberty's butt is pointed right at New Jersey?" Grayson asked. "I mean, that's their view."

"Maybe they should put that on the license plates," replied Alex. "New Jersey—the Butt of Liberty."

We were waiting in Battery Park at the southernmost tip of Manhattan. In addition to its view of the harbor, the park is the starting point of the George Washington walking tour of New York City. The tour was laid on the map that my anonymous informant mailed to me. I wanted to walk it as part of my search to see what the father of our country had to do with Marek Blackwell's plan to reinvent underground New York. But, since we didn't know when Marek was going to strike back, the others thought it would be safer if they came along.

"You know, I've never even been there," I said, pointing at the statue. "My whole life in New York and I've never been to the Statue of Liberty."

"Me neither," said Alex.

Grayson shook his head. "Molly I understand, because she's terrified of heights, but why not you?"

"No reason," Alex said. "It's just something you figure you'll get around to one day, so there's no rush. Every time

I thought about going, I put it off because I knew I'd get another chance."

We were all quiet for a moment, and then Grayson said something that revealed what was on all of our minds.

"I wonder if Natalie thought the same thing," he said. "I wonder if she thought she'd do it sometime and never got around to it. 'Cause she sure can't do it now."

The three of us had not really talked about Natalie's situation yet.

"I think about stuff like that all the time," Alex said. "I think about all the things she can't do. All the places she'll never get to go."

"Do her parents know?" asked Grayson.

"They must," said Alex. "After all, they moved from the twelfth to the second floor."

They both turned to me. "How'd they take it?" asked Grayson.

I shrugged. "I don't know," I said. "Natalie and I weren't really talking much in the month and a half after I found out, so I never got the chance to ask her about her parents."

"Why weren't you talking?" asked Alex.

I took a deep breath and closed my eyes, embarrassed by what I was about to say. "I accused her of being a Level 2."

They both laughed.

"That must have been fun," said Grayson.

"Did she try to rearrange your face?" asked Alex.

I thought about it for a moment, then asked them, "Is it really that impossible to believe? I mean, did either of you two think she might be an L2?"

"For about a nanosecond," said Grayson. "But we were about to fight the Dead Squad. It was pretty obvious what side she was on. I might have wondered about it if it had just come up in conversation."

"Not me," said Alex. "But I can understand why you would."

"Why not you?" I asked.

Alex thought about it for a moment. "The best that I can understand is that the person's state of mind at the moment of death is what determines whether or not they become a Level 2. So it comes down to this: Does she have the type of heart that forgives or the type of heart that blames? And when you think of it that way, it's not even a question."

He was absolutely right. Before I could reply, we were interrupted.

"I hope you guys don't mind, but I brought a friend," Natalie said as she walked up with Liberty.

"Not at all!" I replied, happy to see him. He gave me

a hug and then did the whole fist bump, handshake thing with the boys.

"We can use the help," I continued. "I've already done this tour twice and come up empty both times."

Left unsaid was the full reason he was with her. He'd been protecting her in the one place we couldn't. Every day when Natalie went underground into Dead City to recharge her energy levels, Liberty went with her.

"So what brings us to the Battery?" he asked.

"This," I said, handing him the envelope. "It came addressed to me and contained a map of the George Washington walking tour and a note."

He pulled out the note and read it aloud.

"'Reserve a place in history.'"

He looked up at us and asked, "What does that even mean?"

"I wish I knew," I replied. "I thought maybe I needed to reserve a spot on an official tour of the locations, but there isn't one. Then I looked into getting reservations at different places along the route, but that didn't lead anywhere. So basically I'm stumped."

"That's why we're here," Natalie said, taking charge. "With four really smart people working together, we should be able to figure it out."

"You know there are five of us, right?" said Alex.

"I know," she said as she put an arm around him. "I'm sure you'll help too."

I absolutely loved the fact that they were able to joke the same as always. It was a sign their friendship was strong no matter what. That same relaxed mood continued as we followed the map from the Battery up to Bowling Green Park. I acted as tour guide, since I'd already walked it twice before and because I had been reading up on New York during the Revolution ever since I got the assignment months earlier.

"This is where they used to have a statue of King George III riding a horse," I said as we entered the park. "And don't ask me which way the horse's rear end was facing."

Natalie and Liberty exchanged confused looks, but I didn't bother to explain. Instead I told them a story that I'd learned in the history book about the city during the Revolution.

"Washington and his troops were in Manhattan when the Declaration of Independence was signed. And after he had it read to the troops and the local citizens, a bunch of people came here to the park, toppled the statue, and melted it down."

"What did they do with it after they melted it?" asked Natalie.

"They made it into forty thousand musket balls for the Continental Army."

"Hey, maybe that's what Marek's doing with all of that Tungsten he's melting down," Grayson said. "Turning it into musket balls."

"Is that what you think he's doing?" asked Natalie. "Melting it?"

"I know he is," Grayson responded. "I've gone through all the files that Beth got on the flash drive and can track all of the shipments from the moment he buys it up until he melts it."

"And then?" asked Alex.

"And then . . . nothing," said Grayson. "He just buys it and melts it down. I can't find any record of what he does with it after that. I don't know if he's turning it into something or if he's just storing it to use later."

Grayson was down. Despite his lighthearted observations about the Statue of Liberty, he'd been in a funk for a while. First he was upset that he hadn't been more "heroic" (his words not mine) during the fight on New Year's. Then Natalie had to rescue him when the cop from the Dead Squad was trying to throw him off the Chrysler Building. And now he was struggling to solve what was going on with Empire State Tungsten, even though he had tons of data. He felt like he wasn't helping the team at all, even though we all knew that wasn't the case.

"If anyone can figure it out, it's you," I said, trying to boost his morale.

"This conversation has gotten me hungry for cheeseburgers," Alex said. "Did George Washington have a favorite cheeseburger joint?"

Natalie stopped and looked at him. "In what way did this conversation make you think of cheeseburgers?"

"Melted statue, melted cheese," he explained, incredulous. "It's kind of obvious."

"Only to you," she said.

"Maybe," I added. "But a cheeseburger does sound really good."

We took a break from the walking tour and found a burger place that was just greasy enough to be delicious. This was also important for Natalie and Liberty because, while the undead crave different tastes than us, they do like greasy foods. We all crowded around a table as we ate our burgers and shared a couple large orders of fries.

"So do you suppose old George liked burgers?" asked Alex right before he took a big chomp out of his.

"We can check," I said. "One of his favorite places to

eat is still open over on Pearl Street. It's also where the Sons of Liberty held their secret meetings."

"I didn't know you had any sons," Natalie joked to Liberty.

"Neither did I," he replied.

"The Sons of Liberty were a secret society of patriots," I explained. "They were the ones who toppled the statue of King George and had it melted down."

"*They* were a secret society, *we're* a secret society," Alex said. "We should call ourselves The Friends of Liberty."

Liberty looked both embarrassed and pleased. We held up our sodas in a toast and said, "The Friends of Liberty."

We continued eating, and a couple moments later Grayson was nibbling on a fry when he looked at Natalie.

"Can I ask something personal?"

Natalie shrugged. "I've been wondering when you would."

He hesitated for a moment, then asked, "How did you tell your parents?"

She chuckled for a moment and looked at Liberty before answering.

"I didn't."

"They don't know?" I asked surprised.

"They know," she said. "But I didn't tell them."

"Then who did?" asked Alex.

Natalie nodded to Liberty.

"First of all you have to remember that her parents are surgeons," he said. "They knew something was wrong with what they were reading in her medical charts and I knew that they'd have to change their whole world for her to survive. So I got my mother to come with me and we met with them in the hospital."

"And you just blurted out that Natalie was undead?" Grayson asked, incredulous.

"I was a little more subtle than that. Although, I couldn't be too subtle. At one point I performed a couple demonstrations to show them my state of undeadness," he said. "I think it was my ability to completely dislocate my fingers and snap them back into place without screaming that really convinced them."

"And then?" asked Alex.

"Then my mom came in and told them the parents' side of it all," he said.

"They came around amazingly well," Natalie said. "It's funny, because when you think of them being plastic surgeons on Fifth Avenue, you think about all the rich women who come in for facelifts and nose jobs. But every year they go down to Haiti and spend two weeks helping children and really saving lives. That's the side of them I've been seeing. I think the medical component helps. Sometimes I have to remind them that I'm their daughter and not an experiment. But they've done great."

Not only did this surprise me, but so did Alex's response. He turned to Liberty.

"Thank you for looking out for her," he said. "I really am proud to be a Friend of Liberty."

Liberty smiled.

All That Glitters

After we ate, we resumed our tour and continued on to Trinity Church and St. Paul's Chapel. Trinity is where some Revolutionary War heroes like Alexander Hamilton are buried, and St. Paul's is where Washington went to church every Sunday when he was President. (New York City was the capital back then.)

"What does any of this have to do with reserving a place in history?" Grayson asked, trying to solve the mystery of the note.

"Think about what the word means," Natalie suggested. "How can you reserve something if it's already happened?"

"I know what it could be," Alex said, getting our hopes up. "Molly said that the tavern where George Washington liked to eat is still operating. Maybe we need to make a reservation there. Oooh, we can eat dinner there tonight. I could use a good meal."

"Seriously? You're already thinking about dinner?" Natalie said. "You just ate. You still have a little burger juice on your chin."

"I can't help it," he complained. "You guys keep bringing up food."

"Actually," she said, "you're the only one who's bringing up food."

"About his idea, though," I said. "You can make reservations there. It's called the Fraunces Tavern and it's a museum and a restaurant. They serve old-style food from the Colonial era. That might be the solution."

"You see?" Alex said to Natalie. "You're welcome."

"We'll look into it," she said begrudgingly, "but let's keep on with the tour for now."

Our next stop was Federal Hall. When the United States began, New York was the capital and Federal Hall was where George Washington took the oath of office as the first president. We were walking down Nassau Street toward the building when I pointed something out to the others.

"This street is where my anonymous letters supposedly came from," I said.

"What do you mean?" asked Grayson.

"Both envelopes had a return address on Nassau Street."

"Did you try to find it?" asked Grayson.

"No, that never occurred to me," I said, giving him the stink eye. "Of course I did. But it's phony. It doesn't make any sense."

I handed him the envelope and he read it aloud. "356852 Nassau Street."

"See what I mean? It's way too high a number to be an actual address," I explained. "The longest addresses on Nassau are only three digits."

"Maybe it's the number of an office in one of these buildings," Natalie said. "If we can find the office, we can find the answer."

"Nope," Liberty said, interrupting. "It's not an address and it's not an office."

I stopped and gave him a look too. "How do you know that?"

"Because it's my name," he said with a cheesy smile.

Now I was even more confused.

"It was one of the first things I memorized when I

learned the Omega code," he said. "3, 5, 68, 52 is lithium, boron, erbium, tellurium. Li, B, Er, Te, that spells Liberte. It's the French spelling, but still the best way to spell my name in the code."

I couldn't believe I hadn't figured that out. "How did I miss that?" I said, taking the envelope and looking down at it. "It's as plain as day."

"No it's not," said Alex. "The numbers aren't split, so you don't know if they're one digit or two. And it's not part of any other coded material. I wouldn't have thought it was code if I saw it."

"But if it is code, that's huge," said Natalie. "That means 'liberty' is part of the clue."

"It could be the Statue of Liberty," suggested Grayson. "Does Nassau Street run all the way?"

"Yes," said Alex. "But you have to take a submarine for the part that goes under New York Harbor."

Grayson rolled his eyes. "I meant does it run all the way to Battery Park, where we were looking at the statue earlier this morning. Maybe if you stand there on the street and look at the statue it all lines up and makes sense."

"No," I said. "Nassau only goes to Wall Street. There's no way you could see the statue from there."

"It could be the Sons of Liberty," Alex said. "You said

they used to meet at the Fraunces Tavern. That gets back to that whole reserve a place in history thing."

"That's good," Liberty said. "That makes a lot of sense."

"Let me see the note again," Natalie said, a hint of excitement in her voice.

I handed it to her and she held it up so that the sunlight shined through the paper. She looked at it for a second and smiled.

"There's a comma," she said, her excitement building. "It's faint but it's definitely there."

"A comma? That's why you made the big smiley face?" Alex said. "Because there's a comma?"

"Don't you see, Alex," she replied, playing up the moment. "A comma changes everything."

"I think it's safe to say that none of us see that," he answered. "How does a comma change everything?"

"Because without a comma in the sentence 'Reserve a place in history,' 'reserve' is a verb," she said. "That's what we've been trying to figure out. How you can make a reservation. But if there is a comma, as in 'Reserve, comma, a place in history,' then 'reserve' is a noun, an actual place in history."

And that's when I realized where we were standing.

"You are a total genius!" I said.

She flashed a grin. "I know, but don't get discouraged. I had to develop the skills."

"Okay," Alex said. "For us mere mortals, do you want to explain?"

"Look where we are," I said. "It's the Federal Reserve."

Sure enough, we were standing right next to the Federal Reserve Bank of New York.

"This is the Reserve! It's a place in history." I continued, thrilled that we'd finally figured it out.

"And check out the address," added Natalie. "We are at the intersection of Nassau Street and . . ."

We all looked up at the street sign and smiled.

It was Liberty.

"This must be where Marek is getting his money," I said as we stood looking up at the massive Federal Reserve Bank. "Remember what Milton said, the money is the key to everything."

"I don't know," said Grayson. "It's not that kind of bank. The Federal Reserve isn't for people to use. It's for giant banks and the governments of countries to use. Marek's not a country. He can't just go in and open an account or take out a loan."

"Yes, but that's not all it is," said Alex. "The Federal Reserve is also home to the world's largest . . ."

He stopped midsentence and left us hanging.

". . . never mind."

"Never mind?! The world's largest what?" asked Natalie.

"Four really smart people and me," he said, referring to her joke from earlier. "I'd hate to embarrass you all by solving the big mystery. I'll just go lift weights and eat cheeseburgers until you geniuses figure it out."

"Okay, okay, okay," she said with exaggerated emphasis. "I was joking and I'm sorry. *Five* really smart people."

"How about four really smart people and one Albert Einstein level supergenius?"

She gave him a look. "You're pushing it."

"Okay, five really smart people will do. As I was saying, the Federal Reserve isn't just a bank. It's also home to the world's largest gold deposit." The mention of gold caught our attention and Alex took a dramatic pause before he continued. "Almost a quarter of the world's gold is in the basement of that building."

"That's a lot," Natalie said, laughing. "That's a whole lot."

"Yeah, but I'm pretty sure they keep it locked up tight," said Liberty. "How would he even get in to see it, much less have access to it?"

"That's the best part," said Alex. "They give tours. I saw a documentary about it on television."

"I think we should take that tour," Natalie said as she started walking toward the entrance. "By the way, super-geniuses don't sit around watching TV."

"It was a documentary," Alex corrected as we all followed her. "Supergeniuses watch documentaries."

Considering what's inside, it's no surprise that we had to go through some major security hurdles just to get into the building. It took about twenty minutes to make it through the first wave of armed guards, metal detectors, and bag searches. At one point I think they took our pictures and ran them through facial recognition software, but I couldn't tell for sure because it was all kind of top secret-y and they weren't exactly talkative.

Finally, we made it to the end of the line. There was a woman at the counter in a crisp blue uniform with her hair pulled back tight in a bun. She wasn't what you'd call friendly.

"Tickets?"

That's all she said. Unfortunately, we didn't know what she was talking about. Natalie was in front, so she took the lead. "How much are they?"

"They're free."

"Great," she said. "We'll take five."

"No," the woman corrected. "You must already have them.

Tickets are ordered online at least one month in advance."

"Well," Natalie said, trying to charm her a little. "Since we're here and have already gone through the security line . . . and since they're free . . . is there any way we can get them now?"

"No."

Alex started to try a follow-up but it was obvious Ms. Single Syllable wasn't going to change her mind. Luckily, her supervisor was a little nicer. He was older, his hair and moustache on the silver side of gray, and his smile was welcoming.

"What seems to be the problem?" he asked as he walked up behind her.

"No tickets," she explained curtly.

He looked at us for a moment, and I used my best pleading eyes. We all did.

"Wait a second, I think they're part of that school group from Texas," he said as he winked at Natalie. "Isn't that right? Aren't you from Texas?"

"Yee haw," said Natalie with a drawl. "We sure are."

Before the woman could protest, the supervisor told her that he'd watch the counter for fifteen minutes so she could take a break. That took care of her, and once she was gone, he turned to us and asked, "You're not going to make me regret this, are you?"

"No, sir," we said in unison.

He smiled and handed each one of us a ticket and directed us to join a group of sixth-graders who were wearing matching purple MANSFIELD TAKES MANHATTAN T-shirts.

"Yee haw?" I said to Natalie as we walked over.

She shrugged and laughed. "It was the best I could think of."

We had to wait about ten minutes for the tour to begin, so we bonded with the school group. And by "bonded," I mean all their girls looked dreamily at Alex while Natalie and I helped their teachers with directions to their next stop. Finally, a tour guide came out and led us toward the vault.

"Welcome to the Federal Reserve Bank of New York's gold vault," he said, his Brooklyn accent making it sound like there was a *w* in the middle of "vault." "It holds more than half a million gold bars, weighing approximately 6,700 tons."

It took Grayson less than thirty seconds to say, "That's over $380 billion. Billion with a *b*."

The guard stopped and smiled. "Very good math. $382 billion to be exact."

I don't know which impressed me more: the money or Grayson's math skills.

"All of the gold in the vault belongs to foreign countries," he continued. "Much of it came here around World War II, when European governments wanted to make sure that their money was secure."

As he talked, he led us through a series of massive steel doors, past many more armed guards, and finally to a long hallway where the gold is held. It's kept in blue cages with numbers and multiple padlocks on the doors. He talked about the meticulous way in which each bar is tracked, measured, weighed, and reweighed.

"Now I have a question for you," the man said as he looked out at us. "We are eighty feet below ground and there is one important thing that makes this gold vault possible. Does anyone know what it is?"

He looked first at all the kids in the school group, but they just shook their heads. Then he looked at us. We were equally stumped until Natalie came up with the answer.

"Manhattan schist?"

He smiled. "What a smart group this is. Good with math, good with geology. Manhattan schist is exactly right. If it weren't for New York's superstrong bedrock, this vault could not exist, because the weight of the gold would cause it to sink deeper into the ground."

We all exchanged looks at the mention of Manhattan schist. Everything was tantalizingly close to coming together. As for the tour, it was interesting and the gold was impressive, but it seemed like the Federal Reserve might be a dead end. For the life of us, we couldn't figure out how Marek could get so much as a single bar out of the vault. There were too many safety measures. And even if he could steal some, any missing gold would be noticed within forty-eight hours.

"It's impossible," Natalie said as we walked around the museum exhibit at the end of the tour. The exhibit had archival pictures, old scales, and equipment used for measuring the gold. There was even a mountain of shredded cash. (Shredding old bills is one of the things the bank is in charge of doing.) "With the gates and the vaults and the many people with big guns, I don't see how he could get any of it."

"It's not like he can come in at night, either," Grayson said, motioning to a display about the massive vault door. "The only way into that vault is through a ninety-ton steel door that is locked air-tight every night. In fact, it's shut so tightly that one time a paper clip got in the door and shut the entire system down. There's no getting through it."

"Then why do I still think that it's exactly what he's doing?" I asked.

"Because it's Marek," said Natalie. "And he always seems to figure out how to pull off the impossible."

"Check it out," Alex called to us.

We walked over to where he and Liberty were looking at a display featuring a timeline of the building's construction.

"This is the vault being built in the early 1920s," he said, pointing at a large brown-tinted photo of the construction crew hard at work. "They're eighty feet underground, blasting their way through the Manhattan schist."

"Okay," said Natalie. "Why is that important?"

"Look at the man in charge." Alex pointed to a man in a hardhat. We recognized him instantly.

"Marek Blackwell," said Grayson.

"It makes sense," said Liberty. "Marek worked underground for almost a century. He worked on a lot of the big projects."

"And he wasn't alone," said Grayson, pointing to another face.

I expected to see that it was another of the Unlucky 13. But it wasn't. Still, it was a face that we all recognized.

"Is that the guard?" asked Alex. "The one who let us in without the tickets?"

We looked closely, and one by one came to the conclusion that it was in fact the guard. His hair and moustache were darker, but there was no denying who it was.

"You think he's friends with Marek?" asked Grayson.

"If he is, then why did he help us?" I asked. "You'd think we'd be the last people he'd help.

Natalie had a look of concern. "Maybe he didn't help us. Maybe he put us on that tour so he'd know where we'd be for the next hour."

"Why?" I asked, still not getting it.

"So he'd have time to call in reinforcements," she said.

We looked toward the exit. There was only one way out of the building. We looked back at the guard station, but the supervisor was no longer there.

"So you think he recognized us, made sure we got in, and then called his friends?" asked Alex.

"That's exactly what I think," she replied. "It's brilliant. There's only one way in and out. The street's narrow, so we don't have a lot of options. It's the perfect place to set a trap."

We all nodded in agreement and looked to the door. We didn't have a lot of options. We were going to have to go out and face whatever was there. Marek's war was about to begin.

Trinity

So what do you guys think?" asked Natalie as we looked out toward the doorway that exited onto Liberty Street. "Are they out there waiting for us?"

"My guess is yes," said Grayson.

"Mine too," I added.

"Maybe we should just fight them," suggested Alex. "We know they're going to attack at some point, maybe we should just stand tall and fight back now."

I didn't like this idea at all. "There are only five of us," I said. "They'll have us outnumbered, and probably by a lot."

"That's what happened to George Washington, isn't

it?" Grayson asked me. "You've been studying the Revolutionary War, what did he do when the British had him outnumbered?"

"When he realized he couldn't win, he escaped instead," I said. "The British had him trapped in Brooklyn and he got away right from under their noses by sneaking his troops across the river in the middle of the night. By the time the redcoats woke up and realized what had happened, it was too late."

"I think that's what we should do too," said Natalie. "We've got to figure out a way to sneak out of here."

"Okay, but we won't be able to wait until the middle of the night like Washington did," Alex said. "So we're not going to be able to hide in the dark."

"True," she said with a smile. "But we can hide in the sixth grade."

She nodded toward all the purple-shirted sixth graders who were mobbed together about to leave. There was another group in addition to the ones who were with us on the tour, so there were about forty of them all together.

"You think we can blend in with them?" Liberty asked. "They're all wearing matching shirts and we're not."

"True, but all we have to do is blend in long enough to

make it to the corner," she said. "Once we're that far, we can make a run for it."

"Just like George did," I added.

Alex thought it over and nodded. "I like it. But we need a plan for where we go once we make it to the corner. This should give us a head start, but they're going to chase after us."

"I don't think the subway's safe," Natalie said. "It's too easy to get slowed down waiting for a train."

"Besides," Grayson added, "the subway's kind of their home turf."

"I have an idea," I said cautiously. "But it will only work if we can make it to Trinity Church."

The school group started moving toward the door, so there wasn't really any time for me to explain it.

"I vote Trinity Church," Natalie said.

"Agreed," said the others.

I felt a lump in my throat and said a silent prayer that my plan would actually work. Lately it felt like most of them hadn't.

The school group was like a floating blob as it worked its way out the door, and we tried to mix in and spread out so we didn't draw attention to ourselves. Some of the kids recognized us and started up conversations, which helped us blend in a little more.

"Keep your eyes down and faces covered as much as you can," Natalie whispered to Grayson and me as she walked passed us. "Until we make it to the corner."

We caught our first break when we stepped outside and saw two tour buses dropping people off. The buses helped us hide, because they blocked the view of the sidewalk we were on.

"I see four bad guys directly across the street," Alex said in a low voice. "They're still watching the door. I don't think they noticed us."

"There's another pair back behind us by the pretzel vendor," added Natalie. "I saw their reflection in the windshield of the tour bus."

We knew there were at least six of them there for us, but so far none of them seemed to be aware that we'd exited the building. We were almost to the corner when one of the teachers spoke up.

"All right, Mansfield, everybody line up!" she called out to the school kids. "We need to do a head count."

The students started lining up alongside the building, and there was no way we could stay with them without really sticking out, so we had to keep walking.

"Pick up the pace," said Liberty, who was behind me.

"Three on the opposite corner," said Grayson, turning

his face down and away from them. It seemed like the undead were everywhere.

We were almost to Nassau Street when I made eye contact with none other than my favorite Dead Squad member. It was one-eared Officer Pell, standing directly in front of us. He seemed surprised that we'd gotten that far without anyone noticing, but pleased nonetheless to see me.

"Hello, Molly," he said with a raspy hiss as he moved right toward me. He reached out to grab me by the shoulder, but out of nowhere Alex clocked him with a punch across the jaw that knocked him down flat. Just like that three more zombies noticed us and leapt out.

Our head start wouldn't mean anything if we couldn't get past them in a hurry. In a flash I took out one at the knee, Natalie knocked down another with a crack of her elbow against his jaw, and Liberty did a nifty move when the last one tried to punch him. He spun around like a dancer and managed to stomp on the back of his calf, snapping his leg bone in half. They weren't down for good, but we had our opening and we burst out into a full sprint.

We caught some luck when the traffic light changed just as we reached the corner, so that we didn't even have to break stride as we bolted toward the church two blocks away. My pulse quickened as we ran, in part because of the excitement but even more out of nervousness. The others were counting on my plan working. I couldn't mess up again.

It took about two and a half minutes until we were running up to the iron gate that marks the entrance of the church. When we reached it, we stopped for a second to take a quick breath and to look back over our shoulders.

"I don't see anyone," said Grayson.

"You don't see them," Liberty said, "but they're there. I guarantee it."

"It's all you," Natalie said to me. "Save the day."

"Follow me," I instructed them confidently. "I've got this."

Trinity is a beautiful gothic church that I'm sure was impressive when it first opened, but now it's dwarfed by skyscrapers on all sides. The churchyard serves as a cemetery and has many famous early American heroes buried in it. When you add up all the tourists and the tombstones, it's a crowded place to be in a hurry. We tried to be respectful without being slow.

I led the others inside the church and down a stairway to a basement vault. Crypts lined the walls and marble markers signified who was buried in them. This was my first time coming down here, so I hoped that I had my facts right.

I turned a corner, worried that we might run into a dead end, but was relieved to see another set of stairs descending farther down.

"Is anyone following us?" Natalie asked.

Alex looked back as we turned the corner. "Not that I can see."

The stairwell emptied out into a darker crypt. The tombstones on the wall in here dated back to the late 1600s.

"This is the oldest part of the church," I said. "We're almost there."

We entered the final vault, and there, in addition to the crypts, was a small construction area in the corner marked off with bright orange tape and thick layers of plastic sheeting. I got down on my hands and knees and pulled up the bottom of the plastic.

"In here," I said as I crawled under.

The others followed, and when we came up on the other side we were in a sub-basement with a dirt floor. It was only about four feet high, so we had to sort of walk and crawl half bent over in between the brick pilings that held up the building.

"There it is," I said, pointing toward an old stone doorway that had been dug out. Carved into the keystone at the top of the entry was the phrase TUTUS LOCUS.

"What is *tutus locus*?" asked Natalie.

"It's Latin," said Grayson. "It means 'safe passage'."

"That's right," I told them. "The Sons of Liberty built this during the Revolution. They would have their meetings in the church, and if the redcoats came, they'd escape through here. It was used again during the Civil War as part of the Underground Railroad."

"Then how come we've never heard of it?" asked Alex.

"Because it was lost and forgotten for more than 125 years," I explained. "It was just rediscovered a few months ago."

"Where does it lead?" asked Natalie.

"Away from the Dead Squad," I answered.

She smiled. "That's good enough for me."

We passed through the doorway and entered a centuries-old tunnel lined with brick walls. There was absolutely no light, so we took turns illuminating the way with our phones. It was hot and sweaty, and my face was caked with dirt and dust. After about fifteen minutes we stopped to catch our breaths and to listen for any Dead Squad members who may have figured it out and followed us down here.

"I don't hear anything," Natalie said happily after about thirty seconds of silence. "Except maybe a couple of rats in the distance."

"Speaking of rodents," Alex said, "let's hear it for our one and only Gopher."

They all did quiet little golf claps and tried to fist-bump me in the dark. For the first time I didn't mind the nickname. (Well, not much anyway.)

"How did you find out about this place, anyway?" Grayson asked. "You said it was just discovered a few months ago?"

"That's right," I answered. "The professor at CCNY, the one I've been studying, she found it in some old papers she was researching. In fact, she was arranging to lead a thorough archeological dig of the entire passageway."

"*Was* arranging?" Natalie asked. "What stopped her?"

"Marek," I answered. "Or rather, his funding. He donated a ton of money to support her research for the new George Washington book, so the excavation of the tunnel has been postponed until that's done."

"When I first put you on this assignment to study her and what she was doing, you weren't happy," said Natalie. "You thought it was going to be boring and that I was punishing you."

"You could tell that?" I said, thinking that I had kept my emotions hidden.

"I could tell," she said. "But, this is why. None of us would have read it carefully enough to find this and remember it when we needed it most."

After more than a few mistakes, it felt good to get something right.

"All right," Alex said. "We better keep following this thing until we can find a safe way back up to the surface."

We started walking again, although not as rushed as before.

"You'd think that studying this tunnel would be more important than her book on Washington," Grayson said. "I wonder why she didn't do this first and then write the book later."

"That's back to Marek," I replied. "His financial support specified that the book had to come first and then this."

"He's really weird, isn't he?" said Alex.

"Usually I've found him to be more smart than weird," Liberty said. "There's always a reason for what he does. Even if we don't always see it right away."

A couple minutes later we reached a junction where the tunnel joined up with another one that was bigger. It was the underground equivalent of going from a side street to a major road. It was about ten feet by ten feet and there was even a little light.

"Wait a second," Liberty said as he rapped the walls and the ceiling with his knuckles. "It's all wood."

"Is that important?" asked Alex.

"Have you ever been in an all-wooden tunnel before?"

Alex shrugged. "I guess not."

"I think this may be a cattle tunnel," Liberty said. "I've heard about them, but I didn't know if they were real or it was just a legend."

"What's a cattle tunnel?" asked Natalie.

"Back before refrigeration they needed to bring the cattle from the boats on the river to the slaughterhouses in the Meat-packing District," Liberty said. "They couldn't risk them stampeding down the streets of New York, so they drove them through underground tunnels made out of wood. They had cowboys and everything."

"Are you being serious?" I asked.

"Totally," he said. "When they stopped needing them, the tunnels were built over and people lost track of where they are."

"That means this should take us out to the river if we go that way," Alex said pointing to the left.

We all started that way but stopped a few moments later when we heard a squeaking noise coming toward us.

"I hope it's not ghost cows," joked Grayson.

"Whatever it is, we don't want to come face to face with it," said Natalie. "Let's get back in the other tunnel."

"You mean the dark and dirty one?" I asked.

"No, I mean the safe one," corrected Natalie.

"Good point."

We hurried back to the other tunnel and disappeared into the darkness. Then we watched to see who was coming.

The creaking got louder and louder, and soon we could tell it was the sound of metal wheels going over the wooden floor. Every now and then there was a little conversation between two people, although we couldn't make it out.

Finally we saw two men, big strong Level 2s, dressed almost like miners with hardhats and lights. They were pulling an old metal flatbed cart, one of its wheels squeaking with every rotation. And even though it was dark, the cargo was bright and impossible to miss.

Six shining gold bars.

Wolfram

We sat quietly in the tunnel until the two men and their cargo were long gone. Other than the steady squeak, squeak, squeak of their wheels fading in the distance, there was no other sound except for the occasional deep breath as we considered the magnitude of what we'd just seen. We crawled out and back into the cattle tunnel.

"Okay, Mr. Math," Natalie said, turning to Grayson. "How much are we talking about there?"

"Let's see," he said. "According to what they told us on the tour each bar weighs twenty-seven pounds. That's about $640,000 per bar. Multiply that by six bars and they were carrying around 3.8 million dollars in gold."

"Why are two L2s moving nearly four million dollars in gold?" asked Alex.

"I imagine they're stealing it," Natalie said.

"You'd think that," answered Alex. "But they're walking toward the gold vault, not away from it. They were coming from the river."

"Should we follow them?" I asked.

Natalie shook her head. "No, that's way too risky. I think we need to get back to the surface and get home."

"Home sounds good," Grayson said.

Alex's sense of direction was right on. After about fifteen minutes of walking, the tunnel dumped us out next to the Hudson River.

"This must have been where the cows were unloaded from the boats," said Liberty.

"Mmmm, that makes me think of hamburgers," said Alex.

Natalie laughed. "Everything makes you think of hamburgers."

"That's not true," he replied. "Little Italy makes me think of lasagna."

"Okay," she said. "Everything makes you think of food."

Alex thought about this. "That's probably true."

We were covered in dirt, dust, and sweat, but it felt good. We'd managed to escape the Dead Squad's trap and I'd played a big part in that. We also knew that Marek was doing something with the gold from the Federal Reserve.

"I'll get word to your mother about what we found and see what she wants us to do next," Liberty said.

I was jealous that he had more access to Mom than I did, but I understood. "Great," I said.

"Let's get home and get some rest," Natalie said. "Good job, everyone."

"Especially you, Gopher," Alex said with a wink.

The others headed uptown while Grayson and I went south toward Battery Park, which is where the morning began. I could tell he was feeling down and wanted someone to talk to.

"My dad's working late tonight and my sister's out with friends," I said. "Mind if I come hang out with you?"

"That'd be great," he said.

We took the subway to Fort Greene and walked toward Grayson's neighborhood. After a few minutes without either of us saying a word, he looked up at me, his eyes red.

"I'm quitting," he said.

"Quitting what?" I asked.

"Omega."

"You can't."

"I'm holding everyone back," he said. "You've got Liberty. You've got Beth. They're not even part of the team but they do more to help than I do."

There was a bench on the edge of the park and we sat down there.

"I don't get it," I said. "You're so important to everything we're doing. You're . . . essential."

He laughed. "For someone who is so good at seeing things that are hidden, how can you possibly miss something so obvious? It happened again today. We got attacked on the corner and everybody took someone out but me."

"Yes, but . . ."

"And at the Chrysler Building everyone was great . . . but me. Even Beth, who minutes earlier didn't even know that the undead existed, fought like a pro. Me? I would have been thrown off the Chrysler Building if Natalie hadn't come back."

His face was pained and heartbroken. I knew that Omega meant as much to him as it did to me. This was really hard for him.

"We all help in different ways," I tried to explain.

"That's a nice way of saying I can't fight," he replied.

"Do you know I've never killed one? In two years I've never once killed a zombie. And on New Year's Eve, I was the one fighting Edmund first. I didn't even slow him down, which is why he was able to do that to Natalie. It is one hundred percent my fault that she is undead."

"That's absolutely not true," I told him. "Believe me, because I think it's one hundred percent my fault. You are so valuable to this team, Grayson. You have to see that. I understand why you're upset, but you can't leave us. We need you."

"I can't even figure out why the tungsten's important, and I've spent months on it. I've studied their records. I've researched geology books. And I'm stumped."

"Let's solve it right now," I said. "Tell me everything you know about tungsten."

"There's too much to even tell."

"Just start talking," I said. "What are the basics?"

"Tungsten is a rare, hard metal most often found in Canada, China, and Russia," he said. "It's gray and shiny. It's used as the filament in lightbulbs and X-ray tubes, none of which have anything to do with Marek."

"Forget trying to connect it to Marek," I said. "Just keep telling me about tungsten. It starts with a *T* but its chemical symbol is *W*. What's that about?"

"It comes from the Swedish word *wolfram*," he said. "Tungsten's chemical number is seventy-four. Its standard atomic weight is 183.84 and its density is 19.25 grams per centimeter cubed."

And that's where he stopped.

The eyes that were red with tears suddenly turned bright.

"That's it," he said. "That's how he's doing it."

I smiled along with him and said, "You know I have absolutely no idea what you're talking about, right? You know this is exactly why I said we needed you?"

He looked at me, the white of his teeth appearing brighter than usual because of the remnants of dirt and dust on his face.

"It's *exactly* the same as gold," he said. "Tungsten's density and its properties are identical to gold. That's what he's doing. He's swapping the tungsten with the gold in the Federal Reserve!"

Back to School

I don't know how you go to school here," Beth said as we walked across the campus. "It looks like it belongs in a horror movie."

She had a point. Once the home of a notorious mental hospital, MIST's gothic architecture was scary enough on bright sunny days. But a fast-approaching storm had filled the sky with dark clouds, and the first week of summer vacation had given the school a certain level of abandoned eeriness.

"Believe it or not, you get used to it," I said as I typed a code into a keypad by the door to the library.

"What's the code?" she asked.

I thought I'd give her a chance to test her code-breaking skills. "3, 35, 18, 39."

"Lithium, bromine, argon, yttrium," she replied. "Li, Br, Ar, Y. Library. That's easy enough."

Just as we had that first day beneath CCNY, our Omega team was arriving separately. We walked through the library without turning on any lights, navigating the stacks and the bookcases quickly. We took the stairs down to special collections, where the air had the scent of dust and old literature.

"Look at those girls!"

We looked across the room to see Mom waiting for us. The security light over her head gave her a slight green haze.

"I miss you two so much."

She came over and hugged us, and before the others arrived we spent a few minutes talking about mundane things like our plans for the summer and the particulars of Beth's job at the drama camp. Those are the details that meant the most to her, the little things that filled in the pictures of our lives.

Alex and Grayson joined us a few minutes later. And a few minutes after that Natalie arrived with Liberty.

"So I hear you guys have been busy," Mom said.

"Let's see if we can figure out what to do next."

She led us back through the special collections to a small reading room. It looked like something you'd find in an old English manor, with a pair of overstuffed chairs, floor to ceiling oak bookcases, and even a fireplace. Without hesitating she walked right up to the fireplace, ducked down, and entered it. She pushed on the brick wall in the back and it opened up onto a staircase.

"This way," she said, directing us down the staircase.

This led us to a cozy studio apartment that had a similar vibe as the reading room. There were bookcases and books everywhere.

"Welcome to my home," said Milton Blackwell as he greeted each one of us with a hearty handshake.

"I thought your home was the lab underneath CCNY," I said.

He laughed. "When you're over 140 years old, you get to have more than one. That's more my home to work and this is more my home to relax and think. It's where I lived the whole time I was principal of MIST. I like it because it keeps me close to school and because it comes with a fully-stocked library upstairs."

We all settled down on comfortable couches, and he poured us hot tea and served cookies.

"Liberty filled us in on most of what you've learned, but we wanted to get everybody together," Mom said. "Let's go around the room and try to paint a full picture of what Marek's up to."

"First of all, he's stealing hundreds of millions of dollars from the Federal Reserve Bank," Grayson said. "He was part of the construction team that built the vault back in the 1920s and he must have left some sort of back door entrance that cuts through the Manhattan schist. All the security is focused on protecting it from above ground. No one would have thought you could come from underneath."

"That's not even the brilliant part," said Alex. "Tell him how he's beating all the checks and balances."

"He's swapping the gold bars a few at a time with bars made out of tungsten and coated with a layer of gold."

Milton's head bobbed up and down as he did some mental calculations. "That *is* brilliant. Their properties are almost identical. They'd pass a lot of tests."

"That's exactly right," said Grayson.

"How does this involve the historian from CCNY?" asked Mom.

"She uncovered a secret tunnel the Sons of Liberty

built during the Revolutionary War," I explained. "She was planning to excavate and study it. If she did that, she would have found the old cattle tunnels Marek is using to move his tungsten and gold. By paying her to do something else, he protected his secret."

"I think there may be more to it than that," Natalie said. "Molly was explaining how the forts were arranged on Manhattan during the Revolution. This professor is an expert in that and I think Marek is trying to borrow that knowledge."

This was a new revelation to me.

"How?" I asked.

"I saw it last night," she said. "I was looking at a map of all the RUNY construction sites and I noticed it looked a lot like the map you showed me of the Revolutionary War forts. The layout is the same."

"I don't get it," said Liberty.

"I don't think he's building entertainment centers underground," she said. "I think that's what they'll look like."

"But they'll really be forts," I said, getting her point.

"Think about it," she said. "He has hundreds of millions of dollars to build underground forts and arm an undead army."

"This is freaky stuff," Beth said. "How are we going to stop him?"

"We may not have to," Alex said. "The Dead Squad changed the frequency of their communication channel after our little battle at the Chrysler Building, but after some searching I found the new one and have been able to listen in on their conversations for the last couple days. They don't talk as much as they used to, but I can tell one thing for sure. Marek is sick."

"That's what we understand too," Mom said.

"His body is rejecting most of the transplants," Alex replied. "And they are searching for the two of you around the clock."

"Why are they looking for Mom and Milton?" asked Beth. "What do they have to do with Marek being sick?"

There was a slight pause in the conversation, and then Milton answered, "My brother needs my body parts in order to survive."

Beth's eyes opened wide. She went to say something, but she couldn't make the words.

"We know," I said. "It's beyond gross."

Everyone was silent for a minute, then I shook my head and went on. "He may be sick," I said. "But he's making a public appearance tomorrow."

"Where?" asked Mom.

"The Central Park Zoo," I said. "I got another letter yesterday."

I handed the envelope to my mother. Inside there was a map of the Central Park Zoo and a press release that said Marek Blackwell was going to break ground on construction for a new exhibit at the zoo. There was also a note, which Mom read aloud.

"When Marek makes his announcement, everything will be clear."

"Scary, huh?" I said.

"Yes," replied my mother.

"It has shades of New Year's Eve," added Alex. "We go expecting one announcement, and it turns out to be something else."

"I know," I answered. "That's why I don't want to make any recommendation about what we should do. I just thought I should share it with all of you."

"First of all, what happened on New Year's wasn't your fault," said Natalie. "And secondly, you know what we have to do."

"She's right," said Mom. "We have to be there."

Ω 24

Groundbreaking Development

It was a beautiful June day and crowds packed the Central Park Zoo. There were seven of us there. Alex, Beth, and I were together near the sea lion exhibit while Natalie, Grayson, and Liberty were over by the snow monkeys. My mom was the wildcard; she was taking advantage of the fact that you can look into the zoo from the walkway that runs through the park. She blended in with the tourists hanging out by the Delacorte Clock.

None of us were next to the penguins, which is where Marek was making his announcement. We wanted to be close enough to see and hear what was going on but not where he'd be likely to see us. Although we were somewhat exposed, we felt comfortable that the undead weren't going to attack us in front of a bunch of kids on summer vacation at the zoo. Marek was building a new reputation as a civic leader and couldn't let anything he was involved with become too messy.

"Anything interesting?" I asked Alex, who was listening in on the Dead Squad's communications.

"Nope," he said. "Hardly any chatter at all."

I gave him a look. "Chatter? Did you learn that reading some book about cops?"

He looked a little hurt at the dig. "That's what my uncle Paul calls it."

"I'm just kidding," I said. "I do that when I'm nervous."

"There's Mr. Evil," said Beth.

Marek Blackwell arrived with the zoo director, and the two of them approached a small podium and microphone. Like always, he was well dressed with a crisp coat and tie despite the hot June afternoon. They stood in front of a few dozen people, including some members of the press. Among them were some television news crews, including one with Brock Hampton, the local reporter who often broadcasts coded messages to the undead.

"I'd like to welcome everyone and thank you for coming," the director said into the microphone. "We are going to have a short presentation today about an exciting new addition we're adding to the zoo. Marek Blackwell has donated a very generous sum of money to support a new habitat for the penguins here at the Central Park Zoo. Today we are breaking ground on what will be a state-of-the-art facility for some of the zoo's most popular residents. I'd like to introduce Marek Blackwell."

There was applause as Marek moved to the microphone. He seemed frail and uneasy.

"I think you're right," I said to Alex. "He looks sick."

Someone handed him a gold-plated shovel, and he said, "I know a little something about digging."

This elicited polite laughter from the people in the crowd.

"I've spent most of my life under this great city, digging holes to carry everything from drinking water to subways," he continued. "And now I am reinventing underground New York, but that doesn't mean I'm not concerned about what happens up here on the surface."

There was some more laughter, and I had to admit that he had undeniable charm. It was easy to see how he got people to support him.

"When I put this shovel into the ground, it will mark the beginning of a new habitat for the zoo's penguins. It's my hope that it will be a treasure for the families of New York but also for the scientists who study these amazing animals. That means so much to me because of my brother Milton."

Alex and I exchanged looks. We had no idea what he was talking about.

"He was very special to me. But he wasn't just family, he was also a great scientist. That's why this center is so important to me, and that's why it will be named the Milton Blackwell Penguin Research Center."

More applause and more confusion on our part.

"I cannot think of a more appropriate way to honor his memory. He will be missed."

"Why is he speaking of him in the past tense like he's dead?" I asked.

I looked up at Marek, and I swear that he was looking right at me as he shook hands with well wishers and left the podium. Before I could even react, Alex grabbed me by the arm and pulled me closer to him.

"What? What?" I asked nervous.

He held up his finger to shush me for a moment while he listened to something over the radio. "They just arrested your mother."

"They what?" Beth and I said in unison.

"The call just came in over the radio," he said. "They just arrested your mother."

We looked over toward the Delacorte Clock and saw that two police officers, both with Dead Squad patches on their shoulders, had my mother handcuffed and were taking her away. Even though we were close enough to see, the railing around the zoo made it impossible for us to chase after her. We'd have to run all the way over to the entrance.

"What are they arresting her for?" I said to Alex.

"Yeah," said Beth, "what could the charge possibly be?"

"Does it matter?"

I turned to see that Marek Blackwell had now come over to us.

"You must be Beth," he said, offering his hand to my sister.

"If you think I'm shaking your hand, you're crazy," she said.

"Haven't they told you, young lady?" he said. "I'm as crazy as a loon. Or is that crazy as a fox? The fox is the one who acts crazy but gets his way. Just like I did with the letters I sent to Molly."

"You wrote them?"

He nodded. "I wanted to make sure that you were close but not too close. And then, of course, when the time was right, I needed to make sure that you brought your mother to me so that she couldn't be protecting my brother."

Now it made sense. He needed to get her away from Milton so that his men could get to him. Once again, I'd played right into his trap.

"I'm going to make the same offer to you that I made to her six months ago," he said. "We can have peace. I have no interest in fighting you or your friends. I have no interest in fighting anyone."

"What about my mother and Milton?" I demanded.

He made a sheepish expression. "I'm afraid it's too late for both of them. I need my brother for health reasons, and I need your mother because . . . well, let's just face it . . . I want her out of the picture for good. I named the Penguin habitat for Milton. I figured I owed him at least that much. I'll figure out some way to memorialize your mother, too."

I think any one of us would have killed him there on the spot, but in addition to being surrounded by the media, he was protected by four of his biggest Dead Squad members, including Officer Pell. The whole time Marek talked, Pell stared daggers at me.

"I'll be seeing you around," Pell said as he started to walk away with Marek. As he did, he threw a punch into Alex's gut. "That's for the sucker punch you threw at my jaw the other day."

They escorted Marek away, and I started hyperventilating as I tried to figure out what to do next. Natalie, Liberty, and Grayson rushed over to us.

"What just happened?" asked Natalie.

"They arrested my mom and I think they have captured Milton," I told them.

Alex was still recovering from the sucker punch, but once he got his breath back he said, "We don't know that for sure. I haven't heard anything on the radio about them getting their hands on him. But that's definitely their plan. That's why they have your mom in custody, so she can't help him."

"What are they going to do with Mom?" asked Beth. "Just take her somewhere and kill her?"

"They can't do that," said Alex. "They had to call in the arrest. That means there's a record and they have to follow procedures. My guess is that they'll keep her locked up for now and transfer her to the Tombs tonight."

"The what?" I asked.

"The Tombs," he said. "It's what they call the main city

jail. It's bad news. It would be incredibly easy for them to fake an accident in there and make it look like another prisoner killed her."

Everything seemed grim, but for some reason I was more focused than ever. I know that Natalie is our team captain, but I thought it was time for me to take charge.

"Okay, here's what we're going to do," I said. "But it's going to take all of us at the top of our game. Natalie, Alex, and Liberty, you three get over to MIST and see if you can help Milton. They have him outnumbered, but he's smart. Smarter than all of us combined. He may be able to hold them off until help arrives. Listen in on the radio so you know what the bad guys are up to."

"Got it," said Natalie, no hesitation about taking orders from me. "What are you three going to do?"

I looked at her and smiled. "We're going to break my mother out of jail."

25

Jailbirds (We Return to Where the Story Began)

The Central Garden & Sea Lion Pool is at the heart of the Central Park Zoo. It features a rocky island surrounded by water and is home to eight California sea lions. Every afternoon at one thirty an animal keeper climbs up onto the island to feed the sea lions and talk about them. It's incredibly popular, which is why the crowd was three people deep all the way around the tank.

A sea lion name Scooter was demonstrating his ability to stand up on his fore-flippers, when there was a loud gasp in the crowd.

"Mom!" cried out a young boy. "What's that girl doing?"

I was the girl, and the thing I was doing was balancing on the rail that ringed the pool. Embarrassingly, my balance was worse than Scooter's.

"Please get down from there," the keeper directed me in a forceful voice.

Despite my wobbly beginning I finally managed to stand up straight.

"It is not safe for you or the animals if you encroach upon an exhibit," he continued. "You must stay on public paths!"

Satisfied that I had everybody's attention and was the focus of more than a few video cameras, I was ready to make a splash. (Sorry, puns are a weakness of mine.) I thought it would be a good touch to shout something as I did it, and for some reason my mind went back to the Sons of Liberty and their safe passage tunnel.

"Tutus locus!"

It didn't make sense, but I thought it sounded good. And before anyone could ask me what it meant, I leapt into the air and cannonballed into the nearly freezing water. An instant shock ran through my body as I submerged for a moment of silence before I started to float back to the surface. When I came back up, it was anything but quiet.

I heard laughter, yelling, and lots of vigorous instructions from the keeper up on the rocky island.

In addition to being surprised at the water tempera-ture, I was caught off guard by the fact that it was salt water. This should have been obvious, considering that California sea lions live off the coast of California in the Pacific Ocean, but in my mind the water looked fresh, not salty.

Two of the sea lions, I think their names were April and Clarisse, swam alongside me as I dog paddled through the water until the police arrived. As I expected, it wasn't a member of the Dead Squad that came, but instead a regu-lar cop, a female officer named Strickland.

When she showed up on the scene, I happily swam back to the edge, climbed out of the pool, and surrendered myself to her.

I find it interesting that while the keepers and many of the mothers sneered at me like I belonged on the FBI's Most Wanted List, Officer Strickland took it all in stride.

"Try not to slide all over the seat," she said as she put me in the back of her squad car. "I'm going to have to come back out and dry it later."

"Yes, ma'am," I said. "I'm very sorry about that."

It was a short drive from the zoo to the Central Park Precinct of the NYPD. Alex had told me about the pre-cinct, and it was actually quite pretty. In order to maintain the beauty of the park, the precinct was housed in a series of buildings that were once horse stables. Many of the structures had been built out of Manhattan schist, which is why the Dead Squad had selected it as the ideal place for their headquarters.

"Several people reported you shouting some kind of threat when you stood up on the rail," she said to me when she was writing her report. "What was it?"

"*Tutus locus,*" I said. "It's Latin for 'safe passage'."

She snickered. "And who were you threatening?"

"No one intentionally."

She stopped writing her report for a moment and looked at me. It was clear she didn't know what to make of the whole situation.

"Where do you go to school?" she asked.

"MIST," I said. "The Metropolitan Institute of Science and Technology."

"That's a prestigous school," she said. "You get good grades there?"

I nodded. "Yes, ma'am. All As."

"All As means you're smart," she said. "But what you did today was not smart."

"No, ma'am. It was stupid."

"Do you have an explanation?"

I shook my head.

"I'll tell you what I think it is," she said. "I think you had some kind of crazy idea that it would be funny, and you made a mistake."

"That's pretty accurate," I told her.

"What do your parents do?" she asked.

"Well, there's just my dad," I said. "He's a paramedic with the FDNY."

That caught her attention, which is exactly what I was hoping for. The police and fire departments were part of the same extended family, which kind of made us related.

I can't say enough about how great she was. We talked for a little while more and then she had me call my dad. He explained that he couldn't come to pick me up until his shift was over. As a bonus, while I was at her desk, I could hear the communications over the radio and knew that the Dead Squad was having trouble finding Milton.

Then she brought me here to the cell where I am right now. Like I said when I started to explain all of this, it was my intention to get arrested and wind up here. So that part of my plan worked. But for everything to work out, a lot of other pieces are going to have to fall into place.

The first is that my sister has to be able to explain everything to my father. Or at least, she has to explain enough to get him to play along. It's going to take a leap of faith for him to buy into the plan, but Beth can be amazingly persuasive. And Dad's always had a soft spot for his daughters. The second, harder to predict portion, is that the Dead Squad is going to have to follow police procedures, like Alex said they would.

I was hoping that Mom would be in one of the holding cells, but I don't see her anywhere. I'm trying to stay upbeat, but it isn't easy. If I've miscalculated then the only thing I've accomplished is getting locked up so that I can't help at all.

I look across the squad room and notice that there's some activity in one of the interrogation rooms. Finally, the door opens and I see Mom in handcuffs being led out of the room. I turn my back to them so that the two Dead Squadders can't see my face. They lock her into the cell right next to mine.

"You're going to wait here for a little bit and then you're going to visit the Tombs," one of them tells her. "I think you're really going to enjoy it there."

Alex had it down perfectly. They're doing exactly what he said they would do.

I continue to look the other way so that they won't notice me, but once they're gone I walk over to where the two cells join.

"Mom," I whisper.

"Molly?" she says in total shock. "What in the world are you doing here?"

She comes over to me and we talk in whispers.

"I'm here to rescue you," I say.

"That's crazy," she tells me. "This is why I should never have let you do this. You aren't ready. It's not safe."

"You're right, it isn't safe," I say. "But I *am* ready and this is going to work. I was meant for this. Just like you. There aren't a lot of things that I'm really good at. But being an Omega, that's one that I am."

She looks at me for a moment and considers what I said. After a moment she smiles. "Okay, Molly Koala," she says. "What's the plan?"

26

The Great Escape

My name is Michael Bigelow and I'm here to pick up my daughter. You know, the girl who is going to be grounded for the rest of her life."

I look up from inside the holding cell and see my father in the precinct's main squad room. He's still wearing his navy-blue paramedic's uniform, and his expression is impossible to read. I can't tell if Beth has been successful in convincing him, but I'll know in a couple seconds.

"She's right over here," says Officer Strickland.

The police officer escorts him toward me, and I watch his eyes as he scans the other cells. It takes a moment before they lock on Mom. They open wide in disbelief. He can't say anything. He can't react. It will ruin the plan. He has to direct all of his anger at me, and I'm not sure he can pull it off.

"I'm really sorry, Dad," I say, my voice full of remorse. "I don't know what came over me at the zoo."

He tries to respond but he stammers, his focus still directed at Mom. He looks like he might cry.

"Are you going to be okay?" I ask.

He hesitates, but then finally answers.

"I don't know," he replies, and I have no idea if it's because of my arrest or because he sees Mom, but it's convincing. "I'm angry and I'm heartbroken and I'm trying to understand how all of this happened."

Finally he turns to look at me. "But we're a family and we are going to work this out no matter what."

I breathe a sigh of relief. That's the phrase I told Beth to give him. That's the signal that he's on board with the plan and we're ready to start.

"Well, I understand your frustration, Mr. Bigelow," says Officer Strickland. "But I get the feeling that this is a one-time only occurrence for your daughter. Isn't that right, Molly?"

"Yes, ma'am," I respond. "It will never happen again. That's a guarantee."

She unlocks the door, and I rush into my father's arms and hug him as tightly as I can. It's part of my plan, but it couldn't be more real.

"I'm so sorry, Dad," I say, looking up at his eyes, which are welling with tears. "I'm so sorry about everything."

"All I care about is that you're safe," he says. "All I care about is our family."

There's the second cue.

Suddenly my mother screams in agony and collapses to the floor. She lets out another wail and her entire body tenses up so that she's as stiff as a board.

"Are you okay?" Officer Strickland calls, jumping into action.

Mom's body begins to shake in a seizure and she starts to cough up black liquid. She's acting, but she is pulling it off with unbelievable realism.

"She's having a severe anaphylaxis episode," my dad says, breaking into paramedic lingo. "She needs to get to a hospital immediately."

It is sudden and total chaos, and Officer Strickland unlocks the door to help my mother. She bends down to assist her, but Dad stops her by grabbing her shoulder.

"Have you been inoculated against hyponeurological nanovirus?"

The police officer flashes a look of total confusion. "What?"

"Hyponeurological nanovirus? It's highly contagious and it's demonstrated by black liquid being produced by the lungs."

"No!" she says. "I haven't."

"Then do not touch her," he instructs. "I drove straight here at the end of my shift so my ambulance is in the parking lot. Let me carry her out and I'll drive her to the hospital."

Without waiting for permission Dad steps into the cell and scoops Mom up in his arms. Even in the turmoil of our little drama, I see the tender moment of connection as she slides her head onto his shoulder and he tells her, "It's going to be okay. Everything's going to be okay."

Within seconds I'm running alongside my father as he carries my mother down the long hallway toward the exit. (I told you I wouldn't be walking out the door.) I think my plan is going to work until I hear another scream from behind me.

It's one of the Dead Squad officers. He's stumbled onto the scene and sees what's happening.

"We better hurry," I say. "We've got bad guys hot on our tail."

In one swift motion my mom swings down from my father's arms like a ballroom dancer and lands on her feet in a full sprint as we rush out the door.

The ambulance is parked right by the entrance, and as we run toward it the back door flies open to reveal Beth and Grayson waiting for us. Mom and I dive in with them while Dad climbs into the driver's seat and starts the engine.

The Dead Squadder is right behind us, and he leaps onto the back bumper while I'm trying to close the door. He grabs at me and I slam the door shut, chopping off his hand so that it falls in with us.

"I think I'm going to be sick," says Beth, getting her first close-up look at zombie body parts.

"Go, go, go!" I shout, and Dad takes off across the parking lot.

Even though I've chopped off his hand, the zombie is still hanging on to the back, trying to open the door. Beth and I clamp onto the handle with all our might to keep it from opening.

"Look at that!" Grayson says, pointing out the side window.

I look up in time to see Officer Pell chasing after us along the roof of the precinct house. When he reaches the edge, he leaps into the air and lands on top of the ambulance with a huge thud.

"Keep driving!" Mom tells Dad. "Do! Not! Stop!"

She climbs up into the front passenger seat.

It the middle of all the mayhem, Dad turns to Mom as he speeds along the road.

"Last year on our anniversary," he says to her. "I swear I saw your face in the crowd."

"Outside Lincoln Center," she replies, happy at the memory.

"I knew it was you! I knew it was you!"

"You guys do realize that we have two zombies trying to beat their way into this ambulance," Beth says.

Pell's on top of the ambulance, pounding the roof, and his one-handed partner is still trying to come in the back door.

"I've got an idea," I say to Beth. "Let go of the handle."

"What?" she says as she gives me an "are you crazy?" look.

"Trust me."

We both let go at the same time and the latch opens. The zombie smiles for a second before I kick the door as hard as I can, making it fly open all the way. It knocks him off the bumper and he slams onto the street.

"Nice move!" says Beth.

I don't even have a chance to respond before Pell swings down from the roof and flings himself through the now open door like an undead gymnast. His face is contorted with rage, and he starts swinging wildly as purple spittle shoots out of his mouth.

Grayson tries to fight him but Pell slams him against the wall of the ambulance, causing medical supplies to scatter all over. He head butts Beth and knocks her down hard onto the floor.

He is completely unstoppable.

"Hello, Molly!" he hisses as he looks at me with wild eyes. His orange and yellow teeth shine bright as he reaches down and grabs me by the throat.

I gasp for air, completely unable to breathe, and flail my arms at him.

None of it matters. He just continues to tighten his grip.

My eyes start to roll back and I catch a glimpse of my mom trying to crawl back toward us to help. It doesn't seem to matter. It's too late.

I open my mouth to scream but no sound comes out, just the hiss of air escaping.

"I should have done this a long time ago!" he says, tightening his grip even more.

I start to black out, and the last image I see is his smiling face.

Then I hear an electric charge and Pell begins to convulse. It lasts about a second or two, and his eyes go wild as he tries to figure out what's happening. He has no idea, and then, without warning, his chest explodes and purple slime spews everywhere.

He just hangs there frozen in midair for a moment before his body falls dead.

As he does, he reveals Grayson, standing behind him with the electric paddles of a defibrillator in his hands. He has a look of wonder on his face, and I cannot begin to express how grateful I am that he has finally killed his first zombie.

He looks at me and I look at him, our eyes locking for a moment.

"Well, look who the hero is now," I finally manage to say.

Cain and Abel

It all started ten months ago on the first day of school. I entered the Roosevelt Island subway station wearing a necklace that once belonged to my mother. I'd worn it because it had a charm that looked like a horseshoe and I thought it might bring me luck. What I didn't know at the time is that it was actually an omega symbol, a memento of my mother's status as a zeke, or zombie killer.

A Level 3 saw it around my neck and attacked me. I was completely overmatched and survived only because

Natalie came to my rescue. Since then, whenever I return to that station, I can't help but think back to the day that changed my life forever.

I'm heading there right now, but this time everything is different. Now I'm the one looking for a fight. I'm the one planning to do the rescuing.

"All units descend on Roosevelt Island subway station, northbound platform."

That's the emergency call we hear minutes after we busted my mom out of jail and Grayson killed Officer Pell. The radio scanner in my dad's ambulance is tuned to listen in on the Dead Squad and their communications. We know they're trying to capture Milton Blackwell, and this sounds like they're getting close.

Thirty seconds later I get a call from Natalie and I put it on speaker. The reception is bad because she's in the subway station, but she's able to give us basic information about the situation.

"They've got Milton cornered on the northbound platform," she tells us. "There are three Dead Squad cops down there with him, but they're staying about ten feet away from him."

"Why aren't they just taking him?" asks Mom.

"He's got something in a vial or a test tube," she explains. "It's hard to tell exactly what it is from here, but it sure has them scared."

She explains that the Dead Squad found Milton's secret home beneath the MIST Library and chased him through a series of tunnels that ultimately led to the subway station.

"How close can you get to him?" asks my mother.

"Just to the mezzanine overlooking the platform," she replies. "They're using their status as NYPD to close down access to the stairs. We can't help him."

Before we can ask anything else, we lose the connection.

"There's no telling how long he can hold them off," says Mom. "We better get there in a hurry."

"But how can we help if they're blocking off the stairs?" I ask.

"We're not taking the stairs," Mom says. "We're taking the train."

One of the advantages of driving around in an ambulance is that you can park it almost anywhere. Minutes later we're at the Lexington Ave–63rd Street subway station, getting onto the F train. We are less than two minutes away from Roosevelt Island.

"What do you think is in the vial?" I ask my mother.

She shakes her head. "I don't know. All of his experiments are about figuring out how the Manhattan schist affects the undead."

It is so surreal to see all four members of my family together again. It's something I've dreamed about ever since we said good-bye to Mom in the hospital. Unfortunately, we don't have any time to actually be together. Mom is trying to explain some of this to Dad, but it's more than you can cover in two minutes while you're rushing to fight a zombie police force.

We're in the front car of the train, so we have a good view of the situation the moment we pull into the station.

"There they are," I say, pointing. "In the far corner."

The scene is still pretty much the same as Natalie described it. Milton is in the northernmost corner of the subway station. There are three Dead Squad cops who are blocking his way, but they're also remaining at least ten feet away. And there are more even farther back than that. Milton is disheveled, but he seems focused as he holds a vial containing a bright blue liquid.

The subway doors hiss open and the five of us step out. It's Mom, Dad, Beth, Grayson, and me. We only make it a couple of steps toward Milton before a handful of Dead Squadders come down to block our way.

"You're going to be real cool and back away," Mom instructs them. "Because Milton is going to get out of here right now."

"I'm afraid we can't let that happen."

It's Marek, and he's walking down the platform right toward us.

"I just can't seem to get you to die," he says to my mom, his voice a mixture of frustration and admiration. "I'd kill you myself, but frankly I'm not feeling my best right now."

"Clear everyone else out, Marek," Milton says the moment he sees his older brother. "This is between you and me."

"And if I don't clear them out?" Marek asks.

"Then I'll drop this and end it all."

Marek laughs and shakes his head as he continues to walk toward him. "That's the problem with baby brothers. They're always such . . . babies. Please enlighten us as to what's in your test tube?"

"It's a synthetic pathogen," he says. "The moment the liquid is exposed to air it will vaporize."

"And what will the vapor do?" Marek asks condescendingly.

"Neutralize the Manhattan schist," says Milton. "That

means it will kill the undead. Within two minutes every zombie in this room would be dead. You and me included."

This is pretty frightening. I assumed that Milton was trying to figure out how the schist kept the undead from dying in order to help them. It hadn't dawned on me that by doing so he could also counteract its power.

Unlike me, Marek isn't worried in the least. "No way," he says. "You don't have that in you. You're the lover of people, the nurturer. I'm the monster, not you."

"That all changed the moment you started to build an undead army," Milton replies. "I knew you needed to be stopped once and for all, so I built the perfect weapon for the job."

Marek is now about five feet away from Milton, and he's having trouble telling if his threat is real or not. Milton senses this hesitation and adds, "Are you willing to risk everybody's life, including your own? It's the same mistake you made when we were digging the tunnel."

This enrages Marek. "I didn't make a mistake in the tunnel! That was all you, little brother. You're the one who started all of this."

"And I'm the one who will end it."

Milton accentuates his threat by dangling the vial between his thumb and forefinger.

Marek regains his composure and turns to look at us for a moment. He locks eyes with my mother and smiles. Then he turns back to Milton.

"I don't believe for one second that you would create such a weapon, but if you did, I know you wouldn't use it here and now. It would kill your prized student right in front of her family."

"Go right ahead, Milton," says my mom. "I've been reunited with my family one last time. They know that I love them. You can drop the vial. I'm willing to be sacrificed if it means stopping him."

I see the look of devastation in my father's eyes as he clutches her hand. He's just gotten her back. He can't lose her again just moments later. Beth takes her other hand.

"It's okay," Mom reassures them.

I make eye contact with Milton, and I think he can read my panic.

"I'll do it, Marek," he replies. "I will expose everyone to *Saccharomyces cerevisiae*."

I have to fight the urge to smile the moment I recognize the name.

The deadly pathogen is actually the harmless bacteria commonly known as yeast. I know this because every year Milton uses a vial of it as part of his first day of school lecture. He's bluffing, and the only ones that know it are my friends and family. It gives us a slight advantage.

"I do have an offer for you, though," says Milton. "Clear out all of your people, and I'll do the same. Let's just leave it to the two of us to resolve."

Marek laughs. "You want to fight? Me?"

"That's what you want, isn't it?" says Milton. "That's what you've wanted every day since that explosion."

"You mean the explosion you caused?" he replies.

"I mean the accident that did this to us, our brothers, and our cousins."

"Do you think you can fight me?" Marek asks. "Does my little scientist brother actually think he can fight big, evil Marek?"

"There's only one way to find out," says Milton.

Marek cannot resist the opportunity. He tells everyone on the Dead Squad to move back, and Milton tells us to do likewise.

Milton carefully places the vial on the ground and the two of them start to size each other up, stalking around like boxers in a ring.

"I have to be careful," says Marek. "I don't want to damage the body parts I need to have transplanted."

Milton suddenly makes a charge and throws a punch

at Marek, who simply catches the fist in his hand and stops it in midair. Then he counters with a punch that staggers Milton.

"This is just like when you were twenty," Marek says. "You think you are so much more than you actually are. Then you thought you were smart enough to build a better explosive, but you weren't. Now you think you are strong enough to fight me, but you aren't."

Marek throws another punch but Milton dodges this one and catches Marek with a punch to the jaw. Reflexively Beth, Grayson, and I let out a cheer.

"Get him, Milton!" shouts Natalie from the mezzanine.

Marek is furious and determined. "Playtime is over!"

I realize that Marek might be at his breaking point, so I step forward and march right toward the two of them.

"So this is the way the world ends," I say, reciting from the poem "The Hollow Men." "Not with a bang, but a whimper."

They both look at me in total confusion, but they stop fighting so I have my opening.

"Is there a reason you're reciting poetry?" asks Marek.

"Yes," I say. "It's from 'The Hollow Men.' Natalie says that it reminds her of you two. She says you're hollow because your life has been taken out of you. But I don't think that's why you're hollow."

I wait for either one of them to respond, but neither does, so I just keep going.

"I think you're hollow because you're missing from each other's lives," I explain, trying to think fast and keep talking. "Despite everything you've said and done, Marek, Milton is still your brother. You still love him."

He laughs derisively. "And what led you to this conclusion?"

I have now reached them, and the three of us are standing in a little triangle a few feet from each other.

"You did," I say. "That day in Central Park by the statue of Alice in Wonderland. "You said you'd like to think that your family could reunite."

Now he laughs even louder. "I was lying to you. It was a manipulation."

"That's what you tell yourself, but you weren't lying. I could see it in your eyes. It was the most honest thing I ever heard you say. It's also why you sent me those letters. Deep down there's a part of you that wanted us to figure it all out. Maybe you don't even realize it, but it's there."

He shakes his head. "You couldn't be more wrong."

"My sister and I fight," I reply. "Nothing like the two

of you. It's usually about clothes or whose turn it is to do the dishes, but we fight. And sometimes I can't stand her."

I look over at my sister and smile.

"But she's my sister and I love her more than anyone on earth."

Beth smiles back at me.

"When you were little and Milton was trampled by the horse, who rescued him? Who carried him to safety?"

I notice a change in Marek's expression. It's slight, but it's there.

"I should have left him there in the street," he says. "Then none of this would've happened."

"But you didn't leave him," I say. "Because you couldn't. He's your brother. You were heroic in his rescue. And when he became a scientist, you were proud. That's why you wanted him to make the explosive. And earlier today, that's why you named the research center at the zoo after him. He's your brother and he's a part of you."

The two of them look at each other, and I can't tell if anything I've said has made a difference.

"Could it be true?" asks Milton. "Could you still think of me as a brother?"

Marek shook his head. "Even if I could, it wouldn't matter. If I don't get your body parts, I'll be dead in a matter of days. So I guess we are going to be reunited, the two of us forming one person."

Just then there is the whoosh of a subway train as it enters the station.

"No, we won't," says Milton.

When the doors open, he surprises all of us by stepping on board.

"As soon as this train leaves the station, it will take me out of Manhattan," he says. "I will die instantly. And when I do, you will no longer be able to transplant my body parts. That means you will also die, in a matter of days."

"No!" screams Marek. "Get off the train!"

There is at most another twenty seconds before the train doors close and seal both of their fates.

"Believe it or not, I still love you," Milton says. "She's right about us always being brothers. I am forever sorry about what has happened. We should never have lived like this. We should have died in the subway tunnel all those years ago. We should have died together. Come with me. Let's leave this world as brothers and not enemies."

Milton reaches out toward him, but Marek is frozen by indecision. He does not know what to do. Then, as the train doors start to close, he leaps on board.

I look through the window right at them. They stand

face to face for a moment, and then they embrace. The last thing I see is Milton's eyes as they close and he rests his head on his brother's shoulder.

A rush of air roars out of the station as the F train departs and disappears into the darkened tunnel that leads to Queens. Moments later it passes beyond the protective blanket of the Manhattan schist.

Marek and Milton Blackwell are dead.

Ωmega

My family will never be . . . *normal.* That was true even before the undead disrupted our lives. But now, we'll be even less normal than before. It's been an odd couple of weeks since that day we broke Mom out of jail and watched Milton and Marek ride off in the subway.

Don't get me wrong; it's great that the four of us are together. But there are still a lot of adjustments that have to be made. After all, my mom is undead, and even though there isn't an evil dark lord of the underworld trying to kill her, there will be some complications. My dad thought he had buried her forever, but he never stopped loving her. That's the key to all of it . . . love. If you love someone, nothing else really matters.

My family is everything to me, and when I use that word I don't just mean the people who share the same blood that I do. (In fact, some of them don't even have blood.) No, I use it to mean the people who share my heart. All the people I love.

We are gathered together at the moment because this is family night. Well, technically it's family day, and the rules are both simple and ironclad. When it's my turn to pick what we do, then you have to do what I say. That's why all of us are out on the Great Lawn in Central Park.

We had to spread out three blankets just to hold all the food that Dad made for the picnic. Alex is devouring fried chicken at a record pace while he talks to Beth about the play she's directing at drama camp. Grayson and Liberty are locked in an epic match of One Foot Trivia as Natalie does everything she can to come up with questions to stump them. And my parents are holding hands, laughing at each other's stories and listening to *La Traviata*.

In other words, even though it's not normal, it's still pretty close to perfect.

I close my eyes and turn my face toward the sun so that

its warmth radiates through my body. I inhale the delicious aromas of food and fresh air, and I listen to the music of people laughing and having fun.

I'm wearing my mother's necklace, the one that started me on this adventure, and I reach up and press the omega symbol between my thumb and finger.

Omega is the last letter of the Greek alphabet, and it's often used to signify the end of something. It was chosen as the name of our secret society because we were to be the last word on the undead. But omega is also the first letter of the Greek word for family. So, in that way, what is an ending is also a beginning.

I open my eyes and look at my family and know that I am the person I am supposed to be. I think back to when we used to come here and my mom would read *Alice's Adventures in Wonderland* to us. I remember her favorite line from the book: *It's no use going back to yesterday, because I was a different person then.*

It really is no use going back, and I have no interest in doing so.

My name is Molly Bigelow, and I am ready for whatever comes next.

The City Spies are on the case!
From bestselling author
JAMES PONTI
comes another must-read,
action-packed mystery series
that is sure to thrill.